THE MONARCH OF KEY WEST

THE MONARCH OF KEY WEST

D.M. Paule

Writers Club Press
San Jose New York Lincoln Shanghai

The Monarch of Key West

Writers Club Press
an imprint of iUniverse, Inc.

For information address:
iUniverse, Inc.
5220 S. 16th St., Suite 200
Lincoln, NE 68512
www.iuniverse.com

Any resemblence to actual people and events is purely coincidental. This is a work of fiction.

ISBN: 0-595-22290-0

Printed in the United States of America

For Gary, Sean and Jimmy Buffett.
It all started with them.

Life…is a tale
told by an idiot.

—William Shakespeare

CONTENTS

▼

Acknowledgements

A lot of people had a hand in helping edit both the book and the story. My thanks go out to Gary Mann, Sean Dolan, Paige Norwood, my parents and family (especially, Cathi), Laverne Mann, and the members of the all-powerful Emmanuel Lutheran Church Book Club of Virginia Beach, Virginia.

Finally, and most especially, my thanks to Dana Dolan, the world's foremost expert on the Chicago Manual of Style, who took on the formidable task of editing my use of the comma.

ALBERT

I *hate* television.

I *hate* suburbs.

I *hate* malls.

I could not have written three more inflammatory statements for white, middle-class America if I had suggested that Ronald Reagan had been a cross-dresser. Unfortunately (or *fortunately*, depending on your perspective) they are true. I am a traitor to my middle class upbringing. I have renounced the golden goal of complacent *Bradydom*, which my generation was supposed to hold sacred, and thrown away career and prospects in search of something more tangible. Happiness.

If I had been older, say, in my forties, they would have called it a midlife crisis. However, at twenty-eight circumstances conspired to prevent me from having a midlife crisis, and I've successfully avoided it ever since. I'm not sure exactly when I came to this realization, but somewhere in the complex interactions that define my life I had come to understand that there had to be more to life than what I had.

Not that I didn't have it good. I was actually quite successful. I had been promoted twice at the airline where I worked. I was happily ensconced in Boston. I had just earned my private pilot's license, and was working on my commercial rating. I had good friends and a new little red convertible. I had even saved enough money to be in the market for a condo.

Someone once told me that dissatisfaction is characteristic of my generation. Those of us who were born on the cusp of the baby boom grew up in a world of diminishing opportunities where we thought life was supposed to be like television. Happy families, witty repartee and problems that can be resolved in thirty minutes with two commercial breaks.

I had a stereotypical childhood for middle America. Home in the suburbs, away from the disruptive elements of the city. Teenage years which centered on cars and girls and hanging out in the mall. College, which centered on beer and general malaise. Career ripe with the potential of inflicting this legacy on my yet-to-be-conceived progeny.

I think I realized I didn't belong to Middle Class America when I stopped watching television. My first two years at the airline, I was a constant source of amazement to my friends and coworkers whose sole topic of morning conversation centered around what had happened on the previous evening's shows. I never watched these shows. Indeed, I seldom watched television at all, and so was at a loss and unable to carry on a conversation with these people.

In the beginning it was considered an eccentricity. But, as the years passed and I never moved to the suburbs, never settled down with the little woman, never took to shopping at the mall and buying clothes at Sears, I became suspect in the eyes of my colleagues. And, I in turn began to suffocate under the crushing boredom which the people around me embraced.

Fortunately, my Uncle Albert came to my rescue. He died.

Growing up, I never really knew Uncle Albert that well. He was my mom's older brother. He wasn't really the black sheep of the family, but he had different priorities and so was the "misunderstood" child. He had left Chicago and moved to Key West over forty years ago where he ran an import/export business. His visits back to Illinois when I was a kid were seldom, but he did seem to have a particular fondness for me. One of my only memories of him from those days is when he tried to talk my mother into letting me accompany him to Caracas over summer vacation. I was ten.

I was in college and looking for a warm beach upon which to spend spring break when I decided to meet my uncle as an adult. I was certainly wary of him. I knew nothing about his life in Key West except that my parents didn't approve of it. That made it all the more alluring.

The man I met in Key West was old, but old in a way that only Irishmen can be. He had developed the red cheeks and the white hair and that perpetual goddamn twinkle in his eye that makes all of us look like demented leprechauns as we get older. Uncle Albert was a man who lived life to the fullest. He had been around the world seven or eight times. He was the only man I knew who could claim to have walked on all seven continents. He was a pilot, a fisherman, an occasional small-time smuggler and a hell of a guy. I wish you could have met him, because I certainly can't do him justice typing into a word processor.

Over the years, he became my mentor and confidant. He frequently broke his cardinal rule against writing letters to anyone, and I would receive long missives from him telling me to live my life on my own terms, to believe in myself, and to come to Key West whenever I needed to escape an increasingly complacent world.

I heard of his death just three weeks before I was to visit him. Although I had been out of college for years, I still returned to Key West for a week every spring for my own "spring break." In his last letter, he told me that he had decided to build a small six-room hotel in his back yard. In his letter he wrote "Key West is full of these goddamn bed-and-breakfasts where you pay a huge amount of money to sit in frilly rooms and talk about some bowl that someone's great grandmother carried all the way from Romania. There's no place to stay and have fun. So I'm going to open a bed-and-beer." My plan had been to help him get things ready to open when I went down over spring break.

Word of his death came while I was at work. It was after lunch, and I was writing a particularly uninteresting memo. I was daydreaming, in the middle of my favorite fantasy about the sailboat off the coast of Bimini. I was startled out of my reverie by the phone.

"Engineering, Aidan McInnis."

"Aidan, George Kelly." George was Albert's attorney and friend. Before the words, "I'm sorry to have to call you at work like this…" were out of his mouth, I knew. After all, what other reason would George have to call me?

"How did it happen, George?"

"It looks like he had a stroke. It must have been pretty massive. He was at the hangar working on the plane when he collapsed. It was pretty quick, Aidan. He was probably dead by the time he hit the ground."

At least he died doing something he loved. Nothing meant more to him than his plane.

Being Irish, I did what all good Irishmen do when they are faced with a loved one's mortality. I went to a bar. Actually, I had been planning to go there all along. My two best friends, Tony and Scot were planning to go to Key West with me, and we were meeting in the bar for happy hour to discuss our plans. They were already there when I arrived.

The three of us all worked for the same company. In fact, we had met in employee orientation on the day all of us were hired. All of us were just out of college, new to Boston, and looking for friends. We got lucky.

I told them of Albert's death. Tony was sympathetic. He had met Albert two years before, and had come with me on the subsequent trip to the island. His eyes misted a little and he had a hard time saying anything.

Scot was different. He was the dreamer, the idealist in our crowd. He lived his life vicariously through the words and actions of others. He longed for a life of adventure and wild abandon, but unless pushed into action by someone else, remained content to let others do his living for him. He had never met Albert, but the stories that Tony and I told of him had elevated him to legendary status in Scot's mind. He was truly disappointed that he would never get to experience my uncle.

The three of us stayed at the bar until late in the evening. When I got home, there was a message on my answering machine from my mother relaying the news. She sounded tired and I wondered at her emotions. Mother was uncomfortable around people who stepped outside the conventional rules for conducting their lives. I had no doubt that she loved Albert and was saddened by his death, but I wondered if she wasn't the tiniest bit relieved that his "disruptive" influence had been removed from my life.

The following Monday I borrowed a friend's Cessna and flew south. Flying such a small plane made it a several hour trip, but it gave me time to reflect. As I piloted the plane through the high clear springtime skies, I felt close to my uncle. He had been the one who taught me to love flying, and I wondered if he was somewhere in the clouds nearby.

I landed at Key West International Airport and taxied to the small hangar where Albert kept his plane. It was early evening. I was a little uneasy about letting myself into the hangar where he had died, but I needed a place to keep the Cessna.

I removed the combination lock that secured the doors, and opened it up. There, in front of me, was Albert's true treasure: a mint condition 1934 Douglas DC-2. The DC-2 was the smaller forerunner to the DC-3, which became the most famous aircraft ever flown. Many of the original DC-3s are still in operation even today. The DC-2 is smaller, and there are far fewer left. But it was built from the same basic design as the bigger plane. I never understood what Albert needed with a plane that carried fourteen passengers, and I doubt he ever even considered it. Albert lived his life around a much less complicated system of "needs" and "wants."

From the hangar I called the house. My mother and father were already there, and my dad told me he would drive over to pick me up.

I knew it would take him about ten minutes to drive over from the house, but I took my time about getting outside the hangar to meet him. Alone in the dark, musty old building, I took a few minutes to try to come to terms with what Albert's death meant. I walked over to his plane and gently laid a hand on the engine cowling. The plane was immaculate. The old Wright Cyclone engines that they installed on these planes were famous for throwing oil, but the cowling was smooth and clean.

I walked around to the tail and opened the cabin door. It was a steep climb up the aisle to the flight deck. When Albert had bought this plane, a skydiving school had been using it as a dive plane. He had gone to great pains to convert it back to a passenger plane, and had tried, whenever possible, to recapture the look of the 1930s. The cabin had teak trim, and the old airline sleeper seats were marched up the aisle in a proper regiment. Even in the gloom of the hangar, I could see a 1942 copy of *Life* in one of the seatback pockets. I started to pull back the curtain to the flight deck but stopped. It did not feel right. This was still Albert's plane, and I felt like I was trespassing. I walked back down the aisle and left the craft.

I pushed the Cessna into the hangar and chocked the wheels, secured the tail lock, and removed my duffel bag from the back seat. Then, looking back at the space where my uncle and friend died, I pulled the hangar doors closed and secured the lock.

My father was waiting in front of the hangar in Albert's Jeep. He seemed entirely out of context. Dad is not a "Jeep kind of guy." He's driven large Detroit products for most of my life. Surprisingly, he looked very comfortable sitting behind the wheel. I climbed into the passenger seat and we shook hands.

Our drive into town was uneventful. We talked quietly about my flight, his trip down with Mom, and the arrangements for the funeral. Dad said very little about Albert himself.

We drove down Duval, passing the bars and restaurants of modern Key West. Just beyond a small artist market, a narrow, fairly nondescript lane led between two brick houses. We turned into this alley and emerged, a moment later, into Monarch Court.

Albert's house was one of five on the small palm-lined cul-de-sac. The street had not originally been a cul-de-sac; it had been closed off at one end about seventy years ago. Four Monarch Court was an old sea captain's house: a Victorian monstrosity complete with requisite four-story turret and widow's walk. It was unusual from its neighbors in that it was brick instead of whitewashed wood. It was unusual from all of Key West in that it boasted not just one, but three fireplaces. Dad pulled the Jeep into the ground-floor garage.

Albert's house was...*eclectic.* He had preserved most of the original Victorian interior, but every inch of the house was crammed full of stuff. Old diving helmets and airplane radios and musical instruments hung from the walls or resided on tables or, in some rooms, sat defiantly in the middle of the floor. In the foyer alone, one had to circumnavigate an elephant's foot umbrella stand (filled with an dazzling array of golf umbrellas), dodge around a suit of armor holding a mace aloft menacingly, then duck past a palm tree potted in a model light house and dodge a stuffed pelican before managing the assault on the staircase. Just beyond the staircase, inside the kitchen, my mother awaited.

She was in the kitchen washing wine glasses. I'm not sure why since Albert had a perfectly good dishwasher right next to her, but sometimes you just don't question why Mom does things.

When she heard me behind her, she dried her hands on a towel and came to the door to hug me. The hug was tight and affectionate, and the familiar scent of White Shoulders filled my nose. We talked for a few moments, and I declined her immediate offer of food. As soon as it was possible to excuse myself without being rude I did so, and carried my bag upstairs.

I knew my parents would be occupying the bedroom I normally used in the front of the second floor. I suspected Aunt Vivian (Mom's bitchy sister who never misses a funeral) would be occupying the bedroom in the turret. Of course, Albert's bedroom would be sacrosanct. I carried my bag up to the turret room in the attic. Since my brother and sister had elected not to come to the funeral and I was therefore alone in the house with Albert's siblings, the attic seemed to be the best possible refuge.

In the turret room I deposited my bag next to the ancient bed. In the early evening darkness I could see the lights of Duval Street through the window. I opened it to let the fresh ocean breeze into the musty room. I was sweaty from a long day of flying, and so I took off my shirt and pants before unpacking. The breeze felt good against my chest.

After I unpacked, I stole down to the second floor to get cleaned up. In the bathroom I splashed water on my face, brushed my teeth and performed some quick pit maintenance. When I was finished, I emerged back into the upstairs hall and collided with Aunt Vivian as she came up the stairs.

"Aidan," she scolded as soon as she realized I was wearing nothing but a pair of boxers, "you could show a little decorum. Albert is dead. I think it is entirely inappropriate to be wandering his house in your undergarments."

"Yes, Aunt Vivian," I conceded and stole up the stairs to the attic. When I knew I was out of earshot I added, "Grand to see you, too, you old battle ax."

In my room, I finished cleaning up and began to dress for Albert's wake. A wake is truly one of the most civilized Irish traditions. What better way to send off a loved one then by having a big party to celebrate his or her life? As I was buttoning my shirt, there was a knock on the door. "Come in. I'm decent."

The door opened and my mother came in. "It's just me. Your Aunt Vivian seems to be in something of a state over you." She crossed the room and sat on the bed.

"Aunt Vivian is always in a state about someone," I observed. "In this particular case, she did not appreciate me walking about the second floor in my boxers. Sorry."

My mother waved away the apology. "Don't worry about it. I'm sure by now someone else has committed another transgression which has made her forget about you. If she gets to be too much, bring up Uncle Jeff." That was good advice. Uncle Jeff, their other brother, had elected not come to the funeral. Not because he was busy or had to work. He and Albert hadn't spoken in about twenty years, and apparently Jeff saw no reason to make the first move now just because Albert was dead. That should tell you all you need to know about Uncle Jeff.

"Is Uncle Mo here?" Uncle Mo is Aunt Vivian's husband. He is also the single most uninteresting human being I have ever met.

"No he had to stay at home. None of her kids are here either." I silently thanked God. Mom looked around the room and observed, "This room is pretty dusty. I doubt anyone has used it in years. Wouldn't you rather stay downstairs on the couch?"

"I sleep in the nude, Mom. I can just imagine Vivian's reaction if she saw me wandering around the house like that." She laughed. "I'll be fine up here."

Mom looked tired. Albert was the first of her siblings to die (I had always hoped Vivian would take that honor), and I think she may have felt guilty for not being more upset. I asked her if she was holding up okay.

She shrugged without looking up from a threadbare spot of the bedspread, which she was studying intensely. "I'm holding up okay. I just need some sleep. We had a long layover in Miami. Besides, you were much closer to Albert. How are you holding up?"

I stopped brushing my hair and thought about that. I'm a man. How was I supposed to be holding up? Men don't admit their feelings to themselves, much less to their mothers. "I'm okay." I resumed brushing my hair.

Mom took this rather noncommittal answer in stride. She has a husband and two sons. She's accustomed to uninformative answers. She nodded, and got up to leave. "We're going to be leaving for the mortuary in about ten minutes."

I nodded. "Where's the wake at?"

"I'm not sure. I don't even know if there is going to be one." She walked through the door and pulled it shut behind her. "See you downstairs."

How could there *not* be a wake, I wondered. A few moments later, I followed her downstairs. We would be walking to the mortuary since Aunt Vivian refused to ride in the Jeep. ("After all, they tip *over*.") The four of us met in the foyer and proceeded in solemn procession down the front steps and out of the cul-de-sac.

"Mom, what did you mean you don't know if there is going to be a wake?" I asked as we walked.

My mother looked uncomfortable. "Oh, you know. Those things are in such poor taste. I can't imagine anyone throwing one for poor Albert."

I knew very well that Albert had indeed wanted a wake and I said so. "You mean you didn't arrange one?"

"Certainly *not!*" Aunt Vivian sniffed. "Those things are barbaric. No brother of mine is going to paraded in front of a bunch of drunks!"

I couldn't believe what I was hearing. "Even though it is precisely what he wanted?"

"Oh, Albert liked to talk," Mom said. "I'm sure he never really cared if he had a wake or not."

We arrived at the mortuary. The building was shocking pink stucco, a little alarming for a mortuary but perfectly in keeping with Key West's personality. We went inside. We were, of course, the first to arrive. The mortician met us and escorted us into what Albert used to refer to as "the showroom." There, at the end on a small table was a simple silver urn. Flowers surrounded it.

Aunt Vivian sniffed. "I can't believe he was *cremated*. Mother must be rolling in her grave."

I thought about pointing out to Aunt Vivian that burial was an inefficient use of land and cremation more ecologically sound but decided against it. In truth, I was sure Albert chose to be cremated *precisely* because it would have caused his mother to roll over in her grave. The four of us approached my uncle's earthly remains. As we inspected the setting, it quickly became obvious that there was something unusual about it. My mother gasped.

Behind the urn were three huge wreaths. The first read "*Bon Voyage*"; the second, "*Happy Haunting*"; and the third "*Good Luck In Your New Location!*" I laughed out loud. Both of my parents shot me stern looks of disapproval. I have discovered that one of the nicest things about being an adult is that you are perfectly free to ignore stern looks of disapproval from your parents.

Aunt Vivian pronounced her judgment, her voice fairly dripping with horror. "How *inappropriate!*" She commanded me to remove the wreaths from the room.

I refused and three faces spun on me.

"I'm not removing them. In the first place, Albert would have *loved* these. In the second, you will offend his friends if you throw away these wreaths."

Aunt Vivian launched into an acid tirade against me, Albert's "riff-raff" friends, and my parents for raising such a disrespectful son. I remained steadfast and held my own with the old harridan. Eventually, my father suggested a compromise. The wreaths were moved to the side of the room, still visible, but well away from the urn.

The mourners began to arrive. I recognized many of them. Albert collected people the same way he collected things. He had many friends, and they were a varied and interesting lot. When his attorney, George, entered, he ignored my parents and aunt and walked straight to me to offer his condolences. After the few polite words spoken loud enough for my family to overhear, he led me aside and spoke to me in a hushed whisper.

"I have been arguing with your aunt all day. She is making my life a living hell."

"I'm sorry, George," I replied. "I wish we had some excuse for her. Unfortunately, we just all accept that she's a bitch."

"Albert left very explicit instructions about how his funeral was to be conducted and Vivian wants to change everything. And your parents are no help. They keep suggesting we *compromise*."

I nodded. That was my parents' solution to almost every conflict. "I'll have a word with my dad."

George waved my offer away. "I think we've got most of it settled. Are you aware of the part you're supposed to play in this circus?"

I looked at him blankly.

"Apparently not. Albert's will states that, after the funeral, you are to take the urn up in his plane and dump him over the gulf."

"You're kidding."

"I'm not. Of course, Vivian would prefer that we inter him somewhere, something about Catholicism not acknowledging it as an appropriate burial. But I cannot authorize that kind of variance from the will, and can take her to court if she tries to interfere. I just wanted to give you the head's up so you could file the flight plan."

I considered this. "That's pretty brave of Albert. I've only flown his plane three or four times, and never alone."

George smiled. "What's he got to lose?"

I laughed. "Good point."

"Listen," he said, suddenly all business again, "When are you going back to Boston?"

"I dunno. Wednesday maybe."

"Do me a favor. Don't go back until at least Thursday evening. We're doing the will Wednesday, and you should be here for it."

I considered that. "Why? Afraid Aunt Vivian is going to try to make off with his silverware?"

He chuckled. "Something like that. Oh, one other thing. I assume you're aware that Vivian nixed the wake." I nodded. "Well, we've decided to have one anyway. It's at Seamus Weinstein's bar at 10:00."

I smiled. Albert and I had spent many evenings discussing life over red ale at Seamus'. "I'll be there."

"Good. I was also hoping that you could help us out."

I'm sure my eyes narrowed. "How?"

"Bring Albert."

"*WHAT*?!?"

"Shhh!" George commanded. "I've talked to Ethan D'Vey. He's the mortician. He can't take the remains out of the mortuary without the family's consent. You're family, so you can. He says that if you take the urn to the bar, he can bring it back and no one will be the wiser."

"George," I rasped. "How am I going to get that urn past my parents?"

George reached up and patted my temple with his index and middle fingers. "You went to college. I'm sure you'll figure it out." With that, he walked away.

I considered what he was asking as I walked back towards my family. The larceny part itself didn't bother me terribly since it was proposed by the executor of Albert's will (George) and the mortician was in on it. I knew my parents and aunt would have a collective stroke if they found out. I dwelt on the idea of Aunt Vivian having a stroke as I rejoined my parents.

"What are you grinning about?" my father asked me.

"Oh, nothing. How's it going?"

He shrugged. "Okay, I guess. Don't know a damn person here."

"I hear I'm supposed to dispose of the remains tomorrow."

Dad nodded. "Didn't you know that?"

"How would I?"

He shrugged again. "I don't know. You spent so much time with Albert, I just assumed it was something he arranged with you."

I said nothing. After a few moments, Dad asked, "Have you ever flown his plane before?"

I nodded. "A couple of times. It was the plane I used to get my twin-engine rating." Dad is not a pilot, so I'm not sure this statement had any meaning to him, but I think he appreciated the fact that I didn't explain further.

The viewing ground along. As I said earlier, Albert collected an interesting group of people as friends. Somehow, though, none of them were acting particularly colorful this evening. The viewing was entirely out of character. Funerals in Key West often take on a Mardi Gras flavor. But Albert's otherwise interesting friends were behaving as though they had been in the embalming fluid.

Eventually, the viewing drew to a close. The last of the guests drifted out into the night (bound for Seamus', I hoped) and the four of us were left alone in the room. I heard Ethan D'Vey quietly clear his throat in the next room.

"Well," Dad observed. "I guess we should get back to the house."

"Why don't you all go ahead," I ventured. "I think I'm going to hang around here for a while."

"*What?*" Aunt Vivian practically shrieked. "Why on earth would you want to hang around a mortuary alone at night?"

"I don't want to hang around a mortuary. I just want some time to say good-bye."

Vivian rolled her beady little eyes into her puffy, red head, turned on her heel and lumbered towards the foyer. As she passed my mother she offered, "Honestly, Elaine. Your kids are so *weird!*"

Mom looked at me with concern. "Are you going to be okay? Should we wait?"

I smiled and shook my head. "I'm fine, Mom. I want to say good-bye to Albert, and then I'm going to stop by a friend's bar for a beer and then I'll come back to the house."

The concern remained on her face, but she kissed my cheek and took her leave by saying, "Well, okay. Just be careful. Key West is a dangerous place."

My parents followed Vivian out into the night. I was alone with Albert. I turned and walked towards the urn, gently running my fingers along the silver face of it. Inside was all that was left of my uncle. I tried hard to summon up some feelings, something to say, some act that would give me closure, but none came. I don't know how long I stood there caressing the urn, but I eventually became aware of someone standing behind me.

"Aidan," Ethan D'Vey ventured. "Everyone's waiting."

I smiled and nodded. I gently hefted the urn. It was heavier than I had expected. "He must have put on some weight since I last saw him."

Ethan chuckled a polite little mortician's chuckle. We walked towards the doors and he extinguished the light.

"C'mon Albert," I said to the urn as we walked out into the night. "Let's go party."

I'm sure I made quite a sight that evening, walking down Duval with what was left of Albert's mortal coil, but I really was unaware of any attention. Fortunately, Seamus' was only a few blocks away, and the two of us arrived safely.

As soon as I entered the bar, I was greeted by my uncle's friends in their true environment. There was a lot of laughing and shouting and singing. George was at a table in a corner dispensing free legal advice to a hooker. At another table, Sam Kinner, the mechanic who usually worked on Albert's plane, was having a beer with Sister Mary Rose. I was never certain if Sister Mary Rose was really a nun. She had a saintly demeanor and wore a habit, but she could also hold her liquor and had drunk Albert under the table more than once. By the bar, Simone du Champs, a local drag queen was comparing makeup notes with one of the waitresses. There were a host of others there who I didn't recognize, but who George later explained included the mayor, most of the city council, the director of financial aid from the local college and a guy who performed with trained cats on Mallory Square.

Seamus himself came to the door and handed me a beer while simultaneously relieving me of Albert. He placed the urn on the bar with a shot of rye in front of it. The wake could now officially begin.

Webster's defines a wake as a "watch over a dead body." I'm sure that is the least common denominator definition, but it is sadly lacking when applied to an Irish wake. An Irish wake is a party that is specifically designed to deteriorate into drunken maudlinism. This allows us (the Irish) to simultaneously celebrate the life of the deceased, mourn his passing and, if we're lucky, remember to celebrate the lives of the rest of our loved ones while they're still alive.

The wake was truly a party to be remembered. I'm sure that, wherever he was, Albert loved it. One beer led to several beers, led to shots of rye and, after about three hours, I was arm-in-arm with other Irish Conchs (the term for a person who makes his or her home in Key West) singing "Danny Boy." By the end of the song, everyone was crying. It was a great party.

Until Albert fell off the bar.

No one is sure how it happened. He had been moved several times in order to make room for the pitchers of beer. Somehow, he had been moved progressively closer to the edge, and finally he just toppled over.

I don't care how good a wake is or how determined the mourners are to give their loved one a glorious sendoff; dumping the deceased's remains out in the middle of the room is going to break up the party. George, Seamus, Ethan and I examined the dented urn and pile of ashes while the guests quietly, but rapidly, said their good-byes and quickly made their way out into the street.

None of the four of us was exactly sober. In fact, the term *shit-faced* seems entirely more appropriate. After a while, we all agreed that the unthinkable had indeed happened, and that we must now return Albert back to his vessel. We tried scooping him up with ice scoops, and sweeping him up with a dust tray, but both seemed largely ineffective. Eventually, it was decided that Seamus' wet/dry vacuum was the best solution.

We were able to restore Albert to the crumpled urn, or, at least, *most of him*. But the dent was severe enough that we were unable to re-secure the top. Ethan clearly looked nervous. We sent him back to the mortuary with Albert's remains to try and disguise the damage, and the rest of us departed for bed.

It was well past one a.m. when I wandered back into Monarch Court. Despite the lateness of the hour, I was not really sleepy, so instead of going into the house, I wandered into the back yard to check out the *bed'n'beer*.

The pool behind the old house looked the same. When I had last been in Key West, the rest of Albert's lot had been a few palm trees and a seriously overgrown wisteria. Now, all of that had been replaced with a two-story white frame building. It had been built to maintain the same Victorian look as the rest of the neighborhood, and a great verandah ran along the entire front of both floors. I promised myself I would explore it after the funeral tomorrow.

As I turned to walk back towards the house, I saw someone standing at the gate watching me. I immediately thought of my mother's warning that Key West was a dangerous place, and considered what I would do when this person attacked or mugged me. I considered running, but the entire back yard was enclosed. I considered jumping into the pool, but sitting on the bottom and waiting for this person to leave was a temporary solution at best. I considered panicking. I finally decided to greet the person instead.

"Uh, hello," I ventured. "Can I help you?"

"No, probably not," came the reply. The figure did not move from the gate, but continued to watch me.

I considered my next move. "Um, I'm Aidan. This is my uncle's house."

"Was," he corrected.

"Well, yes. I suppose that's true." I began to walk tentatively towards the figure at the gate.

Slowly, I drew up near him. He was probably in his late sixties. A tall, thin chap with a bony face and long white hair pulled back into a ponytail. He wore a velvet jacket, tweed pants and a white linen shirt. All were impeccably cut. He was carrying a walking stick with what looked like a large silver griffin for a handle. He was barefoot.

"I, uh, don't suppose you would care to tell me who you are?" I asked.

He considered a moment. "No, not really."

"Oh." This conversation had clearly run its course. "Well, um, I guess I'll be going inside now."

"That seems wise," the stranger agreed. As I started to walk past him, he held something out. I jumped back, startled.

"Our condolences on your loss, young Aidan," he said. "We were unable to come to the viewing. Please leave our card for your parents." I took the card and continued to stare at him blankly. Who in the hell was this guy? He then placed a top hat, of all things on his head, touched its brim to me, and turned around. A moment later, he disappeared up the walk.

After the adrenaline subsided, I was able to collect my thoughts. I walked around to the front of the house, climbed the front steps and let myself into the foyer. There, in the dim light falling from the upstairs landing, I read the card. It was printed with gold ink on purple, silk-faced card stock and read simply:

> *Louis Of Robideau*
> *Monarch of Key West*

I was too tired to contemplate what the encounter meant. I left the card and my keys on the hall table and stumbled upstairs to bed.

The next morning, I awoke early and immediately wished I hadn't. My head felt like it was about to explode. As I began to approach consciousness, I felt a deep, drilling pain in each of my temples, and a visceral grip at the back of my skull. The inside of my mouth tasted like a wet mitten. I pulled on a pair of shorts and stumbled downstairs to the bathroom, all the time trying to keep my head as still as possible. After a shower, I didn't feel better but I at least felt human. I was also able to keep both eyes open simultaneously, which was a major accomplishment. I got dressed and inched downstairs to the kitchen. The house, mercifully, was quiet.

My dad was in the kitchen standing at the counter, quietly sipping his coffee while he read the paper. I have seen my dad stand like this in the morning perhaps ten thousand times. He looked around as I entered the kitchen.

"Good morning."

"Mornin'," I muttered.

"You're up early."

I nodded as I retrieved a bagel and the cream cheese from the refrigerator. "I want to file the flight plan before we leave for the funeral."

"Ah." He took a sip of coffee and turned to look out the window over the sink. "How was the wake?"

Busted! I thought to myself as I put the bagel into the toaster. There was no point in lying about it. "It was fine."

Dad nodded again. After a long pause, I asked, "How did you know?"

He smiled. "I've been Irish a lot longer than you. A man like Albert doesn't die without his friends holding a wake."

Since my father is so reserved and unemotional, I tend to forget that he is also Irish. "Do Mom and Vivian know?"

Dad laughed. "If they did, do you think there would have been a wake?"

I conceded the point. The toaster delivered my bagel to me and I spread a generous amount of cream cheese on top. Dad resumed reading his paper. Nothing was said, but it was one of those few times when I felt a sense of camaraderie with my father.

After I finished my bagel and a mug of coffee, I informed Dad that I was taking the Jeep to the airport. He nodded, and I left the kitchen. In the foyer, I retrieved Albert's spare set of keys from where I had left them on the table, and again noticed *Louis Of Robideau's* card. It was no longer where I had left it, but in a brass bowl so I assumed my father had examined it. I stuck it in my pocket and left for the airport.

The morning was bright and clear. I parked in front of the hangar and let myself in through the back door. The DC-2 and the Cessna sat where I had left them the previous evening. I went to Albert's plane, climbed inside and made my way to the flight deck. I was less apprehensive about entering the flight deck this morning, I suppose, because I knew Albert wanted me there. Behind the captain's seat was Albert's flight bag. I retrieved it and made my way back to the hangar office.

The flight manuals were old, which I guess was appropriate since the plane was old. It took me about and hour and a half to get the weather forecast, plan the flight, and file the appropriate documents with the FAA. When I had everything arranged, I returned the bag to the flight deck, and drove back to the house.

George picked up my parents and Aunt Vivian and me for the funeral at 11:00. Since Vivian wouldn't ride in the Jeep, he had volunteered his Lincoln. I followed behind in the Jeep.

When we arrived at the church, the urn was already present and sat on a small pedestal in front of the altar. I overheard Aunt Vivian whisper to my mother "Does the urn look *different* to you?"

The urn was indeed different. It was similar to the one which Albert had previously occupied, but the handles were a different shape. The whole thing looked a little tarnished.

"It's probably the light in here," my mother whispered back to Aunt Vivian. I excused myself and walked to the back of the church.

George and Ethan were standing in the vestibule. They both looked like hell. I greeted them and then politely mentioned the urn to Ethan. "That *is* him, isn't it?"

Ethan looked annoyed. "*Yes* Aidan. It's him. I couldn't fix the urn so I transferred him to that one. I expect you to bring it back after you dump him."

The funeral was typically Catholic. The church was *packed*, and George delivered the eulogy. While he spoke I looked around the crowd. Among the people in attendance was Louis Of Robideau. I made a mental note to ask George who he was. Instead of going to the cemetery after the service, the procession of cars drove to the hangar.

Since the priest did not like to fly, he performed all of the rites of burial next to the plane. When he finished, George and I pushed the Cessna outside. Then, Albert's mechanic Sam Kinner and I each took a wing and pushed the DC-2 out of the hangar. I did a quick pre-flight walk around of the aircraft while George carried Albert inside. My parents stood next to the plane speaking softly with the priest, and Aunt Vivian watched everything everyone did like a hawk. As I prepared to board, the priest performed a quick blessing of both me and the airplane.

Inside, I saw that George had strapped Albert into the seat by the flight deck door. I gave the urn a snappy little salute and went through the curtain. George was already strapped into the copilot's seat.

I completed my preflight checks. Although the plane was old, Albert had certainly added some expensive enhancements. There was a decent radio altimeter, a Loran, and about as sophisticated an autopilot as you could expect on a plane of this vintage. When the checks were complete, I opened the window and asked everyone to move away from the plane. Sam pulled the wheel chocks and gave me the thumbs up when everyone was clear of the aircraft. I switched on the fuel pumps and batteries and held down the starter for the Number One engine.

Outside the plane, the left propeller began to turn slowly. As it picked up speed, I held down the starter for the other engine and radioed to the tower to request permission to taxi. It was granted, and I eased the throttles forward slowly. The plane began to roll.

We left the hangar and turned onto the taxiway. Instead of a nose gear and two under-wing main landing gear, these old planes have their third wheel in the tail, and are hence known as *tail draggers*. While this configuration makes them extremely graceful on takeoff, they are tricky to land and just a downright bitch to taxi. Fortunately, Key West is not the busiest of airports (with a 4,600 foot runway, only so many planes can even operate there), and we were cleared as second for departure on Runway 27.

The plane ahead of us departed and I was cleared to taxi into position. I did so, and did my magneto check. After a moment, the control tower gave us clearance for departure. Before I could radio my acknowledgment, the air traffic controller on the other end of the radio added, "And Godspeed, Albert."

I applied the throttles and we began to roll down the runway. At 75 knots, I felt the tail leave the ground. I eased the yoke towards me and we were in the air. We flew over the island and turned northwest into the gulf. My flight plan took us on a circular route out over the gulf, then down to the Dry Tortugas, and then back home. George and I sat in silence for a while as the plane cut through the bright blue sky, each lost in our own thoughts. Eventually, my thoughts turned to my encounter from the previous evening.

"Hey George," I said as I retrieved the small silk card from pocket and handed it to him. "Do you know this guy?"

George examined it. "Oh. So you've met Mad King Louis?"

"So you know him? Who is he?"

"Oh, this is a long story. Years ago, I guess it was about 1982, Key West was going to secede from the country…"

"Oh yeah. I remember Albert talking about that. Weren't they going to do something like put a toll gate on Highway One?"

"That's exactly what was going to happen. Anyway, the mayor declared that we were going to secede. We were going to call ourselves the Conch Republic. We even planned to declare war. Well, some of us who were friends of the mayor decided this was a good reason to have a party."

"You guys think everything is a good reason to have a party."

"True. Anyway, we formed the Conch Republic Government in Exile."

"But you're not in exile. You're right here."

He turned and gave me a cross look. Since George has enormous bushy white eyebrows of sufficient length that he can probably use them to drive, his cross looks are immensely funny. "Would you let me finish this story?"

"Sorry."

"Anyway, we formed the government in exile. Albert was the Prime Minister. I am the First Lord of the Admiralty. Well, all of us have positions, and the G.I.E..."

"G.I.E.?"

"Government in exile. Anyway, it's been kind of a standing club for years now. Well, Louie Robideau was one of the original founders, and he declared himself king. No one felt like arguing about it since we thought, in case of revolution, we could throw him to masses and escape with our own heads."

I laughed. "Very pragmatic. Ruthless, but pragmatic."

"Louie is an artist; actually lives in the house that backs up to Albert's property. As he's gotten older, he's had to build on his reputation each year. He even had his middle name legally changed to "Of.""

"You're joking."

"I'm not. In a place like Key West, you have to work harder to be eccentric."

About forty minutes into the flight, I informed George that we had another ten minutes before I turned south. We agreed that this was probably the best place to dump the remains. George went into the cabin and returned with the urn. The silence was awkward.

Eventually, George cleared his throat. "Should we, uh, *say* something?"

I didn't answer right away. The men in my family don't do these things well. I was grateful that none of the women in my family were there to point it out.

"I think," I said, "that Albert would have liked it if we related our favorite memory of him."

George thought about it for a minute. "I guess my favorite memory of him was a fishing trip we took a few years ago. There is this little abandoned airstrip on one of the smaller islands in the Tortugas. About five of us took the plane, flew down there one morning, and spent the day drinking and fishing. We slept that night beneath the wing. Anyway, right at sunset this beautiful big schooner sails by the beach. It was an extremely peaceful moment. And Albert says to me, 'Home is the sailor, home from the sea, and the hunter home from the hill.' I've heard that before, although I'm not sure where it's from, but it was very appropriate."

I smiled. "It's the epitaph from Robert Louis Stevenson's tombstone."

He looked sideways at me. "No shit?"

"Nope. Albert visited his grave in Samoa."

"Wow. That, I did not know." He paused, and then turned to face me. "Your turn."

There was no question in my mind what my favorite memory was. "It was during my first summer visiting him. We were sitting up on the widow's walk of the house, drinking margaritas, playing Jimmy Buffett. All very Key West. Anyway, Albert's asking me all kinds of questions about what I'm going to do with my life. I tell him I'm going to be an engineer. He asks why, and I tell him that the money's good and I think I would be pretty good at it. He asks me, if the money wasn't that good, would I still want to do it. I think about it and tell him, no, probably not. Then he tells me 'Aidan, the worst thing you can ever do is choose a life for yourself because it's the easiest alternative. It's every bit as important to love what you do as to love what it buys you.'"

George looked confused. "But I thought you are an engineer?"

"I am," I conceded. "But, for an airline, so at least I'm exposed to flying, which is something I love."

George looked dubious. "I'm not sure that was exactly what he meant."

I nodded. "No, it's probably not. But I had Albert on one hand telling me to do what I loved and I had my parents on the other telling me to pick a career where I could make a decent living. I think I chose the best compromise I could."

George thought about this for a minute. "And, if you didn't have to worry about money, what would you do?"

Again, I knew right away. "I'd take a plane and retire to an island somewhere just like Albert and be a writer."

George smiled. "What would you write about?"

"I dunno. I haven't had that many interesting experiences in my life so far. I guess I'd have to write about Albert's life."

George chuckled. I looked at the instruments and told him we were about in position. He nodded and asked "Well, do you want to do the honors or shall I?"

"I guess I'd like to do them," I said. The plane was on autopilot. I accepted the urn from George and opened the window. We were only at five thousand feet, so the depressurization was insignificant. I opened the top of the urn and looked at the ashes. I couldn't think of anything more appropriate than to echo the air traffic controller's words. "Godspeed, Uncle Albert." I held the urn out the window and poured the ashes into the wind.

That done, I took control of the airplane again. George put the urn behind his seat and began to chuckle. "We should tell Ethan you accidentally dropped the urn into the ocean."

I began to laugh. The somber and respectful portion of the day over, I realized I was extremely hot. I hate flying in a tie, and had taken precautions against being uncomfortable on the trip home. Underneath my dress clothes I was wearing a tank top and a pair of running shorts. After turning the plane south and verifying our heading, I took off my "funeral wear."

"That looks better," George concurred, taking a flask out of his jacket pocket. He took a swig and offered it to me. I shook my head.

"If you're going to drink," I said, "I wish you wouldn't do it on the flight deck. It's illegal."

George rolled his eyes. "I'm an attorney, Aidan. I assure you I've gotten away with far more illegal things."

I didn't have a good argument for that. We flew on to the Dry Tortugas.

"You know," I mused, "it's too bad Albert never took me to this island you're talking about. It sounds like a great place for a party."

George reached behind my seat and pulled out Albert's flight kit. "I'm not a pilot, but it seems to me that he had it marked on a chart in here." After rummaging around a bit, he produced a badly wrinkled airman's map with "Runner's Island" circled in pencil.

"Runner's Island?"

George nodded. "That's what we called it. Not sure if it has a proper name, but it must have been used for drug running at one time. Anyone who tells you the Coast Guard did nothing in the eighties to stop drug trafficking needs to see the number of abandoned airstrips throughout the Keys and Caribbean. Nowadays, it's mostly used by pilots looking for a deserted stretch of beach."

After dumping the ashes, we had climbed to 10,000 feet. Looking out the window, I couldn't really make out where the airstrip was on the islands below, but I could determine the general area in which to look. "Maybe I'll go there some day." We flew back to Key West.

It was early evening when I returned home. My mother and aunt greeted me with horrified looks. "That's *not* what you wore when you dumped the ashes, is it?" my mother asked.

"No, Mother. It's what I wore afterwards." I started for the stairs. I heard my mother thank God, and Aunt Vivian launch into some whispered tirade, I'm sure against me. I detoured through the dining room and made myself a drink before escaping to the attic. In my tiny turret room I felt like a prisoner in the Tower of London. I stalked around, trying to relax, but I was soon climbing the walls. I finally decided that I had to get some air.

The attic itself was lit by a skylight in the roof. An ancient wrought-iron staircase wound up to a hatch which led onto the widow's walk. I took my drink and went up there.

The roof of the house itself was copper. The wood floor of the widow's walk, after a day baking in the Key West sun, was as hot beneath my bare feet as the copper would have been. I walked quickly to a chaise lounge that sat perched next to the skylight, facing west. I sat down to watch the sun drop into the Gulf.

From my rooftop vantage point, I had a beautiful view of the island. In the distance, I could hear the sounds of people gathering at Mallory Square to watch the sunset. I loved Key West, and I wondered for the first time if, now that Albert was dead, I would ever return. The thought depressed me.

Dinner was singularly uneventful. Mom prepared some steaks that she had found in the freezer and Aunt Vivian reviled red meat. I could tell that they were starting to get on each other's nerves.

The next morning, I again awoke early and went swimming. I was quite surprised that Vivian did not rebuke me for showing disrespect by swimming in the deceased's pool. She seemed strangely distant. It wasn't until my father mentioned the reading of the will at 1:30 that I understood *what* she was thinking about.

Albert was not a poor man. For all of his hobbies and eccentricities, he was an extremely good businessman. Mom and Aunt Vivian, along with their brother Jeff (who lived in California) stood to make a bundle from the inheritance. I know Mom didn't like to think about such things, but I'm positive Vivian did.

That afternoon, we walked to George's office. Dad wore gray slacks and a twill jacket. Mom wore a conservative navy pants suit and Vivian wore a loud, ill-fitting, yellow floral dress. Since I had thus far been unable to bait Aunt Vivian into reprimanding me that day, I wore another tank top, the same running shorts and a pair of flip-flops.

At George's office, we were escorted into a conference room and seated around the table. George joined us after a few minutes. He was wearing what must have been a $300 suit, and I realized that, until the funeral, I had never seen George wear anything but shorts and a tee shirt. Judging by the quality of the suit, he must have been somewhat more successful than I had imagined.

"You all should understand that this is just a reading," George said. "It is, by no means, the settlement of Albert's estate. As Albert's executor, he has left me instructions to pay off certain bills and expenses before releasing any properties or moneys to individual heirs. Is that clear to everyone?"

The family all nodded their assent. I was bored. George began reading the will. There were the usual "I, Albert Cochran Fitzgerald"'s and the "of sound mind"'s and so forth. It was almost an hour before we got into any of the good stuff.

The first surprise was Albert's net worth. It greatly exceeded what any of us had thought. Unbeknownst to any of us (except George), Albert had sold his business earlier that year for quite a substantial sum. Almost all of his net worth was in the form of cash.

The second (and bigger) surprise was the identity of his principal heir. When George read the words "do hereby acknowledge Jason A. Metior of New Orleans as my son and principal heir," Aunt Vivian came out of her chair.

"His *what!?!*" she cried. "He has a son?!"

George put down the will. "Yes Vivian, he has a son. I think he may be fourteen now. Albert has always acknowledged him, and has paid support to the child's mother since before he was born. But he was adamant that his family never be told."

I certainly saw why George had suggested I stay. This was better than theater. I watched avidly as Aunt Vivian threatened to contest the will.

"You can certainly do that, Vivian," George said with exaggerated calmness. "But I'm afraid you will have a very hard time making a case in court that an acknowledged child of the deceased is not entitled to inherit his father's estate."

Vivian's face was almost purple (which really *clashed* with her dress). George added, "There are other heirs named and other assets to be disbursed. May I continue?"

Vivian said nothing, but slammed her substantial fanny back down into her chair. George continued. He detailed everything that my cousin Jason was to inherit, including the bulk of Albert's cash to be paid out through a trust administered by his mother, as well as several very valuable stocks, partnerships, and other financial instruments. I was impressed. Jason A. Metior would be a fabulously wealthy teenager.

More money was left to Jason's mother, and $999,999.99 was to be divided among Mom, Aunt Vivian and Uncle Jeff. I was not really paying attention since I was contemplating my new cousin and was therefore startled when George mentioned my name.

"To my nephew, Aidan Fitzgerald McInnis, I bequeath my house at Four Monarch Court, Key West, Florida. Also to Aidan F. McInnis, I bequeath the amount of $61,591.34 to be used towards the completion of my guesthouse."

Now it was my turn to be shocked. I could do nothing but sit there and blink. And then, I heard the words I would have never even dared hope to hear. "Also to Aidan F. McInnis, I bequeath my 1934 Douglas DC-2, Registry Number ZK010."

I was stunned, and more than a little confused. The house, the money and the plane; I had no idea what Albert was thinking when he left these things to me. I certainly couldn't get the house to Boston, and I couldn't afford to keep a plane hangared in Boston. All of my assets would be tied up in Florida, two-thousand miles away from home.

The rest of Albert's assets, mostly his furniture and personal possessions were to be divided among the family, and everything that no one wanted was to be auctioned and the money given to the Key West Historic Preservation Society. As you might have suspected, Vivian's children were not mentioned in the will, nor were my sister or brother.

Also as you might have suspected, the dinner discussion that evening was, well, *colorful.*

While I may have been clueless as to what Albert had been thinking when he left me the house and plane, there was absolutely no question in my mind what he had been thinking when he left nothing specifically to Vivian's kids. Aunt Vivian is a positive joy to be around compared to her two children. I was also not terribly surprised that my brother and sister were not mentioned: not because there was any animosity between them and Albert (or anyone else in the family) but simply because they had never really spent any time with Albert and he hardly knew them. Therefore, when my mother suggested at dinner that I consider selling the house and the plane and sharing the proceeds with my sister, brother and Vivian's brats, I almost spit a mouthful of food across the table.

"I beg your pardon?" I asked, choking down some baked potato.

"Well," she began, "it would be very nice of you to share, and I'm sure Albert would have wanted them to have *something.*" Aunt Vivian was uncharacteristically silent, but watched me like a hawk.

"If Albert wanted them to have something," I said, "he would have mentioned them in the will. Besides, it's not like they were left out in the cold. You and Vivian each came out of this with over three-hundred grand. They're going to receive some benefit from that."

"Well, yes…" Mom began, looking for a defensible position. "But I'm sure he wanted all of you to have the benefit of at least the house."

I couldn't believe she was putting me in this position. Not only was she asking me to sell off two things that I valued, she was asking me to do it in front of Vivian. If I refused, it would certainly make it back to the family how mean-spirited and cheap I was, and how little concern I had for the rest of my family. While I didn't give a damn what Vivian's kids thought of me, I would prefer not to have my own brother and sister feeling that I had screwed them.

I was carefully weighing my response when my dad spoke up. Ordinarily, he defers to my mother on all matters of family protocol, so I was surprised when he came to my defense. "I don't think Aidan should have to do anything of the sort," Dad began. "First of all, no one else in the family is a pilot, so it was only right that Albert left the plane to someone who would use it and get some pleasure out of it."

"Well, yes..." Mom began, "but the house..."

"What to do with the house is Aidan's decision. None of the other kids have ever even seen it. Albert and Aidan had a special relationship, and I don't think it is fair of you to ask him to sell it. If he does, that is his business."

My dad doesn't usually take strong positions like this, so when he does it carries some weight. The rest of the dinner was mostly conducted in silence. Afterwards, I made myself a stiff drink and walked outside to inspect the guesthouse, *my* guesthouse now.

It is amazing how differently one looks at a property when it is his. I noticed details that would have completely escaped me before. I saw that the trim on the main house needed to be painted. There was a crack in the concrete around the pool. While the guesthouse was almost completely done on the outside, most of the rooms inside still needed a great deal of work. It was going to take a good bit of work to finish this place. I decided I needed to talk to George and find out exactly what Albert had been thinking by unloading this place on me.

I had no desire to go back into the house yet, so I walked out of the court to Duval to use a payphone.

George answered on the second ring. "Hi, it's Aidan. I need to talk to you."

"About?"

"About exactly what in the *hell* Albert was thinking when he left me this place."

"Well, that didn't take long."

"What didn't?"

"For you to go over the edge. Let's have lunch tomorrow."

I returned to the house. Mom and Aunt Vivian were waiting.

"Since this is *your* house now," the sarcasm fairly dripped out of Vivian's mouth, "we thought we'd wait until you were here to divide up the furniture and such."

Mom tried to be conciliatory. "Is there anything in here you especially want to stay?"

The last thing in the world I wanted was to be part of this division of spoils. "I want all of the yard tools, everything in the garage and all the pool equipment. That way, I'll at least be able to care for this place." I started to leave the room. "Oh, and everything in Albert's study. I'll need to go through his papers." I left them to split up everything else.

I crossed the foyer, heading for the stairs. It was my intent to pack my clothes so I could get off the island as quickly as possible tomorrow. However, as I passed the door to the study, I paused and decided to enter.

The study was in the first floor of the turret. It was round, and bookcases stretched the entire twelve feet to the ceiling. It was one of the three rooms with a fireplace, the others being the living room and Albert's bedroom. There was a beat-up leather sofa against one wall, an old wing chair by the fireplace, and a battered desk in front of the window. I closed the door silently behind me, sat down at the desk and took in the place.

I had not asked for anything that Mom or Vivian would value; Vivian had precious little use for books. I had never sat at Albert's desk before, so I never noticed the two small photographs that he had stuck into the corner of the blotter. One was of Albert with a teenage boy, maybe thirteen. I wondered if this was my cousin Jason. The other was a picture of him with me, taken when I was nineteen. Both pictures were remarkably similar. Albert standing with his son or his nephew, on a pier in front of a sailboat. I remembered well that day the one was taken with me. It was my first spring break in Key West and I was so full of hero worship, I could hardly see straight.

I took the pictures out of the blotter and tucked them into my shirt pocket. As I left the library, I could hear my mom wondering aloud if Uncle Jeff would want all of Albert's clothes. I went upstairs.

I met George the next day on Mallory Square. We had lunch at a small *Miami Subs* that was nearby. Over our sandwiches, I repeated my question of the previous evening.

"Isn't it interesting," George mused, "that we usually discover that we did not know a person close to us until after he has died?"

"Very philosophical," I replied, impatiently. "Let's get down to basics. I've suddenly acquired a lot of assets. How much trouble am I in financially?"

"Well, it depends how much you make at work. I'll be honest Aidan, I'm not sure *what* Albert was thinking leaving you the house and the plane. His primary concern when he made out the will was to make sure that Jason got most of the estate. Frankly, I think the only reason he left anything to his sisters and brother was to keep them from going after Jason. But you're a different matter.

"You see, I agree with you that he had *something* in mind, because of the amount of money he left. Everyone else got nice, round, evenly dividable figures except you. He did not arrive at sixty-one thousand five hundred and ninety-one dollars and however many cents by whim. When he wrote this last will, he calculated the exact amount of inheritance taxes you would have to pay."

"You mean," I asked as a sinking feeling washed over me, "that, once I pay the taxes, I'll have nothing left?"

"No, you'll still have two things left. The house and the plane."

I dropped my face into my hands. He continued.

"It's not as bad as you think. Both are paid for. There are no liens against either. He even paid cash for the construction of the guest-house. The annual property taxes on the house are high, but not outrageous and certainly more economical than the mortgage payments would be. The biggest monthly expense is the rent on the hangar, but I would imagine you're paying a good deal more than that just to rent planes."

I thought this over while I ate. I wasn't necessarily any better or worse off than I was when I started. I had acquired some of Albert's assets and still maintained my status quo.

"What about Jason?" I asked. "Why didn't Albert ever tell anyone in the family that he had a son?"

George shrugged. "Why did Albert do anything that he did? Albert did not have a high opinion of his family, your family. Albert detested complacency. I think he was probably afraid that your aunt or some other relative would make his life a living hell for having a son and not being married to the mother." I certainly couldn't argue with his reasoning.

George was able to provide me with some papers that helped me handle business, and I retained him as my attorney. After lunch, I said good-bye to my parents and my aunt, and flew home.

Compared to the DC-2, the Cessna felt light and fragile. Although the weather was mild all the way up the east coast, it seemed as though the slightest winds buffeted the plane. I looked forward to again flying Albert's plane, my plane now.

I am generally not the kind of person who likes to operate without a plan. I was uncertain what I was going to be able to do with the house or the plane. The plane was the easier of the two, since I could at least bring it to Boston. However, like everything else in Boston, the cost to rent hangar space is outrageous, and I was sure I couldn't afford the amount of space that a plane sixty feet long would require. The house was a different matter entirely. It could not be brought to Boston. And I had no idea how I was going to be able to care for it from two thousand miles away, much less carry out Albert's wish that I finish the guesthouse.

Albert's wish. Again I wondered what Albert was thinking. Did he have some grand plan in mind that I was simply unaware of? Did he assume I would understand what he meant by leaving me the house?

Or, did he just want to leave me *something* in the will, and the house and plane were all that was left. Whatever it was, he was dead, and I would never know his intentions.

KEY WEST

The next day was Friday. I considered not going in to work, but realized I had already presumed on my boss' good nature by staying in Key West one day longer than I had intended. I had not been back in my office for more than five minutes when Tony and Scot were there, hounding me for details. I told them about the funeral, about Albert falling off the bar at the wake, and about my inheritance. I could have predicted their reactions.

"Cool," Tony declared. "A place to party in the sun!"

"Wow," Scot enthused, "what a great thing to inherit."

"When are we going down to get the plane?" Tony asked.

"Not until I figure out where I can keep it," I told him. "Besides, the estate still hasn't released it to me. It may take months for that part to be settled."

I was, in fact, wrong.

Friday was nothing if not an eventful day. Just before lunch, George called me to inform me that he had pulled some strings and that the house and plane would be released to me on Monday. The money would be held up a few weeks, but I would not have to pay the inheritance tax for three months yet. I immediately faxed him my power of attorney to handle the legal matters of the inheritance.

Also that afternoon, the airline posted its results for the fiscal year. As airlines are occasionally wont to do in these heady, post-deregulation times, it posted a loss. In fact, it announced that it was hemor-rhaging money. In fact, later that same day, it declared bankruptcy.

Everyone knew that the company was struggling. We had had three money-losing quarters in a row. But, no one expected the end-of-the-year numbers to be that bad. Everyone in the office was dazed and stunned. Then, we received the news that everyone with less than five years seniority would be furloughed on Monday. For many, that was all it took to push them from dazed and stunned into catato-nia.

I had been with the company four years.

The three of us met at a bar near the office. No one said anything for a long time. We just stared into our beers and tried to sort out how all of our lives had collapsed in one afternoon. And, somewhere in the back of my mind, I wondered if Albert had orchestrated all of this from beyond the grave just to further complicate my life.

All three of us were in trouble. I had the money I had saved for the down payment on a condo. It would last about four months. Tony and Scot were in similar situations. But, the airline industry was in chaos, and there was little chance of finding another airline job. In fact, at that time, there was little chance of finding another job in Boston, period.

It was as obvious to me as it surely must be to you reading this what I had to do. I put down my beer and said, "Well, I'd say this is proba-bly as blatant an omen as possible that we move to Key West."

The two of them were not enthusiastic. Tony does not do spontane-ity well. He believes in well-orchestrated spontaneity, and an upheaval of the magnitude I was proposing was well outside his comfort zone. Similarly, Scot was not anxious to walk away from his girlfriend. To be perfectly accurate, his girlfriend was not *actually* his girlfriend. She was a cold, domineering, unpleasant waste of carbon who had actually ended their relationship about four months earlier. However Scot has a hard time coping when he's not in a relationship so he still stayed in regular contact with her, and felt they might get back together one day. I prayed he would be disappointed.

As I said, each of us had a reason why he needed to stay in Boston, including me. But, as we debated the possibility late into the night and over the rest of the weekend, we all began to agree that none of the things holding us here were important or even substantial. We turned our attention to the guesthouse.

The three of us had very different skills. I was an engineer and a pilot. Tony was an accountant. Scot was a computer programmer. None of us knew anything about launching a business. In fact, people like us launched businesses every day with catastrophic results. We should, of course, have forgotten the idea that very minute.

I had other pressures not to do it. On Sunday evening, when I spoke to my parents (who had just returned to Chicago), they let me know in no uncertain terms that they thought this was just about the dumbest thing they had ever heard. Their idea was, if I could not find a job in Boston before my money ran out, to move back home to Chicago (and, I presume, in with them) and look for a job from there. That was, of course, just about the dumbest idea *I* had ever heard.

On Monday, I called George at his office, explained the situation to him, and told him I would be arriving some time the following week to take up residence.

"You realize," he snarled at me, "that your parents and aunt have had the place mothballed, and now you want to reopen it?" I confirmed that I did. George sounded as though he had had enough of the Fitzgeralds and McInnises and the rest of our sundry relations.

It did not take any of the three of us long to close out our affairs. Since so many people were leaving the airline, there were no farewell parties, although many tearful good-byes. Truthfully, I was glad to be leaving Boston altogether.

We left the following Monday at about four a.m. I drove my little red convertible, Tony followed in his Toyota, and Scot brought up the rear in his truck. He had the undesirable task of pulling the U-Haul containing all of the large pieces of our furniture including miscellaneous couches, dressers and beds. Everything else we owned was stacked in a friend's garage. Our intention was to fly back before the end of the week, load everything that was left into the plane and return to Florida.

Spring had not penetrated as far north as Massachusetts, and we left the city in a cold, biting drizzle. Our drive took us straight down Interstate 95. Seven hours later, we saw the first tentative signs of the new season in Washington. Three hours after that, the last of the rain clouds disappeared, and we were greeted by sunshine as we entered North Carolina. In South Carolina, it was warm enough for me to put the roof of my car down, although we only had about another four hours of light. At nine that night, we pulled into a rest stop two hours north of Savannah, Georgia and decided to call it a day.

Since we were all pretty tight on funds, we elected to sleep in the trailer. I was able to climb under Tony's dining room table and find a spot to curl up on the cushions from my couch. Tony slept between two old chairs and my drawing table. Scot rolled out his futon (his only piece of furniture besides a truly monumental stereo cabinet) on top of the table above me. As I curled down into my sleeping bag, I momentarily relived a childhood game of building forts from couch cushions and blankets and card tables. I must have found the memory reassuring because I was soon fast asleep.

We awoke at about five the next morning and set out again. After a quick McBreakfast, we passed through Savannah and entered the great void of coastal Georgia. At noon, we had left Daytona Beach far behind us and were just on the outskirts of Melbourne. Interstate 95 ended on the south side of Miami at 3:30, and we picked up Highway 1, which would lead us across the keys and to the house.

At five we stopped on a tiny island just before Marathon Key. Our intention was to eat in Marathon and then push out the last ninety minutes of the drive. Since none of us had showered in two days, we were all a bit aromatic. We pulled off the road and down beneath the bridge to the next island. Here, we shed most of our clothes and took a quick swim to wash away the road dirt. By six, we were seated on the deck of a small, nameless fish shop in Marathon enjoying grouper sandwiches and big glasses of Miller. We pulled into Key West at ten o'clock.

Tony and Scot drove on to the house, and I cut down some back streets to George's house. I was still smelly and looked like hell, but the maid who greeted me escorted me into his study just the same. George appeared a few minutes later with a large envelope. He looked slightly disoriented, and I could smell the bourbon on him. He was also in a chatty mood. It was almost thirty minutes before I could get the keys for the house and be on my way. At 11:07 p.m., I came home for the first time to Four Monarch Court.

At that hour, the house looked dark and foreboding. Albert almost always kept all of the lights on, and I had always suspected he was afraid of the dark. But no cheery lights shone through the windows. Instead, the hurricane shutters were tightly closed and the yard was dark. Tony's car, Scot's truck and the trailer were parked in front, but Tony and Scot were nowhere to be seen. I pulled the car into the driveway and got out. There was music coming from behind the house, and I assumed that was where they were. I considered going back to join them, but decided to open up the house first.

A small fenced yard separated the front steps from the driveway and stoop. I unlocked the gate and walked into the yard. It had once been filled with pots overflowing with flowers. Now, Albert's terra cotta pots were neatly stacked beside the steps.

Albert's house was built in the manner of many houses from the late nineteenth century. The "basement" actually sat on the ground, and one climbed a flight of steps to the front door of the house. I ascended the steps and gently touched the wood of the door before unlocking it.

Mom and Aunt Vivian had certainly been thorough. The foyer was empty, as was the living room. Nothing remained except some marks on the walls indicating where paintings had once hung. Dad had warned me on the phone that Vivian had laid claim to almost every stick of furniture in the house, but I hadn't really expected to find it so completely empty. I opened the door of the study to verify that every-thing in there remained, and then set about exploring the rest of the vacated rooms.

In the dining room, I opened one of the three pairs of French doors which led onto a wrought-iron balcony overlooking the backyard pool. Below, Tony and Scot were skinny-dipping while Jimmy Buffett crooned from my boom box. I noticed that the patio had also been stripped of its furniture and I cursed myself for not including it in my list of things that were to remain.

"Hey," Scot called when he saw me emerge onto the balcony. "C'mon down. We stopped on the way here to get some beer."

I smiled and leaned on the railing. "Isn't the water a little cold?"

"Nah," Tony replied as he swam to the side. "Someone must have left the heat on. If anything, it's a little hot."

Great. My pool had been running hot for more than a week. I couldn't wait to see the utility bills. I wondered if I had Aunt Vivian to thank for that.

"You guys keep swimming," I told them. "I'm gonna finish check-ing things out up here." I wandered back inside.

I meandered through the rooms of the first floor, turning on lights as I went. The house smelled musty, as only an old house can when it has been closed up. In each room I opened the windows and then sweated through the laborious process of opening the storm shutters. The evening breeze felt good when it could finally drift through.

Upstairs, I opened up the front bedroom and the tower room first. There was one small window in the hall bathroom that hadn't opened in probably thirty years so I didn't try, but I did switch on the light and give the room a quick once-over.

We had divided up the rooms when we agreed to move in together. Tony was going to take the front bedroom and use the tower as a sit-ting room. Scot was going to take the tower room above as his bed-room, and use the attic beneath the widow's walk as his sitting room. I would take Albert's room. The door stood in front of me, closed and foreboding, and I wondered if even Aunt Vivian hadn't had the gall to sort through the man's most personal possessions. I went in and switched on the light.

I should know Vivian's gall better than that.

My bedroom was over the top of the dining room. I had the same three French doors, each of which opened onto one of three smaller wrought-iron balconies. I opened each and walked onto a balcony. Tony and Scot were drying off beside the pool.

"How's the house?" Tony asked as he pulled his shorts back on.

"Empty," I replied. "Hurricane Vivian didn't miss much."

"Well, maybe that's better. Without all of Albert's stuff, maybe it will make this place feel more like your home."

That thought had crossed my mind also. "Maybe," I conceded. "If you guys are ready to come in, I'll unlock the kitchen door."

I went back downstairs. By the time I reached the kitchen, the guys were standing on the back stoop. I undid the six or so locks (you'd think Albert lived in Boston instead of paradise) and let them in. Scot carried a case of beer, and Tony a bottle of champagne. "We were going to cool this in the pool," he explained, "but it wasn't very cool. Anyway, here." He handed it to me.

Scot opened the refrigerator door and slid the beer inside. "Boy, you weren't kidding. She cleaned you out. Even took your *last can of Who Hash.*"

I laughed. "Should we open this now?" I asked, holding up the bottle, "Or, should we wait until we've got glasses?"

The consensus was to open it now. I popped the cork, and the three of us sat in the middle of the living room floor passing the bottle to each other.

Since it was late, we decided to unpack the van in the morning. We did, however, drag out Scot's futon and Tony's mattress. My bed was buried somewhere in the front of the truck. As soon as their beds were in their rooms, both of them disappeared, exhausted.

I checked all of the doors to make sure they were locked before carrying my sleeping bag up to my room. Years ago, Albert had converted an old sewing room into a half bath for the master bedroom, and here I quietly unpacked my shaving kit into the medicine chest. I brushed my teeth, turned off the light, and took off my clothes. I unrolled the sleeping bag, but knew immediately that I was still too wired to sleep. I walked out onto the balcony. The night air felt good against my body.

My bedroom was the only one at the back of the house. As I stood there, nude, I realized I was looking straight into the unfinished guesthouse. Well, I thought to myself, I better enjoy this while I can.

I studied the guesthouse. As I have said, it was mostly finished on the outside, but still needed a great deal of work on the inside. All of the plumbing fixtures had been purchased and even installed in a couple of the rooms but, for the most part, every room needed to have its bathroom installed, its plugs and light fixtures installed, walls plastered and painted, and floors either tiled or carpeted. Not to mention furnished. And, after I paid the inheritance taxes, I would have a grand total of about five thousand dollars to my name.

For the first time since I lost my job, I considered what I was doing. I had, with very little money in the bank, moved to another state to open a guesthouse. I had roped my two best friends into coming with me. None of us had enough money. None of us had any building experience. None of us had any experience running a guesthouse. Nor did we have a plan of how to accomplish this grand scheme.

I wonder how many people in the world give up their "rat race" existence to run away to the tropics on some half-assed idea of going into business for themselves. However many there are, their ranks had now been increased by three. Needless to say, I didn't sleep very well that night.

I awoke early the next morning. I pulled on a pair of shorts and quietly walked downstairs. After a quick swim, I toweled off and let myself into the study to try and figure out what we were going to do next. I went through Albert's files to find old bills so I could get an approximate idea of how much this place was going to cost me. I spread all of the bills out on the floor before me.

One of the few things I had brought inside with me last night was my notebook computer. It's an old, outdated model, yet the size of it is extremely convenient, and I seldom go anywhere without it. I sat it on the hearth of the fireplace and began building a spreadsheet of expenses. After about an hour, I determined that it would cost the three of us about one thousand dollars a month just to keep up the house. I figured we could get by on about three hundred dollars for food. And since Key West is not large, I figured my own gas expense would not be exorbitant.

Next, I began to forecast expenses. I knew that my property taxes would come due in nine months, and that they would cost me twenty-one hundred dollars. In addition, Albert had legally subdivided the lot, so I would have to pay an additional nineteen hundred dollars on the guesthouse. I had no idea what it was going to cost to finish the guesthouse and get it operational, so I took a guess, and allowed twelve thousand dollars. Once it was completed, we were going to have to advertise in some national magazines to get the winter tourist trade, so I allotted another twenty thousand for that. By the time I was finished, I was forecasting net expenditures of over sixty-five thousand dollars between now and the end of the year. And, that didn't include the amount of additional money I was going to have to lay out to maintain the plane, let alone fly it. I lay down on the floor, demoralized. This is probably why so few engineers go into business for themselves.

Scot and Tony wandered in. Both were drinking beers, and they brought me one. Although I usually detest drinking in the morning, I didn't want to look at these figures sober.

I explained to the guys what I was doing and what I forecast. To my surprise, they did not bolt, screaming, into the street. Instead they listened intently. When I had finished, Tony excused himself and ran upstairs. Scot looked at the numbers.

"I dunno, Aidan. Sixty-five is high, but not undoable. I think the three of us can probably make a go of it." I love Scot because he not only believes *anything* is possible, he believes *everything* is possible.

Tony returned with a book. He held it up for us to see. It was the *National Chamber Of Commerce Guide To Starting A Small Business.* "I've been reading this ever since we started talking about this. I think we may be able to use it to build a business plan." He explained some of the initial steps we had to go through to set up the business. Okay, maybe one of us wasn't approaching this in a half-assed fashion.

All that morning as we unpacked the truck and trailer and cars, we talked about the business plan. Everyone came up with good ideas, and every few minutes someone darted into the study to record something on the computer lest we forget it. The house, the business plan, and my spirits all began to take a turn for the better that day.

By two o'clock, we had finished carting everything into the house. We had not eaten since the previous afternoon and the beer was starting to make us lightheaded. We locked up the house and walked up to a small sandwich shop on Duval for lunch.

The three of us were a study in contrasts on that walk. Tony was still talking about the business plan, already going over some of the minutiae. He was obviously excited about this, and enjoyed being the expert. Scot, on the other hand, was by-and-large ignoring him. He had never been to Key West before, and was focused on the sights and sounds and smells of the place. I again marveled at his faith in Tony and me. I'm not sure I would have moved to a place I had never been on the word of my two best friends.

I, too, was getting excited. Not so much by Key West and not so much by the idea of going into business, but by the idea of starting a new chapter in my life. I wondered if Albert would have approved of how I was doing it.

The sandwich shop was mostly empty. We ordered our lunches and then looked around. In the corner, dressed in a flowered shirt and a pair of clam diggers sat Louis Of Robideau. Our eyes met over his newspaper. I wasn't sure how seriously anyone took his *monarchy*, but out of respect I inclined my head slightly. He appeared to be pleased with the deference, and smiled. Then he turned his attention back to the paper.

Our sandwiches arrived. While we ate, Louis Of Robideau arose, paid his bill and stopped by our table. "Master Aidan, welcome back to the island. The first Lord of the Admiralty told us that you might be returning soon."

I decided there was no harm in playing along. "Yes Sire. It's good to be back. These are my roommates, Tony and Scot."

Louis inclined his head. "Gentlemen. We welcome you to the Conch Republic. We hope you will, at some point in the future, avail yourselves to visiting us at court."

Scot looked slightly amused. Tony, who truly lives up the title accountant, was definitely taken aback. "Uh, what?"

Louis smiled. I interceded and told him, "We would certainly enjoy that, Sire."

"Good, we will look forward to it. Until then, gentlemen." He left the sandwich shop.

"What in the hell was that all about?" Tony asked around a mouth full of falafel. I explained to him the whole story of the Conch Republic Government in Exile and the role their somewhat addled monarch played. Scot found it very interesting. Tony expressed his hope that the monarch did not have free and easy access to our house.

That afternoon, we returned the trailer to U-Haul, and then unpacked most of the house. Although none of Albert's rooms were large, my furniture spread thinly across the main floor of the house. Upstairs, Scot's and Tony's rooms filled up much more quickly.

That evening, after we had all showered and cleaned up, we decided to take Scot to participate in one of Key West's most respected traditions. Our house was at the Atlantic end of Duval Street, so we walked the eight blocks to Mallory Square at the Gulf end.

Almost nightly, Mallory Square celebrates the sunset. Everywhere on the square are street musicians, performers, craftsmen, and food vendors. Some of the best food I have ever eaten has come out of the least hygienic looking vendor carts on Mallory Square.

We stopped at one cart and I bought the three of us frozen margaritas. At the next cart, Tony bought a big plate of conch fritters. We wandered around the square, stopping only to watch a local animal trainer who had taught some of Key West's indigenous six-toed cats to perform tricks. Later, we listened to a steel drum band playing calypso. We made fun of the tourists. We were entitled to do this now that we were locals. Meanwhile, the sun slowly dropped into the Gulf of Mexico in a blaze of crimson and purple. That evening, we splurged a little and grilled steaks on the patio. Even Tony, who purports to be a vegetarian, savored his. Most of my earlier fears began to subside, and I submerged myself in the...oh, I don't know, the *rightness* of it all.

We got up early the next morning and headed for the airport. Although all of our furniture was here, some important things were still in Boston. Books, computers, clothes; stuff like that.

Tony is not much of a morning person, and Scot is downright mean, so the drive to the airport took place largely in silence. I pulled the car into the hangar. Sam Kinner had serviced and fueled the plane. While I calculated my flight plan and filed the paperwork with the FAA, Scot and Tony put the sleeper seats to their intended use.

It was cloudy as I taxied the plane out onto runway 27. The tower gave me clearance, and I pushed the throttles forward. We left the ground in a smooth line and I pulled the lever to retract the gear. Once I heard the reassuring sound of the wheels taking their place in the engine nacelles, I called Miami Center to inform them of my presence. I had estimated that we were going to put in ten hours of flying time, and had scheduled a twenty-minute fueling stop in North Carolina. But, with the low cloud cover over Florida and Georgia, as well as most of the northeast, the flight might take considerably longer.

Alone on the flight deck, I had an opportunity to think. Despite a chronic lack of money, a very rudimentary business plan and the general chaos that currently characterized my life, I was actually in pretty good spirits. It probably had something to do with the plane. Flying always creates a kind of euphoria for me.

Around eleven o'clock, we were flying through Savannah airspace when Tony stumbled into the flight deck. He was carrying a plastic cup that he had liberated from the small galley, and he filled it with coffee from my thermos. He then sat down in the co-pilot seat, and sipped it while scanning the horizon in silence. After a few minutes he observed, "We need a lawyer."

"Right now?" I asked. "I can radio ahead."

He gave me a snarly sidelong look that indicated he was not amused. "I mean to draw up the paperwork for our partnership."

"Got one," I informed him. He nodded, and continued to gaze through the windshield.

Since the DC-2 is an unpressurized aircraft, you can only operate below a 10,000-foot altitude. This means you can very seldom climb above weather. While not outrageous, we had been gently buffeted by winds since leaving Key West. Now, as we passed over Charleston, the winds calmed and the cloud cover broke, offering us clear skies. As the flight smoothed out, Scot came forward and joined us in the cockpit.

"I couldn't sleep once the turbulence stopped," he volunteered.

We landed at a little public field near Kittyhawk, North Carolina, and took on fuel. It also gave us a chance to use the restroom (a convenience sadly lacking on a plane this old), and eat lunch. Then we were back into the air for the trip up the coast. As we flew, the temperature dropped steadily. Tony and Scot, who had dressed appropriately for Key West in shorts, tank tops and sandals, now found themselves rapidly adding layers of clothes for every state we crossed. Although the skies clouded back up, we still made relatively good time and landed outside Boston a little after five.

At the airport, my friend Mike greeted us. Much of our stuff was in his garage, and he had agreed to chauffeur us around the city while we gathered the rest. Mike had just passed his five-year anniversary with the airline when the layoff came down and had therefore narrowly missed getting canned himself. He was waiting by the fence as I taxied the plane to the parking area. While I secured the plane for the night, he walked over to greet us.

"My God. What a motley-looking crew," he observed. "Three days in Florida can certainly change you."

The three of us exchanged glances. We were, indeed, motley look-ing, even without comparing ourselves to Mike in his pilot uniform. As we drove into the city, he pumped us for details about the house, the guesthouse and the island in general. Scot answered all of his questions enthusiastically, while Tony and I mostly listened. For reasons I couldn't fathom, a deep depression began to wash over me.

Mike dropped me off at my apartment first to pick up the things that I hadn't moved to his garage. His plan was to drop the others off next, then circle back around while I finished packing the last of my stuff. He would then pick up the others and we would put all of our remaining baggage on the plane, and then spend the night at his house.

I walked up the stairs to my flat and let myself in. Most of my stuff was ready to go. There wasn't much left: two boxes of books, a large box of floppy disks and my clothes. I finished cramming some suits into a garment bag, and then settled down to wait.

The apartment had served me well during my life in Boston, but there was nothing special about it. It was just a typical one-bedroom box, really. I walked around and inspected it closely, amazed at how empty and uninteresting it looked. "No turrets here," I mused aloud.

Mike buzzed the apartment from the front door, and I began to carry my stuff down. He was waiting on the front sidewalk and, as I handed him the first box, it began to sleet. "Three years I've been com-ing here," he observed, "and today is the first time I've ever found a space in front of your building."

The last thing I did before I left was check my mailbox. Inside was the notice from the FAA that I had passed the written test for my commercial pilot rating. A commercial rating is not of much use to a private pilot, and I had only gone after it in the hopes the airline would let me transfer from my office job to a job flying the line. I sighed. Nothing in my life was turning out the way I had expected.

It took about two hours to make the circuit and load all of our stuff. During that time, Mike kept up a nonstop conversation about how much he envied us for "just taking off and starting over like this." We delivered our cargo to the plane and then went on to his house.

We were greeted at the door with a cool reception from his wife, Susan. Susan was one of those wives that single men always use as the prototype for the kind of woman they are *not* going to marry. While she was pretty, she was always a little distant to begin with, and I always came away with the impression that she preferred that Mike only associate with *married* men. Tony, Scot and I had a pool going as to how long the marriage would last.

Dinner was uneventful, and the three of us went to bed early. The last few days had been eventful enough and none of us had had all that much sleep. The next morning as we loaded the last of our worldly goods from their garage, we got an eloquent sendoff from Susan (which Tony interpreted as "go and have a wonderful life and *never* contact my husband again"). Mike drove us to the airport on his way to work, and we were back in the air by eight o'clock.

The DC-2 was rated for 12,000 pounds of payload. Although we did not have quite that much aboard, she handled like she was dragging an anchor. It took me a while to realize that I had never flown her with full payload (most of which was in the cargo compartment), and what I was interpreting as sluggishness was just an old plane loaded to the gills.

I did not have the opportunity for private reflection on the flight deck this morning. Tony and Scot were in a much more pleasant mood, and kept me company from the moment we were off the ground. One would sit in the copilot seat and the other sat cross-legged on the floor, and we all traded opinions concerning what a frigid bitch Susan was.

When we were passing over the Hudson River Valley Scot, who had been exploring every inch of the cabin, came onto the flight deck and observed, "This is really a beautiful plane."

"That it is," I concurred. Outside, the plane itself was painted white on the upper half of the fuselage. A blue stripe divided that half from the lower, silver half. At the back of the plane, the stripe turned and ran up the white tail. Inside, the cabin was trimmed in teak. The carpet was a deep burgundy, and all of the sleepers were navy blue. Little brass fittings were everywhere. The only concessions to modern convenience (other than on the flight deck) were a small electric cooler and food warmer in the galley. "This plane was Albert's pride and joy."

"Does it have a name?" Tony asked.

That one caught me off guard. I had no idea. Albert had never mentioned a name for her. "I don't know. Maybe we should come up with one."

That discussion lasted for almost two hours as we tried to find a name in keeping with the plane's character. While I leaned towards something like the *Millennium Limited,* Scot argued vigorously that she should be called *Albert's Albatross.* Tony, who was studying an airman's chart of the Florida Keys finally picked the appropriate name. We called her the *Biscayne Voyager.*

We landed back in Key West in the early evening and unloaded our cargo. Later, after we had hauled everything to the house, we all sat around the pool, sipping screwdrivers and listening to Buffett croon from the back yard sound system about how he once fell in love in a library. It was a mellow night, and a thousand stars sparkled in the sky above Monarch Court.

"Tomorrow," Tony observed, "we get to work."

I nodded. "I figure, before we can get a small business loan, we better go through the guesthouse and figure out exactly how much there's

left to do. Then we can go to the hardware store and get some estimates on supplies."

"Sounds like a plan," Tony agreed. "We also need to go talk to the
lawyer about the partnership papers."

"I'll call him tomorrow and have him get started on them."

Buffett was now finished in the library and moving into the next
song. As we sat in silence and gazed at our guesthouse, none of us
heard the gate open or the sounds of footsteps behind us. All of us
jumped up when a voice behind us said, "Gentlemen."

The Monarch of Key West was dressed just had he had been the
night I met him. "Where the hell did you come from?" Tony
demanded.

The Monarch was not at all taken aback by this and replied, "Vermont." He turned his attention to me. "Master Aidan, you have not
yet presented yourself at court."

"Uh, my apologies," I offered. "We just today returned from Boston. I thought it would be inappropriate to arrive unannounced."

"Nonsense," the king scolded. "No one ever announces their intention to visit me. They just do it. I'll expect the same behavior from
you."

"Um, okay."

"Where do you live?" Scot asked.

"Court is just behind this monstrosity." He waved his cane at the
guesthouse.

"Oh."

There was an awkward silence; made much more awkward by the
fact that the king did not seem to be blinking. He finally turned on his
heel and said over his shoulder, "Well, see to it you present yourself
directly." He disappeared around the side of the house.

"I'm going to have to install a lock on that gate," I said.

"He's not going to keep popping in like that, is he?" Tony asked. "It
could be bad for business."

"I'm not sure. I guess the best thing I can do is present myself at court occasionally, whatever the hell that means."

"You're not going to humor him like that, are you?"

"Why not? He's just a harmless old guy."

"He's a psychopath. If you humor him, he'll keep popping in here every night."

"Well, what do you suggest I do?"

"Have him arrested the next time he trespasses."

I collapsed back into my chair. "Jeez, Tony. We've lived here two days and you want to imprison the king? What kind of neighbor are you?"

Scot laughed. Tony was clearly annoyed, and did not reply. They both returned to their chairs, and the mood subsided, although I did notice that Tony moved his chair so he could keep an eye on the gate.

"What are we going to use for collateral for the loan?" Scot asked.

That question had been haunting me, too. My best guess at this point was that we were going to have to borrow almost one hundred thousand dollars. I was hoping that I could mortgage the guesthouse for that amount without having to touch the house or the plane. But, if that didn't work, the house was worth at least that much and, to some collectors, so was the plane. I knew that, if my father had to choose which of these properties to risk on such a venture, it would be the plane. Common sense argued that I should also borrow against the plane. However, I loved the plane, so I didn't want to consider it. I felt as if it would be mortgaging Albert.

The next day, we got our estimates together. As far as building materials went, we were in pretty good shape. Two of the bathrooms were completely finished, and the tubs had been installed in the remaining four. We had most of the building materials we needed, so all we really needed to buy was paint and floor coverings. That came out to about eight hundred dollars.

Next, we drove to Miami to find furniture. Tony had looked through a tourist guide to Key West and determined that most guesthouses had refrigerators, televisions and VCRs in each room. In order to be competitive, we would at least have to have televisions and VCRs. Six of each would run us twelve hundred dollars.

We found a used furniture dealer and determined that we could get beds and lamps for about another eight hundred. Linens and sundries would run about six hundred more.

All of these costs found their way into our business plan. We estimated that, from the time we actually started working on the building until the time we were ready to open for occupancy would take about three months. That would put us at the end of June, with three months to go before the tourist season began.

George drew up the partnership agreement. I retained ownership of the property, and "leased" it to our company on an annual basis. The first year's rent would be one dollar. Each of the three of us had equal ownership of the business, and would evenly divide the profits, if any.

On the Thursday night following our return from Boston, Tony went to a meeting of the Key West Chamber of Commerce. Scot and I made drinks and wandered out into the street. It was our intention to visit Louis Of Robideau at court before he wandered into our back yard again. I was afraid that such an action on his part would put his person in grave danger of harm from Tony.

We walked around the block and identified the house we thought most likely to back up against the guesthouse. It was a two-story wood frame house with a verandah wrapping around both floors. The entire house was painted a truly unpleasant shade of orange. From a bracket over the front steps flew one of the few Conch Republic flags in existence. We opened the front gate and walked up the walk. From the upper verandah, two women and a man looked down at us with no particular interest. We walked up onto the front porch and rang the doorbell. From inside, we could hear the sounds of a number of people, but no one made any effort to open the door.

"What do you suppose we should do?" Scot asked.

I thought for a second. "Well, since he feels he has the run of my property, I guess I have the run of his. Let's check out the back yard."

We wandered around the house and found a number of other people in the pool in the back yard. All of them appeared to be nude. A young women with hair a shade of red which is not found in nature noticed us and called out hello.

"Hi," I replied, trying to make sure I kept eye contact and did not let my gaze wander to where it was going naturally. "We're looking for Louie Robideau."

She smiled. "Here to see the king? Are you cops?"

"Nope. Just neighbors."

"Oh, okay. In that case, he should be inside some place."

Scot asked, "If we were cops, what would you have told us?"

"That he's inside someplace, but I would have demanded to see your warrant before letting you go in."

I must have looked somewhat surprised, because she added, "I'm his lawyer."

We climbed the steps to the back verandah, and let ourselves into the kitchen. There were people everywhere. The house could almost have been a show place. Beautiful high ceilings held up expensive crystal chandeliers above rooms crammed full of Sheraton period furniture. Oil portraits of various European monarchs stared down from all the walls. The only thing that ruined the effect was that every room was painted in a different, very bright neon color.

We wandered into a Post-It Note yellow dining room where a group of men and women were clearly involved in a high-stakes poker game from the shocking-purple kitchen where a very old gentleman was washing crystal by hand. "Waterford," he told us as we walked past. In the red and aqua foyer, several women were in a heated discussion concerning the sexual orientation of someone named Olivia.

No one really seemed to notice our presence. We continued onward into the front parlor. In this room, all of the walls had been spray-painted gold. At one end, on a small raised dais sat Louie's throne. It was a high-backed chair, also painted gold, and upholstered with the Conch Republic flag. A harried-looking young woman in full business attire was sitting on the dais muttering into a cellular phone. No sign of Louie.

I wished I had brought one of my old business cards. I would have left one on his front table, and my duty would have been done. We were about to leave when Scot noticed that there was a door partially hidden behind the throne. We opened it and found ourselves in the king's presence.

"So," he cried, looking up from the easel where he was painting, "Young Aidan and Master Scot have finally elected to present themselves at court. Welcome." He stood, wiped his hands on a rag and shook ours.

We exchanged pleasantries of a rather mundane sort. I asked what he was painting, and he turned the easel to show me a very detailed portrait of Queen Elizabeth II. He was clearly proud of it and told us that he had painted it from memory. Since there was no photograph of the queen readily apparent and she was not with us in the room, I decided to believe him.

"When you were wandering through the house, did you happen to notice a severe-looking woman who obviously does not belong in Key West?" he asked us.

"Do you mean the one sitting on the dais talking on a portable phone?" Scot asked.

"Probably. She's my agent. She's here for the painting but I'm just not ready to let it go yet."

"Where's she taking it?" Scot asked.

"To Washington. It's supposed to hang in some office of the British embassy."

We learned that Louie was something of a sought-after portrait painter. He had been commissioned by the British ambassador to paint the queen several times. Ordinarily, only British citizens were commissioned to paint the queen, and it was considered quite an honor to award the commission to an American. Or, a Conchian, I guess.

The woman with the phone came stomping into the study. She was clearly annoyed. "My plane leaves in a hour. Can I have it now?"

Louie shook his head. "I'm not ready yet."

"Louie, please," the woman pleaded. "I don't want to spend the night here. It's the last flight I can take."

Louie looked cross. "Olivia, you don't understand. This is a sovereign, like myself. Every time I paint her, I invest the portrait with the full fiber and being of my soul. I'd expect the same from her if she had any talent." He winked as he turned aside to us. "So much inbreeding in that blood line. It just *kills* any genetic hope for creativity."

Olivia threw her hands up. "When are you going to be done?"

Louie stared at the painting. "I don't know. It may take several more days."

She folded her arms in front of her. "Louie, I'm not going to miss this flight. You can give me the painting now, or I can return to Washington with your check. After all, it's only fifteen thousand dollars. What does money like that mean to the great Louie Robideau?"

"Of," Louie corrected without taking his eyes off the painting.

"Oh, right. Sorry, *Of.* What could it mean to you, *Of?* Something frivolous like paying off your back taxes, *Of?*"

Louie closed his eyes and sighed. "Fine. It's done. Take it."

Olivia yanked the painting off the easel and stuffed it in a case that must have been especially designed to transport it. "I'll have it framed in DC. We're not taking the ambassador another painting in one of your frames."

Louie smiled at us mischievously. "I rather thought he would have liked the argyle one I sent last year."

Olivia rolled her eyes as she finished sealing the box. "Can you call me a cab?"

"Nope," the king responded.

"Oh, c'mon Louie. I don't have time for games."

"No game, my sweet. I'd love to call you a cab, but the phone's been disconnected. Some misunderstanding about my long distance company."

Olivia slumped over the box, clearly defeated. A single lock of her dark hair worked its way free from her impossibly severe chignon and fell forward over her face.

"I can drive you to the airport," Louie offered.

"Not without a license you can't," she snarled. She picked up the box. "Fine, I'll use one of the neighbor's phones." As she turned to go, I interceded.

"You're not going to get a cab here in time to take you to the airport. I can drive you, if you like."

She looked at me, and I got the impression it was the first time that she noticed there were other people in the room. "Who the hell are you?"

I had only been out of Boston for a week so I should have been accustomed to her rudeness. How quickly we forget such things. "A neighbor," I snarled back. "Who the hell are you?"

She recovered herself, brushing the renegade lock off her forehead. "I'm sorry. I'm Olivia, and yes, thank you, I would very much appreciate a ride."

We left Scot with Louie and walked around the block back to my house. She looked up at it as I wedged the painting behind the front seats of my car. "You live in old Albert Fitzgerald's house?" she asked.

I nodded as we got into the car. "I own it. You knew Albert?"

"Yep," she said as we drove out of the cul-de-sac. "He was a wonderful man. I was very sorry to hear he had died."

"I was too," I told her as we turned right onto Duval. "He was my uncle."

She extended her condolences. "He was a wonderful man. When I was a little girl, I always remember that his house was the most fun to go to at trick-or-treat. We used to go back to it seven or eight times during the night, and he always acted like he didn't recognize us. He was a very giving man."

"Whoa. You mean you grew up here?" We turned left onto South Street.

She nodded. "Unfortunately. I got out about ten years ago when I went to college. I only come back when I have to deal with Louie."

"Is it always as much of an ordeal to get the painting away from him?"

She smiled. "Actually, it was fairly easy this time. You should have seen him when I had to wrestle away a painting of JFK."

We turned right onto Bertha. "That must make him very hard to represent."

She sighed and leaned her head back against the seat. The top was down and several other locks of her hair had escaped their bondage and were becoming quite unruly. "No, not difficult to represent. I've been watching him work my whole life. He truly is brilliant. He's just very difficult to work with."

I stopped for a red light. To our left was the salt pond, and on the opposite side sat the airport. "Well, I hope you get a good commission for your troubles."

She laughed. "Hardly."

I was confused. "Why put up with it if there's nothing in it for you?"

She shrugged. "To make sure he eats. Family loyalty. He's my father."

I almost drove into the ocean. "Oh."

We turned onto the road which led to the terminal. She gave me a sidelong look. "You didn't know he had a kid, did you?"

"Nope. Not that there is any reason why I should. I only met him a couple of weeks ago."

We pulled up to the terminal and she released her seat belt. "Well, Aidan, thanks very much for the ride. I hope you enjoy living in Key West." She got out of the car and retrieved the painting from behind the seat. "If I were you though, I'd beware of your neighbors. After all, its a well known fact that insanity runs in all royal families." She winked at me and walked away towards the door.

I drove home in the fading light of the evening. As I passed the salt pond, I could see a Comair Embraer pull away from the gate and taxi towards the runway. I hoped she made the flight. I had a feeling that, if she did not, her wrath would be mighty.

THE OCEAN NIGHTS INN

In retrospect, given his relative lack of psychosexual sophistication, leaving Scot alone at Louie's house that evening may not have been my brightest move ever. He was not at the house when I returned home. Tony and I had dinner, and then retired to the widow's walk to have a nightcap. He still did not return. From beyond the guesthouse, I heard the sounds of ongoing revelry at Louie's, occasionally punctuated by the sound of Scot's voice yelling something. "At least we know he's still alive," Tony observed. He was still not home when I went to bed at one.

We found him the next morning, passed out on the grass next to the pool. He seemed to have lost his pants during the evening. We later learned that Louie's vivid-haired attorney had won them from him early in the evening in a game of strip bocce.

When we found him, shortly after breakfast, we roused him as best we could. He rolled onto his back and squinted against the sunlight, clearly befuddled as to where he was and, possibly, even *who* he was. Tony and I both noticed a small stain of red on his shirt at his left pec, and speculated on whether he had been shot with an extremely small caliber bullet. This caused us some concern, so we made him strip off his shirt, revealing that, at some point during the evening, he had elected to have his left nipple pierced.

He did not remember having the nipple pierced, and studied the small silver hoop as though it was a trigonometry problem. "It must have been after the Jaegermeister," he speculated. When pressed on what he did remember of the previous evening, he was extremely circumspect. He did acknowledge having had a copious amount to drink, and to eating a Scottish haggis, which is a sheep's stomach stuffed with a wide assortment of other, equally unpleasant parts of the sheep. Since haggis, generally, is not readily available in Key West, we were somewhat surprised. He couldn't offer much more insight, except to say that it tasted *nothing* like chicken. He never shared any more details of what had happened that night, but he still has the nipple ring to this day. He treats it as sort of a badge of honor, I presume for having survived one of Louie's debauches.

That day, we had our business plan completed and we went to the bank to apply for a loan. Since I had lost my job, I had seldom worn anything besides shorts, tank tops and flip-flops. It felt strange to be back in a suit again. The application process was relatively painless, and we scheduled a date to have the guesthouse appraised. That afternoon, we actually began work on the building itself.

We elected to start by installing a bathroom on the second floor. Plumbing is not one of my favorite activities, so I wanted to get the unpleasant projects over with first. Installing the toilet was fairly simple once we worked out how the three of us were going to participate in what is basically a one-man job. It took a little under two hours, six beers, and twelve Tylenol. (For the record, Tony and I consumed the beers.)

When it was done, Tony turned the valve with some trepidation. We were rewarded with the sound of water running into the tank. A moment later, the three of us put our hands on the handle and flushed. It worked, and there was much rejoicing. We had to forcibly restrain Tony from breaking a bottle of champagne over the john. Our first project was a success.

Three toilets later, I never wanted to see another piece of porcelain again as long as I lived.

For three days, we struggled through the hells of installing toilets and sinks and faucets and hoses. A great deal of colorful language was used that weekend. However, when the appraiser came the following Tuesday, we were able to proudly show off six completed and functional bathrooms.

We had applied for a loan of one hundred thousand. The appraisal on the property came back at ninety-two thousand, so we had to come up with seven thousand dollars of collateral. We offered to use all three of our cars but the bank declined.

I went to George for help. As I sat in his musty old lawyer's office I asked if there wasn't any way I could get them to up the appraisal of the guesthouse.

"I doubt it," George observed. "Do you all have anything else you could put up as collateral?"

"My house and my plane," I replied unhappily. "And I'm not terribly anxious to do either."

George sat back in his chair. "Well, I can certainly understand that, but some might interpret your unwillingness to put either of those things up as collateral as a sign that you don't have much faith in the venture."

That certainly hit home. I was not, in fact, confident that we would succeed. I was hedging my bets. My father certainly would have approved.

That night it rained. I sat alone in the study, fingering the two photographs I had removed from the desk blotter a few weeks before. I looked at Jason, Albert and myself. It was certainly easy to see that we were related. Jason was slender with longish, dark brown hair and bright blue eyes. He looked an awful lot like I did as a teenager, and I am told that I look a good deal like Albert did when he was my age.

Looking closer at the three of us, I could see more subtle differences. There was something in Albert's eyes that was missing in my own. A certain daring? A devil-may-care attitude? An understanding that life is risk?

I put down the pictures and walked to the window. The rain splattered against it fitfully. "What would you have done, Albert?" I asked out loud.

No one answered.

Would Albert have risked his plane? Would he have risked his house? I was pondering these questions when an absolute heresy crossed my mind: did it *matter* what he would have done?

Albert was, after all, my hero. But when it came right down to it, he was dead and this was my decision. George's words echoed in my ears. Not putting up anything I cared about did indicate that I didn't have confidence in our ability to succeed. Well, it was time to get confident or get out.

I walked into the dining room and made a drink. The bar sat in the exact same place where Albert had kept his. I walked into the living room and looked around. It was all my furniture, but I had put the couch where he had put his couch. I had put the TV where had had put his. I even had a palm tree next the fireplace just like he had. Defiantly, I moved the palm tree next to the couch. It was a sad and pathetic rebellion, but God it felt good.

I returned to the study and considered my options. Tony was confident we were going to succeed. Scot was confident we were going to succeed. Why wasn't I? I could find no reason for it, so I pushed down to the very lowest level of my soul and committed myself to the project.

I considered which item to borrow money against. If we did default on the loan (and I was absolutely committed that we would not), the bank would take the guesthouse property. If I borrowed against the plane, I would still have the house. But, would I want the house if the guesthouse in my back yard belonged to someone else? If I borrowed against the house, I would still have the plane, but I certainly couldn't live out of the plane (although I have known people who have tried).

Besides, the plane was nothing but an expense. The house gave me something solid.

I wrestled over which one to borrow against for about three hours. As I was ready to give up and go to bed, I asked myself one last question: which one would more effectively demonstrate to myself my belief in our success?

The plane.

Having decided to borrow the money against the plane, I went to bed.

It was not a restful sleep. All night long I had dreams of Albert yelling at me for risking his plane. In my dreams, I calmly told him that it was my plane now and, if he didn't want me to risk it, he should have left me more money. In my dream this just made him angrier.

I awoke the next morning exhausted. Looking up at the ceiling I announced, "Albert, you are no longer welcome in my subconscious."

At breakfast, I announced to Tony and Scot that I intended to borrow the rest of the money against my plane. They started to argue with me, so I told them that I had absolute faith that we were going to succeed and that there was no danger of losing my plane.

Later that morning, George called me to find out if I wanted him to try and find another bank that might consider the cars as collateral. I told him no, I would borrow the money against the plane. He asked if I was sure I wanted to do that, and I told him it was important that I demonstrate my absolute confidence in what we were doing.

After lunch, my father called. Things had been a little strained with my parents since I had lost my job and we had not spoken much. I was frankly surprised to hear from him since he hates to be bothered with personal business while he's at work.

"I was just thinking about you," he said on the phone, "and I wanted to make sure you were okay."

"Yeah, I'm fine, Dad," I told him while mixing tile grout. "Things here have just been very busy."

He cleared his throat. "How are things coming with the guest-house?"

When my parents don't approve of something, the subject is never mentioned, so I was not expecting a question so direct. I decided to be equally direct in return. "Well, it looks like the bank is going to loan us the money. I'm using the guesthouse as collateral for the bulk of the loan, and I'll borrow the remaining seven thousand against the plane."

My dad was quiet a moment. "Are you sure you want to do that?"

"Of course. The guesthouse is the most logical asset to use to borrow the money and…"

Dad interrupted. "No, I mean use the plane. The plane means a lot to you, doesn't it?"

I gave him my now rote speech about how using the plane demonstrated my absolute commitment to the project. He accepted everything I had to say and asked me more and more detailed questions about the project. I was happy to fill him in and, to my surprise, he gave me some very useful advice on how to insure the property. I wasn't certain I had his approval for the project, but I walked back to the guesthouse after we hung up feeling like I at least had his respect.

Later that afternoon, I called the bank to change the loan arrangements. I would borrow the remaining money myself against my airplane. The loan officer took all the necessary information and said she would draw up the paperwork.

That night, Albert stayed out of my dreams as I had instructed. I felt good about the project. I felt good about the work the three of us had done that day. I even felt good about my relationship with my father, which is not something that had happened very often in my life. I slept soundly.

The next morning, we finished grouting the tile in all of the bathrooms. They were now complete, and we were prepared to start working on the bedrooms. We had bought most of the paint using the money we had between us, and so we constantly admonished each other to use it sparingly.

When we went into the house for lunch, there was a message on the answering machine that our loan had been approved and we could come in that afternoon to sign the papers. I was also told that I needed to make an appointment to have the airplane appraised.

While we were eating, the doorbell rang. Tony answered it and returned a moment later with a FedEx envelope addressed to me. It was from my father.

I opened it. The letter inside read:

Dear Aidan,

When I was twenty, I used to dream about having a sailboat. All I really wanted was to move to San Diego and live on my boat and make money by taking people out for sails. Instead, I got married, raised a family and did everything that was expected of me. I do not, for one minute, regret any of the choices I have made in my life. If you judge every choice you make in your life by how happy you are at this moment, than I have made every one right so far. While the decisions you are making are not necessarily the ones I would have made, I also understand the dreams that are driving you, and I believe in you as much as you believe in them.

Attached to this letter is an insurance policy which your mother and I took out on you when you were born. It is fully paid and we have been allowing the dividends to accrue for the last fifteen years. While it may not be all the money you need, I hope it will help you accomplish what you are working towards.

Love, Dad.

My father does not come across as a sentimental man. He is sometimes cold and distant, and I sure as hell never knew he dreamed about having a sailboat. You can imagine the effect that his letter had on me. As I dried my eyes, I looked at the insurance policy. In good Catholic fashion, it was with the Knights of Columbus. I finished lunch, then called the local Knights office and asked them to find out how much it was worth.

A few minutes later the agent told me that the policy itself was worth ten thousand dollars, and there were currently four thousand dollars in dividends available to me. He asked if I wanted to cash in the policy. I told him that I did not, but I made arrangements to collect the dividends that afternoon.

The three of us talked it over. We were still three thousand short, but we decided to try and do without it. Once we picked up the money that afternoon, we would have enough to finish the guesthouse, place ads and get the operation running. We would just have to live lean for the next few months until we started making money.

That afternoon, we picked up the check at the bank and I canceled the loan on my plane. I wondered briefly if Albert's ghost had had a hand in this, but decided not to think about it. Albert was dead and Aidan was in charge now.

Our lives soon fell into a regular pattern of work. We started work on the guesthouse every morning by nine, had lunch at one, and finished by five. We would then get cleaned up and walk down to Mallory Square for the island's daily sunset fix.

Tony continued the business arrangements. In addition to joining the Chamber of Commerce, we also joined a local association of guesthouses. The owners and managers of the other guesthouses were extremely helpful and gave us advice on everything from how to deal with building inspectors to the kinds of washing machines that were best suited for large loads of sheets.

June rolled around, and we could see the beginning of the end. For the most part, Tony stopped working on the building with Scot and me, and concentrated more on making business arrangements. On a Thursday afternoon early in the month, Scot and I were drenched in sweat from the sweltering summer sun so we quit work early and dove into the pool. Tony came outside with a sheaf of papers and sat in a lawn chair nearby. He looked uptight.

"Okay, we've avoided this as long as we can. I can do no more until we resolve this issue."

"What issue is that?" Scot asked as he rolled over to float on his back.

"We've got to come up with a name for this place."

It was a sticky problem. We had been discussing it for more than three months and still not resolved it. Key West was full of guesthouses with interesting and exciting names. So far, everything we had come up with sounded about as romantic as Howard Johnson's. Scot favored calling it "Uncle Albert's," but I was still in the midst of my Albert rebellion and would have none of it. We had flirted with "The Waldorf Hysteria," but decided it probably wouldn't attract the kind of clientele we were looking for.

Tony was in favor of something a little more dignified. He didn't have any ideas yet, he was just in favor of something a little more dignified. The three of us stared at each other blankly.

"Are you sure we have to have a name?" Scot asked hopefully.

Tony gave him an icy stare. "How are we supposed to advertise without a name? We can't even put it in the phone book without a name."

"Jeez, you're in a bitchy mood today."

"All I know," I offered as I pulled myself up onto a raft, "is that I don't want to cop out and name it something like 'Three Guys Guesthouse.'"

"Look, we all know what we don't want to name it," Tony snarled, "how about coming up with some suggestions for what we do?"

Scot and I exchanged looks. There had been an obvious tension growing between all of us for about two weeks. I hadn't really noticed it before now, but it was there. As I thought back over the day, I could think of at least three separate instances where I nearly threw a hammer at Scot.

"Y'know," I began, "I think we may all be a little too consumed with the project right now. We've done nothing for the last six weeks except work on this place. I think it's got all our nerves a little frayed."

Tony relaxed a little. "Yeah. You're right. I can't even remember the last time I thought about something else."

"Maybe we should lay off for the weekend," Scot suggested.

"What I need is a beach," Tony said, leaning back in his chair. Tony grew up at a beach, and this was one of his lines from Boston that indicated he was stressed.

"You live at a beach," I pointed out.

"Well, kinda," he mused. "But not really. There really isn't a good beach on the island."

"Maybe we ought to drive up to Miami for the weekend," Scot suggested.

"We don't have the money."

I considered getting away for the weekend. I did need to get away from the place. All of us did. As I floated on my back I stared up into the infinite blue sky and considered how we could get off the island. A plane flew overhead.

A plane. I had not taken the plane up in weeks. Planes are unique machines. They are at their best when they are being worked hard. If you let them sit, they begin to decay. I have always found them to be a good analogy for people.

"I need to take the plane up," I said. "It's been almost three weeks. She needs a workout."

"I wish there was some place we could fly into and just sleep on the beach for the night." Scot again.

I thought back to Albert's funeral and remembered George telling me about a trip to some island in the Tortugas with Albert where they did precisely that. "I think there is."

I pulled myself out of the pool and retrieved my clothes. As the three of us climbed the steps to the kitchen door, I told them about Runner's Island. My flight kit was in the study, and I retrieved Albert's old airman's charts from the bag. I spread them out on the floor and located the faded pencil marks indicating where it was on the map.

"This could be great," Scot enthused.

Tony and I concurred. We didn't need to take much really, just some sleeping bags and food. Maybe a lantern.

"I think Albert had some camping stuff in the garage," I volunteered. Everyone groaned. Since we had moved into the house, dealing with the garage had been something we had actively avoided. Albert was a packrat of the worse sort. The garage was filled with all kinds of old equipment, old furniture, old luggage, old tools, old *stuff.* You could almost always find something interesting down there. You just couldn't find anything you were looking for.

After dinner that evening, I decided to dig through the garage (after all, it was full of *my* stuff, now) and try to locate some camping equipment. The door was open to admit the balmy evening breeze, and Scot was perched on the hood of my car, drinking a beer and offering encouragement. No help, alas, but encouragement. I had been at it an hour and had liberated one Coleman lantern, a camp stove, and two bottles of propane when we heard voices in the driveway.

We had not lived in Key West all these months without making a few friends. As I said earlier, we had joined an organization of guesthouses, and many of the other owners had been quite helpful. There were two guesthouses in our neighborhood. Two women, Elizabeth and Andrea, owned House Diana. Their guesthouse catered exclusively to women. The other was called The Madison Key West and was owned by Jake. It had the dubious honor of being located directly across the street from Louie Robideau's house.

The voices I had heard were Elizabeth and Andrea, out for an evening walk. Elizabeth had a wineskin slung over her shoulder, and both were sipping red wine from plastic goblets. They wandered into the garage and joined Scot on the hood of the car.

"Hail and well met, fine neighbors," Andrea declared. "Why on earth are you tackling this mess on such a fine night?"

"We," Scot declared, "are going camping this weekend."

"Camping?" Elizabeth wondered. "Sounds like fun. You going up to the Everglades?"

"Nope," I said as I uncovered a relatively new Honda generator buried beneath a stack of *National Geographics*. "We be headin' to the Tortugas."

"What, you got a boat you not tellin' us 'bout?" Andrea asked, her eyes narrowing.

"No, a plane." Scot related the whole story of Runner's Island, Uncle Albert and how badly we needed to get away from the island. Tony wandered in, sipping his own glass of wine sometime during the story.

"I wanna go!" Andrea whined.

"Canwehuhcanwehuhcanwe?" Elizabeth asked.

The three of us exchanged looks. "Why not?" I asked.

"It'll cost you though," Tony, our ever-vigilant accountant, declared.

Andrea's almond-shaped eyes narrowed again. "How much?"

"Well," he began. I always wonder that he doesn't wear a green eyeshade. "We'll be expending fuel and wear and tear on the plane, so I think it's only fair that you provide one case of beer. And pretzels."

"Is that all? Hell, we'll bring a whole cooler of food." Andrea is not one of the foremost negotiators of our time.

It was the slow season in Key West. Andrea and Elizabeth's house had no guests. Someone wondered aloud if Jake had any guests at his place. It was immediately decided that we could not go to the Dry Tortugas without Jake. Andrea called him from the small cellular phone that was always in her back pocket. "Hey you big pansy," she said into the receiver, "you have anyone staying at your place? I mean paying guests. Well, do you feel confident leaving him alone with the house over night? A bunch of us are taking Aidan's plane and going camping on a small island they know of in the Tortugas. Wanna come?" It did not take much convincing, and there were six of us heading west. Tony required Jake to bring a bottle of vodka, two bottles of tonic, and six submarine sandwiches.

At about ten the next morning, we left for the airport. When I filed my flight plan, I took the liberty of informing the Coast Guard that it was our intent to be camping on the island for the night. They didn't seem to have any problems with it, but I was still concerned that DEA agents, suspicious of a lone aircraft parked on a deserted airstrip would swarm the island in the middle of the night.

For an overnight camping trip, our luggage certainly told a lot about our personalities. Everyone had sleeping bags. I had my laptop computer in case I felt like writing (as I said, I seldom go anywhere without it), my flight kit, the camping equipment, some extra clothes and a towel. Tony had a magazine and a bag containing nothing but tanning accessories, oils and lotions. Scot brought along three books, his boom box, and about seventy-five CDs. Jake contributed his required alcohol, mixers and sandwiches, along with his own magazine, three changes of clothes, a small, battery-powered blender, some margarita mix and large bottle of tequila. Elizabeth and Andrea brought two enormous coolers, three books, two fishing rods, a small tool kit, a shovel, plastic bags, waterproof matches, flashlights, towels, a radio, a camera and soap.

"Christ!" I declared as we filled up the *Voyager*'s cargo compartment with our equipment. "We're just going to the island to camp, not *colonize* it!"

It was nearly noon when the six of us piled into the plane and I taxied out onto the runway. Noon is a busy time at Key West International, and we had to sit on the taxiway for almost fifteen minutes before we could finally pull into position. Planes the vintage of mine are not well ventilated and do not have little luxuries like air conditioning. My passengers were quite gamy by the time we were airborne.

Despite the load, the plane handled like a dream. At least it did as long as everyone was sitting down. Unfortunately, the level of excitement was a little high, and people moved around the cabin constantly. I was forever compensating for the plane's shifting center of gravity.

The Dry Tortugas are a group of small islands at the western end of the Florida Keys, about 70 miles west off Key West. During the civil war, the government confined prisoners of war at Fort Jefferson on one of the islands, and it has served this same purpose off and on ever since. Since I wasn't exactly sure where I was going, we were flying low over the waters at about ninety miles per hour. I was concentrating on my heading, and Tony sat in the right seat looking for the island.

"Got it," he told me. "About eleven o'clock." For an accountant, he's pretty good on the flight deck. Not only can he navigate, he's not above playing flight attendant. He told everyone in the cabin to sit down and buckle up.

We circled low over the island. Actually, *island* was something of an overstatement. It was a runway with about ten feet of beach surrounding it on all sides. I needed about three thousand feet of runway, and it looked like I barely had it. It was going to have be a slow, careful approach if I didn't want to run off the end of the island.

I circled the island once more, and then eased off the throttle and dropped low over the waves. I fully believe in the symbiosis of man and machine when it comes to pilots and their airplanes. I had never flown this approach before, but the plane had. We came in smooth and the wheels touched about two hundred feet down the runway. We stopped with at least three hundred feet to spare. I taxied the plane to the edge of the runway and cut the engines. There was no room for me to turn it around under power, so we all got out and pushed it 180 degrees to face the other direction.

The island was really not much more than a spit of sand. It was less than a mile long and only about three hundred feet wide. At its highest point I doubt it was more than five feet above high tide. There was no vegetation other than some pampas grass. It was hard to imagine a more desolate or remote place. There would be nothing to indicate a human had ever set foot here were it not for the asphalt runway running down the middle of the island. Someone had devoted a great deal of energy to locating an airstrip out here; but clearly, it was seldom used. Large cracks were beginning to appear in it, and sand had blown up over the edges. It stood now as a testament to a more cavalier day when the extent of the drug-running network was so misunderstood that someone could build an airstrip such as this without attracting the attention of the government.

"Should we explore the island?" Scot asked.

Tony looked disgusted. "Scot, look around. There's nothing here. The rest of the island looks like this part here."

Scot turned to me. "I told you we should have pushed him out of the plane."

It took us about ten minutes to unload the plane and set up camp. Afterwards, all of us stripped down to enjoy the afternoon in the sun. Jake, Scot, Tony and I were all arrayed on beach towels sunning ourselves while Elizabeth and Andrea were out in the water with a lobster trap that they had smuggled aboard.

"Hey Jake," Tony asked, rolling onto his side.

"Hmm?" Jake replied as he turned his head towards my roommate.

"How did you come up with the name for your house?"

Jake smiled and rolled back over so that his face was full in the sun. "My house is named after James Madison. Why do you want to know?"

"Because we're having a hell of a time coming up with a name for ours. Why James Madison?"

He blushed slightly. "Because I lost my virginity at Montpelier, which was his home in Virginia."

All of us laughed. Tony wondered, "The experience was that significant?"

Jake nodded and rolled up onto one arm. "It was. I was there on a field trip when I was seventeen. We wandered away from the crowd. All in all, it was magic."

"Okay, it was a magic experience, but how did you arrive at it for the name of your guesthouse?"

Jake finished the beer he was drinking and retrieved another from the ice chest. "That was courtesy of my illustrious neighbor, King Robideau. I was having the same problem trying to come up with a name. One night, I was in my backyard, relaxing in my jacuzzi, when Louie pops up outta nowhere."

"Does he make a habit of surprising *everyone* in their back yards?" Tony asked, petulantly. Jake didn't hear him and continued with his story.

"Anyway, we got talking and I told him that I was having a hard time naming the place. He told me that a name should come from a significant event in my life. I should think about my life and try to remember a time whose spirit I wanted to recreate. He told me to try to find something in my past that I wanted to carry into my future, and look for a name there."

"So, basically," Tony summarized, "you named your house after a dead president because you associate him with getting laid, which is something you would like to recreate in the future."

Jake looked at me. "Jesus, is he always this cynical?"

"He prefers to call it analytical," I replied. "We've decided to find it charming."

Scot rolled over onto his stomach. "So, we're supposed to name the house after something associated with the first time we got laid?"

Tony and I snickered. Jake rolled off his towel and stood up.

"But I don't want to name our house the 'Back-seat-of-my-father's-Lincoln Inn,'" I whined.

"Look, name your place whatever the fuck you want," Jake snarled. "Mine has a lot of meaning to me." He stomped around the plane.

I got up and walked into the water. It was cool and felt good against my rapidly baking skin. As I floated, I noticed the tan line at my waist. It was only June, and I was considerably dark. For expatriate northerners (especially those of us from Chicago) a really good tan before July is something we can only dream of.

That afternoon was as long and slow and drawn out as a day at the beach should be. Elizabeth and Andrea caught four lobsters in their trap and all of us got very drunk on margaritas from Jake's blender. Around six, we built a fire and roasted the lobsters.

As the sun dropped low in the sky, we began to add layers of clothing against the evening breezes. Everyone wore sweatshirts and shorts and huddled around the fire smelling the roasting lobsters. It was well below the horizon when we broke open the first one.

As we ate, Andrea asked if the plane had a name. Between mouthfuls I informed her that it was named the *Biscayne Voyager*. She asked how it got its name.

"We were flying back from Boston, and Tony was studying the chart for the Keys. He just kinda hit on the word *Biscayne*, and Scot suggested *Voyager* with it, and *Biscayne Voyager* seemed to fit."

"But you haven't been able to do the same thing with the house?"

I shook my head. "Somehow, it hasn't been the same thing. The house has been all work so far. The plane has been all fun."

Before she could indicate where her line of questioning was going, we heard a boat on the far side of the plane. It gunned its engines a couple of times, and we thought we heard someone wading ashore. All of us exchanged alarmed looks, and the *"some drug runner has come to this island to make a pickup and will be very upset to see a bunch of innkeepers from Key West having a picnic and kill all of us"* thought ran through my mind. I stood up and started to tentatively walk around the plane when I heard a halloo from the other side.

"Albert? Where the fuck have you been, man?"

At that moment, a uniformed Coast Guard captain rounded the tail of the plane and saw us. "Albert?" he asked again.

Relief washed over me that this, at least, was not a drug runner here to reclaim the island. I walked towards him and extended my hand like

Robinson Crusoe greeting Friday. "Hello! I'm Aidan McInnis, Albert's nephew."

The captain was middle aged but clearly in his element. He came forward and shook my hand vigorously. Looking at his face, it was immediately obvious that he was Irish. "Glad to meet you son, glad to meet you. I'm Ian Finch. I've heard your uncle talk about you often. Where is the old turd?"

At that moment, a Coast Guard Lieutenant rounded the tail of the plane. I glanced at him, then looked back at Captain Finch. "I'm sorry, Captain. Albert died last March."

The captain was genuinely shocked. He stared at me for a long moment, and then whispered, "I had no idea."

I motioned towards the fire. "Please, come join us. Can we offer you something to eat?" The captain readily followed us to the fire; the Lieutenant was more tentative. I seated the captain on the cooler and walked back to introduce myself to him. His name was Ross McArthur, and he could not have been more than twenty-three. I offered each of them a Coke, which they both accepted, and some of the lobster meat. The captain declined but Ross accepted with gusto.

The captain recovered himself some. "How did he die, Aidan?"

"He collapsed while he was working on the plane. We didn't have him autopsied, but everyone is pretty sure he had a massive stroke. I doubt he even knew what hit him."

The captain nodded as though he was satisfied that Albert had died a fitting death. "That's good. Albert was not the kind of man who should waste away in bed."

"Did you know my uncle well?" I asked, sipping my beer. The captain laughed.

"That I did, sir. That I did. Knew him for years. Bailed him outta jail a couple of times, put him there myself once or twice. Albert's been bringing his friends out to this key for fifteen years, even before it was safe from drug runners. We patrol out here often, and we investigate whenever we see a plane on the strip. Usually, it's Pipers or Cessnas.

But, whenever we saw a silver DC-2, we knew it was your uncle, and it was usually a party." He motioned towards the lieutenant. "Ross here has only been stationed with us a few months and didn't have the opportunity to meet Albert, but he's heard the stories. When I saw the plane tonight, I thought it was his chance."

I smiled. "He left the plane to me in his will, and I had heard he sometimes came out here for the night. I thought I'd check it out."

The captain nodded. "Whenever we'd come out here, he would always have something cooking for us and offer us something to drink. It can get boring patrolling these waters every night, and I always welcomed the diversion." He motioned towards Ross who was finishing his lobster. "I see he taught you some hospitality as well."

Albert was still a sensitive subject with me, but I knew the man meant it as a compliment. "I learned a great deal from him."

The captain finished his Coke and accepted another. "What about Albert's house? He had some crazy scheme to convert it to a bed and breakfast or a bed and beer or some such thing."

Tony piped up. "The dream lives on. We're getting ready to open it up in a month or so."

Finch laughed. "That so? He kept telling me about how, instead of getting a breakfast every morning when you stayed there, you'd get a cocktail hour every night."

Tony, never one to resist a marketing opportunity, began his sales pitch. "Well, actually, we're planning to have both. Breakfast in the morning, and then a free cocktail hour from five until…"

I interrupted. "You really should come by and have a drink with us the next time you're on the island." I looked at Ross. "You as well."

He smiled. "That I will." They stayed with us for perhaps another half hour and Finch regaled us with stories of my uncle. I think there must be an unspoken agreement among Irish men that, when one dies, every other one who knew him must relate these legends. God knows I've heard enough of them since I've been on the island.

Ross and the captain bid us good-bye, and I walked back to their patrol boat with them. They had beached near the plane and, once they were aboard, I pushed them back out into open water. They waved and thanked me for the hospitality, and Ross called "Hope to see you out here again." Then they were gone.

With the plane between me and the fire, I was in almost total darkness. Above me, more stars than I think I have ever seen shimmered in the sky and reflected back from the water. It was not hard to imagine I was standing far out in space instead of on a spit of sand in the Gulf of Mexico.

After a little while, Tony and Scot wandered around the plane and brought me a beer. "Sounds like things quieted down over there," I observed, indicating the other side of the plane.

"Uh huh," Tony confirmed. "Everyone's more or less passed out except us."

"Lightweights," I mocked as I took a swig of the beer.

"What are you over here thinking about?" Scot asked as he sunk into the sand next to me. Tony sat down on the other side and the three of us looked out towards infinity.

"The universe," I replied, "and the plane and the ocean and Uncle Albert and the house and how perfect this very moment of my life is."

Although I couldn't see there faces very well, I knew both of them were smiling. Tony held out his can, and Scot and I touched ours to it in a silent toast to the perfect night.

"This must be one of those moments Louie Robideau told Jake about," Scot observed. "One of those moments you want to recreate all through your life."

It seamed reasonable to me. Then again, at that moment Ethel Merman could have water-skied by while reading aloud from *Ivanhoe* and it would have seemed perfectly reasonable to me.

"Ocean nights," Tony said.

"What?" I asked.

"I understand what Louie meant. Find a perfect moment, and look for a phrase that captures it for you. Ocean Nights. We should call it the Ocean Nights Inn."

Consent was unanimous. We stared out into the night for a while longer, and then wandered off to find our sleeping bags. As he collapsed onto the sand beside the fire, Tony muttered, "I guess I owe Jake an apology."

The next morning, I awoke with the most tremendous hangover. Margaritas always give me headaches, and I raided the plane's medical kit for aspirin. Everyone else was beginning to wake up, so I shook out enough pills for all.

Breakfast that morning was a subdued affair. We ate mostly in silence. We all discussed staying the day briefly but decided that it was time to fly home. Besides, we were extremely low on alcohol.

We loaded the plane amidst my repeated warnings about getting sand inside. At one point, I made Jake hold up a cooler so I could brush sand from the bottom before I would let him put it in the cargo hold. While I was brushing, he observed, "You know, you should consider doing this for money."

"Cleaning coolers?" I asked.

"No, flying people out here for a party."

I took the cooler from him and placed it in the hold. "Who's going to pay to fly out to a barren island to sit on a the beach. They can sit on the beach at Key West."

"Tourists, man," Andrea joined in. "After all, what is there to do on the island itself? Eat, drink, and lie in the sun. Sure there's the Little White House and some museums, but tourists are always looking for something else to do."

"It's true," Jake concurred. "I know a lot of people who make money by having these party boats. You load up ten, twenty tourists and sail out for the day. Feed them beer and soda and sandwiches, and bring them home at the end of the day. Your investment is minimal. And you get cash from them for throwing a party."

I shook my head as I secured the cargo compartment door. "I don't want to fly a whole bunch of strangers around. I'll always be sweeping sand out of my plane." With that, I shepherded everyone inside and we flew home.

But the idea stayed in the back of my mind. It did have certain merits. When I looked through the tourist pamphlets that we were beginning to stock at the front desk, I did notice an awful lot of cruises and such directed at tourists. Maybe there was room for a tour in a vintage aircraft.

But, then again, I really did hate having sand in the plane.

THE BISCAYNE VOYAGER

On July first, the Ocean Nights Inn opened for business. We had finished the building, and had installed all of the furniture and linens. That same week, our first ad appeared in travel magazines up north. It featured our new logo, which consisted of a single palm tree, the moon reflected off the water, and the silhouette of a DC-2 flying overhead.

The problem with opening an inn in Key West in July is that it is the very bottom of the off-season. The tourists have all left the island to the locals who, of course, have places of their own to stay. We knew this would happen, and had budgeted our money to ensure that we would have enough to carry us through to the tourist season. What we hadn't counted on was the sheer, crushing boredom we encountered. With the inn finished, we had nothing to do.

The first few days weren't bad. There were minor projects to be completed. We were able to relax and enjoy our evenings and even attend some social events. But by the twenty-first, the life of leisure began to get to us. Even Tony, who can *always* find some project to obsess over, was at loose ends. I began to spend more time at the airport working on the plane, even though I couldn't really afford to operate it right now. Scot wrote some elaborate office software for making reservations, tracking guest billing and compiling mailing lists, which he was considering marketing to the other inn keepers on the island. Tony began to make noises about cleaning out the garage.

About a month after our camping trip, Jake (who was the newly elected president of the guesthouse and innkeepers association we belonged to) wandered into my back yard while I was floating on a raft in the pool.

"You can always tell when a guesthouse owner has no guests," he observed from the side of the pool.

"How's that?" I asked, looking up from my book

"It's the only time when they feel completely confident sunbathing in the nude." I was, in fact nude, although I had strategically placed my towel to prevent the development of a rather uncomfortable sunburn. Modesty is somewhat anachronistic in Key West, especially during the hot days of a south Florida summer when any clothing is a nuisance.

Jake was not wearing much more than I. He had on some green nylon running shorts and a pair of flip-flops. He left the sandals by the side of the pool and eased himself into the water. "I've come with a business proposition."

I sighed. "It's sad. That's the only thing anyone ever propositions me with anymore."

He ignored me. "I need to throw a party for about ten people and I wanted to know if I could charter your plane."

I considered his offer. "What kind of party?"

He ducked under the water momentarily, and resurfaced next to the raft. "Same kinda thing we did last month. Except we bring the food."

"Who's it for?"

"A group of travel agents and writers from up north. They're in town putting together tours for this winter. I thought it might be a neat idea if we threw them sort of a forties-themed beach party. Fly off in a vintage aircraft to a remote hide-away for a lobster roast. Whadd-aya think?"

It certainly sounded like a good idea, and it would give me a chance to plug the inn to some agents. "I think we can work it out."

"Cool. How much?"

That, I didn't know and told him so. "What we can do is figure out all of the details of the party, and I can come up with a cost. When do you want to do this?"

"Next week."

"Christ, Jake, there's nothing like waiting until the last minute."

He nodded. "I know. I apologize. It's something the association decided at the last minute that they wanted to do."

I rolled off the raft and swam to the edge. "Let's go inside," I told him as I pulled on a pair of shorts. "There's no time like the present to figure this out."

He pulled himself out of the pool and followed me into the kitchen. Tony was seated on the counter, drinking a beer and reading over some letter from the bank. Tony loves mail.

I explained Jake's proposition to him. One of the reasons I enjoy being in business with Tony is that, while I've got a good head for operations and *how* to do things, he has a much better grasp of *why* to do things; namely, for money. Better yet, how to make them profitable.

I gave Jake a beer and the three of us trooped into the study to work out the details. What he had in mind was a five-hour party, beginning at two and ending at seven. He wanted Tony, Scot and me to handle the arrangements for the food, and the flight. Jake would handle getting the guests to the airport. I would then fly them to the island where the three of us would feed them, serve them beverages, and fly them back that evening.

Tony and I exchanged glances. The three of us worked out a quick menu and a list of things we would need to supply. "Oh," Jake added as the list was completed, "You'll also need a dining fly or some kind of shelter. Some of these people have never been out in the sun and they may fry without shade."

I added "awning" to the list. I then told Jake that I would need to figure out what it would cost to actually fly them to the island. Tony and I promised to have a cost figure back to him the next afternoon.

He appeared satisfied, and I him escorted to the front door and sent him back out into the blistering afternoon heat.

"This could be interesting," I observed as I returned to the study.

Tony nodded and handed me the letter he had been reading. "We can use the money. We need to take out hurricane insurance." I scanned the letter. The bank was offering certain incentives to businesses that increased their hurricane coverage. We did not have any on the guesthouse building.

"Well, I guess we better find a way to make this profitable."

We did a quick cost analysis. It was not a long flight, and I was sure that the actual trip wouldn't cost more than about twenty dollars per person. We made a couple of calls to determine how much it would cost to cater the party. Scot came in as we were finishing the estimate and we filled him in on what we were doing.

"All we have left is to rent a dining fly," I observed.

"No, you don't," Scot replied. "Elizabeth and Andrea have one that they use in their back yard. I'm sure we could borrow it."

Our final projections came out to forty-five dollars a person. At Tony's insistence, we would tell Jake that we could do it for seventy. If he bargained, we would settle for fifty-five.

The three of us wandered over to his house the next morning with a letter to the association that contained our bid. Jake took the letter and read it while eating his breakfast. When he finished, he looked up smiling and said "Fantastic. We were sure you were going to want a hundred per person. Seventy is great."

I heard Tony say "Shit!" under his breath.

The association would pay us half of the money in advance, and the other half when we landed back in Key West. We took the check and set about getting things ready for the party. We borrowed the dining fly, liberated some card tables from the garage, and ordered the food. The party was scheduled for the following Friday. On Sunday, Jake called and told me that he had to include two more people, so there would be eleven guests, himself, Tony, Scot and I. The plane had fourteen passenger seats, plus a flight attendant seat, so seating would be tight, but not ridiculous. We upped our price accordingly.

On Tuesday, two other guesthouse owners had to be included on the flight. Now, every seat on the plane was filled.

On Wednesday, he called again to see if he could add two more people.

"Jake," I told him on the phone, "every seat is filled."

"I know, Aidan, but people keep hearing about this and want to come. Can't someone just sit in the aisle?"

I rolled my eyes. "It's not that simple. In the first place, it's illegal. In the second place, you're getting close to the maximum amount of weight I can land on the island with."

Tony was sitting next to me, and I could tell he didn't want to give up the revenue that two more people would bring in. I put my hand over the receiver and we discussed it quickly. Between the three of us, we agreed that the association would pay for me to fly Tony and Scot to the island first, then come back for the guests. When we left, I would do the same thing in reverse.

"This is getting to be a major yabaho pain in the ass," I snarled as I hung up the phone.

"It's more money," Tony replied flatly. The discussion was ended.

On Friday, we got up early, loaded the plane and the three of us flew to the key. Quickly, we unloaded the supplies and the dining fly. As I prepared to leave, Tony looked around uncomfortably. "This is weird. I mean, what if you have an accident? We'll be stranded here."

I generally don't appreciate people speculating about what will happen if I crash my plane. "It's more money," I growled and climbed back into the plane.

I had never flown the DC-2 alone, and it was a strange experience. Like an old house at night, a plane makes some strange noises when it's empty and I had the uncomfortable sensation that I was going to turn around at some point and see Albert floating in the galley. I reached behind me without looking around and closed the galley curtain.

I made it back to Key West without incident and taxied up to the hangar. In the cabin, I quickly shed the running shorts and sandals that had been my standard outfit for many months now and put on white pants, a white pilot's shirt and a captain's hat (uniform courtesy of Jake). I couldn't remember the last time I had worn socks.

Jake and guests were waiting for me outside the hangar. I escorted them to the plane, and we boarded while Sam Kinner refueled it. A number of the passengers asked if there would be beverage service during the flight, and I could see that Jake was clearly disgusted with himself for not thinking to include this in the plans.

We taxied to the end of the runway while I made the required pre-flight announcements. Jake checked everyone's seatbelts, then came onto the flight deck and latched himself into the co-pilot's seat. Seeing as air travel was not his customary form of locomotion, he sat frozen to one side of the seat, terrified that he might touch one of the controls and send us plunging into the ocean.

We flew back to Runner's Key. All in all, I had logged less than two hours of flying time, but I was already feeling fatigued. Tony and Scot had been busy while I was gone. They had put up the dining fly, set out a buffet of fruit on one card table, and had a bar ready for service on the other. We had even flown in some lawn chairs, so people had places to sit. A fire was burning well away from the party area, and the ice chest containing the lobsters sat next to it.

"Pretty impressive, guys," Jake told us as we got off the airplane. Our travel agents and writers all came off and began to look around.

Tony and Scot were both barefoot and were wearing bathing suits and tank tops. They took in my nautical garb, and immediately burst out laughing. "You look ridiculous," Tony offered.

I glared at Jake. "I'm changing back into my civvies."

"Wait a few minutes," Jake pleaded. "Mingle with the agents and writers first. Then you can do what you want."

I was not happy, but I was clearly the only one on the island who could say that. Our miscellaneous guests looked around tentatively at first, but as soon as they realized they really had the whole island to themselves, both clothes and inhibitions were shed. I wandered among the crowd, accepting compliments on the plane, the flight, the idea and the party.

Scot handled the food and Tony was busy tending bar. I noticed that he had put out a tip cup and it was already half full of ones. "You are planning to divide that three ways, aren't you?"

"Of course not," he told me.

"You want me to come back and pick you up?" I asked.

He rolled his eyes and turned away to take the order of a rather rotund woman in a French-cut bathing suit.

We started the lobsters at about four, and the island was soon filled with their delicious aroma. We set the food out at five, and Jake and I found ourselves sitting with a bald, rather serious looking man who identified himself to me as Earl.

"Have you been putting on parties like this long?" Earl asked between mouthfuls.

"Not really," I replied. Before I could finish my statement, Jake interrupted.

"They've done this a number of times this summer. They're still trying to figure out if it's worthwhile to do it all the time."

"Oh, absolutely," Earl replied. "Tourists eat this kind of thing up. How did you come to be associated with the guesthouse association?"

"Actually, I'm a member. I'm part owner of the Ocean Nights Inn."

A few feet away I saw Tony's head snap up.

"Indeed?" replied Earl. "Well, if you run your guesthouse as well as you run your tour service, you should do quite well."

I thanked him. Earl excused himself to go get more lobster. Jake slapped me on the back. "Do you have any idea who that was?" he demanded excitedly.

"Earl."

"*Earl,*" he told me in an elaborately patronizing tone, "is an editor for Conde Nast. This could be just the write-up you need."

"Write-up I need for what?" I asked. "I wasn't planning to go into a second business."

"You need to do this, Aidan. It's worked out great. How much money are you going to clear off of me on this?"

I didn't answer.

"Oh, c'mon. I'm not going to try to renegotiate. Just tell me."

"With all the additional arrangements we made? A little over a thousand."

He sat back, triumphant. "A little over a thousand, for a few hours work. It's not enough to live off of, but it's definitely cash worth having. Look, you'll learn soon enough that you're not going to get rich running a guesthouse. Any additional income doesn't hurt."

Once the lobsters were finished, I loaded the guests back into the plane and took off for home. The air was rough, and when I tuned in the weather from Miami on the radio, I got word of showers moving into the area.

We landed in Key West, and I rushed the passengers off the plane. I had enough fuel for one more round trip, so I immediately taxied back out and took off. I could see the dark clouds moving in on the horizon.

Ordinarily, I would not have flown into weather like this. Airplanes do much better flying around storms than straight through them. I could not, however, imagine Tony and Scot riding out the storm on the island with no more protection than just the dining fly.

I made it back to Runner's Key at the same time that the storm did. The guys had everything packed and were looking anxious when I taxied up to them. We loaded the plane frantically.

One thing I had not considered was that the runway had no lights on it. The sky was rapidly growing dark, and without lights, I couldn't see well enough to take off. We all climbed into the cabin, but instead of going to the flight deck, I opened the aft storage bin and took out the spare wheel chocks.

"What are we waiting for?" Tony asked.

"I can't take off without lights on the runway. It's too dark for me to even tell which way the wind is blowing."

"You mean we're stuck here?" Scot asked. I nodded. "Until when?"

"Until morning."

"Well, this sucks."

I jumped back out of the plane and chocked the wheels. The wind had really picked up and I looked in vain for something to tie the gear down to the ground. I didn't want the wind to lift one of the wings and smash the other to the ground.

That was not, however, my biggest concern. On an island that sat barely five feet above the high tide, it didn't take much of a storm to wash waves completely over it. A strong enough wave could break one of the gear or, possibly, wash us off the island.

I climbed back into the plane and walked up to the flight deck. I switched off all the systems to save the battery. I then returned to the cabin, opened the locker next to the galley and dug out the flashlights and emergency candles. "Use these sparingly," I told the guys. "We may need them to watch the water." Before I closed the locker, I also made sure that the life raft was in there.

I don't know if the guys sensed my fear, or if they were just too exhausted to talk, but they both collapsed into the seats in the back of the cabin. I walked back up to the flight deck and sat alone in the dark. The winds were picking up outside, and I could feel the old plane rock slightly. I looked out the window, but could see nothing but pitch darkness. I tried to think of a plan.

I hoped we could ride out the storm and the night where we were. But if it looked like the water was rising, or the plane was in danger, I would start the engine to power the generator and radio for help. If the wind really picked up and the plane flipped over, or worse, if we were washed off the island then we would have to use the life raft and take the emergency radio…

I spent a good deal of energy that night planning for all possible eventualities except, maybe, an invasion of the island by Haitian nationals. Every fifteen minutes or so, I would shine my flashlight out of the window and check the location of the water level. There was a good chop on the waves, and they were breaking progressively closer to the plane. The wind howled around us and I found myself in the unusual position of having to manipulate the rudder and wing surfaces in order to keep us on the ground. I also found myself digging around in the pouch behind the pilot's seat for the rosary that Albert had placed there years ago, and that I had elected to leave there.

About an hour and a half into the storm, the waves had advanced far enough to be breaking against the right landing gear. I had the radio on and was monitoring the storm's progress. Back in the cabin, Scot and Tony were sound asleep.

Around midnight, the storm began to abate. The radio reported that the worst of it was bearing down on Sarasota, and that the gulf was beginning to clear. I silently thanked God, and began to loosen the death grip I had on the controls. I fell asleep shortly after one as the first stars were winking into view above the plane.

I awoke to pounding. I was sprawled across both seats with my head wedged between the edge of the seat and the left window. My neck was incredibly stiff. Behind me, someone pounded again. I twisted myself out of the flight deck. Scot and Tony were yawning and beginning to stir. Someone was pounding on the hatch.

I opened the door to see the concerned faces of Captain Ian Finch and Lieutenant Ross McArthur.

"Thank God you're still here," Finch declared as I emerged, blinking, into the bright morning light. "We got a call that your plane was missing."

"A call from who?" I asked. Tony dropped out of the plane behind me.

"Some guy," Ross volunteered, "I think his name was Jake."

I nodded. "He kinda got me into this. The storm hit last night before we could get off the island."

"So you decided to ride it out?" Finch asked. "That was a dangerous decision. It doesn't take much of a wave to wash across these keys."

"I know. I spent all night watching them." I explained my various evacuation plans. "How long have you been looking for us?"

"Not long. I was about to give Ross here a ride into Key West when the call came in. We decided to look for you while we were on our way."

I apologized to Finch for having caused him any trouble and asked him to relay my apology to the entire United States Coast Guard. He laughed and informed me that there was one thing I could do to pay him back. "Ross here is going on a week's leave. With looking for you all, I'm really pressed for time to get him into town and get back to the base. Would you mind giving him a lift?"

My mind was beginning to clear, and for the first time, I realized that Ross was wearing civvies. "We'd be happy to."

We gathered Ross's gear from the boat and transferred it into the hold of the plane. While Scot walked the runway to make sure it was clear of debris, I made a quick inspection to make sure the *Voyager* had weathered the storm all right. She had a little water in the hold, which Tony blotted up with his beach towel, and there was some sand inside the engine cowling that I would have Sam Kinner take care of for me, but otherwise, she seemed to be in pretty good condition. Finch pushed off the island, and a few minutes later I was starting the number one engine.

"Pratts?" Ross asked from the flight deck door as the giant propeller began to turn.

I shook my head. "Pratt and Whitneys were used on the DC-3. The DC-2 runs Wright Cyclones."

Tony offered Ross the co-pilot's seat, which he gladly accepted. I started the number two engine and he scanned the instrument panel. "Pretty sophisticated avionics for a plane this old," he observed.

I nodded and began to taxi the plane into position. While I ran the checklist I asked, "You a pilot?"

"I managed to get my private when I was in school. Never went on, though."

I finished the checklist and yelled back to Tony and Scot to strap in. I taxied into position and pushed the throttles forward. Since the runway was so short, I waited until the engines reached full power before releasing the brakes. We shot down the runway and into the air. As I circled right, we could see Finch cruising west in his boat below.

"I wasn't aware the DC-2 was such a hot rod," Ross observed.

"She's got some spirit," I confirmed.

"Ever flown an Electra?"

"Nope. Closest I've ever been was to see one in the Air Force Museum." The Electra is also a famous plane. Lockheed introduced it about five years before Douglas introduced the "two." It is the plane Amelia Erhart disappeared in. "Have you?"

He nodded. "Yep. My dad had one. Flew it all over the Southwest when I was a kid."

I was impressed. "That would be a treasure. What did he do with it?"

Ross shrugged. "Flew it into the wall of the Grand Canyon."

I've got to stop trying small talk, I thought. "I'm sorry."

He waved away my condolences with a smile. "It was a long time ago. Neat plane, though."

I confirmed that it was, indeed, a neat plane and tried desperately to find some happier subject. "What are you planning to do with your week off?"

He stretched back in his seat and crossed his arms behind his head. "Sleep. Eat. Drink. Try to get laid. The things you're supposed to do on leave."

Tony, ever the marketer, stuck his head through the curtain. "Got a place to stay yet?"

"Not yet," Ross laughed. "It's summer in Key West. How hard could it be to find a place to stay?"

Tony informed Ross that there were fluctuations in the summer tourist trade (an overstatement), and that sometimes rooms could not be had on the island, even in the summer (a lie). He then pointed out that the Ocean Nights Inn had just opened, and we would certainly welcome the opportunity to have him as our first guest.

Ross blushed, apparently not used to having someone market to him so flagrantly. He asked our going rate for a room, was satisfied when Tony told him, and accepted.

We landed in Key West and returned home. Once there, Tony handled checking Ross in while I called Jake to let him know that we had made it back safely.

"Thank God," he gushed. "I was scared to death that you and that little gold mine had flown off into the Bermuda triangle." I decided that there was nothing to be gained by pointing out to him that the Bermuda Triangle was off the *east* coast of Florida.

Jake informed me that Earl from Conde Nast was planning to write an in-depth article on the plane and wanted to get some pictures of it tomorrow. I reminded him that I had not planned to go into business.

"Aidan, this is *Conde Nast!* What does it take with you to make you recognize a good opportunity?"

We debated the issue for a few more minutes, and I promised I would think about it over night. He wasn't happy, but grudgingly accepted the promise. I then told him we had our first guest and asked him over that evening for the house christening.

We were, after all, an innovation in Key West. There are lots of bed and breakfasts in the world, but not many bed-and-beers. We offered a free happy hour to our guests each evening from five until seven. I knew it wouldn't be long before the other guesthouses started doing the same, but we decided to play it for what it was worth in the short term.

Ross understood that he was to play a key role in all of this. At five o'clock, the three of us were gathered around the bar that was in a small gazebo next to the pool. Jake, Elizabeth and Andrea had joined us, as well as our august monarch. Ross, who had taken a room on the top floor, was in a chaise lounge, trying to squeeze in every last minute of tanning time possible before the shadow of the mangroves extended over the pool.

We called him over to the gazebo. There, he was handed a bottle and asked to christen the guesthouse. "But don't hit it with the bottle," Scot warned. "I'm not sure it's strong enough to survive the impact."

Ross poured some champagne into a glass and tossed the glass against the wall of the building. It shattered in a burst of crystal and amber liquid and everyone cheered. We then all shared the bottle of champagne while Louie rambled through a three-page toast. Afterwards, we invited Ross to join us and we all went out to dinner. "After all," Tony explained to him, "you're basically paying for it."

During dinner, we discussed the merits of running a tour using the *Voyager*. I would certainly have to increase my insurance, and there were a few minor things I would have to do in order to comply with the federal aviation regulations governing such activities, but otherwise the obstacles were not significant. And, I had to admit, the prospect of it did sound like fun. It would allow me to fly on a regular basis, and there was no doubt that the cash would come in handy.

Ross suggested that, initially, I could limit operation to one or two days a week. That way, I still had time to devote to the inn. Finally, I succumbed. *Biscayne Voyager Airways* was born over dessert.

After dinner that evening I went to Jake's house, where the two of us sat at his computer and designed a promotional flyer and some business cards. I had to cut the cards out by hand so they did not look incredibly professional, but at least I would have something to hand Earl tomorrow.

The next day in the hangar, Earl was all business. He asked me a series of questions about the history of the plane, the history of air travel in the Keys, and about the inn. I fielded most of the questions, and took him up to the flight deck and explained some of the controls to him. I showed him the airman's charts and gave him a little bit of the history of Runner's Key. He then took a series of pictures of the plane, including one of me leaning against the wing with my arms crossed which I thought was very flattering.

When I returned to the house that afternoon, it was empty. From the dining room windows, I could see Tony, Scot and Ross lounging about the pool in Key West fashion. I took a beer from the refrigerator and walked down the back steps to join them.

"How did it go?" Scot asked as I stripped off my clothes poolside.

"Great! He seemed really impressed. He couldn't tell me when the article would run, but he said he would try to get it in the September issue. That way, travel agents will see it before the tourist season." I dove into the pool.

"Fantastic!" Tony declared. "We need to get word out about this. I'll make up a brochure." He may have said something else, but I dove below the surface and couldn't hear it. When I came back up, I swam to the side and asked him "Did you deposit Jake's check?" He nodded.

"What are you going to use the money for?" Ross asked from the raft behind me. I turned around and propped myself against the sides of the pool.

"Survival. We need the money to carry us through until tourist season gets underway."

He nodded. "I can understand that. I'm scraping every cent together that I can for the day when I get out of the Guard."

I asked Scot to hand me my beer. "How far away is that?"

"December first. You can expect to see me back here then. I intend to spend most of my first month free completely drunk."

"You're kinda young to be getting out, aren't you?" Scot asked as he slid into the water next to me. Again, Ross nodded.

"I guess. The Guard is great. But being stationed on a bare rock in the Tortugas is not what I want from life. Besides, I have some personal reasons to get out."

He took a sip of his beer and then continued. "And, I need to find a gig like you guys have got. You three are livin' in paradise."

"It's not completely paradise," Tony interjected. "We're living hand to mouth until we can get some sustainable cash flow."

Over the next few weeks, word got around the island about my new business, and people began dropping by the house in the hopes of getting a free ride. I had a very good incentive not to offer them one since I knew Tony would break both of my legs if I did so.

My friends are natural promoters. Tony did a great job of selling the plane to the innkeeper's association. Scot had managed to post flyers on every bulletin board on the island. Large posters advertising the *Biscayne Voyager* hung in the lobbies of House Diana and the Madison Key West. As you might suspect, it was only a matter of time before the king dropped in on me.

It was mid-August and the evening was truly stifling. Tony and I were seated on the widow's walk splitting a bottle of wine and quietly speculating on the number of bottles of wine we had split over the years we had been friends. We heard the doorbell ring below us. I leaned over the rail and yelled hello to whoever was below us.

"Master McInnis!" the king hollered. "Please come down here. We would like to discuss a business proposition with you."

"Jesus," Tony snarled. "Why does this guy only come out at night? It's like living next to a bat." I yelled to the king that I would be right down.

Outside, Tony and I found the king seated in one of the wrought-iron chairs on the front terrace. We sat in the other chairs.

"Young Aidan," the king began. "We have been informed that you have gone into the aviation business. We would like to retain your services to take the court to Runner's Key."

Tony was immediately businesslike. "How many people?"

"Twelve."

"That's good," I informed him, "we only have fourteen seats."

"I know. It won't be the first time I've been on your plane."

Tony informed him that it would cost one hundred dollars a person, payable in advance. Louie consented and a date was set. It looked like I was really in business.

The flight was set for the following weekend. Catering would be much more simple. Louie was much less interested in the lobster, much more interested in how the bar was stocked.

In order to legitimately run a charter business like this, I really needed to have another pilot fly with me. That week, I made the rounds at the airport looking for someone who wanted to fly with me that weekend. There were no takers. Not because I was that undesirable to fly with, but because most of the local pilots were flying charters of their own.

By Wednesday night I was getting desperate. I was about to call Louie and ask if he would consider rescheduling when our *reservations* phone rang. I picked it up and dug out the reservations book.

"Aidan," Ross said from the other end of the phone quietly, "think you can squeeze me in this weekend?"

Ross! Ross could fly it with me. This would be his third time staying with us. I offered him half-priced lodging if he would help me fly on Saturday. He accepted, promised to be there Friday, and then hung up. I guess I noticed that he was somewhat somber, but didn't really pay attention to it. I was elated that I wouldn't have to cancel the gig.

I spent Thursday at the hangar, devoting attention to the plane with a tenderness I must someday learn to apply to my human relationships. Sam Kinner took care of the engines, the airframe and the control systems for me, but I liked to actually take care of the plane's aesthetics. That afternoon, I serviced the tires and gave all the landing gear a quick check, tightened some bolts on the engine cowlings, washed all the windows, vacuumed out the interior, and oiled all of the teak paneling. I was sitting cross-legged on the flight deck floor digging some sand out from around the yoke when I heard a voice behind me say, "Hey, flyboy."

I turned around and saw Olivia Robideau's head and shoulders sticking through the hatch. She wasn't exactly smiling (indeed, island lore said she *never* smiled), but she looked pleasant enough. "Miz. Robideau. What are you doing here?"

She climbed aboard and walked up the aisle towards me. "My father said you might be found here. I just flew in and was wondering if you could give me a lift to his house. There don't appear to be any cabs available."

I agreed. "Whose portrait are you here to claim this time?"

"Queen Julianna of the Netherlands. It's also an obligation visit. Saturday is Dad's birthday."

"That would explain the party," I said as I stood up and wiped off my hands. "Let me lock everything up, and then we'll go."

I closed up the hangar and we walked to my car. She had left her luggage beside it, so I loaded her bags into the small trunk. We then drove to her father's house, talking of nothing important. When we pulled up, the front yard was full of thousands of plastic flamingos, each painted a different color. She sighed, rolled her eyes and shook her head simultaneously. "Any vacancies at your place tonight?"

I laughed. "It's the off season. It would probably be more accurate to ask if there were any guests, instead." I handed over her bags and added, "If things get too crazy, give us a call. We'll cut you a good rate." She nodded and picked her way through the chaos of the front yard. I drove home.

I saw her again that evening. The three of us were walking back from watching the sunset at Mallory Square, and we saw her turn into Monarch Court ahead of us. We were about twenty yards behind her, so she was already on the front steps, knocking on our door when we reached the driveway.

"No one's home," I said as I climbed the steps behind her. She turned around and looked at me with a tense face.

"Too bad," she said. "I've got Louie's check for tomorrow's party. I believe Tony told him 'payable in advance'?"

Tony reached past me and snatched the envelope from her hand. I unlocked the door, and he disappeared upstairs with it to lock it into the safe in his office.

"You'll have to excuse him," Scot told Olivia as we walked into the living room. "He was raised by wolves."

Olivia looked around. "I haven't been in here in forever. What did you do with all of Albert's stuff?"

"I believe my aunt pawned it all," I replied. "Why'd you bring the check down here tonight? We would have taken it tomorrow at the airport."

"I needed to get out of the house for a while. The problem with Louie is he's terrified to be alone. He won't even be alone with someone else. Unless he's painting, he must always have fifty or sixty people around him. Every once in a while, it just gets to be too much for me and I have to get out of the house."

"You want a drink?"

"I'd love a beer," she said. I led her to the kitchen. In the hall, I could hear Scot checking the messages on the answering machine.

"Hey Aidan!" he called. "Message from your mom. She wants a reservation."

I gave Olivia her beer, and we returned to the front hall as Tony was coming down the stairs. I punched the play button on the machine, and my mother's voice informed me that the whole family would like to help inaugurate my new inn. She and my dad, my sister and my brother, Aunt Vivian and Uncle Mo and their wretched offspring would like to book all six rooms for the first weekend in October. "Sort of a family reunion," she laughed in her strained voice, which indicated to me that someone, probably Aunt Vivian, was in earshot. The message ended with a request from her to call so we could work out the details. "I love you," she said, and the tape stopped with three beeps.

I looked at Tony. "We've got to get a restraining order."

He sat on the steps. "We need the business," he reminded me gently.

"I know we need business, but not *this* kind of business."

"Not fond of your family either?" Olivia asked as she took a sip of the beer.

I sank down at sat with my back against the front door. "Oh, they're okay. My parents are sometimes a little stiff, but I like them. And I would love to see my brother and sister. But my Aunt Vivian is the single most unpleasant woman on earth. She's something of a back-stabber, and she's beside herself that Albert left me the house and plane."

"That's been months," Tony said. "Don't you think she's over it by now?"

"No. People in my family don't 'get over' things. They carry everything around for years after it has any meaning. If they want to come here, they either expect to stay for free, or they're up to something else."

"We need the business," Tony repeated. "At least call your mother back."

Before I could protest further, the doorbell rang. I stood up and opened it. Ross stood on the porch with an inordinate amount of luggage. "You guys always hang out in the foyer?"

"I thought you weren't getting here until tomorrow morning," Scot said as he retrieved the book from the desk.

"I was," Ross confirmed as he came inside. I closed the door and introduced him to Olivia.

"The Coast Guard decide that they didn't need you tonight?" Tony asked from the steps.

"Well, actually, they've pretty much decided they don't need me period. They're discharging me early."

"How'd you work that?" I asked. He grimaced.

"You've heard of 'don't ask, don't tell?' Well, they asked, and I told."

The silence in the hall was immensely awkward. Finally, Olivia looked at me and said, "Y'know, you guys lead real interesting lives."

I got Ross a beer, and all of us moved out into the back yard. He really wasn't in much of a mood to talk, so the rest of us wandered from one mundane subject to another. Well after midnight, Olivia stood up and excused herself to leave. She said her good-byes, and I walked her around the house to the front yard.

When we reached the driveway, she asked, "How long have you known Ross?"

"Not long. A couple of weeks."

"Did you know he was gay?"

I shook my head. "I'm never any good at figuring that stuff out. Don't really care much either. I'm really not very interested in what goes on in other people's bedrooms."

She smiled a good-bye and walked down the driveway. I turned and went back to the pool, but no one was there. A light was on in the guesthouse, so I assumed Ross had retired. I walked up the back steps and into the kitchen. Tony and Scot were sitting on the counters, quietly finishing their beers.

The atmosphere in the kitchen was extremely interesting. Men, in general, when faced with some friend's tragedy will often gather together to commiserate, and brainstorm ideas for how to address it. But when faced with news the that there is more to the friend than one supposed (especially the *big* news), guys often have no idea how to react. In the kitchen, there was an overwhelming sense that *something* should be said but, honestly, each of us was at a loss for what it was.

I didn't sleep well that night. Thoughts of Ross and my family and the overall purpose of my life kept floating through my head. Around three, I got out of bed, slipped into a pair of shorts and wandered downstairs for some milk. I carried it into the study and switched on the light on my desk. I sat there for a long minute, thinking about anything, nothing. Eventually, my gaze came to rest on my cousin Jason.

I knew my family wondered about this kid, our now-rich cousin in New Orleans. Privately, I did too. I'm not much surprised that Albert had chosen to keep him a secret from the rest of the family, but I was a little insulted that he had chosen to keep him a secret from me. After all, in my vainer moments, I had fancied myself as the son Albert never had.

Early the next morning, I poured myself a big cup of coffee and took the phone out onto the porch. I dialed my parents' phone number.

My mother was cheerful. She usually is in the morning. We had a nice conversation in which she filled me in on all the family news and gossip. Eventually we got around to the subject of their visit.

"You realize that this is a partnership," I began. "While I would love to let you stay here free," *oh I would, would I?* "It wouldn't be fair to Scot or Tony."

"Oh, your father and I understand that, dear. And we'll make sure Aunt Vivian understands it, too."

"Well, I'm glad to hear that."

While we spoke, I went back inside and put their names in the reservation book. "Are you sure you can't discourage Aunt Vivian from coming?"

"I doubt it. She needs to talk to Albert's attorney…what's his name? George? Any way she wants to talk to him about Albert's son."

Alarms went off throughout my head. "What about his son?"

"Well, she wants to meet him. All of us do, actually. Vivian mentioned that, after all, he's family, and we should make sure that he's well taken care of."

I put my face in my hands. "Jesus, Mother. He's got almost four million dollars in a trust fund. Of course he's being taken care of. Was this Vivian's idea?"

"Well, yes…"

"Mom, Vivian has no interest in making sure Jason is taken care of. Her only interest is to see if she can find a way to get her hands on the money."

"Oh, Aidan. What a terrible thing to say. You should be ashamed of yourself. Vivian may be difficult to get along with, but she certainly is not that conniving. Why on earth would you think such a thing?"

"Because, Mom, Vivian *is* that conniving." I considered telling her that we would not accept their reservation, but quickly decided that it would probably be better to have them here where I could keep an eye on them. Per family protocol, the subject was changed. We spoke a few minutes longer before I made an excuse to get off the phone. I dialed George's office.

"Hello, Aidan." George sounded merry. I hated to ruin his mood.

"George, my family wants to get hold of Jason."

"What do you mean 'get hold'?"

"They want to meet him. To check up on him. 'He's family, you know.' Is there a way to stop them?"

George was quiet for a moment. "No, not really. I'm under no legal obligation to provide them with his address and number, but they could certainly try to subpoena it. But I doubt that they would go to that much trouble. They know his name and they know that he's in New Orleans. All they really need to do is hire an investigator to find him. Why do they really want to meet him?"

"It's Aunt Viv's idea. I'm sure she's looking for a way to get to his money."

"As your attorney, I have to advise you not to say those kinds of things out loud, Aidan. She's the kind of woman who might try to come after you on a slander charge."

"Certainly," I mumbled. Keeping my mouth shut about Vivian would be no small task.

"As far as Jason is concerned, we must be very careful how we play this. All of my dealings with him have been through his mother's attorney. I think the kid knows his dad left him some money, but I'm pretty sure he doesn't know how much. I can call the attorney so he at least has a heads-up on this."

An idea occurred to me. "George, can you give me his address and phone number?"

An uncomfortable silence ensued. "No."

"Um, what if…"

"Aidan, look…Albert was very specific on one point. He didn't want his family to contact Jason. I don't know if he meant that to extend to you, but you are family and I must abide by the letter of Albert's wishes."

"I understand, George. I just thought that, maybe, if I could get to him first…"

"That's exactly the wrong thing to think!" His voice was stern. "In the first place, it could only make matters worse, and put you in your aunt's line of fire. In the second place, it's exactly this kind of family politics that Albert wanted to protect Jason from." His voice softened a bit. "And, in the third place. It's none of your business. If your aunt does decide to go after Jason or his money, it will be between the two of them. You have no business getting involved, and could stand to lose a great deal if you did."

It was true. I had automatically slipped into my family's standard operating procedure. "I understand, George. I'll stay out of it. But, one thing? If he ever comes to you looking for some of his father's family to contact, give him my name first."

"I will, Aidan. I will." We hung up.

Most of that Friday was devoted to getting things ready for the party. We laid in a heavy supply of liquor, and a decent spread. I went out and bought a new dining fly and some new lawn chairs. Tony got the food together while Scot handled the daily inn routine. Ross spent the day lying by the pool, not saying much.

The next morning, I went out to the guesthouse, climbed to the second floor, and pounded on Ross's door. He yelled "Come in," and I opened the door. He was seated on the bed wearing a pair of khaki shorts, and was bent over tying his sneakers.

"Ready to fly?" I asked.

"Definitely. I need to do something or I'll probably go crazy." Despite his words, he certainly sounded in a good mood. He stood up, pulled on a blue golf shirt and grabbed his aviator sunglasses off the bed. "Ready, Captain."

The four of us drove to the airport in Tony's car since it's the only one with an adequate back seat. Some of the King's party were already gathered outside the hangar. I recognized a couple of people, but the King and Olivia were not among them.

We hauled the coolers out of the trunk and into the hangar. While members of the party milled about, Ross and I did the walk-around inspection. "I love this plane," I told him.

"Apparently she's always been loved," he commented. "She wouldn't be in this good condition if she hadn't."

We climbed on board and began to run the pre-flight inspection. Ross had only flown single engine airplanes, so he mostly watched as I completed the checks. Then, the four of us rolled her out of the hangar.

As you might expect, the King and the majority of his retinue arrived in style. I'm not sure where he found the trumpeter, but the opening stanza of a march by Chopin announced his arrival. Everyone in his crowd looked excited, and I suspected that they had begun celebrating long before they arrived at the hangar. Even Olivia looked unusually pleasant, albeit somewhat embarrassed. She wore a pair of cutoff denim shorts, a loose cotton blouse, and a pair of Jackie-O sunglasses. Her dark hair fell loosely about her shoulders. Scot just stared at her.

I greeted them at the hatch. "Joyous birthday wishes, your majesty," I said.

"We thank you," the King replied, raising a champagne flute of mimosa in my direction. "We are most pleased." I stood aside, and he stumbled up the aisle and collapsed into a seat. Olivia followed him onboard.

"I thought you detested *court* functions," I said as I followed her up the aisle.

"Well, I do," she replied. "But a day on the beach on a desert island sounds like a lot of fun. I'll just sit on the other side of the island from everyone else."

Tony and Scot shepherded the passengers on board and pulled the wheel chocks. I started one engine and called into the tower for permission to taxi. A few minutes later, we were high in the air over the island.

"Beautiful takeoff," Ross commented from the co-pilot's seat. "She really climbs smoothly."

"I'm learning that it depends on how you load her. There's an invisible line in the hold. If you get the cargo ahead of it, she really gets up." I looked sideways at him. "You want to take her?"

"You're kidding, right? You're going to let me fly your great treasure?" It was friendly sarcasm.

"I have no problem if you fly it. Just don't land it." He put his hands on his yoke and I released mine. "Copilot's plane."

It took him a few minutes to adjust to the sensitivity of the controls. Having only flown single engine planes before, he did not know how to trim it to adjust for uneven engine thrust. Nonetheless, within fifteen minutes, his flying smoothed out, and he relaxed with the controls.

It was a beautiful day for flying, but it would be a hot one on the ground. Even at our speed and altitude, it was getting stuffy in the plane. Ross and I talked mostly about incidentals. The weather. The calibration of the gyroscopes. The ocean. The flight went by quickly, and soon I took back control of the plane and put it down on the island.

It didn't take us long to set up at all, and the party was underway. The majority of guests settled onto the south side of the island. Olivia took her towel and disappeared behind the plane to the north. Tony, Scot, Ross and I went about the necessary hosting duties.

Around noon, I asked Tony if he had seen Scot.

"He's probably over bugging Olivia. I keep seeing him disappear around the plane. I think he may be smitten." The two of us were behind our makeshift bar making margaritas. I poured one for some inebriate friend of the king, while Ross came by to bring us two hot dogs. He had spent the day tending the grill (a thankless job on a day like this), and his chest glistened with sweat. As he returned to the fire-pit, Tony said in an offhand way, "He's pretty useful to have around."

I nodded. "Too bad we're not making money. I'd offer him a job."

"Yeah," Tony agreed. "Well, maybe we can at least recruit him for these parties."

"I would like to. I definitely need another pilot to keep this legal."

I heard a boat engine from the far side of the plane. Tony and I exchanged glances. It could only be Finch. At the fire pit, Ross was staring in the direction of the plane. Obviously, he knew who it was also. I left the bar to Tony and walked around the plane.

Scot was helping Finch pull his boat aground. The old guy was as red and merry as ever. He dropped over the side and strode ashore like MacArthur. The years I have spent in the islands have since taught me that most naval men like to do this.

I greeted him, and he walked up the beach to speak with me. We talked for a few minutes, and then the king came staggering around the plane.

"Finch!" he hollered. "You old sot. Where the hell have you been?"

"Happy birthday, Louie." Finch said warmly. "I thought I might find you here...." His words trailed off, as he saw Ross round the corner of the plane. Their eyes locked, and Ross crossed his arms and leaned against the horizontal stabilizer.

"Of course you'd find me here," Louie replied, oblivious to the mounting tension. "I've spent every goddamn birthday of the last decade on this God forsaken piece of rock."

Finch turned his attention back to the king. "Sand."

"Huh?"

"God forsaken spit of sand. There's not much rock here."

Louie stared at Finch for a minute, then dismissed the comment. "C'mon 'round to the other side of the plane. Have a drink."

"I better not," Finch replied. "I need to get back to the base."

"You must. I'll take it as an insult."

Finch smiled, glanced sideways at Ross, then looked back at the king. "Nonetheless, I must go. Have a good birthday, Louie." He turned and waded back out to the boat.

"That's strange," the king confided in a voice that let me know he was perfectly sober, after all. We watched Finch turn and drive away, then walked back up the beach towards Ross. "He always has a drink to celebrate my birthday. Something seems to be making him uncomfortable."

I glanced at Ross and told Louie, "I'm sure it was just some business back at the base, like he said. I'd chalk it up to nothing more than a tight schedule."

Louie said nothing and walked on around the plane. I stopped next to Ross and said, "So hello, Sailor. Come here often?"

He smiled, but said nothing, and strode away towards the fire pit.

The rest of the party went off well, if somewhat predictably. As the sun dropped close to the horizon, we packed the trash, the gear and the revelers into the plane and flew home.

Once we cleared the end of the runway and were on course for Key West, I looked at Ross and asked, "Wanna talk?"

He smiled that same wan smile and said, "Nothing really to talk about. Finch trained me. We were more than colleagues, he was like my mentor. He's the one who asked. I never dreamt he would turn me in."

I nodded, and adjusted the rudder slightly. "It's a bizarre subject with men. It either elicits absolute apathy or pretty severe emotions. No one is ever *slightly* uncomfortable with it."

He nodded. "That's for sure. Least of all in the military."

Tony came forward with two cups of coffee. "I hate playing flight attendant."

I took one cup; Ross took the other. "It *is* a pretty thankless job," I observed. When we were still at the airline, I remember one flight attendant who quit. On her last flight she poured coffee on a passenger and told him 'Look, you wouldn't be acting like this in Denny's.'"

"'Tis true," Tony said. "And I'm *so* fond of the king to begin with." He returned to the cabin.

I looked at Ross and asked, "So, what's next for you?"

He shrugged. "I haven't got a clue. All my reasons for wanting to get out of the guard were personal. I'm not sure I have any idea what I want to *do* with the rest of my life."

"Didn't you ever have any dreams, man? It would seem that now's the opportunity to pursue one."

He shrugged. "Sailing mostly. I always wanted to sail around the world. What about you?"

"What, sail around the world?"

"No. I mean, what are your dreams?"

That caught me off guard. No one had ever asked me that before. In the hard-edged, practical McInnis family, dreams were looked at with some derision. We are *planners* and *doers*, not dreamers. "Well, there was one. I wanted to be the next Kerouac. I used to dream about owning a seaplane and flying around the world having grand adventures and writing stories about them. Maybe even be a correspondent for *National Geographic* or some other magazine while I was working on my stories.

"I used to have it all planned out. I'd live out of my plane. It'd be big enough to carry a few books and my clothes and maybe an old Underwood typewriter and the other bare essentials of an eccentric's subsistence lifestyle. I'd fly to the Galapagos, or to Europe, or anywhere else on the planet that my interest took me."

"Why didn't you do it?"

"I don't know," I replied truthfully. "I'm not sure I ever really took time to think about it."

"You know, it's funny. You're living the kind of life *other* people dream about. Are you living the life that you dream about?"

"I don't know. I've come about as close to it as I can, I guess. I mean, the only thing missing is money."

He nodded and leaned forward in his seat to get a better view through the windscreen. "I know what you mean. I've got some stashed away, but not nearly enough to sail around the world."

"Or fly it."

We flew on in silence for a few moments.

"You know," Ross volunteered as we began our descent into Key West, "this plane is big enough for books and a typewriter."

I nodded. "The thought's crossed my mind many times. Except the Underwood. I've replaced it with an old laptop."

"So you still write?"

"Oh yeah. When I have time."

Of course, when did I ever have time?

It rained that night in Key West; a long, steady rain that was going to last all night. The house was unusually still, almost as though everyone in it was maintaining a hushed silence in order to listen to the fat, sloppy drops as they hit the high Palladian windows, and the gush of water as it cascaded from the steep hipped roofs to the ancient brick walks and terraces below. Each of us was holed up in the tower, but on a different floor. Scot was in his room in the attic reading a novel. Tony was in his office on the second floor, setting up spreadsheets. I was locked in the library.

I truly felt more at home in that room than in any other room in the house. The musty smell of books and wood and varnish and old leather created an almost chemical reaction within me. On this particular night, I had closed the doors, lit the small oil lamps and candles that were scattered around the room, and lay down on the battered leather sofa with a glass of red wine and my laptop.

My writing has forever been a passion of convenience. It is something I truly love when I have the time to play at it, but also something I never go to great pains to make time for. Still, rainy nights were created for writers to retire away to musty rooms with a glass of liquor and tirade against writer's block. I had been staring at the screen for about an hour when I heard someone splashing up the front steps. I stood up and opened the glass doors to the foyer just as the bell rang. Through the window of the front door I saw Olivia standing in the arch of the porch closing her umbrella. Under one arm was tucked a book.

"'Not a night fit for man nor beast...'" I observed as I opened the door.

"You're not kidding. I wouldn't be out in it either if the beasts weren't all hanging out at my dad's place. Do you have a room available for the night?"

"It's summer in Key West. Of course I have a room." I went to the desk, pulled out a key and had her sign the guest book. "You want something to drink?"

"Beer'd be good." We walked into the kitchen and I gave her a beer. "What are you working on tonight?"

"Trying to write," I told her. "Mostly just staring at a blank computer screen." We walked back towards the library.

"I didn't know you wrote. Have you published anything?"

"Not in years. I wrote for the paper when I was in school and published a few short stories after I graduated, but nothing else. I never really get the time to finish my stories. Most of them are just sloms."

"Sloms?" She sat in the chair by the fireplace and curled her legs up beneath her. The book lay in her lap. I collapsed back onto the couch.

"I read a story once in which the writer talks about how she is always looking forward to the day when she can get around to finding out what is in a mysterious box in her attic marked 'sloms, drinds, and blue jeans.' When I was in college and didn't have time to write, if I would get a story idea, I'd take an hour and rough out as much about it as I could and then put it in a notebook labeled 'sloms, drinds, and blue jeans.' Any unfinished story is a slom."

"And a drind?"

"Some observation about life or misplaced journal entry."

"Ah. So tell me what do you write about?"

"Anything I happen to think about. Or, in tonight's case, nothing."

She took a sip of her beer. "What do you eventually want to do? Publish a novel or something?"

"I dunno. I kind of like the idea of never publishing anything except posthumously. I think it'd be cool to die and then have my heirs discover that I had written ten novels during my brief but merry life."

We talked a few minutes more about writing, and I asked about the book in her lap. She showed me its title, which I didn't recognize. "It's really the reason I'm here tonight. I've been dying to finish it, and there is no place in our house quiet enough to do so."

"I see." We spoke a few minutes more, and then she abruptly changed the subject.

"Do you think my father looks well?"

I blinked a few times as I mentally changed gears. "I dunno. I've only known your dad a couple of months, but I haven't really seen a change. Although you have to keep in mind that I see him quite frequently and I might not notice a change. Does he look sick to you?"

"I don't know if I would say sick. I think he looks tired. And he's not quite focused."

I laughed. "Olivia, no one has *ever* accused your father of being focused. And, frankly, if I lived his lifestyle *I* would look tired. Hell, I'd probably be dead."

She pondered that a minute and then waved the subject away. At once she was on her feet. "Well, my book is calling. Thanks for the beer. Do you mind if I let myself out through the kitchen?"

I told her I did not, and without so much as another word, she turned and was gone.

A few minutes later I heard footsteps on the stairs. The library doors opened and in walked Tony and Scot. Outside, the storm was growing in intensity.

"Who was at the door?" Tony asked as he sat on the floor.

Scot sniffed the air. "Was it Olivia? I smell her cologne."

I confirmed that it was. "Jeez, how hung up on her are you if you can recognize her cologne?"

He just smiled and sat in the chair she had vacated.

"I don't know what you see in her anyhow," Tony observed. "The woman *never* smiles."

"You never smile either," Scot replied evenly, "but we keep you around."

"So," I asked as I switched off the computer, "you find her attractive because she reminds you of Tony?"

"I do so smile," Tony replied defensively.

"Don't go there," Scot pointed his finger at me with narrow eyes.

"I smile all the time."

A sudden clap of lightning prevented this conversation from going any further. The lights blinked out and then returned a few moments later. "I hate lightning," Tony observed. As if on cue, another bolt burst directly over the house and this time the lights went out for good. I got up and walked to the window.

"It's out all over the street."

Without power, there is no air-conditioning, and without air-conditioning, houses in Key West can become almost unbearable. Even with the full fury of the storm outside, our rooms immediately began to grow stuffy.

Our house must have a thousand candles in it. The power was only out a few minutes before Tony had enough lit to say mass. I took one and went downstairs to the garage. As I have said, Albert was a packrat, and I am forever finding things in the garage that are mind-bogglingly useful. One thing that I knew was down there was a small electric generator. We had discussed taking this to the island with us to power a blender, but then decided that we could do without. I was also hoping that, amid all the piles of junk, Albert might have hidden a small window air conditioner. I only had to dig for about twenty minutes before I found it.

"I have brought salvation from the heat," I cried triumphantly as I returned to the first floor with my prize. Ross and Olivia were in the living room with the guys. They had wandered in from the guesthouse while I was downstairs.

"I'm not an engineer," Ross observed, "but isn't that thing kinda useless without electricity?"

"I've got a small generator in the garage. And if I were you, I'd watch the sarcasm. Nothing says I have to let you stay in the house."

We ran an extension cord from the generator in the garage up the stairs and into the living room. With all the French doors closed, it became a tiny oasis of cool air in my otherwise sweltering brick hulk of a house. It was agreed that all of us would sleep on the floor in that room in order to stay cool.

Being faced with an adverse situation, Tony suggested we deal with it in the age old accepted Key West tradition. We broke out the tequila and made drinks. In Key West, there is no tragedy, no crisis and no situation so bleak that it cannot be improved with drinks. Tony has long been fond of misquoting Dow's slogan; "Key West believes in better living through cocktails."

We made alarmingly strong margaritas with a battery-powered blender and sat in the dark discussing life.

"Do you ever wonder why we are here?" Scot asked. When Scot drinks, he has a compulsive need to discuss philosophy. I have spent many nights with Scot, drunk, floating in a pool discussing some absurd point of philosophy.

"We are here because the power is off," replied Tony, who has very little patience for philosophy, even when sober. "Otherwise, we would all be in our rooms."

"I mean…" Scot began before Ross laid a hand on his arm.

"He knows what you mean, Scot. He just doesn't care."

"I think we are here," Olivia offered, "by pure and random chance. We have to be somewhere, metaphorically speaking, and here was available. Life is transient. You try to get the most out of it that you can, you abide the inconveniences, and when it's over, you've really gained or lost nothing."

"So what you're saying," I asked, "is that life is like getting a really good deal on a sublet?"

In the dark, I could see her pondering this suggestion. "Well, yes. I suppose it is."

Somewhere in the dark, Scot sighed his *I'm smitten and, by the way, horny* sigh. We ignored it. Well, maybe not Ross.

"I think we are here to chase our dreams," Scot offered.

"But suppose we don't know what our dreams are?" Ross countered.

"How can you not know what your dreams are? Everyone dreams. The biggest challenge is finding one to chase."

"I don't," Tony said flatly.

"You don't dream?" Olivia asked.

"Rarely. If ever. I've tried. But I can't."

"Why not?"

"I wish I knew."

"You know," Ross said, sounding disgusted, "you guys live the perfect life. My god, you live the life that Jimmy Buffett promised in all of his songs. You live the life that ninety-nine percent of the world would kill for, and you guys don't even know that you are living out a dream."

"Who says we don't know that?" Scot asked.

"And, more importantly, what is keeping you from doing the same?" I asked.

There was a long, tense silence in the room for a few minutes while all of us contemplated this. Finally, Ross replied in a quiet voice, "Why, nothing. Nothing at all."

We spoke for a few more minutes, but eventually, each of us drifted off into sleep. I guess we slept for several hours, and would certainly have slept through the night if the power hadn't come back on at one, bringing with it the lights and appliances and ceiling fans everything else whose hum people habitually tune out.

The next day, Ross found a job as the first mate on a sailboat offering day cruises out of Key West. "It's a large catamaran," he told us over cocktails around the pool. "There's a crew of twelve, but most of them have never sailed before. All in all, I think they need me."

THE HOUSE OF
FITZGERALD

The weeks rolled by without event. Finally, in early September, our article appeared in Conde Nast. There was a long article titled The Guesthouses of Key West and, while ours was not exactly featured prominently, it was certainly mentioned. More importantly, a separate article described the "excellent day tours and parties offered by Biscayne Voyager Airways in their vintage DC-2." Frankly, we could not have asked for any better publicity. Almost immediately, travel agents began calling about the tours and the guesthouse. We began taking reservations for the autumn. We received deposits on rooms and on trips. Dear God, we actually made our first payment on the loan.

September is a time of activity in Key West. The tourist season begins in October with Halloween and runs full power until early May. September is a time to forget our otherwise lazy lifestyle and actually get to work planning for "the season." We painted the trim on the house. I painted the plane. We painted Ross' new apartment, which was just around the corner from our house and above my favorite pub. Life was incredibly good. I was even beginning to look forward to the visit from my family. Well, *some* of them, anyway

It was early on the morning of the 13th when the phone rang. The guys and I had an understanding that one of us would carry the cordless phone that we had installed on our "reservations" line at all times between nine and six. Our private line, on the other hand, was answered whenever we felt like it. On this particular morning, I was alone in the kitchen after my morning swim when it rang. On a whim, I decided to answer it. It was George.

"You know, Aidan," he began without a greeting, "I have to admit that you do know your family better than I do."

"Why's that?" I asked as I poured myself a glass of milk.

"You guessed right about Vivian. I have in front of me a letter from her attorney requesting Jason's address and his mother's name."

"I'm not surprised," I told him. And I wasn't. Disgusted but not surprised. "Are you going to give it to her?"

"I've already told you I'm not. Nor am I going to give it to you." He paused for a long moment, then asked, "Do you really think she would try to interfere with Jason and his mother?"

"George, you're an attorney for chrissakes. Don't be naïve. My aunt is perfectly capable of interfering in Jason's life. Frankly, my aunt is perfectly capable of suing for custody of Jason if she thought she could get away with it. She has steamrolled her way over every member of this family except my father, and frankly, that's just a stalemate."

There was another long silence on the other end of the phone. "I hate to think of her going against that boy and his mother."

"Deal with it, Counselor. As you told me, mind your own business." I knew I sounded flippant but, at the moment I didn't care. I am, after all, a member of my family. Although I did not have designs on Jason's money, I did want to know who he was and, frankly, was jealous as hell that a fourteen-year old had almost four million dollars in the bank while I was desperate to make my next loan payment.

George took the flippancy in stride. After all, he knew Albert for thirty years; he had heard far worse flippancy. He ended the conversation and I went about my day. There was a plane to be maintained, a house to be looked after, and most importantly, a sunset to enjoy.

I spoke to George again two days later. "I have spoken to Jason's mother and her lawyer," he began without greeting when I answered his call. "All of us agree that it is important to treat Vivian as a serious threat. She may prove to be nothing but an old windbag, but we would rather prepare for the worst than underestimate her."

"I think that is extremely wise," I replied evenly. I was sitting in the library, paying bills.

"The problem that Phoebe...I mean *Jason's mother*...is facing is that she has not led a, um, conventional, lifestyle by Midwest standards."

"Define unconventional," I instructed George as I took a sip of the vodka tonic that Tony had just handed me.

"Unconventional in the sense that she is a waitress and that she had a son out of wedlock and that she refused to marry the father."

"Well, yes, that is somewhat unconventional in Illinois," I observed as I wrote out the insurance check for the plane. "But, from everything I have ever heard, that is not all that unconventional by Louisiana standards."

"Stop being an asshole," George instructed me. I was sitting at my desk and my eyes drifted to the pictures of Albert and me, and Jason. I decided to, indeed, stop being an asshole.

"The *big* problem," he continued, "is that she has not told Jason about the money. He can't touch any of it until he's in his twenties, so she doesn't want him to even know he has it. She is of the opinion that, if he doesn't know, he may decide to actually do something with his life."

"She sounds like a very wise lady," I remarked. "So what is the problem?"

"The problem," he explained to me patiently, "is that they live with her mother in a tiny house across the river from the French Quarter. She leaves him alone until late in the evening while she is at work, and, most importantly, she is using none of the money to improve his quality of life at this moment."

"So?"

"So, juries don't take kindly to parents who do not use available funds to help their children."

"But the funds aren't available. They're in trust."

"She could borrow against them in his name to take care of him."

I closed the checkbook and rubbed my eyes. "George, I'm confused. Is she neglecting the child?"

"No."

"Then the problem is…?"

"Aidan, the problem is that she is not giving the child everything that he *could* have. Admittedly, she is not doing so for the right reasons but, nonetheless, she is not doing so. And a lawyer could persuade a jury that that makes her unfit."

"I guess I understand. So, tell her to spoil the kid. Then Vivian can't touch her."

"Yes she can. Then Vivian can argue that his mother is needlessly squandering his inheritance."

I began to understand. "Damned if you do, damned if you don't."

"Exactly. Which is why we need you."

"Goddamn it, George. Not three weeks ago you told me to mind my own business and now you need me? I don't like this."

"Look. If Vivian does try to go after Jason, his mother can't just defend herself. She has got to demonstrate that Vivian is the greater of two evils. You can help her do that. No matter what a court may think of Phoebe, we can prove that Vivian is worse. If you, her nephew, were to testify *against* Vivian, that would only help the mother."

I thought about this. It made sense to me. "There's only one problem. How do I know Vivian is worse than Phoebe?"

"Oh come on, Aidan. You…"

"Wait, George. There is a certain degree of credibility involved in what you are asking. It is no secret in my family that I detest my aunt. My own parents would, under oath, tell you that. So I'm not going to be a very credible witness if I know only one of them. But if I *know* both Jason and his mother, and I am the *only one* in the family that knows both of them, then…"

I could hear the anger in George's voice. He wasn't listening to the logic of my argument. "You're hell bent to force me to let you meet Jason, aren't you."

"Yep."

"But Albert didn't want…"

I was suddenly very angry as well. "George! Albert is dead! Frankly, I don't give a flying *fuck* what he wanted. We are here. He's not. If you want my help, that's the price. I've got to know someone before I testify for them."

"Goddamn it, Aidan…"

"Goddamn yourself, George!" I fairly screamed into the phone. "You can't play God in these matters. Albert's will is not some fucking covenant with God that lets you manipulate us. You want my help, fine. I'll be happy to help. But you're not going to keep me in the fucking dark about my cousin! And, frankly, who the fuck are you to pass judgment about how *every member* of my family will treat him? More importantly, who the fuck are you to pass judgment about how *I'll* treat him? I'm part of his family. You are not. Before I testify for this Phoebe person, you better fucking believe I want to know that she's taking care of my cousin. You want my help? Well, those are my fucking terms!" I slammed the phone into the cradle.

"Jesus!" Tony exclaimed as he walked back into the library. "What the hell is your problem?"

"Nothing," I snarled as I brushed past him and out through the front door. I had no idea where the hell I was going, so I just sat down on the front steps and tried to calm down. As I sat there and looked about, I noticed how mossy the bricks of the front terrace were, and the first faint rust stains on the wrought-iron fence.

"I sure wish someone was keeping a secret four million dollars for me," I thought sourly. I almost immediately regretted the thought. Even though we were struggling for money, I knew that I still had one hell of a lot more than many people.

I wondered if I had done the right thing to demand to meet Jason. I wasn't honestly interested in his money. I guess I was more interested in another ally in the family. Although my sister and brother and I all got along pretty well, the three of us lived in an armed truce with our cousins, our aunt and our uncle. It would have been nice to feel like someone else in the family was on my side.

I walked back inside and apologized to Tony. I then returned to my desk and tried to concentrate on the rest of my bills, but my gaze kept drifting back to the picture of Jason. After a while, Tony came in and asked if I needed to talk.

I explained the whole sordid thing to him. "Are you sure you want Vivian staying here?" he asked. In truth, I did not, but felt like I needed to keep an eye on her.

"I dunno, Aidan," he observed, "I think you should stay the hell out of it. Let your aunt and this Phoebe person duke it out. Frankly, I'm surprised that your parents aren't more involved. It seems to me that they would be more genuinely concerned about Jason's welfare."

I had not thought of that before. My mother valued family above all else. She did seem somewhat removed from all this. Tony and I talked for a while longer, before a guest checking in distracted him. I sat alone in the now dark library and continued to mull over what to do.

Jason's picture sits beneath the glass of my desktop, just adjacent to the phone. My eyes drifted from his picture to the phone and an idea occurred to me. I knew Jason's last name and his mother's first name. I picked the phone up, pressed zero, and asked the operator to connect me to New Orleans Information.

"What city please?" asked the mechanical voice at the other end.

"New Orleans."

"What listing?"

"Phoebe Metior."

There was silence, and then the call rang through to a real human being. A pleasant sounding woman with a thick accent told me, "I don't have a Phoebe Metior. Do you have a street address?"

"No, I'm afraid I don't."

"I have nine listings for a 'P. Metior.' Do you want those?"

"Yes, please." I took down the nine phone numbers. I knew nothing about New Orleans, so I asked the operator, "Do you recognize any of the street names?"

"Come again?" she asked in a confused tone.

"Well, I know that the person I'm looking for lives somewhere across the river from the French Quarter. I was just wondering if any of these were obviously in that part of town."

"Hmm," she replied. There was a moment of silence. "I don't recognize any of the streets, but two of the phone numbers are in the exchange for the quarter. And three are in the exchange for Old Algiers. Those might be worth looking at first."

"Which ones?" She told me, and I made marks beside them. "Thanks. You've been extremely helpful."

I hung up and proceeded to dial the first number for the French Quarter. A very gruff sounding male voice answered. "Um, hi," I said. "I'm trying to reach a Phoebe Metior."

"Wrong number," the voice replied and hung up. I dialed the second. This time a very elderly woman answered. I repeated my request. Another wrong number, but the woman was obviously anxious to talk. It took me almost ten minutes to get off the phone with her.

I dialed one of the numbers in Old Algiers. This time, another woman answered. She sounded middle-aged. I asked again.

"No, Phoebe doesn't live here anymore," the woman replied. "This is her cousin."

Pay dirt! "Yes ma'am. Would you have her new number?"

She sounded doubtful. "Well, I don't like to give it out…"

I had to think up a lie and think it up quick. "I understand. I'm with the IRS. I am calling to complete some tax paperwork involving her son's inheritance, and this is the phone number I had listed for her."

I heard suspicion in her voice. "The IRS calls at eight o'clock at night?"

"Well ma'am, she spoke with our office earlier and told us that she works days and can only be reached at night. If you would rather not give out her number, I guess I could pull her tax records…"

It is amazing the effect the word *tax* has. "No, don't do that. I guess there's no harm in giving it to you since you can probably get it easy enough anyhow." She gave me the number. It matched the third Old Algiers number. I thanked her and hung up.

"I see my 'staying out of it' advice will not be heeded," Tony observed from the doorway where he had been watching me.

I looked at him, knew he was right and said nothing. I folded the slip of paper with Phoebe's number on it and slipped it into the lap drawer of my desk, feeling chagrined.

Guests continued to arrive, and we were busy enough to keep my attention, for the most part, away from New Orleans. I heard nothing from George for over two weeks, and began wondering if I should call him and apologize. After all, it is generally preferable to be on speaking terms with your attorney. Ross and I took the plane out a couple of times so he could get used to handling it. We flew our first private party of the season to the island the last week in September, and the money was enough of a windfall that we actually paid ourselves small salaries and went out to eat. And, despite the fact that my family's visit continued to approach, I felt surprisingly cheerful. I was due to pick them up with the plane in Sarasota on Friday afternoon. George broke radio silence on Monday.

"Hello, Aidan," he said in his most severe professional manner. For some reason, I suddenly found the whole situation extraordinarily amusing.

"Hello, George," I replied, mimicking his severity while trying to keep the laughter out of my voice.

"As I am sure you are aware, your family arrives in Key West on Friday…"

"Do they?" I asked with a slight snicker. "That doesn't leave me much time to move."

He ignored me. "And your aunt has scheduled an appointment with me at 5:30."

"Want me to make sure she doesn't make it?"

I could hear the beginning of a smile in his voice. "That won't be necessary. I have discussed the matter with Jason's attorney and we would prefer to hold you in reserve until we need you."

"Sounds grim."

"While I can't in any way require you to avoid the subject with your aunt, I would like to request that you not mention or discuss any of this with her. I'd prefer not to tip my hand to her side yet."

"Gosh, George, that will be hard. You know how close she and I are."

I heard a small snort of laughter quickly choked off. "Yes, um, well, I appreciate your cooperation."

"No problem. Oh and George..."

"Yes?"

"If Phoebe is going to get into wranglings with my aunt, you might want to suggest that she instruct her family to stop giving out her phone number."

"Oh shit...Did you call her?"

"No. I just wanted you to know that I could if I wanted to."

"Aidan..."

"George, don't *worry*. You didn't give it to me. Your conscience is clear." I laughed as I placed the phone back in its cradle. "You should know better than to dick around with *this* family, George."

In my family, we always refer to the day before a visit from my parents as *Mother's Eve*. That day is reserved for quiet contemplation on the fact that *mater immaculata* is coming and you live like a pig. It's a day for doing all those little things that you put off during the year, like cleaning beneath the refrigerator.

I roused Tony and Scot early that day. Fortunately, they have known me long enough to know better than to expect to sleep in on Mother's Eve. Tony got the job of washing all the windows in the house, while Scot was instructed to go clean all the bathrooms in the guesthouse, and I oiled all the hardwood floors in the main house. After that, Scot had to vacuum and dust all the guest rooms, Tony had to clean and chlorinate the pool, and I scoured the kitchen.

We took a break for breakfast and then resumed. While Tony cleaned the front terrace, Scot dusted and vacuumed the main house, and I disinfected the ice machine. After lunch, we were going to take it easy, but I saw a cobweb in the corner of the kitchen and went berserk. We took down all the drapes and vacuumed them, went over the grout in the bathrooms with a toothbrush (I suspect it was mine), vacuumed the dead bugs out from behind the storm windows, and hid the garbage cans. Don't ask me why. I just felt that my mother would somehow be disappointed to learn I had garbage.

Now you might say that, being innkeepers, we should have been doing all this anyhow (except maybe the garbage thing). And, we were. We tried to keep a very neat inn. But, on Mother's Eve, you do everything you normally do anyhow, only *more so*. At a little before five, when I was considering whether I needed to floss the neighbor's cat, Tony and Scot forced me to sit down and have a drink. The house reeked of disinfectant.

The phone rang. I started to get up and Tony shot me a warning finger. "Sit. I'll get it."

He returned a moment later. "It was your brother. He knew you were freaking out, so he called with a dose of perspective. He wanted me to remind you that your mom once found a dead rat behind her washer." I laughed. I was looking forward to seeing him.

My siblings and I are a testament to the system of order that my parents are forever attempting to impose on a turbulent and uncooperative universe. They had had one child every four years for eight years, thus preventing the unfortunate circumstance of having to pay two college tuitions at the same time. Their three children were all named for deceased Irish ancestors and (no small accomplishment) in alphabetical order. At the time, I was twenty-eight. Bartholomew ("Bart") was twenty-four and was a pharmacist in Chicago. Caitlin was twenty, and was studying commercial art in New York. All of us had remarkably similar personalities.

On Friday morning, Ross and I took off from Key West at eight and made our way up the west coast to Sarasota. My sister was flying in from New York via Atlanta and would arrive at eleven. There is an old joke in the airline industry that, when you die, before going to either Heaven or Hell, you must first change planes in Atlanta. Anyway, she, Ross and I were planning to have lunch and then meet Bart, my parents and my aunt and uncle who were flying direct from Chicago at one. At ten o'clock, Ross and I taxied the plane to the general aviation terminal at the far end of the airport and secured it on the ramp. We wandered into the airport and through the main terminal. After passing through security, we walked down the green and teal concourse and settled down at the Delta gate to wait for her flight.

"You know," Ross observed as we watched people wander through the concourse, "I wonder how much demand there would be for shuttle flights between Key West and Sarasota?"

"I dunno. Why?"

"You know how everyone who wants to fly to Key West has to go through either Miami or Orlando to get to the island? Well, it costs a hell of a lot less to fly to Sarasota or Tampa than Miami. Maybe if we could set something up where we ran a twice daily shuttle back and forth between the island and one of those cities, we could pick up some more business for the airline."

"The *airline?*" I asked incredulously. "We have one plane and we fly small-time charter service to one destination which, *technically*, is not even a real airport. We are *not* an airline. Besides, I worked for a scheduled service once. I am not about to deal with all that FAA regulation again."

"Maybe we could fly it and just not tell the FAA?" he said, smiling.

I rolled my eyes and said nothing. At that moment, a pretty gate agent took the podium and announced the arrival of my sister's flight. A 757, decked out in one of Delta's many liveries, taxied to the gate and the jetway nuzzled alongside of it. A moment later, the plane began to disgorge its first class passengers. Ordinarily, first class passengers are a proud, orderly lot who move up the jetway in a dignified march like the Order of the Garter. Consequently, one young art student who was laughing loudly as she shoved businessmen out of the way and ran up the ramp, generated a host of facial expressions which ranged from amused to homicidal.

Although my sister and I are somewhat different physically, it would be hard for anyone to mistake us for anything but Irish. I am five-six, with dark brown hair and blue eyes. I am certainly not hideous, but my looks are pretty unremarkable. Caitlin is barely five-feet tall and has bright red hair and green eyes. She is extremely fair, but has managed to avoid the freckled complexion often associated with redheads. She was definitely an art student, however. She wore an oversized man's white oxford shirt, un-tucked over black jeans. At her throat hung the ugliest tie I have ever seen. She was carrying a knit purse large enough to hold a Buick.

"Aidan!" She squealed as she leapt into my arms. "Aidanaidanaidan-aidan!"

"*This* is my kind of greeting!" I said proudly to Ross and introduced Caitlin to him.

"So will your Aunt Vivian also be leaping into your arms?" he asked, bemused.

Caitlin snorted. "I'm sure United had enough problems getting her airborne."

We laughed and proceeded down to baggage claim to get her luggage. She reached up and played with my hair, which had grown down to my shoulders in the back.

"Look at you! Your hair has never been this long. And where's that pasty Irish complexion we all know and love? You know Aunt Viv is just going to be appalled with how you look."

I smiled and nodded. "Haircuts are one of those luxuries that I cannot afford at the moment."

We reached baggage claim and waited for the bags to arrive from the bowels of the airport. Caitlin rummaged through her huge bag and produced a bottle of vodka, which she presented to me. "For you. I figure this weekend will be easier for us if we aren't sober."

"You know," Ross observed, "it's fun to be around a family that enjoys each other's company so much."

A bell rang, and the conveyors started turning. A moment later the bags began to arrive from below. An enormous, green army duffel bag arrived and Caitlin pointed to it. "That's mine." We pulled it of the carrousel and started back towards the plane. Sarasota-Bradenton International Airport is one of the few airports in the world where the general aviation terminals are conveniently located near the main terminal. We walked out onto the tarmac and into the warm morning. The *Voyager* gleamed in the sun.

"So that's the famous plane," Caitlin observed. "It looks old."

"It is old," I said, probably defensively. "That's what makes it a classic."

We stored her stuff in the hold and climbed inside the plane. We had about an hour until the rest of the family arrived from Chicago. I pulled a picnic hamper out of the galley and passed out sandwiches. While we ate we discussed the coming weekend.

"Well," Caitlin began, "the family gossip is that Aunt Vivian and Mom are dying to meet this new cousin of ours. And Bart told me that Valerie and Roy are pretty anxious to see everything Uncle Albert left you. Bart said they are pretty steamed that you got something and they didn't."

Valerie and Roy were the unfortunate by-products of a brief, but apparently convivial period in Vivian and Mo's marriage. "How about you? Are you unhappy that Albert left me something and not you?"

"God no," she said around a mouthful of sandwich. "It's not like he left you anything I'd want. I have no use for the plane, and I don't want to live in South Florida, so I don't begrudge you any of this. I'm glad you've got something that makes you happy."

"What about Bart?"

"I think the only thing Bart begrudges is that you are in Florida, I'm in New York, and he's in Chicago with the family. He hears more of this crap than I do. But I don't think he's unhappy."

We killed the next hour talking family politics, then wandered back into the terminal. Once through the security check, we went to the United gates, where the gate agents ignored the few people in the gatehouse with their usual, brisk efficiency. A plane pulled up to the jetway unannounced.

"And the games begin…" Caitlin said under her breath.

My mother, father, aunt and uncle arrived with the first class passengers, all courtesy of Dad's frequent flyer upgrades. My dad led the pack down the jetway. He was dressed, rather uncharacteristically, in white Dockers and a golf shirt. He looked very relaxed. It was unnatural. He and Mom kissed Caitlin and me, and then stood aside for us to greet Mo and Viv.

My mother is a tall, slender, professional-looking woman. Her shoulder-length hair is shot through with an attractive amount of gray, and she generally wears it pulled back in a simple barrette. She is fond of long summery cotton pants and knit blouses, and often wears a sweater tied around her neck. She exudes self-confidence. Picture the exact opposite woman and you have Aunt Viv. She wore a frumpy cotton sundress and absurdly large sunglasses. She proffered her cheek for the required peck. Caitlin and I complied with protocol.

I shook hands with Uncle Mo and Caitlin kissed him on the cheek as well. I actually sort of wish he hadn't come because he has so little personality, it makes him difficult to write about. He is medium build with a roundish, bald sort of head. He has a mustache and a potbelly. In my entire life, I have probably heard him say twenty words, and none of them expressed an opinion. For all the impact he has had on this story, or for that matter, my life in general, my aunt could just as easily been accompanied by a large pot of begonias.

I introduced Ross to my parents, aunt and uncle while we waited for the coach passengers. After an interminable amount of time, Valerie, Bart and Roy came down the jetway. Bart had a small flight bag, while both of Viv's rat-faced children were pulling wheeled luggage the size of kitchen appliances.

I hugged and kissed my brother. As I did so, he whispered in my ear, "We would have been off the plane sooner if they didn't try to wedge those monstrosities into the overhead bin. I think one of the flight attendants may try to have Roy killed." My brother had been trapped in the middle seat between Roy and Valerie for an entire two-hour flight, which I suspect is why he smelled vaguely of bourbon.

I kissed Valerie and shook Roy's hand. They smiled weak smiles that never reached their beady little rat eyes. Although I would never describe our relationship as warm, I sensed more coldness than usual from them, which made me wary. I was not happy to see them along.

We walked down the concourse slowly to accommodate the huge bags Ratface One and Two were hauling, as well as Aunt Viv's waddle. By the time we got *the rest* of their luggage from the carousel and out to my plane, almost two hours had passed.

My parents and aunt had seen the plane before, but my brother and cousins had not. "Wow!" Bart exclaimed, hitting me on the back, "she is beautiful. Not bad for your first plane."

"Hopefully my only plane," I replied. "It's an expensive hobby."

"But one you can no doubt afford," my aunt sniped. I chose to ignore her.

"Are you sure this thing is safe?" Roy asked, looking at the plane dubiously.

"I'll stake my life on it," I replied as I heaved his bag into the hold. "In fact, I'm even going to stake yours."

Bart and Caitlin snickered. Roy did not. My mother gave me a warning look.

After about another ten minutes, we had all the bags loaded, everyone strapped into their seats, and were ready to depart. In the cabin, my family had taken the first four seats, and my aunt's had taken the next four. My father and brother were seated in the first two seats behind the flight deck, and they asked me to leave the curtain open so they could see the takeoff. Behind them, I could hear the nervous mutterings of my aunt and cousins.

The air-traffic controllers in Sarasota are extremely friendly, and they worked me into the busy departure traffic in a few short minutes. I called back to everyone to make sure they had their seat belts fastened as we turned onto the runway. Then, feeling a little jaunty, I gunned the throttles and began a much more rapid takeoff run than I usually do. Ross gave me a sidelong look of surprise but said nothing. I personally feel that the plane actually enjoyed being given the chance to show off. As we picked up speed, the tail came up quickly. Whereas I usually enjoy a graceful, gentle arc of departure, today I pulled the yoke back hard. The *Voyager* came up obediently and rotated into a steep climb. The engines purred loudly as I kept the plane at maximum thrust and banked sharply into the departure path. Over the radio, the Sarasota controller commented "Pretty sporty departure. Hope your passengers are insured against whiplash." I laughed and followed the vector until I was flying south back down the coast.

Once we were at cruising altitude, I announced it to my passengers, but asked them to stay seated unless they wanted to come up to the flight deck. My dad and Bart were immediately in the door.

"Was that takeoff for our benefit?" Dad asked with a mischievous smile in his eyes.

"Absolutely," I confirmed as I turned control over to Ross. "Copilot's plane."

"She seems a little sluggish," Ross commented to me as he checked the rudder movements.

"Probably," I replied quietly. "She's got a lot of weight on board between all that luggage and Viv."

Our flight to Key West went without incident and by four I was padlocking the plane in its hangar. As I secured the tail lock, I received a question I wasn't expecting from Valerie.

"Have you had the plane appraised?" she asked as she looked up the fuselage speculatively.

"Of course," I lied. "I needed to for insurance. Why?"

"Oh, I was just wondering," she continued, still not looking at me. "I guess a plane this old is worth a good bit of money."

"Some are," *time for another lie*, "but not this one. There were relatively few DC-2s built, so it is extremely difficult to get parts for them. Collectors avoid them like the plague."

She nodded, clearly not believing me. Outside, a horn blared. I had called three cabs to the airport (a substantial portion of the island's fleet), and sent everyone back to the house ahead of me except Bart and Ross. I said good-bye to Ross in the parking lot, and Bart and I climbed into my car to drive home.

"Any idea why Valerie would be interested in my plane?"

"It's worth money," Bart replied evenly as we drove up Bertha. "You must know that she and Roy the Rat Faced Boy are here for one reason alone."

"Which is?"

"To determine whether it is worth it to contest your inheritance."

"You're joking."

"Well, obviously they haven't *told* me that. But they have definitely tried to pump me for information on your relative worth...not to mention tried to inspire a good deal of resentment in me for you."

I remained concerned. "And do you resent me?"

Bart rolled his eyes. "Yeah, Aidan, right," he said sarcastically. "I sympathize with my cousins. We, who had no idea who the hell Uncle

Albert even *was,* richly deserved his house and plane more than you, who spent every spring with him, are a pilot, and, by the way, had the balls to move to Florida and try to make something out of it."

I smiled and relaxed. Bart was still Bart. "I'm not sure balls had anything to do with it. It's not like I had a lot of other options in Boston."

"You had the balls to leave and try something different. Hell, you had the balls to leave Chicago. I haven't even mustered that yet."

"But you love Chicago."

"Chicago is safe. I'm a McInnis. We love safety. You, son, are clearly a Fitzgerald."

I laughed. "I'm not sure about that." We pulled into Monarch Court.

"Not too shabby," Bart said playfully as he stared up the full four stories of the house. "A mansion in the tropics. Maybe I *should* kick in with Roy and Valerie."

We had one non-family reservation, so Bart had agreed to give up his room (along with the fee) and was going to sleep in my room with me. We hauled his bag up the stoop and into the foyer. Tony sat on the steps looking positively frazzled. "You were not kidding about your aunt," he groaned.

"Where is she?" I asked as I dropped Bart's bag.

"She and your uncle just blew back out of here in a taxi, heading for George's office."

I sighed. "What room did you put them in?"

"Number two. We started out in number four, but she can't climb stairs. She wanted number one, but we've already got the Willamettes in there, so I offered her number three. Too close to the ice machine. Your mother finally said to put her in number two, and put them in three. Your sister's in four, and your cousins are in five and six. Your cousin Roy wanted to know when we open the bar. I just sent Scot out to do it."

I nodded. "Thanks, bud. I'd tell you that you'll warm up to them, but you won't. It's only going to get worse."

Bart and I took his bag up to my room. I went into my closet to change clothes, while he opened his bag. "I hope this is not going to be a formal weekend, because I brought nothing but shorts and tank tops."

I emerged from my closet in green shorts and a blue tank top. "I'm certainly not planning on it. If we do anything that requires more clothes, you can borrow something of mine."

"Jammin'," he replied as he pulled off his shirt. "I'll meet you down by the pool."

I went downstairs. Tony was nowhere to be seen. My parents, my sister and my cousins were seated at a table by the pool. Scot was cleaning glasses at the bar. He was not smiling.

"I've got to hand it to you," my dad said as I walked onto the patio, "You guys have really performed miracles with this place. I never would have believed you would be able to do all the work on the guest-house yourselves."

"Thanks, Dad."

"It really is lovely," Mom added. I blushed, and waited for compliments from my cousins. Instead, Roy held up his glass and whistled for Scot.

"Another margarita!"

I took the glass from his hand and tried to sound amicable as I said, "He's a bartender, not a waiter. He's also one of my partners, so don't piss him off. He's not above spitting in your drink."

I walked over to the bar and started mixing the margarita myself. "I apologize in advance. Roy is an insufferable boor."

"It's not in advance," Scot replied through clenched teeth.

I made the margarita relatively weak, but used cheap tequila so it tasted stronger. The last thing I needed was Roy drunk. I wouldn't have objected to being drunk myself, however.

When I delivered the drink back to him, he took it, drank, and nodded approvingly. "You make a mean margarita, Aidan. Not like your friend over there."

Idiot! I thought to myself. "Thanks Roy. Did all of you get settled into your rooms?"

Before Valerie or Roy could whine about anything else, Mom said, "We certainly did. And they are all just fine."

Bart joined us. I asked him what I could get him to drink.

"Um, bourbon and Seven," he replied with a sidelong glance at Mom. He walked with me over to the bar. "I think Mom is counting how many drinks I've had."

"Mom needs a hobby," I replied. "Scot, this is my brother Bart. Bart, Scot." They shook hands.

"Do I need to apologize to *you* for anything my family has done so far?" Bart asked. Scot smiled.

"No, your brother has already taken care of that."

I made Bart a bourbon and Seven, and we wandered back over to the table. My parents were looking through some of the tourist books that we stock in the lobby.

"I was thinking that tomorrow we might tour the Little White House, and then take a catamaran tour of the island," my dad told us. "Don't want to spend too much time around the house."

"That would be great," I told them as Bart and I sat down next to each other on the same chaise lounge. "And I was thinking that tonight we might walk down to Mallory Square for the sunset and then have dinner at a little Mexican place on Duval."

"What's so special about sunset on Mallory Square?" Caitlin asked.

I explained the entire end-of-the-day celebration which occurs each evening in Key West. My sister and brother were impressed. My parents looked politely interested. My cousins were clearly bored.

We sat around the pool making small talk until about six o'clock, at which time I suggested we walk down to the square. My cousins begged off and said they would wait until their parents got home, and then meet us at the restaurant. My parents also begged off. Mom wanted to be there when Aunt Viv returned.

Caitlin, Bart and I walked towards the path that leads to the front yard. My father followed a few feet behind and appeared to be studying the house. Once we were in the alley, however, it was clear that he was making himself available to talk to me alone if I wished. Bart and Caitlin continued on down the alley.

"Dad, why exactly is everyone here?"

My dad leaned against the stone foundation of the house. He is a tall angular man, with bright white hair. He looked at me in a very serious manner. "Well, this started out as a trip for your mom and me. Bart and Caitlin wanted to come along, and then so did your aunt. Your mother and I and the kids are really here to relax. Your aunt is hell bent on finding out who your cousin is."

"And what do you think of that?"

My dad closed his eyes and looked frustrated. "Aidan, you know what your mom's family is like. Everyone has to be in everyone else's business. I don't, for one-minute trust your aunt as far as your cousin is concerned, or as far as you're concerned either. But I've been around the Fitzgeralds long enough to know that they play a particularly lethal game of family politics."

"Mom doesn't."

"No, your mother does not. But your mother also has a very big heart, and refuses to acknowledge that this kind of game playing occurs. That's why she is occasionally an unwitting pawn in your aunt's games."

I know the frustration was plainly evident in my voice as I said, "This is bullshit, Dad. She's going to go after Jason for his money, and you know it. We've got to stop her."

My dad scowled at me. "I know that as well as you do, Aidan. What do you suggest we do? Have her killed? There is no way we *can* stop her if that is what she decides to do. This is her game right now. The best we can do is stay out of it."

I sighed. "I know. That's what's so damn frustrating. I hate waiting for her to make the next move."

He laughed a mirthless laugh. "You get used to it. Look, the best thing you can do is watch your own back. You are not immune from family intrigues. Your cousins would love to get their hands on the money that was left you. I'd say you've got enough to worry about."

Bart stuck his head back into the alley. "Hey, are you coming or what?"

"I'm coming," I yelled back. Then, to my father, "Do Bart and Caitlin know what all is going on?"

"They know about your mother's inheritance, and they know about yours, and they know they have a cousin. That's about it, although I suspect they know what is going on with Vivian."

I nodded and walked out of the alley. The three of us walked up the street and turned left on Duval.

"Okay, so is anyone going to explain all of the tension?" Caitlin asked. "Everyone is so tightly wound I'm afraid to open my mouth."

"Come on, Cait," Bart replied, "when have our two families ever been together without feeling like we were about to witness a mafia hit?"

"No, it's different this time. Usually, it's always been something between Vivian and Mom or Dad." She stopped and looked directly at me. "This time, you are clearly at the center of it."

I sighed. "That I am. How much did Mom and Dad tell you about the inheritance?"

"Next to nothing," Bart replied.

"Well, here's the deal. Albert left me the house and the plane. All the money he left me went to paying the inheritance taxes. I have two extremely expensive assets with no money to maintain them.

"Albert left Mom, Viv and Uncle Jeff a little over three hundred grand each. Jason inherited the bulk of Albert's estate, about four million in cash."

"Four *million?*" Bart asked, wide eyed.

"Wait a minute," Caitlin said. "I knew Mom got some money, although not how much. But she never said anything about Aunt Viv or Uncle Jeff getting any."

We had reached Mallory Square by this time, and we wandered in. I stopped at the first booth and bought each of us a margarita. We walked down to the seawall and sat on some rocks to watch the sun. Bart looked out to sea pensively as he sipped his drink. "You know, I'm reasonably certain that Roy and Valerie have no idea that their mother inherited anything. They keep talking about the injustice that our family got something and theirs didn't."

"I gather Viv got more than that, because she took almost all of Albert's personal belongings out of the house. My guess is she sold them in Miami."

"So if you've got nothing but the house and the plane," Caitlin began, "and Jason's got four million dollars, why would Roy and Valerie care about you? Jason's the big prize."

"And, how could Viv even touch Jason?" Bart asked as he flipped a pebble into the water with his big toe. "He's in New Orleans with his mother."

I repeated George's explanation of how she could, indeed, go after Jason. They listened in silence. We sat there for a long time, staring out to sea. Finally, Caitlin asked, "Bart, how well did you know Albert?"

Bart snorted and finished his margarita with a loud slurp. "The last time Albert came to Chicago was when? Grandma Fitzgerald's funeral? I was maybe eight. I wouldn't say I knew him well. In fact, I scarcely even remember him."

"If you were eight, that means Aidan, you were twelve, Valerie was nine, Roy was seven, and I was four. I don't ever remember even meeting him."

"What's your point?"

"No point. I'm just trying to figure out why Aidan is the target. Viv obviously knows how much you inherited, as well as Jason. Certainly she knows that there is nothing to be gained from you. So why are her kids so interested in getting their hands on your inheritance?"

We pondered that for a while. Since no answer emerged as the last of the sun disappeared below the horizon, we finished our drinks, and left the square to wander back up Duval. About halfway between Mallory Square and Monarch Court, we ran into King Louis.

"Master Aidan, how good to see you. How are you?"

"I am fine, milord. And you?" My sister and brother both gave me curious looks.

"We are quite well. And these young people are obviously related to you somehow?"

I nodded. "My sister, Caitlin, and my brother, Bart. Guys, may I present his serene highness, Louis Of Robideau, Monarch of Key West."

Caitlin smiled, and Bart raised one eyebrow. Louis smiled beatifically. "Please, no need to bow." This, despite the fact that no one had made any movement in that direction. "And the rather feral looking group of people who appear to be poking around your property today?"

"Would be my aunt, uncle and cousins."

"Ah." He regarded Bart and Cait. "Well, we welcome you *all* to our realm. We hope your stay here will be most pleasant."

Cait laughed as she said, "Um, thank you, sire." Bart, who now looked quite amused, also thanked him.

Turning his attention back to me, Louis continued, "Master Aidan, we cannot help but notice that you have appeared more stone faced and serious than usual of late. We are not pleased by this situation. However, we *are* extremely pleased by the hospitality you showed the Princess Olivia, and so we have decided to elevate you to the status of Knight of the Realm."

I was not expecting this, mainly because I was unaware the realm even *had* knights. "Why, thank you, sire. I am honored."

"Yes, I know you are. Expect to be knighted on the Eve of all Hallows."

"I definitely will."

Louis then kissed Caitlin's hand and drifted off into the night. As soon as he was out of earshot, they both turned to me and demanded to know what had just occurred. As we finished the walk home, I recounted the story of King Louis and Uncle Albert and the Key West Government In Exile.

We arrived back at the house as one of Key West's few cabs was depositing my aunt and uncle on the curb. We slowed our pace to allow them time to walk around to the guesthouse. Bart and Cait then followed them into the back, and I climbed the front steps and let myself into the hall. I heard the back door slam. Tony was standing at the base of the stairs glaring at me.

"I just threw your cousin out of the library. She was going through the file drawer of your desk."

"Oh, fuck." I berated myself mentally. I should have known to lock that room up. I turned and went immediately in. Tony followed and closed the frosted glass doors.

My file drawer was open, and one file was out and open on my desk. It was titled *Miscellaneous Expenses,* but all it contained was some invoices for the building products we had used in the guesthouse. Nothing terribly incriminating. My phone book was also open to the *M* page.

"I don't think she was in here long. She was looking through your phone book when I came in."

"Fortunately, I don't keep Jason's number written in here." I opened the lap drawer of my desk and saw the slip of paper where I had written Phoebe Metior's phone number. It was still tucked under my pewter letter opener, undisturbed. I removed it from the drawer and put it in an original edition of Harper Lee's *To Kill a Mockingbird,* one of my prized possessions, which I keep in the bookcase. "What did she say when you found her?"

"I walked in and saw her reading your phone book, and asked her if she needed help. She said no, she had wandered in looking for something to read, and saw my phone book. She was curious about whether you had a phone number for a mutual friend, and I walked in. She was rather arrogant about the whole thing."

"Val *has* no friends," I muttered as I returned the file to the drawer. "It shows how competent she is at spying. She pulled this file out and missed my copy of Albert's will."

There was a knock at the door and Scot came in. "Aidan, your family is asking for you. Apparently they're all ready to go to dinner."

Tony closed the door and quickly told Scot what had just occurred.

"She's been asking a lot of questions about our finances…" Tony observed to me.

"Yeah, Roy's been asking me similar questions," Scot added.

"I'm sure they have. They're trying to determine if there is enough here that's worth contesting the will."

Since Tony keeps all the books and financial information in his office on the second floor, I told him to keep his door locked, and to lock up all of his files. He agreed. The three of us also agreed to act like this never happened, but everyone would exaggerate our difficulties if anyone asked about our finances.

We left the library, and I locked the glass doors. I rejoined my family by the pool. Vivian was notably agitated, and Val didn't meet my eyes. Roy had obviously had several very bad margaritas and was quite lit. My dad looked at me with a twinkle in his eye and gave me a mischievous wink to indicate that things had not gone well at the lawyer's. Uncle Mo was occupying space and consuming oxygen as usual. I suggested that we all go to dinner.

"I assume this place is *casual,*" Vivian sniffed as she regarded Bart and me. Bart was barefoot, and I had on sandals. Both of us wore tank-tops. Roy was dressed the same way, but I decided not to point that out.

"There aren't many places on the island that *aren't* casual," I replied jauntily. "And, frankly, I can't afford any of them. Trying to build a business out of a falling-down Victorian house and an oil-burning airplane doesn't leave me with much disposable income." I motioned for Bart to go get some shoes and he disappeared into the house. "I was thinking we might get some Mexican for dinner."

There was the usual groaning associated with trying to get nine people to agree on dinner, but Mexican appeared to be favored by the majority. Bart returned in flip-flops, and we left the house for the restaurant.

As we walked, Bart sidled up next to me and whispered in my ear, "Cait and I have an idea. Play along." I nodded and he eased away. A moment later, he was walking next to Roy and, loud enough for the group to hear, asked me "Aidan…these are big old places. Do many people use these as seasonal homes?"

Next to me, Val's head snapped up, and she waited attentively for my answer. I thought a minute, and then said, "Not really. These big, old houses require a lot of upkeep." I waved my hands to indicate the houses around Monarch Court. "The youngest house on this court is over eighty years old. So they require a lot of maintenance. Plus, tropical storms and hurricanes come through often enough that insurance is awfully high. No, if you wanted to keep a vacation house on Key West, your best bet would be to have a condo where you pay someone else for the upkeep."

Val looked at me intently. She weighed the answer for a long minute, and then asked her question. She tried to sound casual, but couldn't keep her hidden agenda out of her voice. "Wouldn't that be a better plan for you? I mean, sell the house and buy a condo? I would imagine that the house would command enough money to buy *several* condos."

I finally saw what Bart was up to. "I wish. My house is really something of a white elephant. All of its eccentricities which would make it worth a fortune in Chicago are just annoying down here. For example, it has three fireplaces. In Chicago, that would be worth a fortune. Down here, they never get used, but you still have to pay to keep them up. I've also got twelve-foot ceilings which would be great up north, but down here, they mean it costs a fortune to cool in the summer. No, even with the pool and the guesthouse, I wouldn't clear enough to buy one decent vacation condo."

Val clearly looked discouraged. Caitlin, walking on the other side of her, added casually, "I guess I see why you wrote me last summer you would have been better off financially if Albert had left you the money without the house or plane."

I never wrote her any such thing, but I agreed enthusiastically. We arrived at the restaurant and had a very good dinner. My parents, Mo and Viv sat at one end of the table, and the five kids sat at the other. Val was somber through the whole thing, and Roy was too drunk to form complete sentences, but the rest of us had a great time.

We left the restaurant around ten. As we walked out, my aunt wondered aloud if it was safe to be walking the streets at night and shouldn't we maybe call a cab.

"Truthfully, Aunt Viv," I replied in a voice so pleasant it surprised me, "there just aren't many on the island. Nothing on the island is more than about twenty minutes' walk from anything else, so they don't make a whole lot of money here. Besides, it's too early for anyone to get mugged right now. Key West doesn't start partying until ten or eleven, so the whole island is relatively sober and alert." Except Roy. "Criminals usually wait until much later to stalk their prey."

When we returned to the house, the parents all retired for the night, and the kids all took up stations around the pool. Cait, Bart and I talked a good deal, while Val listened intently. Roy did a surprisingly good imitation of his father. Throughout the conversation, Cait and Bart took turns commenting on what a financial drain the house obviously was, and how I would have been so much better off if Albert had just left me the money. This lasted until about midnight, when Roy passed out and fell out of his chair.

"I guess that's a sign we should call it a night," Val observed, and asked Bart and I to get Roy upstairs. We complied and carried him up to his room, where we deposited him on his bed. Val said goodnight and returned to her room. Cait kissed me and whispered in my ear to leave the back door unlocked. I nodded in silent agreement, and Bart and I retired to my room.

Once we were inside, I asked him what he and Cait were up to. "She'll be here in a minute," he answered as he stripped down to his shorts. "We'll tell you then."

While we waited, I told him about Tony's encounter with Val in my library. He listened intently without comment. I opened the French doors and saw Cait running across the patio towards the kitchen door. A moment later, she was bouncing excitedly on the foot of the bed.

"Bart and I figured out what is going on," she told me excitedly. "Viv's plan is to make *you* do her dirty work."

Bart nodded in agreement as I settled myself into the bed. Much of my life has been spent with the three of us huddled together on my bed after everyone else was asleep. It is one of the few things I miss about childhood.

"While you were in the library with Tony this evening," Bart explained, "Cait overheard Aunt Viv discussing how poorly things went with the lawyer and asking Val if she had found out anything about the value of the house and the plane. She's encouraging Val and Roy to contest the will."

"This is *so* Machiavellian," Cait added. "She can't contest your inheritance, because you could also contest hers. Roy and Val *can* contest it because they got nothing. Then, when they have you convinced that you will lose the plane and the house, they want to force you to help them go after Jason instead."

I thought about it. "But they have access to the same resources I do. They could find him as easily as I could. And they don't need me to be involved."

"But they do. You're the only family member who was close to Albert. You could tell a judge that Albert felt Jason needed to be with our family, not his mother's. On the surface you have nothing to gain by handing custody over to Viv, so you are impartial."

It made sense. It would be true to family form to file a lawsuit against me to blackmail me into cooperating with a lawsuit against the Metiors.

"However, there is hope," Bart said beatifically. "Vivian needs Roy and Val's cooperation, but they aren't going to sue you if there is nothing to gain. So, Cait and I are on a campaign to let them know what a money pit this place is. Vivian won't contradict us too much, because she doesn't want her kids to know that she also got an inheritance. She has more money in cash from the will than you do, and her kids could realize a better *return on investment* by nagging her for money instead of suing you."

"So what we need to do," Cait finished, "is convince them there is nothing to be gained here, while simultaneously letting them know their mother has the money."

I was impressed. "My God. You guys are brilliant. And I know exactly how to let them know. I need to entice Val back into the library to get a look at Albert's will."

Cait returned to her room shortly after that, and Bart and I lay talking until we drifted off to sleep. Over the course of our lives, Bart and I have been forced to share a bed maybe a thousand times. When we were little kids, we shared a room and he used to climb into bed with me when he had nightmares. I always rather liked the role of big-brother-as-protector. I don't know if it was the memory of that role now, or simply the feeling, for once, that I had the upper hand, but I slept better than I had slept in weeks.

The alarm went off at six-thirty. "Christ," Bart muttered. "Don't tell me you get up this early."

"Innkeeper's hours," I replied. He grunted and pulled a pillow over his head. I took a shower, got dressed, and scrambled downstairs to start breakfast.

When we set up the guesthouse, we arranged everything so that no one ever had to come into the main house. The "lobby" was a small gazebo as you came into the back yard. It adjoined a larger gazebo which served as the buffet for breakfast, and the bar in the evening. It, in turn, adjoined the guesthouse via a long, low verandah that was lined with tables and chairs. Behind the bar, we had a large coffee maker, a toaster oven, and a liquor cabinet which was secured with a large, menacing padlock.

Breakfast was my assignment in our morning routine. Each morning, we put out fresh fruit, cereal, bagels, pastries, milk, orange juice, hot tea and coffee. I pulled the food together in the kitchen and then carted it down the back steps to the bar. While I did this, Scot would clean off the patio tables, set out plates, cups and glasses and then skim the pool. At the same time, Tony would set up the front desk and make up our daily to-do list based on the reservations book.

As I carried the first of the two enormous food trays we used down the back steps, I noticed that Scot and Tony had already started the coffee maker and were pouring their first cups. The sun was not yet visible over the banyan trees that divided our lawn from the house to the east.

"Mornin'," I said as I sat the tray on the bar. "Am I late getting to the coffee?"

"No," Scot replied as he ladled sugar into his cup. "We just needed it earlier."

"We were up late discussing how much we hate your cousins," Tony said flatly.

I nodded. "I promise I will make this up to you. Feel free to invite down some genetic or geriatric horrors from your own families." No one had had enough caffeine to laugh yet.

"Have you figured out why Vivian is here yet?" Tony asked as he sank onto one of the chairs by the front desk.

I nodded as I poured my own cup of coffee. I explained what Bart and Cait had figured out, and how I needed to get Val to take a copy of the will from my desk.

"That shouldn't be difficult," Tony observed. "Just let her know where it is."

"That is precisely what I intend to do."

I returned to the kitchen to retrieve the second tray. As I brought it down the steps, my parents came out of their room. My mother was fully dressed and my father wore a bathing suit. They greeted us, and Mom joined me at the bar while Dad dove into the pool and began to swim laps.

"Did you sleep well?" I asked her as I made her cup of coffee.

"Very. Thanks." She took the cup and sat on a bar stool while I finished setting out the food. "Don't you ever wear shoes anymore?" she asked in a pleasantly mocking tone.

"Rarely." It was true. At the house, the three of us were usually barefoot. If we were out, I wore sport sandals, Scot wore flip-flops, and Tony was still usually barefoot. Tony had a personal vendetta against footwear. "Our life style is pretty casual."

"But you own your own business now. You should project a professional image."

I considered telling her that, most afternoons, I also did not wear a shirt, but decided against it. It was true that in the world my mother lived in, the owner of a business would always wear shoes. (After all, she had owned her own business, and *she* had always worn shoes.) But, theoretically, the owner of the business also wouldn't be the one cleaning the bathrooms. Every three days, it was my turn to clean all the bathrooms.

"Maybe in the real world, Mom, but not Key West. Our customers aren't the country club set. They're young, usually under forty. If they are wealthy and have wealthy expectations, they stay in the hotels or the condos. The guesthouse crowd is looking for a funky, laid-back atmosphere. If I present too formal of an image, I will lose clients to the other guesthouses, and I will never be able to be upscale enough to lure the wealthy clients away from the Marriott." All of which was true. In the real world, my parents would never have stayed at the Ocean Nights. In fact, I very much doubt they would have ever spent the night in Key West. They were not the "funky" type.

Unfortunately, the Willamettes, who were the only guests staying at the inn with whom I did not share a gene pool, were *most definitely* the funky type. They generally spent most of their time walking around the inn nude. Most inns in Key West have some form of clothing optional policy, or at least take a relaxed approach to it. I was living in mortal fear, however, that the Willamettes would bump into my family. Not because it would have appalled them, which it would have, but because I was terrified Vivian might decide it was okay for *her* to wander around that way.

Mom shrugged and did not respond; her classic way of disagreeing with her children without provoking an argument. In truth, it is her most maddening habit. After a moment she asked, "So do you like this life?"

Boy, what a question. I knew that one day I had to have this discussion with her. In truth, life was not bad. We were making enough off of the inn to pay ourselves a small salary, but only because we were living in the house. I was very much aware that if Tony or Scot decided that they wanted to move out, they could not afford a rent payment. I was enjoying the challenge of running a business. I liked being my own boss. I liked being out in the sun everyday. I loved having the opportunity to fly and make money doing it. But I was also very much aware that I was not living the life I had been raised to live. I lived in a hundred-year-old house on an island instead of a nice new mass-produced house in a safe suburban subdivision. And, I had a college education in engineering that I was most definitely *not* using. I knew this was probably the thing that upset my mother the most.

"Actually," I replied, "I am enjoying my life. I don't know if this is something I want to do forever, but I do know it is something I want to do right now."

"But if you stay out of engineering too long, you'll have a hard time getting a job when you decide to return to the profession."

"True," I conceded, "but I don't know that I ever want to return to engineering."

My mother looked truly shocked. "So you wasted your college education?"

This was going badly. I absolutely did not waste my college education, nor was I ashamed of being an engineer. My engineering classes had given me a powerful set of problem solving skills, which I used daily. It had also given me a sense of accomplishment. I remembered my first day at the university, when the dean had told all the engineering students to look at the person sitting on each side of them, and then told us only one of us would graduate. He had been right; I was extremely proud that I had been the one who made it.

But I had also worked as an engineer. I had seen what the career could do to you if you weren't careful. It was possible to wind up a stale, bitter old man, so focused on the best technical solution to a problem that you can't see it might not be the best *overall* solution. Or the best for the people involved. I suppose this happens in every profession, but engineers seem to be more susceptible than most.

"No Mom, I didn't waste my education. But I want to build on it. Life is about learning. You don't learn if you do the exact same thing everyday of your life. I'm ready to learn the next thing I need to know."

She was silent again, but this time it was her thoughtful silence. Apparently, this had not occurred to her. After a moment, she smiled at me and said, "I'll have to mull that one over."

My father pulled himself out of the pool and came over to join us. As he dried himself off, I poured him a cup of coffee. "I've got to hand it you, son. It is definitely hard to find fault with your lifestyle." He and Mom had their backs to the guesthouse. As I handed him his coffee, I saw Mrs. Willamette walk out onto the terrace in all of her middle-aged, full-figured glory. She stretched and looked around.

"Glad you think so," I replied, hoping there was no panic in my voice. "It's not a forty-foot sailboat, but it'll do." Mrs. Willamette scratched below her breasts.

Dad winked at me. Tony came out of the kitchen door, paused at the top of the steps and looked from Mrs. Willamette to me and back to her. He then sat down and started laughing. I would have given him the finger if I didn't have my parents' full attention. And, at the moment, my parents' full attention was *exactly* what I wanted.

After an eternity, Mrs. Willamette turned and walked back into her room and closed the door. Tony came down the steps, still laughing to himself and greeted my parents. Another door opened in the guesthouse, and this time, Val emerged. She came down the staircase and joined us at the bar. Tony continued on to the front desk. We said our good mornings, and she poured herself a glass of orange juice. Turning around to lean back on the bar, she gave an appraising look to the back yard.

"You know, Aidan. This is a nice place, but I can see what you were talking about last night. It must be an incredible amount of upkeep."

"That it is. I love the house and I love the plane, but I think Albert was issuing me a challenge when he left them to me." I took a sip of coffee, and then added, "My mom, your mom and Uncle Jeff were the real winners."

My mother shot me her wide eyed, pursed lips, civil defense warning look, but I chose to ignore her. After all, no one had *officially* told me that Viv had never told her children about the will.

Val turned around. "*My* mom?"

"Sure," I beamed. "You know. I mean yes, I got some collateral property, but they got cash. Cash is, after all, always worth more than property."

My dad began smirking and turned away to face the pool. Mother's expression had passed from civil defense warning to DefCon II. I didn't look at her.

"Yeah," I continued on merrily. "I was rereading the will the other day. I've got a copy of it in my desk in the library. It seems pretty clear that Albert unloaded all of this on me for a reason, but I've got no idea what it is. Everyone else just received a benevolence."

My dad was now laughing and had to walk away from the bar. I am sure my mom's expression was showing up on NORAD screens as far away as the Aleutians. Val stared at me wide eyed, but said nothing. Before I could add any more, Cait burst from her room at the same time that Vivian and Mo emerged from theirs. They all joined us at the bar, and Vivian immediately began piling danish on her plate. Val regarded her with a long, cool, appraising look, but said nothing.

I walked around the bar and over to the front desk to look at Tony's to-do list. Scot began sweeping the deck around the pool. A moment later, my mother was behind me, right on schedule.

"You shouldn't have said anything about the inheritance," she said quietly. "Vivian didn't tell her kids about it. She was planning to put the money in trust for them."

I did a very good job of not screaming *Oh Bullshit*, and instead said absently "Oh really? Gosh, I didn't know that."

"Don't say anything else. Maybe Val won't mention it."

My mother, although brilliant and self confident, will never master politics. Fortunately she has Dad to protect her. If anything ever happens to him, I may have her sealed in a plastic bubble for the rest of her life. "Let's hope so."

She rejoined the group and I climbed the back stairs to the kitchen. I walked quickly to the front hall and unlocked the library doors, and opened the left one a crack. From behind me on the stairs, Bart asked "The seed's planted already?"

"Gotta move fast sometimes." I smiled back at him.

"You know," he said sadly as he sank down on the landing. "I hate this. We can't escape family politics. And the fact is, I can see why Viv and Uncle Jeff and half of the Fitzgeralds carry on like this. It's easy."

I nodded and sat next to him on the steps. "You're right. The game is easy and, I suppose, could even become fun. But we're a family. It's not supposed to be like this."

"And it's not for you."

"What do you mean it's not like this for me? I'm playing every game I can to protect my house."

He nodded. "Yeah, but you're removed from it. Once this is over, you'll be like Albert. On the very periphery of things. Over half of the family is in Chicago. I'm in it all the time."

"You don't play games."

"No, but they go on around me. And everyone would like to enlist my help. If Mom and Dad weren't there, I'd be out in a minute."

The virtue of being the oldest is that you are the first one to leave. No one questions it because there are other children at home. But if you are the last one to leave, it is often guilt that keeps you from roaming far.

I put my arm around Bart's shoulder, and we walked back into the back yard. There was nothing I could tell him. If he was going to escape the Fitzgeralds, he would have to find his own way out.

The family spent that day playing tourist in Key West. They would wander out in groups for a couple of hours, return, and leave again in different groupings. I had told Tony and Scot that I wanted all three of us to spend as much time as possible out of the house that day. After three, I wandered into the house and peeked into the foyer. The doors to the library had been moved. I walked in, and it was evident that someone had been using my desk. I opened the file drawer and confirmed that the will had been moved (Val hadn't returned it to its proper spot), and the legal pad I keep in my lap drawer now sat on top of the blotter. I also noticed that one of my good pens was missing.

That night, I had a cookout on the patio for my family and the guys. Val was noticeably cool towards her mother, although Roy seemed totally oblivious to what was going on. At different times, Bart, Cait, Tony and Scot all shot me inquisitive looks with a sidelong glance at Val, and I nodded. That seemed to put everyone in a good mood, and we had a very nice evening. During dinner, Val and Viv seemed to snipe at each other, but the rest of us ignored it. Late that evening, after everyone had gone to bed, Bart and I both heard something on the patio below the French doors. I got out of bed, walked over to them and saw Viv and Val hissing at each other over by the bar. I closed the doors slightly so we couldn't hear what they were saying.

Bart rolled over on his side and looked at me inquisitively. "Not interested?"

I shook my head as I got into bed. "We've won this round. I don't need to keep playing."

The next day, everyone packed up for the flight home. My father surprised me by asking which coast of Florida was the better place to retire. I told him the west coast. When people from the Northeast retire, they move to Miami, Fort Lauderdale and Boca on the east coast. Good solid Midwesterners move to Sarasota, Tampa or St. Petersburg.

We loaded up the plane and flew back to Sarasota. We put Cait on her plane first, and then everyone else on the plane to Chicago. Saying goodbye to Bart was hard. Maybe it was just the big brother thing, but I really knew I was going to miss him.

Their plane must have been late getting away, because it was sitting at the end of the runway as Ross taxied the *Voyager* out. We stayed relatively far back so the blast from the jets didn't flip my plane, but gave it a little salute. Over the radio, ATC invited me onto the runway. "*Biscayne* One cleared for departure."

I thanked the tower over the radio, and Ross advanced the throttles and pulled us into the sky.

I returned to the house at about five. It was quiet. Scot was tending bar in back for the Willamettes and a handful of other guests who had checked in immediately after my family's departure. I walked behind the bar, made myself a vodka tonic and wandered back out into the street. I slowly meandered around the block. In time, I found myself standing in front of King Louis' place. As usual, there was a crowd there. Louis himself sat on the porch, quietly painting and apparently oblivious to the boisterous crowd inside. I walked up the front steps.

"You know, your highness, this isn't so much a residence as a sustained keg party."

Louie smiled and laid down his brush. "That it is. And, what better metaphor for Key West?"

I laughed and gave him a little mock toast with my drink.

"I believe I saw the sunlight glint off of a vintage Douglas DC-2 today as it circled the island and headed north. May I take that to mean that your entire clan has departed?"

I nodded and sat on his front porch. "That they have."

"And you seem less than pleased by it," he observed and took a sip from a martini glass that could easily hold half a gallon.

I shrugged. "I would certainly say that I miss a couple of them."

He nodded. "I'll assume that sentiment doesn't apply to the four in tacky northern white trash tourist attire."

I laughed. "You've got that one pegged. Why is it that I can be a normal, healthy, well-adjusted person any other time, but get me around someone whom I'm related to, and I'm a basket case?"

Louie picked up the large scepter he carried occasionally and used it to stir his martini. "That, my boy, is what makes people family; the ability to know exactly what buttons to push to shut each other down. I'm sure you do it to them as well and don't even realize it. And I hate to break into your wallow in self-pity, but you are not alone. *Every* family does it."

The term *wallow in self-pity* struck me as awfully harsh coming from someone who was clearly insane, but I said nothing. He continued.

"Aidan, do you think Olivia lives in New York because she likes it? I know of no one who likes New York and lives there. She lives there because it is everything I am not. And I live here because it is everything that she is not. Or more accurately, because it is everything my mother was not. Why do you think your uncle came here? He came to build a life without any of the preconceived notions of his family. And, as to being *healthy* and *well-adjusted*, I defy you to define those terms for me. From where I sit, everyone's definitions so far have been clearly lacking."

Louie's house is not far from Ernest Hemingway's house, which is home to...no, which is *infested* with dozens of the island's indigenous six-toed cats. As I pondered Louie's point, one chose that moment to wander into the yard. Sitting next to Louie's chair was a large box full of rubber ducks. Louie picked one out carefully, yelled "Pull!" and lobbed it at the cat. The cat darted into the large wall of shrubs that his neighbor carefully maintained to screen off his property. I noticed that there were about fifty rubber ducks in the yard so far.

"Louie, you seem unusually cynical today."

He looked genuinely shocked and hurt. "Master Aidan! I am *never* cynical! Sir! If all of us did things the same as our parents or families, what would possibly be interesting about the world? What you've got to learn (and, I might add, what my *daughter* needs to learn) is that you can be different from your heritage without hostility. Individuality and rebellion are *not* the same things. Your uncle's life should have taught you that."

For a lunatic, he was a surprisingly wise one. I spent the better part of an hour talking to Louie while he viciously threw rubber ducks at any random wildlife misguided enough to wander into the yard before meandering back to my own house. As I walked, I pondered my uncle's life. I was not sure I had learned anything from it, because I was not sure I had ever been privy to it.

I found George seated in the back yard sipping a drink. We shook hands and I collapsed into a seat across the table from him. We stared at each other for a moment. Since he wasn't volunteering any information, I decided to ask something that was on my mind.

"George, how come I never met Louie Robideau before I moved here? I've been coming here since I was in college, but I don't remember anyone ever even mentioning him."

George took a sip of his drink. "I'm sure Albert knew a lot of people you didn't know."

"No, that's not it. I spent a lot of time here. Albert introduced me to you, to his bartender…*hell,* to drag queens, for God's sake. It seems to me that Louie is a pretty colorful character and his path must have crossed Albert's often. I don't understand how I missed him."

George smiled and set his drink down. "Aidan, you never met him because Albert didn't want you to. Son, if you haven't learned by now, your uncle could be the biggest control freak on the planet."

I was well aware of Albert's need for control. I still tried to wrestle with it on a daily basis. "But why wouldn't he want me to know him?"

George looked down for a second, then looked me in the eye. "A year ago, if I asked you who was the most interesting person you had ever met, what would your answer have been?"

I didn't hesitate. "Albert."

George nodded. "There's your answer. Aidan, I'm not sure you've ever realized what you meant to Albert. You reminded him of himself as a kid. Whenever you came down here, you clearly idolized him. And why?"

I thought for a long time. "I guess it was because I always admired that he lived life on his own terms."

George nodded again. "Please realize something. That is also Louie. They are two of a kind. They live (or lived) by their own rules and when they didn't like the rules, they changed them. Make no mistake, there was a keen competition between Albert and Louie. The one thing Albert wouldn't risk was you."

That did strike me as very Albertian. "So is that why he didn't want the family to ever know about Jason?"

"Precisely. Albert protected what he cherished. In Albert's mind, you were a buried treasure. More so, because you were family. Albert had an acceptance from you that he never had from the rest of the family, and he guarded it. Jason falls into a similar situation."

"Did Albert spend much time with him?"

"He did. He took a very active interest in Jason, and made sure he wanted for nothing. Why do you think he put so many hours on that damn plane? Back and forth to New Orleans. Back and forth."

I looked up and pondered the stars as they winked into view. "Do you know Phoebe?"

"Quite well," he smiled again. "She is…I guess *earthy* would be the term for it. She's hard headed. Stubborn. Lots of street sense, but not a lot of formal education. Very, very, *very* determined to have her own way."

I laughed. "She's Albert."

He touched the tip of his nose with his index finger. "Exactly. Hence why they never married."

I laughed again. We sat silent for a moment. "I expect Vivian to go after her."

George nodded, suddenly very serious. "I as well. *Phoebe* as well. Sometimes, though, we just have to let things play their course."

I agreed. "I will stay out of it. But if you need me, I'm there."

"I appreciate that Aidan. I'll let you know if I do." He got up to go.

"Hey," I suddenly remembered, "Louie says he's planning to 'knight' me on Halloween. What's that all about?"

George laughed his evil attorney's laugh. "The Order of the Conch is a highly secret order. I cannot tell you what you're in for. Suffice to say, I expect you will enjoy it." He turned and walked back up the alley.

THE ORDER OF THE CONCH

The month of October proceeded uneventfully. Tourist bookings on the island steadily increased. A particularly strong hurricane season in the lower Caribbean helped funnel lots of dollars into the Keys, and we were steadily booked for the entire month. We also flew two parties per weekend. With the money we were able to raise, we made a substantial payment on the loan. I also managed to sock away enough money to pay the property taxes.

Olivia came back to the island for a weekend to pick up a painting, and she and Scot went out, but nothing came from it. She was uninterested, but Scot remained smitten. Ross met a guy and they dated briefly, but it didn't take. In the elections for the local chamber of commerce, Tony won the position of treasurer. Halloween approached.

To appreciate Halloween in Key West, you must understand that it is one part Mardi Gras, one part Drag Show and three parts Rum. There are few events in the world more hedonistic, and none more likely to offend the Southern Baptist Convention. It is called, simply, Fantasy Fest.

Fantasy Fest takes place over the entire week leading up to Halloween, and occasionally spills over into the following week. It is characterized by drinking, parades, drinking, costume contests, drinking, and mayhem. It is one of the biggest tourist draws of the year, and small guesthouses like ours clean up.

That year, Halloween fell on a Saturday, so the Fest kicked off the previous weekend. Each year, the organizers merited a theme for the week, and all parades, parties and costumes reflected it. This year the theme was the Roaring Twenties.

Owning a vintage aircraft came in handy, and we scheduled parties almost every day that week. I ruled out Friday and Saturday because Friday night was my induction into the Order of the Conch, and Saturday was just one hell of a party. But, I'm getting ahead of myself.

Monarch Court is conveniently located just off of Duval, the main party-artery of the island. As such, we were completely booked and, frankly, working our butts off. Typically, we would have to do all of our daily chores by noon since we were flying parties each afternoon. Ross was roped into every possible job both at the house and on the plane. We would fly a party from one until five, return to the house and open the bar for happy hour at five-thirty. Ordinarily, we would close the bar at seven-thirty, but during this week we found we had to keep it open until ten. Once it closed, most of the guests would wander up Monarch to Duval to join whatever party had spilled out of a bar onto the street. We would all be in bed by midnight, although the sounds of drunken guests jumping into and out of the pool all night below my bedroom window usually woke me up two or three times during the night.

By Monday night, Ross had moved in with us and was sleeping on the couch downstairs. It was taking too much time for him to get from our house and through the crowds in the street to his own apartment. Moreover, since he lived above a bar, he could get no sleep at all and was technically not legal to fly. While I'm not sure our place was any more restful for him, we definitely needed the help, and we were paying him generously for it.

After finishing a trip Wednesday afternoon, he and I were busy trying to clean the aircraft before returning to the house to help Tony and

Scot. It was filthy, and the crowd that day had been particularly unruly. As I removed an airsickness bag from the galley that reeked of semi-digested margarita, I mused out loud, "If Albert can see this, he's spinning in his grave."

Without looking up from the window he was cleaning, Ross said, "I thought he had been cremated."

"I stand corrected," I said as I threw the bag out the door and into the garbage can. "If Albert can see this, he's making plans to kick my ass when I get to Heaven."

After a moment, I added, "If he's there."

Ross smiled. "Doesn't seem to me he has a case. It's your plane now. If he cared, he should have taken it with him."

"I imagine he tried."

"It's not unprecedented," Ross reflected. "I had a Great-Aunt Mary who died in the 1920s. She was buried in her Dusenberg."

"No way."

"Way. She had this huge mausoleum built, and when she died, the family sat her in the back seat with a magnum of champagne, drove her in, and walled her up. I actually always thought that's how I'd like to go. Cruising through the pearly gates with my champagne in my Dusenberg."

I laughed. He finished the window, stood up and stretched. "I wonder if you can get a DUI in Heaven."

"I'm sure Albert knows by now."

"If he's there," Ross corrected.

"If he's there," I agreed.

We left the plane and locked it up. As we walked across the hangar, Ross asked "Mind a question?"

I shook my head no.

"Well, maybe it's part question, part observation. You seem to have some real issues with your uncle. Why?"

"Why do you think I have issues?"

"Because you never stop talking about him, but you frequently sound angry while you're doing it. It seems to me you were crazy about him, but now you're mad."

I thought for a long moment as we climbed into my car. "Maybe I am. He left me very confused and frustrated. When Albert died, he left me a couple of great things: the house and the plane. But he didn't really leave me money to do anything with them, and he didn't leave me any instructions on what to do with them."

Ross looked sideways at me. "You mean you're upset that he didn't leave you enough? That doesn't sound like you."

I pulled out of the parking lot. "No, that's not it. Believe me, he actually saved my ass. I don't know what I would have done when I lost my job if I hadn't had Key West to come to. I just have felt that he was trying to guide me to something and never took the time to tell me what it was. We play a lot of games in our family, and I felt like he was playing one with me in his will. I guess I was just angry that...that..."

"Oh hell, I don't know why I'm angry with him. I just am."

Ross smiled sardonically. "You know, when my dad died, I was angry. He found out he had cancer, and he took off one day and flew the plane into the Grand Canyon. He didn't try chemo. He didn't go out fighting. He just flew off. I've never known if it was an accident or if he gave up. Part of me thinks that he wanted go out in some blaze of glory rather than as a wasted-away cancer patient. I've never been sure. But, Jesus, I was pissed. For over a year I was pissed at him and I couldn't figure out why. And then I did."

"Why?"

"I was just pissed because he left. I thought it was because he gave up. But in truth I don't know. I was just pissed because I still wanted him here and I didn't understand why he wasn't."

I had nothing to say. I turned left onto Monarch Court.

"How long has Albert been dead?"

"Eight months," I replied quietly.

Ross smiled. "Let's talk on the one-year anniversary and see if you're still mad."

We got out of the car and walked into the house.

Later that night, I lay in bed and reflected on what Ross had said. I remembered something from psych class in college about the stages of mourning. It went something like shock, anger, grief, bargaining…that was as far as I could get. Outside I heard quite a bit of splashing from the pool. I got out of bed and looked out the window. Five or six people were floating in the pool, and there were a number of empty beer bottles on the concrete surrounding it. I groaned at the mess we would have to clean up tomorrow.

I wasn't really in the mood to get back into bed. I pulled on a pair of shorts and walked downstairs to the kitchen. I didn't turn on the lights because they would be visible to the pool below, and I didn't want to invite attention from the guests (or, more accurately, requests to open the bar). I poured a glass of milk and sat on the counter with a bag of Oreos.

My brother and I have good and bad memories of growing up together. There is, however, one great memory that I associate with him; sitting up late at night in the kitchen talking while eating Oreos and milk. They had to be dunked however. Whenever I have Oreos and milk at night, I think of Bart. I considered calling him and glanced at the clock on the microwave. It was two a.m. in Chicago. I decided against it.

Ross wandered into the kitchen. "I thought I heard cookies." I smiled and offered him the bag. There was shriek of laughter from the pool that was quickly muffled.

"Couldn't sleep either?" I asked. He shook his head.

"No. Too much partying going on." He poured himself a glass of milk and sat on the counter next to me, with the Oreos between us. "Let me correct that. Too much partying going on that doesn't involve us."

"I know what you mean. What's the point of living in Key West, if you aren't going to be part of the party?"

"Don't get me wrong, we've made a boat load of money this week, and I've racked up enough flight hours to apply for my multi-engine. But let's face it. Being the only sober people on the island is kind of depressing."

"Well, we're not the only sober ones. I imagine all of the innkeepers are sober. Too many of us are afraid the guests will burn down our businesses."

He smiled.

"Although," I continued, "it's almost over. At least we will be done flying after tomorrow, so we don't have to worry about the minimum sleep requirements. Tomorrow night, I'll take you out and buy you a drink."

"Oh you will, huh? Where?"

"Whadaya mean, where? Anywhere."

"Really? Even one of my bars?"

That caught me off guard. The general motto of Key West could be "*whatever.*" We were so far south on the continent that the Christian Coalition, the Moral Majority, and all those other groups that pander hate in God's name never really made it down here. There was not a lot of moral indignation over things like sexuality here. Moral indignation was reserved for things like *last call,* and a crack down on the illegally imported Cuban cigars that everyone had anyhow.

That said, I had to admit I had never been to a gay bar. I never really even thought about it. We always merrily dragged Ross off to whatever bars we usually went to and assumed he enjoyed them as much as we did. All of them very straight bars.

I must have paused too long before I blurted out, "Uh, sure."

He laughed and said, "I won't do that to you."

Now my pride was on the line. "No, *wherever* you want to go is fine. Even…there."

"Aidan, you don't have to prove your open mindedness to me. I'm sure you're the least judgmental person on the planet."

I smiled. "Who says I'm worried about proving it to you. I may have to prove it to myself."

He leaned back against the cabinets and looked at me. "You guys never, really, talk about this with me. Are you okay with it?"

"With what? You being gay?" He nodded. "Of course we are."

"I mean, you guys have been great friends and you've always gone out of your way to include me in things. You just seem to, I dunno, avoid the subject."

I closed the Oreos and put them away just to have something to do. "Well Ross, it's not like we really care, or are even particularly interested. As you may have noticed the three of us are pretty focused on trying to make the business work, and I'm afraid what goes on in your bedroom just doesn't make our top ten topics of discussion. Those are usually reserved for money, our lack of money, where we intend to find money, and what we will do with the money when we find it."

"Well, I'll give you credit for one thing, at least none of you have ever asked me if I was hitting on you." He slid off the counter.

I laughed and then asked, "Why, did I miss something?"

He laughed as well. "No Aidan, you're not my type. Too clean cut."

"Ah well, your loss."

He pointed at me and said, "Nope. Yours." He walked back into the living room and I returned to my bedroom.

The next morning I cornered Tony. "I promised Ross I'd buy him a drink tonight."

Tony was transferring sheets from the washer to the dryer. "Well, it's the least we could do. We've been working his butt off this week."

"Well, I'm glad you said 'we'."

"Why?"

"He wants to go to one of *his* bars."

Tony looked up from the laundry and stared at me. "One of his..."

I nodded.

"Have fun." He took the laundry basket and walked away. I followed pleading.

"C'mon man. You've got to go."

"I don't *got* to do anything," he replied.

"Look he was telling me last night how he was wondering if we were cool with him because we never asked about his personal life. I told him we were, but we all do kind of avoid the subject like the plague."

Tony stopped and rolled his eyes at me. "Why do I have to go? Take Scot."

I smirked. "Tony. Scot has the sexual sophistication of a garden gnome. I don't think this is the best environment to spring on him."

Tony looked disgusted, but clearly knew I was right. He sighed heavily and said "All right, but so help me if anyone hits on me…"

"I doubt anyone ever would," I cracked. He flipped me off and stomped away.

I'm not sure what I expected the bar to be like, but the Alamo wasn't it. During the entire course of the day, I had concocted elaborate, terrified fantasies of what I would encounter that night. I imagined drag queens and men in leather and a lot of heavy cruising. What I encountered, instead, was a room full of men who looked more like they were about to attend a fraternity meeting.

The three of us walked up to the bar, and Ross ordered us a round of beer. When they arrived, he glanced at me over his beer bottle and smirked. "Not what you were expecting?"

"Is it that obvious?"

"You couldn't look any more shocked if you found Madeleine Albright in here."

I shrugged.

As it turned out, except for the rainbow flag flying by the front door and the preponderance of men in the place, I might never have known it was a gay bar if I had wandered in by accident. We had two beers, during which time no one hit on either Tony or me. While I didn't particularly want anyone to hit on me, I was nonetheless disappointed that no one did. I mean, it's not like I'm hideous or anything. My thoughts must have been obvious because Ross observed, "Don't know how to tell you this, but you're underdressed for this place."

I had to admit that my togs were not up to the standard in the bar, but I had on a clean tee shirt, running shorts and sports sandals. Still, compared to the studied, casual attire of the crowd, I looked like I was there to clean out the storeroom. I glanced at my watch.

Oddly, although the bar was packed, no one seemed to be doing anything. Dance music blared over the sound system, but no one danced. The music was loud enough that no one really seemed to talk either. I asked Ross about this. He shrugged.

"It's an s and m bar."

A wave of shock rolled through me. "S and M? As in sadomasochism?"

He laughed and shook his head. "No, as in 'stand-and-model.'"

Although I found it somewhat fascinating, Tony was clearly bored. I glanced at my watch again. We had told Scot what we were doing that night, and invited him along. As I had suspected, he had turned it down. We had agreed to meet him at Seamus Weinstein's bar at ten. It was nine forty-five.

Ross finished his beer. "Let's go to Seamus'," he said, sounding slightly disgusted.

"Anything wrong?" I asked as we walked outside. He shook his head.

"No, just nothing going on. I was hoping I could at least shock you guys, but how do you shock a couple of straights with a room full of Tommy Hilfiger models?"

Tony and I laughed and we continued down the street. As we turned the corner onto Fleming, Ross got his wish. I was, indeed, shocked.

Because we had been working so hard, none of us had really been out at night, so we had missed all of the large costume parties which the bars host and which spill out onto the streets. However, one was going full force at Weinstein's. Of course, big bar parties were not all that much of a novelty in Key West. But the costumes were. As we rounded the corner, I ran headlong into a man wearing nothing but a garment bag with a sign taped to it identifying him as *Lost Luggage*. Behind him were hundreds of revelers in varying states of costume, dress and undress.

While I have been to costume parties all over the country where the participants sport risqué costumes, nothing prepared me for the concept of body painting. The most predominant costume worn by both men and women was a g-string, and a couple of shades of paint, artfully applied on their skin. As far as I could see, naked breasts adorned in bright colors glittered and bobbed in front of me. I looked at Ross and said, "Well, you got your wish."

We found Scot inside the bar, clearly drunk. He was surrounded by a dozen little shot cups. When he saw us he yelled "Hey!" and fell off his bar stool.

"Jesus, Scot," Tony said, "Isn't it a little early for shots."

"'S'not shots," Scot grinned at me as I helped him up from the floor. "'S'Jell-O."

They were indeed shot cups filled with Jell-O. However, instead of being made with water as all good, god-fearing Jell-O should be, these *Jell-O shooters* had been made with grain alcohol. "'S always room f'Jell-O," Scot slurred as he consumed another shot, offered by a rather buxom young waitress who was painted blue.

Ross, Tony and I shrugged, and each had a shot as well. It tasted like Jell-O, but burned on the way down. The sensation was not all that unpleasant. We each had another.

By one in the morning, I had consumed more Jell-O than all the retirement homes in Boca. A couple of hours before, Scot had made the discovery that Jell-O-shooters were flammable. The four of us began to light the shots on fire before consuming them. Around midnight, it occurred to me that we were basically eating Sterno.

Whether it was the fact that he had spent five nights on our couch, or the fact that I'm pretty sure he was hot for the bartender, Ross told us he would be staying in his own apartment that night. We left him at the bar. When we returned home, we found a large envelope taped to the front door. By large, I don't mean a manila envelope. I mean an envelope that measured twenty-four inches tall and more than thirty-six inches across. Since the three of us were quite drunk, we stared at it for a long time.

"That's a rather large envelope," Tony observed sagely.

"It is," I agreed.

"Perhaps we should open it," Scot offered.

I walked forward. The envelope was addressed to me, with my name embossed in gold. I removed it from the front door, and carried it inside the foyer. Sitting on the bottom step of the staircase, I opened the envelope and removed a large card, also embossed in gold lettering.

To: Mr. Aidan McInnis

HRH Louis Of Robideau, Monarch of Key West, summons you to court on Friday, October 30th, to celebrate your induction into the most solemn Order of the Conch. As a Knight errant, you may bring two gentlemen to serve as your squires during your induction.

You are expected to present yourself to His Royal Highness at the hour of ten p.m. in the throne room of his most serene Palace-in-Dayglo.

"Oh Christ," Tony complained. "You're going to make us go to this thing, aren't you?"

I looked at him. "Maybe not. I'd rather take someone who was going to have fun." Tony looked shocked. I don't think it had occurred to him that he might not be invited. We didn't discuss it further because Scot chose that moment to pass out on the foyer floor.

The next day went as smoothly as a day with a monster hangover could. At lunch, I considered what I should wear to my knighting. After all, Fantasy Fest is a pretty exotic time, even for Key West. Sandals and cut-offs just wouldn't do. I felt compelled to do something that would at least put me in the running with the horde of eccentrics that seemed to share my life now. Tony stumbled on to me as I stood contemplating my closet. I explained my dilemma and, rather than the sarcasm I expected, he studied the closet with me.

"You know," he muttered, "I have a box in the attic that is filled with old costumes I wore in plays in college. Perhaps we can find something in there." We trudged to the attic.

Inside the box, we found several options. I could have gone as a yeoman, a Keystone cop, or The Joker. I finally opted for a brocade frock-coat that Tony had worn when he played Cyrano De Bergerac. Since it was heavy, I wouldn't wear a shirt underneath, but I would wear a pair of white tights. While not exactly accurate, the costume was close enough to something that Charles the First would have worn that I was sure the king would approve.

"Um," Tony asked hesitantly as I modeled the outfit in front of my closet mirror, "am I still invited?"

I smiled. "Only if you agree to have fun."

"I will definitely try," he said and disappeared into his room. He emerged later with two short blue yeoman's jackets that he and Scot would also wear.

That evening, after dinner, I put on my costume, and added my college fencing foil to it. The guys each put on the yeoman's jackets and white pants, which made them look more like cheesy Bahamian bellhops than yeomen, but it really didn't matter. Each of them carried a bottle of champagne, which I felt would be an appropriate display of my gratitude to the monarch.

We left the house at five minutes before ten. As I walked out the front door, the sweltering tropical night hit me like a wet mitten across the face. I took the jacket off for the walk around the block, putting it back on only when we reached the hedge that surrounded Louie's yard. I re-dressed, added my sword and wrapped a red sash around my waist. I must admit that I thought I would have cut quite a dashing figure in the Middle Ages, and I was quite impressed with my costume.

We rounded the hedge, and I realized I shouldn't be. The array of costumes that greeted me in the yard and on the porch was truly astounding. There were women in powdered wigs, and women in nothing but sequins. Some of the women wore huge, Vegas-style head-dresses, as did at least two of the men. Many of the men were dressed in Elizabethan codpieces, and others wore leather vests and pants which would have been at home at some suburban Renaissance festival. There were also people dressed as Middle Eastern sheiks, geishas, wild-life, automotive parts and kitchen appliances. George's words echoed in my head. "In Key West, you have to work harder to be eccentric."

As we came through the gate, an expectant hush fell over the crowd. We paused for a minute, taken aback, and then proceeded up the front walk. Several of the revelers carried Mardi-Gras masks, which they lowered ever so slightly to get a look at the three of us over the tops. I nodded to one or two people I recognized and walked up the front steps and through the front door.

A similar hush fell over the revelers in the hall, and I noted that everyone who had been in the front yard was following close on our heels. I turned and walked into the throne room, attempting not to show my hesitancy.

Again a hush fell over the crowd, and I must say that this group was the most spectacular I had seen by far. Thousands of sequins glittered in the throne room. Candles lighted the room, some in the sconces on the walls, but many more in the hands of the guests.

On the dais at the end of the room, the King sat, conferring with George. George almost looked like pictures I've seen of Benjamin Disraeli: ascot, bowler, umbrella. Pity he wasn't wearing any pants. The green polka dot boxers just didn't fit the picture. George has absurdly skinny legs.

As fabulous as the rest of the crowd's costumes were, nothing could compare with Louie's. He wore a purple cape with an ermine collar over a gold lamé jacket and pants. The lapels of the jacket and the cuffs of both the jacket and his pants were all purple sequins. A bright green sequined sash flowed from his left shoulder to his waist. I'm not sure where he got it, but the Victoria Cross hung on a red ribbon around his neck. On his head was a huge gold and purple crown. For the first time I noticed that, when he wanted, Louie could be a commanding presence.

As the room fell silent, he turned and looked at me, and a genuine smile spread across his face. He picked up his scepter from the table next to him, and walked down the steps, George in tow. A long, red carpet lead from the throne to the far end of the room where I stood.

As he reached me, he looked me up and down, nodding approvingly. Then he did the same to both Tony and Scot. The silence in the room was almost a physical thing, and very intimidating. Finally, he turned to George and said, "You told them to come in costume, didn't you?"

George shook his head. "I did not. They figured it out all on their own."

Louie looked back at me and smiled again. "Well, young Aidan, we are impressed. Over the last thirty-odd years, we've knighted almost a hundred people, but none of them have ever come in costume. We never would have guessed you would. Maybe there is more to you than even we suspected." He took me by the arm, and we walked slowly back up the carpet towards the dais. George and the guys followed close behind.

"Aidan, do you know what a *krewe* is?"

"As in a boat?"

He chuckled. "No, that's crew, with a *c*. This word is Cajun. Krewe, with a k."

"No, I don't."

"A krewe is a secret society. They originated with Mardi Gras in Mobile during the eighteenth century. 'A masked band of revelers, known only to themselves who, in their revels, also do good deeds.' That is what the Order of the Conch is. Everyone here tonight is a member of the order. They were inducted for one reason, and one reason only. They gave a damn about someone else, and from that, a good deed followed.

"Each year, on Halloween, the order throws a huge ball. The proceeds from the ball are donated to charity, this year it's an AIDS charity. One of our members is dying of AIDS. We can't cure him, but we can give money to those who are trying. It's our way of fighting for what is truly right.

"The Order...indeed, the whole monarchy, came about out of a simple group of people fighting for what was right. None of us took ourselves so seriously at it that we didn't have fun. But we didn't give up the fight. Tonight, we want you to join us."

We reached the dais and he let go of my arm, and ascended the steps. He turned around and looked down at me. "Aidan, do you know why we've chosen you?"

I shook my head. "No sir. I don't."

"I do," Tony said behind me quietly. I turned and looked at him. Both he and Scot were smiling.

"Because of us." Scot volunteered.

I was confused. "Huh?"

"Aidan," Tony began, "when we lost our jobs, you didn't need to worry about us. You had a house, a plane, and enough money that you didn't have to worry. Instead, you threw both of us a line without thinking about it, and said that all three of us would make it together." He turned and looked at the king. "That's it, isn't it?"

I turned around and looked at him. He nodded his confirmation to Tony. "It is indeed."

"But that's nothing special," I protested.

"Isn't it?" the king asked. "Well, keep it to yourself, because it impressed the hell out of the rest of us."

The rest of the room laughed and it dawned on me that these people were not hangers-on, as I had so often thought. These people were genuinely Louie's friends. The king continued to stare at me. "Aidan, are you ready to be knighted and inducted into the Most Holy Order of the Conch?"

"I am, sire."

"Then please kneel."

I knelt on the steps of the dais. The king handed a scroll to George, who read it to the assembled crowd. "'Whereas, Aidan McInnis, recently of Boston, has elected to make his home in the Conch Republic, and Whereas he has brought with him friends who have become Useful Citizens of the Republic, and Whereas we deem him to have the spirit and moral context peculiar to the denizens of the Republic, It is therefore our magnanimous royal decision that he be inducted into the Order of the Conch. Signed this thirtieth day of October, by my own hand. Louis Of Robideau, Monarch of Key West.'" He closed the scroll.

"Mister McInnis," the king began. "Do you hereby swear to do good, uphold what is right, and live by what your conscience tells you?"

"I do."

"Do you hereby swear to never take yourself so seriously that you lose your sense of humor about life?"

"I do."

"Do you hereby swear to give a damn?"

"I do."

"My sword." George produced a large gold and chrome sword from somewhere and handed it to the king. He touched the blade first to my right shoulder. "In the name of goodness." He moved it to my left shoulder. "In the name of individuality." He moved it so that the blade lay flat on the top of my head. "And in the name of all who have gone before you, I proclaim that from this day forward, in the Kingdom of Key West and the Conch Republic, you will be known as Sir Aidan the Airborne, Baron of the Biscayne Skies."

The room erupted into thunderous applause, and I stood. I was, to say the least, somewhat abashed by the whole production. The champagne bottles were opened, and a number of toasts were made. Soon, the solemnity was over, and everyone forgot the occasion.

Later, the king came up besides me and touched his glass to mine. "Thanks for the champagne."

I smiled and toasted him back silently. "Not a problem. Thanks for the knighthood."

"Not a problem." We drank. "You know, wherever he is. I'm sure your uncle is quite proud of you."

"I like to think so," I said honestly. At that moment, the large grandfather clock in the hall struck quarter to twelve.

Louie started. "It's time. Come with me, young man. We have work to do."

I had noticed that the guests had been drifting out of the house for about thirty minutes, and George had led Scot and Tony off with him. The king guided me to the back yard, where a parade was being staged. There were three floats, each pulled by a team of men and women. Scot and Tony were standing on the front of the first one with huge barrels of plastic Mardi Gras beads, doubloons and candy. Behind them sat a fourteen-piece brass band. The second float was decked out as a castle, with several women standing on it, positioning themselves so their headdresses didn't collide. Behind that was a third that could only be described as the largest mobile throne chair ever made. Up giant purple and gold steps sat women and men, bedecked as flamingos or swans or leopards. In the center of it all was a great gold chair, which would no doubt be where Louie would sit. On each of the floats burned huge wrought-iron torches.

"Tonight is our night for a parade. We'll travel out of here and down Duval to Mallory Square and then back. I will expect you to ride on the second float and guard the ladies of the court." And with that, he was gone, headed back towards the throne. He yelled back over his should. "Oh yeah, and *have fun!*"

I walked to the guys on the first float. "So, what do you think?"

Tony looked at me and grinned. "I have to admit, this is more fun than I ever expected it would be."

I agreed and headed back to the second float.

About thirty people would ride on floats. The rest would walk along side handing out goodies. I climbed onto my float.

"Hi Aidan," said a woman about my age wearing a sequined g-string and a huge white headdress, "I'm Claudia, the Duchess of Duval. Welcome to the Order."

"Thanks," I told her, trying very hard to keep my eyes locked on hers. She turned to introduce to me to a much older lady who, thankfully, was wearing a little bit more.

"This is Muriel, the Countess of Cashiers." I shook the Countess' hand. I was next introduced to Marchioness of Meter Maids, the Dame of Decorators, and the Tsarina of Tsupermarkets.

"What are we supposed to do up here?" I asked the Duchess, who handed me a facemask.

She shrugged as she secured her own. "It's a parade. You wave and you throw Mardi Gras beads or doubloons."

"That I can do," I replied. At that moment, two trumpeters fired off a stirring herald. The gates of the backyard opened, and the parade began its slow progression into the street as the brass band fired up a piece that I later learned was a Swahili celebration song.

Friday night was a party like nothing I had ever seen. The streets were packed with men and women. As soon as they heard the music, the crowds parted to let the parade through, but it was slow going. Everywhere, people screamed and cheered and loudly demanded that we throw them beads. We did so, and there would be a scramble on the sidewalk for the strings of brightly colored plastic.

Even though it was October, it was still the tropics and it was still hot as hell. I got rid of the jacket, and sweat poured down my chest, but I hardly noticed the heat. Everywhere, people would hand us a beer or some unidentifiable drink. At one point, Ross danced past the float, his chest heavily painted, wearing a pair of jeans. He screamed something at me that I couldn't decipher and handed me a Jell-O shooter, which I politely gave to the Duchess. The music and excitement were everywhere, and I lost myself in the moment. After all, I was the Baron of the Biscayne Skies. I could afford to lose myself.

It took us more than five hours to make it back to the King's house. During that time we had unloaded a huge amount of plastic into the streets. I had lost Scot and Tony, who jumped off of the float as we passed Monarch Court to go handle the setup for breakfast, and then go to sleep.

As the floats were parked, the members of the order quickly drifted off into the night. Soon, I sat alone on the front of my float. Louie came over to me with a fresh bottle of champagne and two glasses.

"You should be home," he observed as he poured me a glass.

"That I should, but I really don't want the evening to end." I took my glass. He toasted me silently and we drank. I was invigorated enough by the evening to be brazen. "Louie, are you really as weird as you appear?"

Louie laughed loud and hard. "I suppose I am. I don't think of it as weird, Aidan. I think of it as free of pretext. I live my life to my own standards, and really don't care whether the rest of society shares them." He took another sip of his champagne, and added quietly, "Much like a relative of yours."

I nodded. Perhaps there was more to Albert than I really had fathomed. Louie took my frock coat off of the float, folded it and handed it to me. "You're a good addition to the Order, young man. Just always remember, be true to yourself, and live your life according to what you believe is right, and God knows where you may wind up. Maybe even as the Monarch of Key West."

I took the coat, finished my champagne, thanked Louie for every-thing, and walked back up the driveway towards home. The sky began to lighten with the pre-dawn glow, and there was an amazing serenity in the streets. Monarch Court was silent except for the wind in the palms and banyan trees. I climbed the front steps of my Victorian monstrosity and looked out over the street. The last eight months had been full of stress and activity. Tonight, for the first time in almost a year, I felt like I had let my hair down. Tonight, for the first time, I felt like I was actually at home in Key West.

I walked into my house and went to bed.

JASON

The next night was the Order of the Conch Ball. It was a costume ball of unimaginable proportions. We raised approximately eleven thousand dollars for the charity that year. It was an impressive affair, but to be perfectly honest, after a week of debauchery, no one really had the energy for it. I had a thoroughly good time, but was home by midnight. And then, it was November.

Our bookings really picked up at that point, and we were actually booked solid every weekend. The weather turned cooler, which in Key West means it dropped below ninety. I was extraordinarily busy, so I was unprepared for the news when George called the Sunday night following Halloween. I was sitting in the library paying bills, and Scot was sprawled across the love seat reading *A Prayer for Owen Meany*, when the phone rang.

"Hello?"

"The opening shot has been fired on Fort Sumter," was George's opening gambit.

"Why can't you say hello like normal people?" I complained. He ignored me.

"I am now reading from the New Orleans court docket. Attorneys today, in the 'Superior Court of New Orleans filed a proxy battle on behalf of one Jason Metior, minor, against his mother, Phoebe Metior, for alleged misuse of funds. The suit was brought by one Vivian

Fitzgerald Medlicott, surviving sister of the child's father, Albert Fitzgerald, who seeks custody of the child.'"

I sighed. "What does 'proxy battle' mean?"

"It means that she is attempting to sue on Jason's behalf that he is being abused."

"Well," I snarled, "who would know that better than an aunt eight hundred miles away who never met the child?"

"Let's hope the court sees that, but we'd be fools to bet on it. For all we know, Jason might be wooed to her side when he discovers how much money he has. After all, he *is* in puberty. He may have some real issues with his mother."

I thought back to puberty and shuddered. I began to come up with plans on how to fight my aunt, before a small voice reminded me that it was not my battle to fight. I asked quietly, "Is there anything I can do to help?"

George didn't answer for quite some time. Finally, he took a deep breath and asked, "What are your plans for Thanksgiving?"

The lawsuit was on the docket for June. Phoebe's attorney was planning to seek a dismissal on the grounds that the suit was meritless. I would be called as a witness to help discredit my aunt. If that failed, we would have to go to court. In order to be credible, I had to spend some time with Phoebe and Jason and determine if I did, indeed, feel she was a competent mother. It had been Phoebe's idea to invite me for Thanksgiving.

I told the guys that I would need to take those days off. They weren't terribly amused since we were heavily booked that weekend. I also think that none of the three of us had been actually looking forward to the holiday, and the fact that I was bailing out on them didn't play well. Nonetheless, they accepted it as something I felt I had to do.

On the Wednesday before Thanksgiving, I packed some Dockers, a few nice shirts and a pair of boat shoes in my duffel bag, said goodbye to the guys, and headed for the airport. When I arrived, I was unexpectedly met by George.

"Okay, remember," he cautioned as I carried my bag onto the aircraft, "don't act like a Fitzgerald. Don't try to improve her life. Don't work to save the world. Just try to form a credible, impartial view point of her competence as a mother."

"Relax," I told him as I stuffed the bag in the galley and walked back down the aisle. "I'm a McInnis. I'll do as I'm told. No hero acts." I walked around the plane and began to do run down the pre-flight checklist.

"Yeah, so you keep telling me. Do you remember her address?"

"107 Huntlee." I wiped some oil from the engine cowling.

"She's going to meet you at the airport and drive you over to her place."

I kicked the left main gear. "Then why does it matter if I know her address?"

He looked cross. "I don't know. It just does."

I finished walking around the aircraft. "Christ, George, have you always been this much of a mother hen?"

George started to say something, then changed his mind. He shook his head as though to banish a thought. "Maybe you're right. Have a good trip. Call me if you need *anything.*" Without waiting for a response, he turned and walked towards the hangar exit.

"I could use some help with the property taxes on the plane," I called after him. He ignored me and left the hangar.

I pulled the chocks and got Sam Kinner to help me roll the plane out onto the apron, and then climbed aboard. Although I flew her a lot, I was almost never aboard the *Biscayne Voyager* alone. I settled myself into my seat, flipped through my charts and did my preflight calculations. After about 30 minutes, I knew precisely where I was going and what I needed to do to get there. I flipped on the batteries, the fuel pumps and started the engines. I called to the tower and requested permission to taxi. It was granted, and I pulled the plane out of the shadow of the hangar. As I emerged into full daylight, a flash of motion caught my eye.

As I have said before, she is a beautiful plane, but a bitch to taxi. It is extremely difficult to see what is in front of you, and so you are always reacting quickly to any flash of movement or random reflection. I stopped momentarily and craned my head in the direction the flash had come from. There was nothing there, but in my imagination I thought I had seen a man in his sixties with white hair, a blue denim shirt and khaki slacks.

I thought I had seen Albert.

"Jesus, Aidan," I berated myself. "Aren't you a little old to be seeing ghosts?"

I taxied to the end of the runway and was given clearance to depart. After doing a quick mag check, I pushed the throttles forward. The plane responded as she always did. About twelve hundred feet down the runway, the rear wheel lifted off, and a moment later, the front gear left the ground. I executed a slow graceful arc to the north, and set my course north by northwest.

As I reached my cruising altitude, I again thought about what I had seen. If I was going to see Albert's ghost anywhere, it would have been in the hangar. After all, he died there, directly beneath the airplane.

Once, when I was a kid, my Boy Scout troop had journeyed from Chicago to Dayton, Ohio for one of those huge, noisy pilgrimages called jamborees. This one was held at the Air Force Museum, which is the government's repository for historic aircraft. For a budding pilot geek like myself, the place was paradise.

Our troop got to spend the night inside the museum, which is a pretty damn spooky place. The reason it is spooky is that a number of the aircraft were returned to service or brought to the museum after a crewmember had been killed in action. There are hundreds of stories of how the planes are haunted, and a distinct melancholy hangs over the place at night. Whenever I am alone on the plane, I remember that place and think of Albert.

"Ever go to Dayton, Albert?" I asked aloud. I heard nothing but the hum of the engines.

"No, huh? Well, you should. It really is the garden spot of western Ohio. Well, garden spot if you're growing smoke stacks. But it's the birthplace of aviation, so I would have thought you might have visited there. I had a friend in college who was from there. He said Wright Brothers worship qualifies as an organized religion. Tax free status and all."

Again, nothing but the hum of the engines. Not even turbulence.

"Was that you I saw on the runway? What's it like to see the plane take off without you? I've never seen that before, but if that was you, I guess you've been watching it for about nine months now."

The radio crackled and directed me to turn north. I complied.

"You know, I am still amazingly pissed at you. Pissed at George. Pissed at Vivian. But especially you. For months now, I've tried to figure out what you had in mind giving me the inn, but not enough money to do anything with it. *Did* you have something in mind? Or did you just give it to me to give me something? I can't help but feel the whole will was some kind of puzzle you wanted me to figure out.

"And while we are on the subject of things I don't understand, why the hell didn't you ever tell me about Jason? Huh? Christ, it is not like I'm Vivian. But I would have liked to know. Now, here I am, heading off to New Orleans to meet this Phoebe person so she can subpoena me to testify on her behalf.

"Hell, why didn't you tell the family? You always complained that we were a family of game players, and then you go off and play the biggest game of all. Does Jason know about his family? I admit, we aren't much at times, but we're better than nothing.

"And hell, what's wrong with us, after all? Vivian has perpetuated most of the games in this family. Well, and Uncle Jeff. But shit, Bart and Caitlin and I turned out okay and you couldn't have been any more surrounded in family politics than we were."

I adjusted the yaw damper. "Of course, you wouldn't know that, would you? Bart and Cait were nothing more than names on the bottom of a Christmas card, and I only visited once a year. But you know, *you* could have made an effort. Was the family so bad that you had to hide from us? You know, in this world you can fight or you can flee. From what I've seen, you fled."

Air Traffic Control asked me to lower my speed and warned me of oncoming aircraft. I eased the throttles back and looked for the plane. He was about twenty thousand feet above me.

"And what did you flee from? Mom doesn't play politics. If anything, Mom said she worshipped you when you were little. Did you run away from her for a reason?"

Again, I was answered only by silence. In the distance, I could make out the gulf coast on the horizon. I would be in New Orleans in about twenty minutes. "Well Albert, I'm about to meet your son. Sorry to break the family moratorium, but apparently the only way to keep him with Phoebe is to turn Fitzgerald against Fitzgerald. So, even though you tried to hide him from the politics, he's now going to be stuck in the very middle of it. This wouldn't have happened if you had just made him part of the family to begin with.

"But, then again, I also don't imagine you expected to die."

The coastline glided beneath the plane, and in the distance I could see the sun shimmering off of Lake Pontchartrain. Air traffic control directed me to my approach vector, and I turned the plane accordingly. "Truly, Albert, now more than ever, I could use your advice."

Albert said nothing.

I forgot about him as I became busy with the landing preparations. As I descended into my final approach, I pulled the gear handle. I heard the reassuring "ka-chunk" as they locked down, and I brought the plane down in New Orleans.

I taxied to a small general aviation hangar and locked up the plane. After paying the exorbitant parking fee to a wizened little man with an impenetrable Cajun accent, I picked up my duffel bag and headed towards the parking lot. There was one woman, sitting against the hood of a dusty old Ford Thunderbird convertible. She was neither old nor young. As is often the case with working southern women, she wore her hair too long for her age. It was brown with a little bit of gray at the roots. She wore jeans and a green golf shirt. She was smoking nervously as she scrutinized everyone who came through the door.

I crossed the parking lot, headed directly towards her. She stood up, threw the cigarette in the grass, and ran her hand down her legs, smoothing the fabric of her jeans.

"Shit, I would know you anywhere," she said as I drew close. "I'm Phoebe."

I extended my hand, and she shook it. It was a strong, no-nonsense handshake.

"I'm Aidan. You would, huh?"

"You look just like Albert. Well, Albert when he was younger. And thinner. And less arrogant." She opened the car door and told me to get in.

I am often amazed by how New Orleans can be suffocatingly humid and still feel dusty at the same time. I dropped my bag in her back seat and got in. "Arrogant?" I asked.

"Oh, hell, yes. Don't tell me you never noticed it. The older he got, the more arrogant he got. The last time I saw him, he was practically swaggering."

Her voice was an interesting mixture of alto, cigarettes and Jack Daniels. It was not unlike trying to imagine Colleen Dewhurst playing Blanche DuBois. Her accent was not pure Cajun, and betrayed a little bit of education. Up close, I could tell that she was only a couple years older than me, which would have made her significantly younger than Albert.

We talked as we drove to Algiers. I learned that she lived with her mother, that she was a waitress in a diner, and that she had taken the day off to get me. As she talked, she fumbled nervously for a cigarette. After failing to light it three times, she muttered "Well, shit," and threw it out of the car.

"Are you okay?" I asked. "You seem nervous."

She smiled and glanced sideways at me. "Of *course* I'm nervous. I feel like I'm auditioning here."

"Auditioning?"

"Sure. If I don't appear to be a good enough mother, I lose my kid."

I stretched. Interstate 10 slid along beneath us, leading towards the river. "I think you are overstating my importance just a bit. I'm not Social Services. All I am is a relative. Best case, you're fit and I testify on your behalf. Worst case, I don't think you're fit, and you never call me to the stand."

"How do I know you won't help out this Vivian person?"

I laughed. "You'd have to meet my aunt to know how truly reprehensible she is. No one in my family is likely to help her. I can't believe Albert never told you about her."

"Who says he didn't? Albert told me all about his family. You don't sound like particularly nice people."

I was growing tired of apologizing for my family. "We're better than Albert gave us credit for. Of the four kids, Albert and my mother were pretty normal. Uncle Jeff is not so much evil as simply unable to abide anyone else's happiness. Only Vivian is the wicked witch of the Midwest. But, I guess you will have to observe me long enough to determine if you can trust me, while I try to determine if you're a fit mother."

"Fair enough." She began to relax a little. We crossed the river, and pulled off the interstate on the General Meyer exit. To our right, an immense housing project loomed over the shore. Broken windows and missing doors opened into an impenetrable blackness. In the center rose an enormous, eerie tower; clearly derelict yet, sadly, also clearly occupied.

I turned my attention back to Phoebe, who had somehow succeeded in getting a cigarette lit while my attention was distracted. "What does Jason know?"

"He knows that his cousin Aidan is coming to visit. He knows that his wicked evil Chicago aunt is suing for custody. He knows there is money involved, but not how much. That's about it."

We turned onto Huntlee and pulled up in front of a tiny ranch house. It was clean, and well maintained, but clearly old and poorly built. I wondered silently that Albert had never bought her a better house. "This the best you could do, Sport?" I asked him silently.

"Did Jason know Albert well?" I asked as I got out of the car.

"Pretty well. As well as he could, given the distance. Much better than I knew my own dad." We walked into the house, and I came face-to-face with the boy whose picture sat in my desk; a boy who, now two years older and in the throes of puberty, very much resembled my side of the family. A boy who, in fact, bore no small resemblance to me.

"Jason," Phoebe said, "This is your cousin Aidan." I held out my hand. He took it and shook it nervously.

"Hi," I offered.

"H'lo," he countered tentatively.

And the relationship began with an awkward silence. The three of us stared at each other for a minute, and then Phoebe said, "Well, Aidan, you'll be sleeping in with Jason. Jase, take Aidan's stuff to your room."

Jason picked up my bag and disappeared into the back of the house. At the same moment, a pair of saloon doors that led to the kitchen swung open, and from them emerged an older, grayer version of Phoebe. She dried her hands on a kitchen towel.

"Aidan, this is my mother, Aileen. Mom, this Aidan, Jase's cousin."

The old lady smiled at me, but a wary look never left her eyes. She held out her hand. "Welcome to 'Nawlins."

I shook her hand. "Thank you. I appreciate the invitation."

Another awkward silence. Again, Phoebe came to the rescue. "Anyone want a drink?"

Aileen shot her daughter a warning look. Phoebe looked panicked for a second.

"Sure," I told her.

She sighed a heavy sigh of relief. "Thank God. I thought I had slipped up for a minute. I had visions of you stomping right back out of the house and going back to Florida."

"Because you offered me a drink? You think maybe family names like McInnis and Fitzgerald mean I'm a teetotaler?"

Everyone laughed and the tension was broken. We all walked back into the kitchen. Phoebe pulled three beers from the refrigerator and handed one to each of us. "I'm Irish as well," Aileen volunteered.

"With a name like Aileen, I would assume you would have to be." I toasted the two ladies. "Happy Thanksgiving." They chimed my toast back at me, and we sat down around a battered aluminum dinette set that was crammed into the dining area. "Native Irish?" I asked.

"Oh no," she replied. "Third generation. My mom's family emigrated during the famine through Savannah. They kept moving west until they ran out of steam in Louisiana."

The sound of the conversation lured Jason from his bedroom. He looked into the kitchen tentatively, and then came in and sat on one of the counters.

Phoebe glanced at her son, then turned her attention to me. "So Albert left you the plane?"

I nodded as I took a sip of the beer. "That he did. I don't know what he had in mind by leaving it to me, but it's come in handy since he's been gone. We use it to fly charters around the Keys. It's a nice supplemental income to the inn."

"George was telling me about that. Albert must be horrified, wherever he is. He hated passengers."

I nodded, but kept my thoughts on what Albert could do with his opinions to myself. I must admit though, the thought came more out of habit than any real spite.

"You run an inn and a charter business?" Aileen asked. "That must take a lot of work."

I told them about Tony and Scot, and about how we divided up the responsibilities. They asked me other questions, and I talked for about an hour about life in Key West. Jason was silent but appeared to hang on every word.

It was about five when I offered to take them to dinner. "After all, it is the least I can do since you're feeding me tomorrow."

Aileen and Phoebe agreed, and disappeared to their bedrooms to change clothes. I looked at Jason and asked, "Can you tell me where to get cleaned up, bud?"

He nodded. "Down here." And led me down the hall. His room was on the front of the house, and the bathroom was directly across the hall. I walked in, opened my duffel bag, and pulled out a clean shirt. I also pulled out a bottle of champagne I had brought for tomorrow. Jason looked at it closely, then quickly lost interest. "Does the plane still leak oil from number two?"

I had my back to him, so he couldn't see me smile. Albert had always cursed the oil leak in the number two engine. It had dogged him for years. Oddly enough, it had cleared up when I inherited the plane. "Not really. Your dad must have done something to it right before he died, because I haven't had any oil leaks since I've owned the plane. Either that, or he's now haunting the number two engine, and it doesn't dare leak."

He smiled. He was looking down at the floor, so his long dark hair fell into his face. He dug into the carpet with one of his toes, apparently lost for small talk to keep the conversation going. I decided to throw him a line. "Did you spend much time on the plane?"

He looked up and smiled. "Yeah. Every year when I would go to Key West in the summer, he would come pick me up in it and bring me back in it. It's a cool old plane."

"That it is," I agreed as I picked up the champagne and walked back down the hall to the kitchen. "You interested in planes?"

"Oh yeah. I think I want to be a pilot some day. Mom says you used to work for an airline. Were you a pilot?"

We were alone in the kitchen. I set the bottle on the table and leaned against the counter. "Close to it. I was just about to transfer to flying the line when I lost my job."

"That sucks," he offered.

"Yeah, it does."

"Would you go back if they asked you?"

I contemplated the question for a moment. The idea never even occurred to me. Airlines lay off lots of people. They don't usually hire them back. I thought about the Boston winters, the traffic out to Logan Airport every single day, having my weekends free. "No, probably not," I said honestly.

Phoebe and Aileen came into the kitchen and I held out the bottle to them. "This is for tomorrow. You know, to celebrate the holiday."

They thanked me and put it in the refrigerator, although I guessed from their reaction that they really weren't champagne people. We went to dinner.

Since I had not spent much time in New Orleans, and none in the French Quarter, it was decided that we would go there for dinner. We piled into Phoebe's car and drove down to the river and the ferry terminal. We had arrived just in time to catch the ferry before it backed out and made the hourly trip across the river to the Quarter. We climbed up to the glass-enclosed deck, and I watched, fascinated, as the ferry slid silently out of dock and steamed across the river. During the entire trip, Jason stood next to me, explaining how New Orleans worked from his perspective.

Once we docked, we walked up Canal Street. Phoebe explained that the intersection of Canal and Bourbon formed the boundary of the French Quarter. We would not, however, be going all the way to Bourbon. Although New Orleans had been cleaned up a good deal in recent years, there was still a lot of booze and pornography readily available in the Quarter, if you looked hard enough. She indicated Jason and said, just loud enough for me to hear, "I'll have a hard enough time keeping him off Bourbon in another year or two, anyhow. There's no need to take him on an advance scouting expedition."

Canal Street was clean, but the buildings were old, and obviously hard used. As a streetcar clattered past us and up the middle of the street, we turned down a small alley. I'm not sure I ever would have noticed it if I had been alone; and if I had, I certainly wouldn't have entered it. The buildings were narrow, and tall, dark windows crossed with iron bars loomed in the walls above. They betrayed no light to the street below. The brick walls were caked with decades of soot and grime. This absence of reflected light spread a pallor across the surroundings. Phoebe expertly led the way down the alley to a spot where a few steps led down from the sidewalk. At the bottom, they met an archway in the base of one of the more forbidding looking structures. The arch was lit with a single exposed bulb which glowed with a sickly, apologetic light. Phoebe opened the door, and a joyful clatter of plates, glasses and conversation spilled into the alley, carried aloft on a steamy blast of Old Bay seasoning.

The door led into a basement restaurant with a bar and maybe twenty tables. Well-worn red-and-black linoleum tiles dully reflected the light from the dusty milk glass fixtures overhead. Phoebe led us to a table covered with newspaper, and explained that this was one of the best places in the entire Quarter for steamed crabs. It may have had a name years ago, but it was lost in the mists of time. Most people simple called it "da place."

Phoebe ordered for all of us, and a pitcher of beer was delivered almost immediately. A few minutes later, an enormous tin tray arrived, piled high with steaming crustaceans. We dug in.

It was an interesting experience being alone with a family of strangers. They were clearly different from my family, but not so different under the surface. Phoebe perpetually corrected Jason's manners. Jason made a careful study of ignoring her instructions. They were working class, but not uneducated. They clearly loved each other, but also clearly got on each other's nerves. And, apparently, they all missed Albert.

As we ate, we reminisced about Albert. Phoebe emphasized it had been her choice not to get married, not Albert's. She had not wanted to leave New Orleans, and because of his business, he couldn't leave Key West. Albert came to New Orleans whenever he could, and had taken reasonably good care of them.

With my lips stinging from the Old Bay, I asked Jason about his trips to Key West. He told me that he had gone every summer up until Albert died. When they were there, Albert would take him up on the plane or out fishing. Jason, like me, detested fishing, but went along because it was one of Albert's favorite pastimes. I asked if Jason had ever met the Monarch of Key West.

"Who's that?" he asked as he wrestled a claw from his fifth crab. I smiled and remembered George's comment that Albert had protected everything he treasured from Louie. "He's one of my neighbors. Crazy old guy who is kind of like the island's mascot."

"Nope. Never met him," he said and immediately lost interest.

Dinner was a long, languorous affair that set me back almost nothing at all. At Jason's request, we detoured into Cafe Du Monde on our way back to the ferry for beignets. I had gorged myself on crabs, so I watched with a mixture of awe and nausea as Jason, who had eaten three crabs more than I had, polished off a plate of a half dozen fried dough triangles. I reminded myself that I had once had a similar appetite. I miss that metabolism.

We returned from dinner around midnight and retired to bed soon after. Jason had bunk beds, and I was consigned to the lower bunk. I smiled as I reflected on the number of times I had made Bart sleep in the lower bunk. He would feel a particular sense of satisfaction at the moment.

Over the course of the evening, Jason had lost all inhibitions towards me. He asked all kinds of questions about the plane and about the inn and about what life was like in Key West. I told him as best I could. After a while, we both grew silent and I began to drift off to sleep. He startled me back to consciousness with a single question. "Is your family really as bad as Dad said they were?"

I thought for a moment about how to phrase my answer. "Well, in the first place, they're *our* family. And truthfully some of them are. Aunt Vivian and her two kids are pretty unpleasant, and Uncle Jeff is just a downright pain in the ass." He snickered. "But my parents are pretty cool. Mom's naïve sometimes. But they are really very kind people. And my sister and brother are two of the finest human beings on the entire planet. You'll like them when you meet them."

"Aunt Vivian is the one who wants to get custody of me, right?"

"Yes, she is."

"Why?"

I thought for a minute. The kid really didn't know how much he was worth. "With Aunt Vivian, it's about control. Like any other human being, I'm sure she has a hidden good side someplace. She just keeps it quite effectively hidden." He laughed again. "Vivian has distinctive ideas about how the universe should work, and who and what everyone should be in relation to her. Unfortunately, God forgot to consult her when he threw it together, and she's been trying to clean up his mess ever since." More laughter.

His tone suddenly grew very serious. "I inherited some money from Dad."

"I know."

"Do you know how much?"

"No, not really," I lied.

"Well, Grandma says she's after the money."

"In truth, Jase, she may be, at least in part. She probably thinks that she knows better how to spend that money than you or your mom."

"I don't want to meet her," he observed.

I thought of Albert and began to realize Albert's decision to isolate Jason from the family was more emotional than logical. A little more of my anger melted away. "No, you probably don't," I told him. We were soon both asleep.

The next day, Jason was never far from me. It occurred to me that his family had been small for all of his life, and his horizons limited to New Orleans and Key West. Then, all of a sudden I appear, with tales of a complex family spread all over the country. He was definitely curious about this tribe of people to whom he was related.

Thanksgiving was an amazing affair. A far cry from the usual fare we had in Illinois, it consisted of jambalaya, corn bread, crayfish, and deep-fried turkey. I had never even heard of deep-fried turkey, and I watched with awe as Aileen dropped a twenty-pound bird into a huge gas-powered deep fryer in the back yard. As you can well imagine, it was delicious. An orgy of cholesterol, mind you, but delicious nonetheless.

During dinner, we opened the champagne, and each of us had a glass. I can only assume that no one had ever offered Jason champagne before, because he made a concerted effort to savor it, and not betray that he didn't like the taste. Phoebe and Aileen drank theirs, and then quickly switched to beer. They allowed Jason to have a second glass to "keep me company."

After Jason and I finished the dinner dishes, I asked Phoebe if I could borrow the phone, so I could call my parents and wish them a happy holiday. Jason perked up and asked if he could speak to my mother. Phoebe and I exchanged glances and, after a long minute, she nodded her approval. "Sure," I told him, and we disappeared into the living room. I dialed my calling card number, and then the number for the house in Chicago. Mom answered.

She and Dad and Bart had had a quiet dinner by themselves. I told her I was in New Orleans and was with someone who wanted to meet her. "Meet me?" she asked, confused.

I held the phone so she could hear me talk into it as I handed it to Jason. "Jason, meet your Aunt Elaine."

He took the phone and said, in a very proper manner, "Hello Aunt Elaine. I'm Albert's son." I glanced towards the kitchen door, where Phoebe leaned in the doorframe, her face a mask of uncertainty and fear.

Mom and Jason talked for a long time. Apparently they had a lot of catching up to do, so I took my champagne and walked back into the kitchen with Phoebe. We sat across the table from each other and sipped our drinks.

"He's a great kid," I offered.

"Thanks. He definitely is."

"And you are quite obviously a great mother."

She smiled at me, relieved, and said, "Thanks again."

"Why haven't you told him about the money?" I asked.

She leaned back in her chair. "Well, it's a long story, but hey, you've got time. I was actually married once. Long time before Albert. I married a man from one of the old New Orleans families. Sort of Cajun aristocracy. Anyway, I married him because of everything he appeared to be. I thought he was a rebel. What he turned out to be was a lazy son of a bitch who never had to work for anything and was happy to be supported by his family while he snorted all of his money up his nose.

"Needless to say, we got divorced. There are a lot of things I'm not really proud of in my life, Aidan. I graduated from high school, but never tried to go beyond that. I got married way too young, and I got divorced way too quickly. But I never stopped working. I've had one job or the other ever since I was fifteen. I've worked hard all my life. No one ever gave me anything. I bought this house myself. I bought my car myself. And, even if Albert had never sent child support, I could have taken care of my family myself. That's what I want for Jase. I want him to be able to take care of himself and never be able to bank on the knowledge that he's got something to carry him through life. If anything is going to carry him through life, it's going to be him."

"You are a very smart lady," I told her.

She shook her head. "Nope. Just stubborn."

Jason stuck his head in the kitchen and said, "Aidan? Your mom wants to talk to you."

I retrieved the phone. "Surprise."

"Surprise indeed," she said, somewhat pensively. "What are you doing there?"

"I was invited," I replied truthfully.

There was a long, awkward silence, before she finally asked, "How is she as a mother?" I was surprised at her directness.

"From what I've seen, about as good as you were, and doing it with a lot less. Much more level headed than Albert, I might add."

Another long silence. "Is it true that Jason doesn't know about the money?"

"It is. For very good reasons. She wants him to make something of himself." More silence. I decided to play my trump card. "Mom, I need to ask you to do something particularly for me. I want you not to tell Vivian I was here." She didn't answer, so I continued. "This isn't about us. It may involve us, but we don't need to involve ourselves. Please. For me."

She took a long deep breath. "Okay. I won't tell her, and I'll ask your father not to as well." One thing about Mom, she doesn't lie.

"Thanks." The subject was closed. We exchanged a few more comments, and then hung up. As I placed the phone back in its cradle, I noticed Phoebe watching me from the kitchen. She had listened to the entire conversation.

"I pass?"

"You pass," I replied. "If you need me, I'll help. Otherwise, I'm going to stay out of it."

She nodded. "Fair enough."

I returned home the next day. Jason accompanied his mother and I to the airport and, while she smoked cigarettes, he followed me around the plane as I did the preflight. He asked a thousand questions about it, and made a point of checking everything I checked. He sat with me on the flight deck while I did the flight plan, talking non-stop. Finally, as I got ready to leave, he ventured, "Maybe I could come visit you some-time over the summer. You know, if you need help at the inn or some-thing."

I looked at him and smiled as I thought of the first time I had sug-gested to Albert that I come visit. "We'll have to talk to your mom about that, but I'd like that."

He smiled, and followed me back down to the tarmac with the enthusiasm of a puppy, making a dozens plans of things we would do when he came to visit. As we reached Phoebe, he told her excitedly, "Aidan says it's okay for me to go visit him this summer if you don't mind."

She glanced at me. "Summer's a long way off. We'll talk about it then."

I held out my hand. "Phoebe, it's been a pleasure." She took it and shook firmly.

"For me as well. Come back and visit us anytime."

"I will." I turned my attention to Jason and rubbed his head play-fully. "Take care of yourself, Sport," I told him.

"I will," he smiled.

With that, I climbed back into the plane and pulled the hatch shut. From the flight deck, I saw them walk back and stare at the plane from a distance. Phoebe was no doubt ready to leave, but Jason obviously wanted to watch the takeoff. I started the number two engine.

SIR AIDAN THE
AIRBORNE

December descended on Key West with a particular fury. Bookings remained high for both the inn and the charter business. Our finances looked healthy, but we were working non-stop. I heard nothing more from New Orleans. In truth, I never expected to.

Christmas in Key West is an odd time. Salvation Army Santas wear board shorts and flip-flops. Christmas wreaths are decorated with seashells. Red and green decorations look oddly out of sorts against the pale pastel backdrop of the city.

I was depressed.

Maybe depressed isn't the right word, but I certainly could not find the Christmas spirit. Christmas had been my favorite time of the year in Boston. The lights, the cold, the music, the food; all of it seemed perfectly choreographed. In Key West, Christmas is geared towards tourists who appreciate none of those things.

None of us would be going home to see our families. I had always stayed in Boston until Christmas Eve and then flown home to Chicago for the week between Christmas and New Years. This would be the first time in my life I had spent Christmas away from my family, and the first time since Caitlin was born that all of us weren't together.

Of course, it would also be the first Christmas Eve I didn't spend with Aunt Vivian and her pack, so there were some benefits. That aside, I was keenly aware of the things that I would miss. For instance, I knew I would miss the holiday music outside Filene's. Of course, inside the store would be overheated and way too crowded. I would also miss having the annual pre-Christmas gift exchange with Tony and Scot at Kincaid's, a small bar near Harvard Square. However, the gift exchange had gotten a little silly since we all gave each other the exact same gifts every year: books and liquor. And, I suspected we would have the exact same gift exchange this year. I would also miss the annual family venture into Marshall Field's for the after-Christmas sales. But, I generally left that sale with sweaters, and wool slacks and lots and lots of tweed. All the booty from years past now hung silently at the back of my closet in a type of cedar-lined suspended animation.

I would also miss New Year's Eve. New Year's Eve had been boys' night out for Bart and I ever since I had been able to drive. It was one night when any rivalry and frustration that we experienced as brothers was put aside and we were genuinely friends. Each year, with dates or without, the two of us spent a lot of that evening talking about our plans and hopes for the next year, and our secrets and accomplishments (or, perhaps, lack thereof) of the past year.

The sense of melancholia must have been apparent to my friends because both of them commented on it. I passed it off as just being tired, but Scot, and especially Tony, knew me well enough to know that that wasn't the case. Tony, in particular, seemed concerned.

It was the Friday afternoon before Christmas, and I had just finished wrapping the few meager presents I could afford for my family and mailed them on to Chicago. As I returned from the post office and was letting myself in the front door, Tony and Scot burst out and hustled me back down the stairs loudly.

"What's going on?" I asked, confused.

"Holiday therapy," Tony replied. At that same moment Ross pulled up in his new Jeep.

"Therapy? I don't need therapy," I protested.

"Yes you do," Scot answered and I was muscled into the back seat of the Jeep. Tony climbed in with me, and Scot jumped into the front seat. We were off before I knew what was happening.

"Where are we going?"

"To get a Christmas tree," Ross replied as he turned right on Duval. That confused me more since I knew the closest tree lot was left on Duval, near Mallory Square.

"Where?"

"South Beach."

"South Beach? *Miami???*"

"You know another South Beach?" Tony asked.

"Hey, we were going to hijack you to Boston, but we didn't think you could get us back in time to set up breakfast tomorrow," Ross observed as he turned on Bertha and headed towards the bridge.

"Especially since the plane's broken," Scot added.

The plane was not, in fact, broken. However, in order to keep its certification, it needed to be inspected before January. So I had elected to have Sam Kinner, my mechanic, give it a good thorough maintenance check. Right now, it was still in the hangar, but both engines were in his small shop on the other side of the airport. Not being able to fly had probably contributed to my sense of ennui.

"They do have Christmas trees in Key West," I observed.

"Yes they do," Tony agreed. However none of them was telling me where we were headed except to South Beach.

The drive up Highway 1 was pleasant enough. The wind was warm and smelled strongly of the ocean. It took us two hours to reach the bridge from Key Largo to the mainland, where we immediately hit Miami rush hour traffic. We didn't pull off onto Ocean Boulevard until sunset.

South Beach is where the beautiful people of Miami hang out. In our cut off shorts, sandals and tank tops, none of us were likely to be mistaken for beautiful people. I mentioned that, but it didn't seem to bother my colleagues. We drove to the north end of the beach, past some of the legendary hotels and clubs like the Colony and the Fontainebleau. Eventually, we pulled up to a large, windowless building that closely resembled a warehouse. It took me a moment to realize it was an ice rink.

We got out of the car, and Ross pulled a gym bag out from behind the back seat. My colleagues escorted me into the lobby. The place was deserted, which surprised me for a Friday. "The place hasn't opened yet," Tony confided in me as Ross disappeared through a single door. "But Ross is dating the Zamboni driver or something."

Ross reappeared. "I am not dating the Zamboni driver," he replied in a disgusted tone of voice. "I used to date the assistant manager. He's letting us break in the ice."

"We thought that there wasn't much we could do to make Key West feel like Christmas…" Scot began.

"So we decided to just beat the snot out of you at hockey," Ross concluded as he tossed me a pair of sweat socks from his bag.

"Excuse me?" I was indignant. "*No one* beats me at hockey."

"Put your money where your mouth is, Tiger," Ross answered as he retrieved some skates from the rental counter. "You get Tony."

Perhaps I should mention that I view hockey with the same reverence some people in the world accord to Islam. It is one of my few passions outside of flying. I think football and baseball are boring, and basketball devotes too much time to foul shots. Hockey, at least, always moves. I have played it ever since I was kid learning how to skate at our local rink. Living in South Florida, however, it's not a passion I often get to indulge.

Playing hockey in shorts and tank tops adds another aspect to the game entirely. Add to that the fact that Tony does not ice skate well, and you begin to get the picture of how the game went. The bet was one beer per goal, losing team buys. Tony and I versus Scot and Ross. The match began simply enough with Ross and I facing off, Tony and Scot playing goal.

Unfortunately, Ross hits for power, while I play more strategy. The downside of playing strategy alone is you can't exactly pass the puck. Consequently, I spent most of my time chasing the puck, which Ross had sent careening wildly across the ice. He scored two points on me almost immediately, mostly because Tony jumped out of the way of the puck every time it came at him.

I had to rethink my strategy. We decided to leave the goal unattended, which was not as much a risk as you might think since Ross doesn't exactly line up his shots. He just hits and allows the puck to ricochet off the boards in whichever direction suits its mood.

Tony playing wing was only slightly better than playing without him. To his credit, however, he scored the first two points, which would have been fine if he hadn't skated into the goal after them. Scot stopped playing goal after Tony plowed over him the second time.

Twice, Ross and I got into a face-off where neither one would surrender the puck. The first time, I succeeded in skating him backwards into the boards to break it free, and scored a goal which took us into the lead. I was pretty damn proud of myself. The second time, he leaned forward and kissed me on the nose, which caused me to lose my balance (not to mention my composure), and he scored a goal on me. Then, to add insult to injury, he followed it up with a figure eight and a poorly executed triple lutz right next to me.

"Would you get serious, you big ice fairy," I growled at him, as he skated another circle around me.

The score stayed tied for the most part of the match. We were finally down to the game point, when Ross broke free of me and made a full-rink press on poor Tony towards our unguarded goal. Tony didn't know how to block; his skill was pretty much limited to body checking. So, he played to his strength and then skated up behind Ross and pulled his shorts down to his ankles. Ross was unable to stop, and fell backwards on his butt, sliding about twenty feet down the ice. Meanwhile, Scot rescued the puck, lined up a shot, and sent it careening majestically into his own goal. Tony and I were exuberant to the point of obnoxiousness.

We had pretty badly scuffed up the ice, and briefly considered taking the Zamboni out to fix it (a childhood fantasy of mine), but we couldn't find the keys. So, we packed up and headed back to Key West. We considered stopping to buy a Christmas tree in Miami, but since we would have to tie it to the roof of the Jeep, we decided against it. A two-hour drive at seventy miles an hour was pretty much guaranteed to remove all of the needles on the side of the tree facing up. Plus, Ross had one hellacious ice burn on his ass, and wasn't in the mood for a lot of moving around.

He and Scot did, however, owe Tony and me drinks to celebrate our victory. We were going to stop at a bar in Miami, but the parking in South Beach is notoriously bad, and Ocean Boulevard was almost impassable, so we went back to the island. Before getting the tree we decided to stop at Sloppy Joe's so Ross could discharge his debt.

The four of us settled in at a corner of the bar and began recounting the match. As Tony and I were regaling the bartender with tales of hockey prowess, Santa Claus came into the bar and sat down next to Ross. He ordered a Canadian Club Manhattan. The four of us exchanged glances, and then continued talking as the bartender delivered Santa his drink.

After a few minutes, a second Santa joined the first and ordered a dirty Bombay martini. He exchanged a few remarks with the first Santa, and then began a long diatribe against the largest department store on the island. The first Santa listened sympathetically, making a few polite remarks at appropriate points.

Ten minutes into the story, the two Santas were joined by two more Santas, an angel and an elf. The second Santa was not at all happy to see the elf (who ordered a gimlet), and began to criticize his prowess as a photographer. The elf was not in the mood to hear it. "Ah, shut your eggnog hole," he snarled back. The first Santa made an off-color joke that seemed to break the tension. Meanwhile, the angel pulled a pack of cigarettes out of her purse and asked Ross for a light.

By now, our conversation had died down, and we were mesmerized by the squad of Santas and their associated hangers-on. We ordered another round. A fifth Santa joined the party. This was clearly the Santa that all the others had been waiting for. They all became more animated, and even the second Santa, the one with the sour disposition, seemed to lighten up and enjoy himself. They all had another drink.

I could see why they had been waiting for the fifth Santa. He was the life of the party. He was everywhere, telling jokes, buying drinks, flirting with the angel. He joined the four of us briefly and asked what we wanted for Christmas. I told him money. Scot told him money. Tony told him money. Ross told him Antonio Banderas.

The Santa promised to see what he could do, and then ordered everyone at the bar a round of Kamikazes. All of us drank the shots, and then he ordered another round for just the Santas. He regaled the bar with a loud tale of how Louie Robideau had come by and related the Monarch's elaborate Christmas wishes which included, among other things, Van Gogh's ear. The Santas, angel and elf treated this as though it was the funniest thing they ever heard. After another round of drinks, they decided that they would head over to Louie's house with a piece of chicken skin and tell him it was Van Gogh's ear. They paid their tab, and stumbled merrily out into the street.

Ross looked at the bartender incredulously. "What was all that?"

The bartender shrugged. "Department store Santas. They need to unwind after work, just like everyone else."

"I bet that last one does great with the kids," Scot observed.

The bartender shook his head. "Oh, that one isn't a department store Santa. He's the Salvation Army Santa that works the corner of Duval and South. He goes off the wagon every Christmas."

We left shortly afterwards, and wandered over to the Christmas tree lot near Mallory Square. We bought one and hauled it back home.

Owning a Victorian house precludes certain problems that people who live in modern homes experience, and creates a whole host of others. My house has twelve-foot ceilings, so almost no Christmas tree is too tall. On the other hand, unless the tree is ten feet tall or more, the high ceilings make it look like a houseplant. Moreover, a ten-foot tall tree requires an ungodly number of decorations.

We bought an eight-foot tree.

"It's too short for in here," Ross observed as we stared at the tree where it stood in front of the living room windows.

"No it's not," I countered. "Besides there is no other room to put it in."

"Put it outside. It just looks silly in here."

I still resisted. "Who puts their Christmas tree outside?" I asked horrified.

"People who live in South Florida. Trust me on this. Times like this are precisely why you have a queen in your life. Put the tree on the patio."

We put the tree outside. Actually, putting it out there had a number of benefits. First of all, there were no needles to clean up. Secondly, it was more to scale in the gazebo next to the bar. Finally, by putting it there, we were able to share it with the guests.

I hated it on the patio. Although the hockey game had done a lot to put me in a good mood, it still didn't feel like Christmas, and having my Christmas tree next to the swimming pool did nothing to improve matters.

Soon it was Thursday, Christmas Eve. Christmas Eve and Christmas night were the only two nights that we weren't booked. Jake explained to me that this is not at all uncommon. Some guesthouses were packed at holidays, but those two days often saw a drop in bookings, depending on where they fell in the week. Christmas at the end of the week usually meant lighter bookings as people decided to celebrate the holiday at home before heading off to the sunshine. They were the only two days of the high season when you could say that.

Christmas Eve morning found me adding my gifts to Tony, Scot and Ross to the meager pile under the tree. As I stood up, someone behind me said, "Merry Christmas, fly-boy." I turned around and saw Olivia standing there. She was smiling and wearing casual clothes, which was an uncommon but flattering look for her.

"Merry Christmas to you as well," I replied. "I didn't expect to see you here. I thought you never came home at the holidays."

"I don't usually. I decided to be different this year. Listen, my father wants to know if you guys have plans tonight for dinner. If not, he'd love to have you 'spend Christmas Eve at court.'" She managed to avoid the usual contempt she reserved for the word *court*.

We had no plans. Ross was going to come over, and we were going to send out for pizza. I accepted the invitation.

The guys had no objections to going to Louie's (including Tony, which made me wonder if he was running a fever), and we presented ourselves at the Palace-in-Dayglo at the appointed hour of 7:00 pm. As you might expect, the Christmas decorations were over the top. As Tony observed, "The whole place looks like some demented idea of a shopping mall Santaland." The entire front yard was full of elves and reindeer and huge wrapped presents. Also prominently featured were menorahs and nutcrackers and several six-foot tall dreidels.

A crèche had been set up in the corner of the front yard. However, the roles of the wise men were being played by three lawn jockeys whose jackets had been painted different, vivid neon colors. In their customary position of one elbow cocked up and one down with out stretched hand, they looked less like they were venerating the Christ-child and more like they were busting a dance move. Ross pointed them out by exclaiming, "Look! Mary, Joseph and the Pips."

What was most odd about the whole scene, however, was the complete absence of people. I had never been to Louie's house when it wasn't just crawling with people. However, there was hardly a sound, and clearly no one was about. It gave the entire scene a kind of surreal quality; but I guessed that even hangers-on have families to spend the holidays with.

We walked up onto the front porch and rang the bell. After a moment, Olivia came and opened the door. She kissed each of us on the cheek as we filed in.

"I've never seen this place so empty," I observed as we gave her the bottle of champagne we had brought.

"Neither have I," she said furtively. "I haven't been alone with him in this house ever since my mother died. It's kind of creepy."

She led us through the dining room into the kitchen where she made us drinks. The smell of something roasting in the oven was heavenly. "Where's your dad?" Scot asked.

"Outside on the back porch. You guys go on out. I'll be there in a minute."

The four of us filed out onto the back porch where Louie was seated in an Adirondack chair, reading. He was wearing a simple golf shirt and a pair of khakis. The whole scene would have seemed unusually mundane and totally out of context for a man so dedicated to being anything *but* mundane if he had not also been wearing a gold turban with an enormous purple stone on the front.

"Gentlemen!" he exclaimed as we came outside. "Merry Christmas. Happy Hanukah. Joyeux Noel. Festive Kwanzaa."

Each of us wished him a happy holiday of some sort. He motioned us to four empty chairs with his scepter. As we sat down, I noticed that he looked a little pale and tired, and my mind flashed back to Olivia asking if I thought her father was well several months ago.

"I trust the holidays are treating you well," I commented.

"That they are, Sir Aidan. That they are. Other than I have a hell of a cold."

It took me about five minutes of diagramming that sentence in my head to realize what was wrong with it. He had neglected to use the royal *we*.

"We were surprised that there was no crowd here tonight," Scot observed.

"No, there's not," Louie replied, sipping his oversized martini. "Olivia hasn't come home for Christmas in several years, and we thought it might be nice to get to know each other all over again without a cast of extras."

Olivia came out onto the porch. "Dinner's in about five minutes," she volunteered as she sank down to sit at the floor at her father's feet. She took a sip of the red wine she was carrying, glanced at me and winked.

We exchanged some pleasant small talk for, perhaps, fifteen minutes which seemed, again, wholly out of context. The conversation was interrupted by the sound of a kitchen buzzer. "That's my cue," Olivia sighed, and stood up. She glanced at me and asked, "Help me get dinner on the table?"

"Sure," I replied and trailed her into the kitchen. Out of the corner of my eye, I caught Scot's forlorn look at not having been chosen.

As she pulled a huge ham out of the oven, I remarked, "You and your dad seem to be getting along much better than usual."

She nodded and smiled as she put the ham on the counter. "You know, on his own, he can be interesting…caring…even quite charming I guess. I just so rarely get to see him without a damn audience around…" She handed me a knife and fork. "Carve the ham for me?"

I took the utensils and cut into the meat. She carried a large green-bean casserole into the dining room, and then continued as she returned. "Although, it *is* funny. Having Christmas alone was his idea, not mine. For the first time in years, I've felt like he really wanted to spend time with me, *just* me. Even when Mom was alive, I never felt like he wanted to focus his attention on anyone in particular. Especially his relatives."

I finished carving the ham and transferred it to a serving platter. "He does look tired. I guess that's his cold."

She nodded and took the platter from me. "I think it is. He certainly seemed full of energy when I got here. Do me a favor and go call everyone in to dinner."

Dinner was a sumptuous affair, much better than what we had become accustomed to. As we ate, Louie asked each of us in-depth questions about our Christmas memories, our families and what we hoped to receive for Christmas. It was an extremely pleasant dinner. As we finished, Louie turned his attention to me and commented, "My daughter tells me you're something of an aspiring writer."

I nodded as I wiped my mouth. "Aspiring is probably accurate. I haven't managed to complete anything in the last couple of years."

"Are you working on anything right now?"

I shook my head. "I've tried a couple of times to write about coming to Key West or my life in Boston, but I really haven't found the story yet. It's hard for me to get started if I don't know how it's going to end."

Louie got up while I was talking and walked over to the sideboard in the dining room. Opening a drawer, he removed a walnut box about the size of a small silverware chest and walked back over to the table. He placed it in front of me and sat back down in his chair.

I smiled at him, confused, and he motioned for me to open it. Inside, I found a partially smoked cigar, a fountain pen and a manuscript. I examined the manuscript more closely.

"It's one of the publisher's galleys for *The Old Man and the Sea*," Louie volunteered. I opened it up and began to flip through the pages, which had comments, instructions and several obscenities scrawled in the margins.

I looked at Louie. "Are these Hemingway's notes?"

He nodded. "They are. When I moved here from Vermont in fifty-two, I worked as a bartender on Duval. I met him while he was working on revising the final draft for publication. He gave me the manuscript a couple years before he died."

I continued to flip through the pages. "You know, I've never particularly enjoyed his works, but, God, I wish I could write like that."

"Well, truthfully, I've never enjoyed them either. But he taught me a lot about the creative process. He didn't sit down with the intent of writing a story. He sat down with the intent of communicating a message. All of his stories are about rather primitive people. Soldiers, hunters, bullfighters. And in all of his stories, the hero's courage and honesty set him at odds with the brutality of modern society and end in hopelessness. Admittedly, not the most upbeat message. But it was the message he wanted to get across, and he did. So maybe, instead of trying to write a story, you should try writing a message."

"Okay," Olivia interrupted. "The painter is telling the writer how to write. It's time to cut off your claret." She stood up and began to clear the dishes. "You guys want dessert?"

Everyone stood up and began to clear except Louie and me. I continued to look through the manuscript at Hemingway's rather drastic handwriting, and Louie continued to watch me from the end of the table. As everyone disappeared into the kitchen, he stood up, took his wine glass, nudged me, and silently motioned for me to follow. Reluctantly, I returned the manuscript to the box, picked up my own wine glass, and followed him out into the hall.

He led me across the foyer and throne room and into his studio, closing the door behind me. "I want to show you something else," he offered. As he began to root around in his amazingly cluttered desk, I leaned my back against the closed door. Perhaps it was the wine, but I felt that Louie was uncharacteristically approachable, which made me bold.

"Louie, what kind of relationship did you have with my Uncle Albert?"

He glanced up from the desk at me for a minute, and then continued to sort through one of the drawers. "Why do you ask?"

I shrugged. "Because I've been coming here for years and never met you until he died. My cousin Jason has been coming here for years and has never met you. Albert apparently worked very hard to keep us from ever even hearing of you."

Louie stopped looking and sat down. He rested his elbow on his desk and his chin on his hand. "Did Albert ever tell you why he came here?"

"To get away from his father and the rest of his family," I replied, from rote.

He shook his head. "That's why he left Chicago. In particular, that's why he left Chicago after a huge fight with your grandfather (which neither of them would ever discuss) on September fifteenth, nineteen fifty. But that's not why he came to Key West."

I marveled that Louie knew that much detail. The Fitzgeralds can be a vicious family, but they don't air their dirty laundry to outsiders. Although I tried, I could not ever remember Albert saying why he had chosen Key West. "I guess I don't know."

Louie finally took his head off of his hand and resumed rummaging in his desk. "Do you see the painting on the wall between the windows?"

I glanced over. "Yeah."

"Go study it while I look for this damn thing."

I walked across the studio to the painting in question. It was a rather nondescript seascape. It depicted the view of land from the sea. The clouds were dark and stormy and, on the right hand of the shoreline were white stucco buildings with red tile roofs...a large collection of Spanish-looking buildings, anyway. "What about it?" I asked.

"Keep looking."

I stared for a while longer, and then noticed that far up in the sky there was a break in the clouds. Upon closer inspection I saw something familiar: a blue, white, and silver airplane. It was, in fact, a DC-2, rendered in significantly more detail than anything else in the painting. I stared for a moment and then looked at the signature in the lower right hand corner. There was a crude outline of a nautical compass and the name A. Fitz.

"A. Fitz?" I asked incredulously.

Louie smiled at me. "He thought it made him look more sophisticated. That is until some old blue hair from Boca looked at one of his paintings and said she felt sorry for anyone named after a garden insect."

I laughed. "Aphids?" Louie nodded. "Albert was a painter?"

"Was being the operative word." Louie took a sip of his wine. "The reason Albert and your grandfather quarreled was that he wanted Albert to go into the family plumbing business and Albert wanted to be an artist. Specifically, Albert wanted to go to Northwestern to get his BFA. Your grandfather was willing to pay for college if he got a degree in business and came back to work in the company, but not otherwise. Since Albert couldn't afford college, he ran away. Became something of a drifter actually. His intention was to run away to Cuba and paint there. Unfortunately, Castro didn't really need artists."

I turned my attention back to the painting. "This is Cuba?"

"Havana, circa 1957. He took a boat over and shot a picture, then hightailed it out of there and painted it from the photograph. I have to admit, I always admired his balls for going there during the revolution."

I looked closely. I don't pretend to know much about art, but I am an engineer and have a strong background in mechanical drawing and drafting. Because of that, I was able to pick out numerous problems with perspective. I mentioned it to Louie. "It doesn't seem to be all that good."

Louie stood up and walked across the room to stand next to me. "It's adequate," he said. "Something that would sell well at one of those *starving artist* sales they have in Ramada Inn ball rooms. If you listen closely, you can even hear the painting say 'feed me.'"

I laughed out loud. "Okay, but that doesn't answer my question about your relationship with Albert. Obviously you were close to know all this detail."

He nodded and finished his wine, then took my empty glass and walked across the room to a decanter on the sideboard. "We were close. Albert and I met in a beat coffee house in D.C., of all places. Kerouac would have been proud. We discovered that both of us were artists, and had some common passions for poetry and music and a common distaste for the way the country was becoming so homogenized after the war. We were soon fast friends. We hitchhiked to Miami together with the idea of stowing away to Cuba. Instead, we just kind of kept going south and westward until we ran out of Keys." He filled the glasses and returned mine to me.

"Key West in the fifties really was still somewhat remote. That's one of the things that appealed to Hemingway. It certainly appealed to us. We would paint and then try to sell our paintings to the few tourists that came here. For the most part, these were wealthy Northeastern types who picked their art with a little more rigid criteria than 'will it match the sofa.' I sold my paintings. He didn't sell his."

"That must have killed him," I observed. Louie nodded.

"It did. Sadly, while Albert wanted to be an artist, he had anything but the artist's temperament. Being insanely competitive and being a painter are not generally a good combination. Ultimately, he went into business, which was suited to his personality. He started out flying rum out of Cuba after the revolution and before long had actually built a profitable legitimate business. He actually helped support me, because while I was a successful artist, until I got into the portrait business, I wasn't making much money. And you can rest assured, Albert loved being my sponsor."

I was certain he had. If someone beat Albert at something, he would not rest until he found something he did better than that person. "How did you finally get into the portrait business?"

"Hemingway. I painted him, he told his friends. I painted Gertrude Stein, Eugene O'Neill, eventually I had a name for myself. Anyway, Albert loved me as a friend. Albert also never forgave me for being better at something he loved. He was a basically good man who had a phenomenal number of talents, but he resented me mine. So, although we would have drinks together, party together, fish together, it always had to be on his terms. And he never, *never,* trusted me with anything he cared about...or anyone.

"The reason Albert never developed a peptic ulcer is because he could delegate blame. Nothing was ever his fault. It was mine, it was George's, it was your grandfather's. I don't think Albert blamed me for my success as a painter, but I think he wanted me to believe that he did. Thankfully, twelve years of Catholic school left me relatively immune to blame and guilt."

I mulled it over in my mind for a while before asking, "What did you want to show me?"

Louie returned to his desk and picked up a nautical sextant. I followed him, and he placed it in my hands gingerly. It was a beautiful tool; highly polished brass with a teak handle. The optics still moved smoothly on their bearings. "It's beautiful," I observed.

"It, my friend, is what Albert used to get himself to Cuba and back. During the Revolution, no one in their right mind went to Cuba except the mafia. He wasn't able to get a plane there. He wasn't able to get a boat there. But he was determined to go.

"Albert had finally made the realization that he wasn't going to make it as an artist. Before he gave it up, though, he wanted to paint Havana. He was *fascinated* with Cuba. But he wasn't going to get there in any conventional way. Well, he had taught himself how to navigate with a sextant on Lake Michigan as a kid. So he rented a boat and set out for Havana on his own one night. Got there the next morning, took the picture, and turned around for home.

"During that trip, I guess you would say he had something of an epiphany. He knew he had to give up painting, but he didn't really know what else he wanted to do. He actually had been floundering a good bit and was obsessed on what he was going *to do* to make a living. The only option that had been cleanly ruled out was plumbing.

"It gradually occurred to him that he was too focused on what he was going to *do*, not on what he wanted to achieve. While he was out there on the ocean, he sat down with a sheet of paper and defined his end game. He wanted to be comfortable enough that he didn't have to work. He wanted a life that was adventurous, but also one that gave him a home base to come back to. He wanted the freedom and means to see the world, and a group of friends to take along. And he wanted, more than anything, to avoid the kind of complacency he felt drove all the back biting in his family.

"When he got back to Key West, his whole outlook on life had changed. He stopped worrying about how he was going to survive. He just began surviving. Albert use to say that, when faced with a momentous decision, he always asked himself "Albert, does this get you closer to *the goal?*" And he always kept the sextant on his desk at work. He said it helped him stay focused on where he was going."

Louie took his wine glass and sat down on the stool in front of his easel. He took a sip of his wine and got a little wistful looking. "About a year before he died, I went over to his place one evening for a drink. It was right after you had gone back to Boston. I had been working on a portrait of King Juan Carlos and I just couldn't get the damn thing right. Olivia was busting my ass about it every single day. So I went over there just to have someone to gripe to. Eventually, we got to talking about old times and about that painting of Cuba. It had taken him almost ten years to paint it. Well, during the course of the evening, Albert really, *really* opened up to me. As you know, Fitzgeralds just don't do that."

I smiled but said nothing. The story appeared to be less about answering my question, and more about Louie needing to recount the past.

"Anyway, he was in a very different mood. He talked about how much he enjoyed your visit. But he also couldn't shake this feeling that he was never going to see you again. Well, the evening became less about me and more about him, but that wasn't uncommon with

Albert. But this time, he's reflecting on his past, and tells me 'Louie, you know what, I think I made it to the goal.' I thought that had happened years ago. Next thing I know, he tells me he's decided to sell the business and enjoy the next phase of his life. And then he gives me the sextant. He told me there were a few things that kept him on track all these years. One had been the sextant. The other was me."

He drifted off into a moment of reverie. A knock at the door suddenly snapped him back to the present. He again squared his shoulders and took on the haughty demeanor I was accustomed to. The door opened and Olivia stuck her head in. "I was wondering what happened to you two. I'm serving dessert."

"We are most pleased," the Monarch replied. "Sir Aidan the Airborne, shall we follow the lovely Lady Olivia?"

Olivia rolled her eyes. "Oh God, he's back."

My evening with Louie Robideau, artist, was over. I was again in the presence of the Monarch of Key West. I gently placed the sextant back on the desk and followed His Royal Highness to dessert.

We were back at the house by eleven, and the guys headed off to bed. I poured myself a glass of wine and carried it into the library. Since it wasn't exactly cold outside, I placed several lit candles in the small fireplace and tuned the radio to a station out of Miami that had been playing Christmas carols since mid-October. I settled onto the small couch and sipped my wine.

I had to admit there was a lot more to my uncle than I had ever imagined; a lot about my uncle which I never thought to ask him while he was alive. The idea that Albert had achieved everything he had ever wanted in life was certainly nothing new to me; it was something I admired about him. The thing that had never occurred to me was that he didn't have it all exactly planned out. I had always tried to live my life according to a set of plans and formulas. How could Albert have achieved such great success without a specific set of objectives and a detailed map of how to get there?

It may have been the wine or the candles or the thoughts circulating through my head, but I was soon fast asleep. Owing to the fact I was sitting on a small love seat, it wasn't a particularly restful sleep, and was filled with half visions and dreams, most of which circulated around the things Louie had told me that evening. I awoke the next morning as the sky was just beginning to lighten over Monarch Court.

Since there were no guests in the inn, the guys would be sleeping in this morning. I got up, went upstairs and took a quick shower. Then, I went back down to the kitchen and made cinnamon rolls, something I only do on rare occasions. Once they were in the oven, I took a cup of coffee out onto the front terrace and watched Christmas morning break over Key West.

I had been out there for about fifteen minutes when Olivia rounded the corner and walked into the court. She was walking aimlessly, not really focused. As she reached the front gate, I startled her by observing, "You're out and about awfully early."

She gave me sort of a wan smile and said, "I like to get up early on some mornings and go for a walk. It often helps clear my head."

I offered her a cup of coffee but she declined. She came up onto the terrace and sat on one of the wrought-iron chairs, but looked to be at a loss for words. "Dinner last night was great," I ventured.

"Thanks. I'm glad you enjoyed it." Again, a long, awkward lull. Eventually, she broke it by venturing, "Aidan, I think my dad is sick."

I noted her obvious concern. "Sick how?"

"Sick as in very sick. Dying maybe."

"What makes you think so?" I asked, leaning forward.

"Pills. He's got all these pills in his bathroom medicine chest. Things I recognize from when my mother died."

"Have you asked him about it?"

She shook her head. "No, I haven't. I doubt he would tell me. Louie kind of maintains this strict code of privacy. He loves being the center of attention, but he doesn't dare risk getting too close to someone by revealing intimate details of his life."

I could believe that about Louie. I had a sneaking suspicion that I had seen more of the real Louie Robideau last night than most other people who had known him for years. "Is there anything I can do?"

She smiled. "I don't know. I don't even know if there is anything I can do."

"The only thing I can suggest is to ask him."

She rolled her eyes and got up to go. "That's what I like about you, Aidan. Nothing is so obvious that it doesn't deserve mentioning. I'll talk to you later."

She walked out the gate and back up the street and I wondered whether or not I should be insulted. In the spirit of Christmas, I decided not to be. I finished my coffee and walked back up the steps. As I came back into the foyer, I met Tony as he came down the stairs.

"Good morning. Merry Christmas."

"Merry Christmas," he replied. "Who were you talking to out front?" Tony's bedroom is on the front of the house, so he can usually hear everything that occurs in the yard.

"Olivia. She's out spreading Christmas joy."

"Really? She must have seen a dead coworker's face in her door knocker last night."

Scot was up soon afterwards, and we took our coffee and cinnamon rolls out to the patio to open our gifts. As I suspected, each of us had given each other books and liquor. I opened my gift from my parents. They had sent me just what I asked for; a new landing gear solenoid for the plane. I couldn't afford to replace the faulty one on my own. Caitlin sent me one of her paintings. There was no gift from Bart.

I didn't view that as particularly odd since Bart is not always the most organized person. Frequently, for example, my birthday card had arrived the week following my birthday. I expected that my gift would arrive some time the following week. It arrived, instead, in a cab at 4:00 p.m.

I was working the desk, checking in a young couple from Chattanooga when I heard a car door close out front. We have a small brass plaque on the front gate directing guests into the back yard, which keeps them from mistakenly climbing the steps to the house itself. I heard the gate open and close, so I assumed someone hadn't bothered to read the plaque.

Tony was setting up the bar for happy hour, and Scot was somewhere in the guesthouse, so I walked around the front to find what I assumed was a wayward guest. I found, instead, my brother.

"Bart!"

He turned at the top of the steps, held up his hand and said "Merry Christmas, mon frère." He smiled and came back down the steps to hug me. He was wearing shorts and the rugby shirt I had sent him for Christmas.

"What are you doing here?" I asked.

"I'm your Christmas present. I didn't think you should spend the holiday alone, so I caught a flight first thing this afternoon."

"This is *fantastic!* God, I'm so happy to see you." I was, too. All of a sudden, it was Christmas. I took his bag from him. "You want a room or you want to bunk in with me?"

"Bunking in with you is fine. Save the rooms for paying guests." He put his arm around my shoulder and we walked up the stairs. I threw his bag on my bed and he opened it up. He produced a bottle of wine. "I thought we could split this tonight. What were you guys planning to do for Christmas dinner?"

I accepted the wine. "Honestly, we didn't have any plans. I guess maybe we'll grill some steaks. Listen, I've got to go finish up at the front desk."

"No prob. I'm going to change, and come down for a swim." He dug back into his duffel bag for his swimsuit.

I took the wine down to the kitchen, then went out back to the front desk. Tony was at the bar, and Scot was sitting on one of the stools. As I walked by I told them, "You'll never guess who was at the front door."

"Your brother," they replied in unison.

"You knew he was coming?"

"Since December first," Tony replied. "He called three times until someone besides you answered." I vaguely remembered three hang-up calls around the beginning of the month.

Bart appeared at the back door in a swimsuit and waved hello to the guys. He came down the steps two at a time and came across the patio. "Hey guys." They shook hands and exchanged small talk. Tony offered Bart a drink. Bart asked for a bourbon and Seven and then dove into the pool and began swimming laps.

"I was thinking I would grill steaks for dinner," I told the guys as I walked over to the desk to check the reservation book. We still had three more guests booked who hadn't arrived.

"Sounds great," Ross said as he walked up the walk towards the desk. "Can I kick in with you guys?"

"Absolutely," I told him. "We'd love to have you."

He was carrying three gifts, which he passed out to Scot, Tony and me. He had bought each of us Christmas ornaments. Mine was a small blue airplane. As we thanked him, Bart pulled himself out of the pool and walked over to the bar to get his drink. Ross looked at him and said "Bart, right?"

Bart smiled back. "Right." He held out his hand. "Is it Ross?"

"It is," Ross shook his hand and, I think, checked my brother out. I had an odd number of emotions sweep over me. I had very little problem with Ross being gay. I am also, however, a very protective big brother. I was used to carefully scrutinizing men who checked out my sister. I had never thought about guys checking out my brother. Bart, for his part, didn't seem to notice; or, if he did, he obviously didn't mind.

The five of us sat around the bar chatting, while the last three guests arrived. I checked them in, plus a fourth guest who was just looking for a place with a vacancy. Other guests wandered down to happy hour. There were a lot of people milling around the bar. Eventually, it was eight o'clock. Tony closed up the bar and the five of us trudged up the back stairs to the kitchen. We made more drinks, and Bart, Ross and I talked about all kinds of things.

I was due to get the plane back on the morning of the twenty-seventh, which was a good thing because I had scheduled a party run for the afternoon of the twenty-seventh. It was actually ready now, but I had made sure I had an extra day in the hopes I would have the landing gear solenoid to install. Bart was enlisted to work the party with us.

We had a late dinner that evening, and then stayed up much later talking. I was surprised that Ross hung out with us as long as he did. He didn't leave until almost midnight. Ordinarily, he cuts out fairly early.

The day after Christmas, we were extraordinarily busy. We were completely booked, and there was a lot of activity. This was the time when I enjoyed the inn the most. In addition to the usual mundane chores, we also had to set up tours, answer questions and provide directions. I enjoyed the interaction with the guests.

Ross came over around noon. Bart was floating in a pool chair, and it soon became apparent that he was the main reason Ross was here. For his part, Bart neither seemed to encourage Ross or to be turned off by the attention.

For *my* part, I was glad to see Ross. Things were too busy for me to get over to the airport with the solenoid. I walked down to the pool with the part and asked him if he would mind running it over to the airport for me.

"Not at all," Ross replied. "I need to go file some papers for tomorrow's flight anyhow." I was confused, because I could not imagine *what* paperwork would need to be filed twenty-four hours in advance. However, before I could ask, he turned his attention back to Bart and asked, "Want to come along for the ride? It'll give you a chance to get out and see the island."

Bart glanced at me, and asked, "Aidan, you care?"

I shrugged and said, "No, of course not. I'm not paying enough attention to you as it is. Go."

He looked back at Ross and nodded, then slipped into the pool, swam to the edge and got out. He dried off, pulled on his shirt and the two of them headed around front to Ross' Jeep.

I was, immediately, a swirl of emotions. This was confusing, and I wondered if I needed to protect my kid brother from one of my good friends. This thought was immediately replaced with a self-admonishment. First of all, I did not believe in the "predatory homosexual." If there was one thing Ross had taught me, the only thing gays preyed on was a good real estate deal. Moreover, Bart was twenty-four. He was more than capable of taking care of himself. I was sure that, if Ross was interested in him, he would find a way to let the poor guy down gently.

"After all," I said out loud to myself as I was doing laundry, "He's a McInnis. We're three damn good-looking kids. It's only natural for Ross to be attracted to him."

The afternoon crawled by.

They eventually returned at about four o'clock. During his last visit, Bart had been taken with the tradition of walking down to Mallory Square for the sunset, and made a point of not wanting to miss it. He jumped out of the Jeep, and waved goodbye as Ross drove off (I'm sure, somewhat reluctantly). It was Scot's turn to tend bar that night, which always makes for an interesting evening. He has a tendency to lose count and therefore pours amazingly strong drinks. Scot poured me a vodka tonic and a bourbon and Seven for Bart, and we walked up the street towards Mallory.

"You know, I am amazingly envious of your life," Bart volunteered as we turned off of Monarch court onto Duval.

"Why?" I asked. "I'm willing to bet you make a much better living than I do."

"Not your living, man, your *life*. Look at us. When was the last time you walked around the streets of Chicago barefoot?"

I had to admit, that did not occur very often. "Still, we're always scrambling to make ends meet. Life here is a little more difficult than it might seem. No one gets rich living like this."

He stopped me and stared at me for a long moment. "Do you *care* about being rich?"

I had to admit, I didn't really. "I used to. I think I really care more about accomplishing something."

We resumed walking and entered the square. "Like what?"

"I don't know. I just want to *create* something. Did you ever hear of a guy named Juan Trippe?" He shook his head no. "Juan Trippe created Pan Am. He is really considered the father of worldwide aviation. He was my hero, really the reason why I got into aviation. He opened up the world, creating air routes to China, and across the Atlantic."

"And creating an inn doesn't qualify?"

I laughed. "I guess that's the problem. I've created something, or at least been part of its creation, but it wasn't my idea. It was Albert's."

"So it's creative ownership you're after."

We took our drinks down to the sea wall and sat down. "I guess it is. Do you remember the guy you met last time you were here, the Monarch?"

"Yeah. Crazy old coot."

"Well, as it turns out, that crazy old coot knew Albert much, *much* better than I did." I recounted the story of Albert wanting to be a painter and going to Cuba. I finished up as the sun first kissed the horizon. "I think that's what the problem is. I live in a romantic paradise, but I don't live a particularly romantic life."

Bart smacked the back of my head.

"Aidan, not every moment of life can be adventurous. You've got to do the mundane things sometimes. You've got to eat, buy groceries, do laundry. I'm sure even this Juan Trippe guy occasionally had to think about his car insurance."

"You're right, of course."

"You're damn right I'm right. You've got everything you ever wanted in life. You've got a great house, your own business, and a plane. Quit whining."

I smiled and finished my drink. He was right. I was whining. Albert had given me the means to have a great life. It was up to me to do something with it. I decided to change the subject. "What did you and Ross do all afternoon?"

He shrugged and looked out over the water. "Nothing really. After the airport, he took me down to the beach for a while, then we went and got a drink. Nothing spectacular."

The next day, Bart got up early with me. The days we fly a party are always busy, because we have to finish up all of the morning work around the inn in two hours as opposed to four. That way, we can get away for a couple hours to go fly. Once Ross began flying with me, we had started making a habit of leaving either Scot or Tony at the inn. That had two advantages: first of all, it meant the inn was always staffed. Secondly, there was always somebody who could call the Coast Guard if we were late getting back. That day, it was Tony's turn to stay at the inn.

In December, Tony had ordered white golf shirts with *Biscayne Voyager* Airways embroidered on the pocket, which had become our uniform while flying to and from the island. Tony lent his shirt to Bart, who seemed excited to be part of the business.

We met Ross at the hangar, and while they loaded up the tables, coolers, and other supplies into the hold, I computed the flight plan and filed the paperwork with the FAA. The guests arrived just as we finished up, and we herded them onto the plane. This part had become a science to us. While I did the walk around, Ross did a quick preflight safety instruction for the passengers. Then, once we buttoned up the aircraft, Scot would walk through to make sure everyone's seat belts were secured. Since we were running a full load of passengers, Bart had to squeeze into the tight jump seat in the galley with Scot.

I taxied to the edge of the apron and radioed for takeoff. Before long, we were climbing out of Key West. Ordinarily, the flight takes about thirty minutes, and so we are busy the entire time on the flight deck. Once the gear are up and the wings cleaned up for flight, we only have about ten minutes before we are beginning to circle down and look for the key. During that ten minutes, Ross and I usually don't talk about much, so I was somewhat surprised when he volunteered, "Your brother is cute."

"Uh, thanks. It runs in the family."

He laughed. "I'm sure it does." A long pause. "Is he gay?"

I wasn't ready for that one. Of course he wasn't gay. "Um, don't you have…what's it called? Gaydar? Can't you tell?"

He smiled and gave me a sidelong glance. "Well, I thought mine was pretty well calibrated, but I can't get a read here. I thought you might know."

"No, he's not gay," I said flatly.

"Pity," he replied, and started looking out the window for the island. "Especially since he has an ass like a marble statue." The silence that followed was long and awkward, and I think both of us were relieved when we sighted the island and began our approach.

The descent over the waves was like silk, and we touched down about fifty feet down the runway. We taxied into position, and Ross jumped up before I was even able to cut the engines, and headed down the aisle to the back hatch. I sensed a certain awkwardness between us, but didn't know how to deal with it. Hell, I thought, why *should* I deal with it? He's the one hitting on my brother.

As Ross dropped the stairs, Scot grabbed Bart and the three of them tumbled out of the back of the plane. I came out of the flight deck and made my usual announcements. "Ladies and Gentlemen, welcome to Runners Key. I need to give you a couple of instructions before you leave the plane.

"First of all, South Florida keys are basically spits of sand. This one is dangerous. Please be careful in the water as the undertow is strong and *Biscayne Voyager* Airways accepts no responsibility for your safety anywhere except on the airplane.

"Your crew, Bart, Ross, Scot and myself are going to need about fifteen minutes to get things set up. We will have a shelter and bar up first, and will then pull together lunch for you. In the meantime, please spread out a beach towel and relax. And, if there is anything we can do to make your afternoon more comfortable, please let us know.

"One final request. This is a vintage aircraft, with limited ventilation, so please watch your alcohol consumption. Airsickness is not a pleasant experience for anyone in the cabin."

This got the laugh it usually did, and the passengers unbuckled their seatbelts and headed out to the beach. I followed them out of the aircraft. Outside, Ross and Scot already had the dining fly set up, and Bart was busy unloading the coolers from the hold. I helped him pull one out and noticed that sweat was already beading up on his forehead. "Jeez, it's hot," he observed.

"Hey, they don't call these the Dry Tortugas for nothing, son. It's only going to get hotter."

We were flying an esoteric crowd that day. A private party made up of six lesbians from House Diana, flying with a private party of four couples in their mid forties from Toledo.

Parties on the island are usually a pretty uninhibited event. We play an assortment of Jimmy Buffett and Bob Marley CDs on the boom box (along with one Michael Penn CD that Scot always insists on bringing along). Once lunch is under way, shirts and shoes come off because, although we're the hosts, it helps the guests relax if they believe this is how we actually live and are including them in our lifestyle. Consequently, they tip better at the end of the trip.

Our division of duties is pretty specific. Ross usually handles the grill, and Scot and I switch off tending bar. Tony, who has two particularly useful skills from an earlier life (he was a waiter and a life guard) generally handles the waiter duties, but also keeps close watch on the guests while they are in the water. Today, those duties fell to Bart.

After lunch, the only thing we generally have to do is man the bar and work on our tans until four, when we begin to tear down for the trip home. That afternoon, Bart took a turn tending bar while Scot and I lay on the sand talking about a book both of us were taking turns reading. Ross spent most of the afternoon sitting on the sand next to the bar, talking to Bart.

When we work a party, none of us usually drink. Legally, Ross and I cannot within eighteen hours of flying, and that is a regulation both of us take pretty seriously. So I was surprised when Scot punched me in the shoulder and motioned to Ross, who was drinking a beer with Bart.

I was on my feet immediately, furious, and stormed across the sand. None of the guests had noticed yet, so I did not want to make a big deal out of it. I simply walked up next to him, took the beer out of his hand, and sat it on the bar.

"What's wrong?" Bart asked.

"FAA regulations," I replied, looking menacingly at Ross.

"Oh," Bart replied, clearly not understanding. I walked around the plane to the beach on the other side. Ross was right on my heels.

"What the fuck, man?" he began. I spun around as soon as the body of the plane was between us and the party.

"Don't 'what the fuck' me. What the fuck do you think you're doing? You know you're not legal as soon as you have one sip of beer."

Ross rolled his eyes. "Oh Aidan, c'mon. This is a charter outfit, not fucking Lufthansa. I had like three sips."

I got right in his face. "Dude, it may be a charter outfit, but it's *my* charter outfit. It's *my* plane. And it's *my* fucking license if I let you on that flight deck."

He was back in my face. "This has nothing to do with the beer, does it? This has to do with me asking about your brother."

"*What?* Bullshit. You're *illegal*, man. You hitting on my brother has nothing to do with it."

"Nothing? I don't think so. Big brother Aidan never thought his brother might be gay, and doesn't appreciate the evil fag…"

"You're out of line, man. I have never once felt like you're evil, and never once treated you like…"

"You never treated me like anything. We're friends, but do you know anything about my goddamn life?"

My head was starting to reel. "About your life? How in the hell did this become about your life? We're talking about the fact you're drinking on the job."

"Are we? Or is that just a clever excuse to get me to leave your brother alone?"

I had had enough. "Look, this is bullshit. Bottom line is you take another drink of beer, you're not getting back on my plane. I'll leave your ass here and radio for the Coast Guard to get you home. Am I clear?"

I have, few times in my life, seen the seething anger I saw in Ross's eyes at that moment. "Yes, *Captain*." He fairly spat at me, and stormed up the beach. I turned around, and saw Scot and Bart standing at the tail, watching. I started to say something, then stomped away in the other direction. Sadly, on an island that's only about a mile long, you really don't have many places to stomp.

Fortunately, for everyone involved, Ross did not have anything more to drink that day. We tore down the setup at four, and departed at four-thirty to have the guests back in Key West by five. Needless to say, the atmosphere on the flight deck was a bit frosty. As soon as we taxied to the hangar at Key West, Ross was out of his seat, out of the plane, and out the door.

We said good-bye to the guests and were tipped well. Bart, because he was acting as the waiter, made out the best in tips. As we drove back to the house, he counted the tips over and over again in the front seat of the car. "You can understand my excitement," he volunteered. "No one ever tips their pharmacist."

When we got to the house, I made myself a drink and headed up to the roof to sit on the widow's walk and think. From the widow's walk, you can see all the way to Mallory Square, and the sounds of the bands and crowds at the square floated back up to me as the sun slowly dipped towards the horizon.

I had been up there about forty minutes when the hatch opened and Tony came up with the bottle of vodka, a bottle of tonic and some ice.

Wordlessly, he sat down next to me, took my glass and mixed me a fresh drink. He handed it back and said, "Sorry. We're out of lime."

I chuckled and raised the glass to him in a silent toast. Among the many irreplaceable roles Tony plays in my life, the fact that he mixes a very good vodka tonic cannot be undervalued. "Is my brother still down there?"

He shook his head. "Nope. He left to walk up to the square about a half hour ago."

I took another sip of my drink. "Did Scot tell you?"

"He did."

"And did I overreact?"

Tony had brought an empty glass up with him and was mixing himself a drink. "Overreact? That's hard for me to say. You know the FAA regs much better than I do." He took a sip of his drink. "Needs lime."

"We don't drink and fly." I said flatly.

"Generally, no," he agreed and took another sip. "But you have. I've seen you take a swig of beer. I've seen you and Ross split a beer when we didn't have many guests. So, while you almost never do, it's not unprecedented."

That point hit home. "So maybe I overreacted."

He shrugged. "Again, I don't know. I guess I'm just wondering if you shouldn't have talked to him about it instead of just taking it away."

"What difference does that make?"

Tony hunched his shoulders. "If he is hitting on your brother, then you just robbed him of his dignity."

"What?"

Tony scratched his head and sat back in the chair. "Do you remember that night in Boston about three years ago when you and Scot and I had to go to that charity event for work?"

"Vaguely," I had to admit. I had been a bit overserved that evening.

"Do you remember humiliating Scot?"

Sadly, that I did. Scot had won tickets to a concert he had been dying to see in a silent auction. Through an odd set of circumstances, he had also won a rhinestone purse, which he was planning to give to his sister. Late in the evening, he had left me alone at the bar with the purse in order to engage in some serious flirting with a young flight attendant.

After sitting alone at the bar for about thirty minutes, I decided to go find Tony. I picked up the purse and carried it over to the table where Scot and the flight attendant were deep in conversation and said absently, "Scot, here's your purse," and dropped it on the table before wandering off.

Needless to say, the conversation died soon afterwards, and Scot, to this day, still blames me for the fact he didn't get laid that night.

I put my hands over my eyes. "Maybe you're right. Maybe I did come down a little hard."

"Maybe." His noncommittal tone told me I had more than come down hard. I had become *da man*.

Later that evening when I finally came down off of the roof, my brother was nowhere in sight. I asked Tony and Scot, but neither of them had seen him since he left to walk up to the square. I thought about going out to look for him, but then reminded myself that he was almost twenty-five, and could take care of himself. I was, however, at a loss for something to do. I knew I should go find Ross and apologize, but I hadn't worked up the nerve yet. I also knew I should go try to write, but I wasn't in the mood. And, as you may have guessed by now, I am not the world's most disciplined writer anyhow.

Having nothing else to do, I made another drink and went out for walk, finding myself ultimately down on Mallory Square. The sun had set, and most of the tourists and locals had gone home. I was surprised to see Louie sitting on a bench on the breakwater, staring out at the sea. I walked up and joined him. By way of greeting, I said simply, "Your Highness."

"Sir Aidan," I received in reply. "How has your holiday been thus far?"

"Complicated, Sire."

The King looked at me. Actually, seemed to study me. "In what ways?"

I recounted the fight with Ross, and the questions about Bart, and my own confused feelings. Louie listened dutifully, and remained silent long after I had run out of things to recount to him. Then, instead of offering me the sage piece of advice I was hoping for, he asked a simple question. "Aidan, are you happy?"

I blinked. "Happy?"

"Yes. Are you happy? At the end of each day, do you feel in some way fulfilled?"

I can only imagine that I had a wholly blank expression on my face. "I don't know. I don't know that I have ever thought about it."

"Why not? Why don't you know?"

"I…I don't know. I've been so busy the last year, I don't think I've ever taken time to think about it. Why?"

He shrugged. "Since I've known you, you've been wrestling with a lot of external conflict, most of it centered around your family. You've had a busy year. Lost your uncle. Lost your job. Started a new life in Key West. You've faced an unusual amount of challenges. But you've not seemed to notice any of them. The only thing that really seems to get you worked up, the only thing you seem to be truly passionate about, is conflict with or within your family."

I started to protest, but he held up a hand to silence me. "Please don't take this as criticism. Just an observation. It just seems to me that all the things most normal people really worry about, how they are going to survive, make ends meet, etcetera, you just take in stride. But you spend a tremendous amount of time and energy on conflicts that, in the end, don't really matter much. That's the reason I ask if you are happy. I'm starting to wonder if your preoccupation with family politics isn't becoming your hobby?"

I felt as though someone had just hit me in the face with a large, dead carp; simultaneously stung and stunned by the unexpected turn of the conversation. I felt like I should say something to defend myself, but I was honestly at a loss for words. "Well, y'know…Albert made my survival so easy…"

"Forget Albert," Louie scolded lightly. "This is about Aidan. Sir Aidan the Airborne. *Are you happy?*"

"I don't know." I said flatly. I honestly didn't. I didn't even know what I expected from happiness.

"I only ask," Louie continued, "Because it seems to me that that needs to be your first priority. Not Bart & Ross. Not Jason. Not even your Aunt Vivian…although I can certainly see why her unhappiness might make you happy." He stood up to leave. "No, it just seems to me that you've got a lot of tremendous opportunities staring you in the face right now, and maybe you should let everyone else work out their own lives for themselves." He patted me on the head.

"Have a good evening, Sir Aidan." He walked around the bench and was gone.

I continued to stare at the ocean for a long time. Louie certainly had a point. The last year had not been easy. We had built a business from the ground up. Admittedly, Albert had made it easy for me, but not *too* easy. He had given us the tools, but we had built the momentum on our own.

But I also had to admit that the guesthouse had never really engaged me one hundred percent mentally. The same thing with the airplane. Although I truly loved it, and probably had more fun flying than running the guesthouse, that too had come easily and never completely engaged me mentally. No, what I had to admit to myself was that the only thing that had truly stimulated me mentally in the last year was developing a strategy to defeat my aunt and meddling in the affairs of my family.

And what the hell kind of thing was *that* to get motivated by?

The realization that I was no better than my aunt hit me like a ton of bricks. A tremendous wave of depression washed over me. How did I reach this point in my life? I couldn't argue with Louie. I was unable to remember the last time something had consumed me. I remembered a quote that used to hang over my desk in my dorm room in college. "We are the makers of music, and we are the dreamers of dreams." That had always seemed to sum up the life I wanted. I had always been full of big dreams as a kid, all the way through college, really. But I couldn't remember the last time I had lost myself in my imagination. Or, more to the point, let my imagination drive what I was trying to accomplish in life.

Jesus, I thought to myself. I sound like I'm having a midlife crisis. How mundane. But I couldn't escape one overwhelming fact. I was living a life that everyone seemed to envy, and I didn't even know if I enjoyed it or not. And my behavior closely resembled my aunt's, which left a sour taste in my mouth.

I sat turning these thoughts over in my mind for a long, long time, and it was nearly midnight before I finally got off of that bench and started towards home. Duval was moderately active that night, but I didn't really notice much. I reached the corner of Monarch and Duval and turned right.

Ahead of me, on the steps of the house, were Ross and Bart. They seemed to be talking pretty intensely. Finally, Bart leaned down and kissed Ross. I couldn't tell if it was on the lips or the cheek. But he kissed him.

Well, that settles that, I thought. *Now I owe Ross two apologies.*

Bart then let himself in through the front door. Ross stared at the door for a moment, then turned and came down the steps.

No time like the present, I thought, and leaned against the lamppost on the sidewalk. Ross came walking up the street, staring down, hands in his pockets, but didn't notice me, until he was almost upon me. He looked up, and I saw his entire body tense up. He stopped and stared at me. After what seemed like a geological age, I finally found the courage to say it. "I'm sorry. I was out of line. I apologize for being 'da man.'"

He stared at me for a moment, and then I saw him relax just a little. "It's about more than just that," he said.

I shrugged. "Maybe you're right. Maybe I was being too defensive of my brother..."

He shook his head. "No, not that. Well, I mean, *yes*, you were being too defensive. But it's not about that. What I'm talking about is that I spend the most time together with you of any of my friends on the island. You never ask about my personal life. You never ask what's going on with me. At times I think we're friends, and at times I think that I'm just a hard-to-replace employee."

I looked at him sheepishly. This day seemed to be just one long litany of my faults and weaknesses. "I don't know what to say."

"All I'm asking is that, maybe once, we find something to talk about besides wind speed and approach vectors. How about getting to know me?"

I slid down the post and sat on the sidewalk. "Fair enough. What do you want me to know about you?"

He smiled and sat down next to me. He ran his hands through his hair and then glanced sideways at me. "I have no fucking idea."

We both laughed.

"I guess we'll figure that out," he said. "Let's talk about you instead. What kind of power trip were you on today?"

I started to get defensive, and a mental imagine of Vivian floated through my mind. I batted her and the defensiveness away. "I don't know. Like I said, I was probably a little hung up on my brother. But you've got to admit, you were out of line, too."

He nodded. "Fair enough. I had about a quarter of a sip of beer, but I shouldn't have been holding it. I know it looks bad and I apologize. But you didn't need to come take it out of my hand like I was..."

"I know. I said I was sorry. I have a bad habit of acting without thinking when it comes to my friends. Just ask Scot."

He looked at me knowingly. "Oh, the purse story."

I was amazed. "You know the purse story?"

Ross laughed. "Dude, everyone on this *island* knows the purse story. It's Scot's favorite story about you."

I put my face in my hands. "Jeez. There's nothing like finding out you're an asshole at Christmas."

Ross rubbed the top of my head. "Well, yes. You can be an asshole. However, you are an endearing asshole, so we all pretty much just put up with it."

"Talk about being damned with faint praise…"

He smiled again. "Dude, not at all. You are an amazingly self-contained person. Very few things get to you emotionally, other than your family, and you make something of a habit of providing a port in the storm for everyone around you. You've thrown lifelines to Tony and Scot and me and even that ice-queen Olivia seems to find some comfort in your company. So we can put up with an occasional bout of *high and mightiness.*"

I shook my head. "How did this get to be about me? I thought we were supposed to be talking about you."

"Oddly enough, just to know that you realize you were an asshole today makes me feel better about everything else."

I shook my head again. "Queen, I am not up to this kind of emotional roller-coaster."

He looked at me as though he knew a secret. "Better get used to it, Sugar."

"Why?"

He smiled, and got up. "I'll see you tomorrow. Have a good evening."

"C'mon. What did you mean by that?"

He started to walk away, and then turned around. He suddenly looked very serious. "Oh, hey Aidan? Thanks. I know how hard it was for you to apologize. I'm sorry as well."

I shrugged. "We're friends. Next time, it's your turn."

He smiled. "Probably." He turned and walked out of the Court.

I made my way to old number four, and let myself in through the wrought-iron gate. The house was quiet, so I locked the doors, and turned off the lights. Upstairs, Bart was standing on one of the balconies outside my bedroom, drinking a glass of wine while leaning with his back against the house. The room was dark. He glanced around when he heard me come in and held a finger up to his lips. He motioned me over to the window.

I peered out. Down below, two of the guests were about to be flagrante delicto on one of the lawn chairs by the pool. I glanced out, and walked back inside. "Sadly," I said quietly, "That's not all that rare of a sight."

He glanced towards me. "I'm sure it's not. It does, however, hold kind of a morbid fascination. Why is it only ugly people who always want to do it in public?"

"It isn't always ugly people, but admittedly the overwhelming majority are. Want to see it get really funny?"

He looked at me and nodded, so I waved him inside. I pulled the flash for my camera out of my bedside table and took him into the bathroom with me. We stood on either side of the window, out of sight, and I held the flash out and pressed the test trigger. For a moment, the whole back yard was lit up, and then it was dark. When we glanced back out, we could see two wide pairs of eyes looking around terrified, followed by a lot of frantic scurrying to put clothing back on.

Bart was doubled over with laughter, and just missed hitting his head on the sink. I blew some imaginary smoke away from the flash, switched it off and put it away. "You don't always do that, do you?" he asked, with tears streaming down his face.

"Not always the flash, per se. But I don't believe guests should be having sex in my back yard. So I usually find some appropriate way to break it up. The flash is especially effective for adultery cases."

"How do you know it was adultery?"

I shrugged. "She checked into room five with her husband. He is staying in room three with his wife. I'm making an educated guess here, but it seems to me something is wrong with these marriages."

He laughed again, and then sat down on the edge of the bed while I got undressed. "Sorry I wasn't around this evening," I said. "I had to get some things cleared up in my own mind."

He nodded and finished his wine. "I guessed. I went out to get a drink and met up with Ross, and we had a couple of drinks. I was really just there to listen while he vented his anger at you."

"I'm sure. He had a right to be."

"Oh, I don't know. It's not like you handed him a purse in a bar and…"

"Shit. You know that story too?"

He screwed up his face. "Aidan. *Everyone* knows that story. I think Scot has it on little cards that he gives to new guests."

I rolled my eyes and pulled my shirt over my head. Bart got into bed. "You know, although he's angry, Ross also thinks you pretty much walk on water."

I smiled and got into bed next to him. "Oh, I don't know. I think his attentions are more focused on the other of the Brothers McInnis."

Bart turned his head and fixed me in a strong, probing look. "What do you mean?"

I smiled at him. "Just what I said. He's gay, and I'm guessing here, but he seems to have a pretty heavy duty crush on you."

He continued to stare at me. I smiled and said as I rolled over, "Do me a favor and don't lead him on. Brother or no brother, I'd have a hard time getting another pilot for what I pay him." I believe Bart was still staring at me as I fell asleep.

I was up well ahead of him the next morning. I had breakfast set up, the pool cleaned and the patio hosed off before he wandered out of the house. He got a cup of coffee from the huge silver coffee urn we kept on the end of the bar and meandered his way over to the front desk where I was tallying bills for checkout. "Morning," he said, while looking around. He seemed to make a study of not making eye contact with me.

"Good morning," I replied. "Did you sleep well?"

"Hmmm." His response may have been affirmative. It was too non-committal to tell. The ensuing silence was long and probably extremely awkward for him. I continued to tally up bills.

"Is there anything you want to do today?"

"Hmm." More non-committal noises.

I finished the tallying, and stuck the bills in the appropriate little slots behind the counter. When I had completed all the busywork I could, I turned to him and said, "You seem to have something on your mind. Anything you want to talk about?"

He looked startled. Again, we don't usually come right out and confront issues in our family. We prefer to dance around and around and around and...

"Um, no. I mean yes, um..."

"Bart, what's wrong?"

He stared at me for a long tortured moment, but said nothing. I was trying to be patient, but I also had work to get done that morning.

"Is it about Ross?"

"Yeah, kinda."

I decided to go for broke. "Is it about your date with Ross last night?"

I could tell by the stunned expression on his face I had hit pay dirt. "It wasn't a date," he stammered. "We just, you know, went out, but..."

I smiled and said "Bart, it's *okay*."

He looked relieved. "You knew?" I shook my head.

"I never knew you were gay. Didn't know you weren't, either. I quite honestly just wasn't paying attention."

"And you don't care?" He was looking for confirmation.

"I wouldn't say I don't care. I'm your brother. I love you. Of course I care. I want you to be happy. If this is what it takes, then I'm totally behind you."

I noticed tears begin to well up in his eyes, and realized I needed to cut the seriousness of the moment. "Well, totally behind you, *except* when you tell Mom and Dad."

The mention of Mom and Dad stunned the tears right back into his head. I laughed, and went to get the first load of laundry started.

Over the course of the next few days, Bart and I got to know each other much better. I learned how he had been fighting admitting to himself that he was gay for years. I also learned how terrified he had been that, when I found out, it would drive a wedge into our relationship. I found that discovery a little disheartening.

I also found out that, while he liked Ross a lot, he wasn't certain he wanted to get involved with him. While he had gone out with a couple of guys, he was still trying to get comfortable with himself before he got into a relationship.

For his part, Bart discovered how upset I had been with myself ever since I had spoken to the king on Mallory Square. As we were sitting in the pool chairs on New Year's Eve afternoon, sipping beers, I told him how Louie had hit home when he pointed out that my only fascination for the last year had been family politics.

"I guess the ultimate frustration is that I had so many big dreams when I was a kid. Now, instead of chasing those dreams, I'm too wrapped up in myself and the lives of everyone around me."

"Then get over yourself," Bart replied.

"I wish it were that easy."

"It is," he said as he slowly paddled his chair over to the cooler beside the pool to retrieve two more beers. "Look, Aidan, I don't mean to be flippant, but let's face it. You've spent the last year chasing Albert's dream, not yours. You never wanted to be an innkeeper. You are now, and I think you enjoy the lifestyle. But you keep looking around you waiting for this place to give you a life. It's not going to.

All this place should do is fund your real life." He paddled back over and handed me the fresh beer.

I took a swig of the beer. "I don't understand what you mean."

"Let me put it another way. I didn't become a pharmacist because I thought it would give me a great, romantic life. I became a pharmacist because it interested me. My real life has nothing to do with pharmacy.

"Ever since I can remember, you've had two interests; airplanes and writing. This place gives you a wonderful amount of freedom. You've got the plane. Start writing again."

"I haven't found anything to write about." I said. No, let's be realistic. I whined.

"Does that matter? Can't you just start writing and wait for the subject to find you?"

Later that evening, I noticed the newspaper sitting on his suitcase. Over the course of the week, he had been pouring over the classified section of the paper. I hadn't really paid any attention until that evening when he and I were getting ready for New Year's Eve. Sitting on top of his suitcase were the want ads with five different pharmacy jobs circled. I held them up. "You thinking of relocating?"

He shrugged. "You never know. This place is a hell of a lot more inviting than Chicago in December. Besides, since you're here I can move down. It's safe now."

That evening, all of us went over to Louie's house. The Order of the Conch was having a New Year's Eve party, and I thought Bart would enjoy the revelry. It was now widely known that Sir Aidan the Airborne *always* traveled with his entourage (Tony, Scot & Ross) so Bart was welcome along with the rest of them.

The guests were decked out in their usual court finery: lots of sequins, lots of feathers. For the occasion, the entire lawn was decorated with enormous martini glasses. In the back yard, several members of the order were busily engaged in using one to make an enormous cosmopolitan.

In the dining room, we each secured drinks from a bartender who was unmistakably dressed as a taco. I recognized the taco. He handed out coupons outside a strip mall on Bertha. I never expected to see the taco in a social setting. On the dining room table, three women dressed as Vegas show girls posed in the middle of the table as one large centerpiece. Each of them held bowls of guacamole. The buffet was laid out between them.

I took a cocktail weenie from a platter being passed by a rather hirsute waiter dressed in a gold lame' Halston who had no business wearing anything backless. I saw Bart looking around wide-eyed. I sidled up next to him and asked, "What do you think?"

Without missing a beat he replied, "I feel like I'm in some post-modern production of *Caligula*. Who are these people?"

"A variety." I pointed to a woman decked out in Christmas tree lights, "That woman is Tony's dentist." I indicated another woman dressed entirely in leopard skin, "She's on the town council." I pointed to a gentleman who appeared to be dressed as a large household appliance, a dishwasher perhaps. "That's the judge of the traffic court. I never understand his costumes."

"Who's the taco?"

"Don't know. He seems nice, though."

We meandered through the other rooms, pausing long enough to say hello to our various neighbors. In the throne room, we paused so Bart could have his tarot cards read. The cards foretold of a troubling altercation with a family member.

"Great," he mused. "Like coming out to Mom and Dad isn't going to be hard enough. I've got the tarot gods working against me as well."

Before I could explain that there are no "tarot gods," the king burst into the room. He was decked out in a white satin suit with gold lapels and gold nautical epaulets and braids at his shoulders. "Sir Aidan, always a pleasure. Master Bartholomew, welcome."

"Sire," I said.

"Uh, hi," Bart offered.

The king got between us and led each of us through the foyer and out onto the back porch. "You must see my latest creation. You arrived after its unveiling, but it should still be awe-inspiring."

On the porch, in the center of a champagne fountain, was a large ice sculpture of a sphinx. Although, instead of the customary face of Rameses, the Sphinx's head was unmistakably Olivia's.

"Um, remarkable likeness, sire," I offered.

"Thank you."

"And Olivia's reaction?" I ventured.

He smirked and shook his head. "Not good, Sir Aidan. Not good."

"Uh oh."

"I was wondering if you might go talk to her. She's upstairs stomping about her bedroom."

I acquiesced. Louie put his arm around Bart's shoulder. "Meanwhile, young man, I think there are several young gentlemen who would like to get a look at you."

Bart shot me an accusing look. I held up my hands to indicate I had not outed him to Louie. Louie laughed and immediately confirmed that to my brother. "Sorry, young Bartholomew. When you've lived in Key West as long as I have, you develop a better gaydar than most queens have."

He led my brother away, and I retrieved a second drink before climbing up the stairs to the second floor. Below me, I could hear Tony winding up in the revelry.

I had never been on the second floor of Louie's house before. There were lots of bedrooms, many more than I would have expected. All of them very small. At then end of the hall was one closed door. I guessed this was Olivia's room. I knocked.

"Dammit Louie! I told you to leave me the *hell* alone." It was Olivia's room.

I knocked again. "It's Aidan."

The door swung open and she stuck her head out. Her eyes were blazing. "Did you see it?"

I handed her the champagne. "I did."

"Is that the most fucking, over the line, piece of bullshit you've ever seen?"

I smiled. "There's no safe answer here. You know that."

She took a drink of the champagne. It mollified her anger not at all. "What brings you up here?"

"You. I didn't see you anywhere and your father said I might find you up here."

She turned and walked into the bedroom. "I can't believe he would do something like this?"

"Like what?"

She looked at me incredulously. "Like mock me in ice! Didn't you see that thing down there? I'm a freaking centerpiece."

"Mock you? Are you sure that's what he intended?"

She rolled her eyes. "Aidan, do you honestly believe that my father thinks before he acts? My father's only intent was 'ho ho ho. She'll look good as the Sphinx.' There's no intent."

"So what are you upset about?"

"What am I upset about? He made me the centerpiece!"

"Actually, um, I think the three babes in the dining room are the centerpiece. I believe you're just a table decoration."

She took off her shoe and threw it at me.

"Not helping, huh?"

"Not helping," she confirmed. "Look, Aidan, you wouldn't under-stand." She turned with her arm crossed tightly over her chest and stared out the window, sipping her champagne glumly. I put my champagne down on her dresser, walked up behind her, and began to massage her shoulders.

"Try me."

She sighed and said nothing. I continued to work her shoulders. The tendons at the base of her neck were like steel bars.

"Hmm, you're pretty good at that."

"I worked for a while as a masseur while I was in college."

She opened her eyes and looked at my reflection in the window. "No shit?"

"No shit. I was also a bartender. If I couldn't get a girl into bed one way, then I would the other." She laughed and closed her eyes again. "Talk to me."

"You wouldn't understand," she repeated. "All my life, I've felt like people were laughing at me because of him. When I was in grade school and high school, it was more than a feeling. My classmates would confirm it freely. 'Hey, Livia. Isn't your old man the crazy coot who thinks he's king?'

"This has been going on for twenty years, Aidan. I've always felt insane by association. He does something outrageous and I'm the one that people laugh at."

I was working a particularly difficult knot at the top of her left scapula, and I felt it begin to break loose. "Olivia, at the risk of sounding insensitive, who gives a shit if they laugh at you?" The knot immediately reasserted itself.

"I do, Aidan. I've worked very hard all my life to be taken seriously. I mean, I've got a fucking MBA from Wharton. All I want is for people to get to know me, to know what I'm about. Not just that I'm this crazy old coot's daughter."

"I can understand that," I lied. "It's like being a celebrity's kid. You're intelligent, and pretty, and have a sense of humor. But, no one will acknowledge the work you put into developing the intelligence or looks or sense of humor, because 'you must just come by them naturally.'" I felt the knot give way.

"You think I'm funny?" she asked. She was watching my reflection in the window intently. I tried not to meet her eyes. For once, I thought I should probably tell someone what they wanted to hear, not what I thought they ought to hear.

"Absolutely. You don't let many people see it. You're pretty guarded after all. But you've made me laugh outright several times."

She turned around and looked in my eyes. "You're not just saying that, right? I mean, just because Louie is my father…"

I shook my head. "Louie has nothing to do with it. Your sense of humor is totally different. Louie's sense of humor is what I call high-brow slapstick. You have to be intelligent to appreciate it, but it's not all that sophisticated. Your sense of humor is one that Louie could never pull off. Very urbane. Dry. Sometimes even acerbic."

She stared into my eyes a long time. I added, "That's why I'm honestly surprised you care about the ice sculpture. You could make mincemeat of your father in a battle of wits. You're right. He doesn't think about these things beforehand. Nor does he believe anyone cares. He assumes that, if he's laughing, then the whole world is laughing with him. There's no one down there that you give a shit about, so laugh along with him. Then, when he least expects it, cut him apart with that rapier tongue of yours."

She giggled. I hardly ever remember her laughing before, much less giggling. "Oh, you're good. You're very good."

"What do you mean?"

"My father put you up to this, didn't he?"

I rolled my eyes and retrieved my drink. "Your father knew you were up here and mad at him. All he did was suggest I come upstairs to check on you."

"And he didn't coach you on what to say?"

"Olivia, I've had a very stressful holiday. I've had a huge fight with my copilot, discovered two thirds of the people who know me think I'm an asshole, and had my brother come out of the closet. While I care a great deal about you, I'm making a concerted effort not to get involved in other people's relationships. I can't seem to even successfully manage my own."

She closed her eyes and laughed again. "I'm sorry. I just had to check."

I held out my hand to her. "My drink's empty. Come down stairs?"

She nodded and took my hand. We walked out of the room and descended the stairs. At the landing as we turned, we could see Louie standing by the front door making a toast. He stopped short when he saw us and called to his daughter.

"'Tis the fair Olivia. Perchance, come to join our merrymaking." I felt her tense up for a second, but then she called back.

"Louie, where the hell did you get that outfit? You look like a seafaring pimp."

There was a moment of silence, and then the room erupted in laughter. For his part, Louie looked stunned. He was, clearly, at a loss for words. He turned back to the crowd and said "Well. Touché," and then went on with the toast.

Later, I found Bart and Ross in a corner of the throne room in intense conversation. I started to join them, but then realized my brother was being hit upon heavily, and enjoying the hell out of it.

Tony and I spent some time flirting with the dining room centerpiece, and Scot got into a spirited discussion with the taco. As soon as I heard him tell the taco "and then he brings it over to us and says 'Scot, here's your purse...'" I immediately hustled him away.

Over the course of the evening, it became apparent that I had created a monster. Poor Louie could find no quarter from his daughter. She joked, mocked and ridiculed him all through the house. People all around were stunned. She was the hit of the party. Finally, at a quarter to midnight, the King mounted the throne and cried out in exasperation. "Where are my knights? I need a champion!"

I called back, "A knight? I'm a knight! Is someone looking for a knight?"

"I'm looking for a knight, you idiot," Louie growled. "Get over here."

I approached the throne. "Are you looking for an idiot or a knight? I'm sure I qualify on either count, but I'd like to know which resume to use."

"Would you shut up?" He picked up his scepter and pointed at Olivia. "Sir Aidan, arrest that traitor!"

I looked around, and then turned back to him. "Which traitor?"

"The traitor to my loins."

I made a sour face. "Oh Louie. That's a mental image that no one needs." The room broke out in uproarious laughter. I realize it wasn't really that funny, but you must remember, vast quantities of alcohol had been consumed.

"Arrest her!" he cried again.

I walked over to her, looked her in the eye, and then turned back to him. "What kind of arrest do you want? Cardiac arrest? Arrested development? Bucharest?"

He slumped down on the throne and leaned his head on the scepter. "I'm surrounded by cut-rate comedians."

"Well, Louie," Olivia observed, "imitation is the highest form of flattery." More laughter.

"Sir Aidan," Louie began again. "My daughter annoys me. Please seal her up in her room."

"Sire, didn't you just send me to fetch her from her room?"

"Yes, but…"

"It seems to me you could have saved everyone a whole lot of time if I had just left her there in the first place."

"That's a good point, Louie," Olivia volunteered. "Once I'm there, will you just send for me again? I mean, Sir Aidan has a lot of drinking to do tonight, and…" The crowd erupted again.

Finally, Louie came down off the dais. "Sir Aidan, what do you want?"

"Sire?"

"What will it take to get you on my side instead of hers?"

"Sides, sir? Why, as I was just telling the lady Olivia, I've been trying to stop taking sides in family arguments. Why just the other day…"

He held up his hand. "Aidan, what…will…it…take?"

"I want a promotion."

"A promotion?"

"Yes a promotion. Once a king, always a king. But once a knight is enough."

He rolled his eyes. "Fine. A promotion to what?"

"Duke."

"Fine. You're now Lord Aidan the Airborne, Baron of the *Biscayne* Skies and Duke of Disrespectful Daughters. Now, for the love of God, would you please *shut her up!*"

"Certainly, Sire." And, with that, I turned around, grabbed Olivia, threw her into a dip, and planted a kiss on her that probably lasted a full sixty seconds.

Behind me, I could hear the King's clearly startled voice. "Well, um…er, well, yes. That has certainly silenced her. Well, okay. Good work, Lord Aidan…Um, I said, GOOD WORK, LORD AIDAN!"

When I stood Olivia back up, she looked at me wild eyed. She started to say something, stopped, and then just said, "Wow."

I turned to the King and leered. "Still want me to take her back to her room?"

"NO!" He fairly shrieked, before regaining his composure. Louie was not used to having competition for the title "life of the party." Moreover, he clearly did not enjoy the competition. All around us, people continued to laugh. "Perhaps having you remove the Lady Olivia to her room was not one of my better ideas."

"I don't know, Louie," Olivia countered as she sidled up next to me and seductively wrapped a leg around my waist. "Seems like a scrumptious idea to me."

Louie looked more exasperated than I had ever seen him. Before he could come up with a response, Tony announced that midnight was in ten seconds. The crowd immediately fell into the mandatory, New Year's Eve rhythmic counting. Olivia leaned over and whispered in my ear. "I don't believe it. He's at a loss for words. My father is at a fucking loss for words."

"Nine…eight…" droned the crowd.

"Hasn't he ever seen you kiss a man before?" I asked.

"Six…five…"

She rolled her eyes and looked at me. "Haven't you heard anything I've said? Do you think I would have ever dared to bring a boy here?"

"Four…three…"

"So, you've found his button?"

"Two…"

"I think so. Let's test our theory."

"One…"

"Stay flexible," she instructed me.

"Happy New Year!!!!" cried the crowd. But then again, what else would they have said?

Olivia grabbed me, spun me around, and threw *me* into a dip. The ensuing kiss lasted approximately thirty seconds, well into "Auld Lang Syne." She let me up, and I looked in her eyes. "Wow," I informed her.

We turned and looked at Louie, who was watching us, clearly not pleased. We both turned away. We walked a few feet away, turned, looked at each other. "Jackpot," we said simultaneously.

Across the room, I could see my brother and Ross. I don't know if they kissed at midnight or not, but they were both smiling at each other intensely. Next to them, Scot and Tony were busy lobbing fistfuls of confetti into the air. Scot's smile convinced me that he had not seen me kiss the great, unrequited love of his life.

Olivia and I walked out into the back yard shortly after our kiss. Everyone was inside, and we sat down next to the mammoth cosmopolitan.

"Aidan, I'm glad you came up and got me. I can't remember a better New Year's Eve."

"Well, I'd like to think it was my charming company. But I know the truth. You just enjoyed getting the best of your father."

She smiled and looked at the ground for a moment. "No, I really *have* enjoyed your company." She began to laugh, and looked up at me. "But I really got him, didn't I? And kissing you just really chapped his ass."

I laughed as well. "Well, if you came home with me tonight, that might push him towards embolism."

She laughed again. "It probably would." Then, still smiling, "but it probably would not be a good idea."

I smiled. I had expected that answer. "No, it probably wouldn't be."

"It's not that I don't care about you," she protested. "And I'm certainly tempted, but…"

I held up my hand. "But, starting a relationship that spans the entire eastern seaboard is not in anyone's best interest."

She smiled and kissed me again. "You're a hell of a guy, Aidan McInnis. I wish you lived in New York."

"And I wish you lived in Key West."

There was a brief silence. Finally, she stood and said, "I'm going to go in and see if I can find him to wish him a happy new year. Come along?"

I shook my head. "No, thanks. I think I'm going to head home. We have a lot of guests right now."

She kissed the top of my head and walked back towards the house.

The party marched on. It would continue to march on and on, until around seven on New Year's morning. But I would not stay for it. I placed my glass on the bench, stood and walked home.

The inn was quiet. Most of the guests were probably out at different bars. I climbed the front steps and let myself into the house. The silence was deafening. I wasn't really tired, even though I knew getting up in the morning would be miserable. I was, however, at a loss for something to do. I let myself into the library and sat down at my desk. From the corner of the blotter, three people stared back at me from dog-eared photographs: Albert, Jason and myself. I stared at Albert for a long time and thought about the last week. I kept turning Louie's question over and over in my head. Was I happy? What would it take to make me happy?

I pulled my ancient laptop out of the bottom drawer of my desk. I opened it and put my hands on the keys. There is something magical about the way a keyboard feels in my hands. There always has been. I switched on the computer and stared at the screen for a few minutes. Perhaps Bart had been right. Maybe I should just start writing, and wait for the story to find me. I began typing.

"Albert Fitzgerald left Chicago on September fifteenth, nineteen fifty, with the intention of becoming a painter in Cuba..."

The Monarch of Key West

Winter in Florida is defined by the presence of tourists. January and February were lucrative for us, and the inn stayed completely full for the entire two months. Our bookings for March also looked strong as the month began, and we were pretty solidly booked into April and May.

Olivia had returned to Manhattan the day after New Year's, and we kept in touch via email. Bart had returned to Chicago the following day, but was due back in March for two or three interviews he had lined up.

He and Ross kept in touch. Judging by the amount of flight-deck conversation Ross devoted to him, he was clearly smitten with my brother. Bart came out to my parents in late February. He told me on the phone that they had apparently known all along, but had been fighting admitting it to themselves mightily. In true family fashion, they were not happy to have the issue dredged up and had immediately gone back to repressing it. Still, although things were strained, Bart felt better for having been honest.

I was still writing about Albert. I spent lots of evenings with Louie, learning details of my uncle's life that I had never known and filling in the blanks of my own understanding of the man wherever possible. As I finished up different stories, I sent them off to Olivia, and she sent back long emails outlining the story problems and edits she felt needed to be made. I generally ignored her advice.

March ninth would be the one-year anniversary of Albert's death. I no longer felt angry with him. Writing about him was helping me process a lot of my emotions, although I still had no idea what the hell he had intended by leaving me the guesthouse.

I did find that the more time I spent with Louie, the more I managed to find a life of my own. During the previous year, Aidan McInnis was pretty much indistinct from the other hundred or so innkeepers on the island. However, Lord Aidan the Airborne began to have a very interesting life. For a secret society, the Order of the Conch was alarmingly public and complex. There were a number of charitable, professional and networking organizations connected or affiliated with it. There was even a writers group that met once a week and where the members would work through story problems together, and critique each other's work.

I began attending the meetings of these organizations with Louie. Who knew Louie had such an amazingly active life? My interviews with him were frequently conducted as we went to one or another of these meetings, and I found myself wondering how he ever had time to paint. As the weeks wore on, however, I began attending more of these meetings myself, often in the company of Scot and Tony. We started to build quite a network of friends across the island. This network proved useful, as it continued to steer business both towards the inn and towards the charter operation. We were flying enough business that I was able to bring Ross on full-time.

One of the advantages of being so busy was that we didn't have time to actually spend much of the money we were acquiring. If the last summer had taught us anything, it was to put all of the money away to get through the lean times, off-season.

On the first Monday of March, George informed me that I was going to be deposed in Vivian's custody battle for Jason. I acknowledged it, but tried not to think about it. I was finding my own life too fascinating to worry about what went on with my family.

Shortly after talking to George, I was finishing up the laundry when Louie wandered into the backyard. "Sir Aidan," he called.

I stuck my head out of the laundry room door. "In here, your highness."

He wandered to the laundry room door. He was dressed in his usual mishmash of styles—tank top, breech coat, bowler—and I couldn't help but notice that they were hanging loosely on him. "What's up, my liege?"

"Aidan, are you aware that the one year anniversary of your uncle's death is upon us?"

I continued folding sheets. "Sure. Next week. Why?"

He leaned against the doorframe. "I've been thinking. As you may remember, I did not attend Albert's wake."

"I do remember."

"The reason I did not attend is that I was so damn angry with the son of a bitch for dying. We had one hell of an argument the weekend before, and I was quite convinced that he died just so I couldn't get the last word in."

I laughed. I could picture Albert sitting somewhere in the great beyond, smugly pleased with himself at achieving just that. "Well, Louie, Albert *was* pretty competitive..."

Louie ignored me. "Anyway, I need some assistance from you. You may find this hard to believe, but I've never been to an Irish wake."

"I don't find it hard to believe at all. Most non-Irish find the whole concept disturbing. Sometimes, even appalling."

He shrugged. "Anyway, that's why I need your help. I want to throw one."

I stopped folding. "*Throw* a wake? For who?"

"For myself."

I stared at him for a long minute. "Go on."

"Albert always said that your wake was the greatest party of your life and you don't get to enjoy it because you're dead. As you know, I hate to miss a good party, so I thought I'd throw my own."

"And what do you need from me?"

"I need you to make it authentic."

A chill ran down my spine. "To make it authentic, you have to be dead."

He laughed. "Okay, maybe not *that* authentic. But I'm French-Canadian. I don't know anything about all this toora-lura-lura and erin-go-bragh shit."

I stood up straight, indignant. "Erin-go-bragh *shit?*"

He waved his hand impatiently. "No disrespect to your noble, Celtic heritage intended. I want to do this on Saint Patrick's Day. It is actually what Albert and I argued about last year. He refused to provide me technical assistance."

"Why?"

"He was jealous," he sat flatly. "He felt that if anyone should get to throw his own wake, it should be him. He always hated it when I came up with an idea first. Then, he went and *died* so he got his damn wake. Now, it's my turn."

I rubbed my eyes. It was only Monday, and the week was already getting unspeakably weird. "Louie, what *exactly* are you asking me to do?"

"Plan a wake for me. Just like the one you gave Albert. All very Irish. I'll pay for the party. I just need you since you know what to do."

The rather unpleasant memory of the urn falling off the bar at Albert's wake flashed through my mind. "I don't think we could recreate Albert's wake exactly…"

"Well, close enough. Just write down everything that is supposed to happen at a wake, and we'll take it from there."

I promised him I would, indeed, jot down a few ideas. He seemed satisfied with the answer and went on his merry way. I walked out onto the patio where Scot and Tony were cleaning up the bar from break-fast.

"What did His Weirdness want?" Tony asked.

I related the nature of Louie's request. Instead of reacting with disdain as I expected, Tony offered, "Seems like a decent idea."

I was shocked. "You're kidding, right?"

He shook his head. "No, I'm not. I think it is a good idea. And if I wanted to throw a wake, I'd ask an Irishman how to do it."

"Besides," Scot added, "you've got to respect him for wanting to see himself off right."

"What do you mean?"

Scot stopped wiping the counter and leaned on it. "C'mon. You've noticed he doesn't look well lately. Olivia told you she thought he was dying. My guess is that he's decided to go out with a bang. And when you consider that his relationship with his own daughter is not exactly what you'd call warm, and that he's established some kind of connection with you, you're the only logical choice."

Later that day, I dropped my laptop in my backpack and headed for the airport. We were flying a group of Jaycees from Cincinnati to the island that day. They didn't drink. I wasn't sure what the hell we were going to do to entertain them for four hours, but I figured that I could probably get a few notes jotted down.

I soon discovered that the Jaycees is a leadership training organization. As soon as we were on the island, they immediately began to organize themselves. There was the volleyball planning team, the snorkeling subcommittee, and sun-block task force. They immediately set out to have highly organized, well managed and administered *fun*.

Sure enough, two hours later as I sat watching fifteen inappropriately sober Jaycees play volleyball on the beach, I definitely had the opportunity to sit and type. I opened a file on the laptop called "Wake" and started to jot down the things that make a great Irish wake. My notes, in no particular order, included the following.

—Beer
—Rampant maudlinism
—Beer
—Testimonials
—Beer
—Danny Boy
—Beer

And so forth. Eventually it occurred to me that Louie's wake would make a great theme party, based on his death. I began working on Louie's obituary. I had been typing diligently for about an hour, when Tony came and sat down next to me.

"Tips are going to suck," he complained. "No one is drinking at all."

"Hmm," I replied.

"What are you working on?"

I wiped the sweat off of my forehead. "I'm brainstorming ideas of how to kill Louie."

"Ooh. Can I help?"

"Sure." I explained my idea of creating a wake theme around a bizarre death. "I've got about fifteen ideas so far. I think my favorite is that Queen Beatrix of the Netherlands beats him to death with her scepter because he paints her nose wrong."

He laughed. "Have you considered having Olivia kill him?"

"Three different ways. She locks him in the attic when he misses a deadline. Or, she accidentally backs over him in the driveway, seventeen times. Or, she goes berserk over last New Year's ice sculpture and flash freezes him into an ice sculpture of Bob Dole."

We kicked different ideas around, and I recorded each of them diligently. Ross came over and joined us. When we had finished, we each picked our favorites. "Now," Tony suggested, "write his obituary for each of the three of them."

I couldn't write the obituaries at that point, because it was time to clean up the island and fly the Jaycees back. I didn't get back to it until later that night when I took a drink and the laptop and camped out on the widow's walk.

In the first obituary, I tried a more metaphorical death for Louie. I had the National Endowment for the Arts cancel a grant to Olivia for Louie's continued existence. At this point we discover that Louie Robideau was never a real person, just an elaborate performance art installation.

In the second obituary, I revised my Queen Beatrix scenario. He and Beatrix get into an ugly altercation over the appropriate dimensions of her nose. Tensions heighten, and she ultimately has him imprisoned until he agrees to repaint it. He expires in a dungeon outside The Hague rather than compromise his artistic principles. His last words were, "I should have given her a bigger ass, too."

In the third obituary, I killed him off in a palace coup. While addressing a convention of produce distributors in Marathon, he unwittingly makes a cruel joke about the Florida citrus industry. The public outcry is immense, and there are demonstrations across the Conch Republic demanding his abdication. When he refuses, he is deposed and assassinated by a militant agri-extremist fringe organization called Fruit Nation.

I have to admit, I had a ball writing these obituaries. I was laughing so hard as I wrote the third, Scot came upstairs to see what all the commotion was about. Admittedly though, he did not find the term "Tangelo Terrorists" quite as amusing as I did.

I finished the last of the three obituaries at about one in the morning. One of the interesting things about writing is that it makes me hyper. I have heard actors and comedians say that, when they come off stage, it takes them two or three hours to wind down before they can go to sleep. Writing has a similar effect on me. By the time I had finished, I was wide-awake, and knew I had to do something to calm down. I took the laptop downstairs and hooked it up to the printer.

My printer is an ancient, cranky thing, and it groaned resentfully when I turned it on. Reluctantly, it selected a sheet of paper from its feeder tray, and began to slowly type out my words. Rather than risk making it more surly by watching it work, I made another drink and went out to sit on the front steps.

A full moon was sailing high into the sky over Monarch Court. Everyone in the neighborhood knew Louie generally took his evening constitutional around midnight. But I had noticed over the last few months, that these evening walks got much longer during the full moon. One weekend in October, I had returned home from a date at about three-thirty and had noticed him ambling out of the cul-de-sac as I drove in. So it came as no surprise to me to see him come strolling up the street as I finished my drink. Louie always circumnavigated the cul-de-sac counter-clockwise, and my house sat at 3:00, so I knew I had a few minutes before he reached my steps. I went inside and retrieved the obituaries from the printer, which looked at me sullenly. I switched it off, and I'm certain I heard it whisper an obscenity as it powered down.

Louie reached the driveway as I came back outside and down the steps. "Duke Aidan, you are up awfully late this evening."

"I am, milord. I have been working on ways to kill you."

A quizzical look crossed his face, and I explained the concept of the wake theme party. He laughed at the idea and rubbed his hands eagerly. I could see the wheels in his mind rev up with ideas. "And, pray tell, how would we expire?"

I handed him the sheaf of papers. "Anyway you like. I've taken the liberty of writing three different obituaries for you. I thought we could stick them in the party invitations."

He smiled, and gladly accepted them. We stood for a moment, and he quickly scanned the first page. He chuckled several times. "We have never read your writing before. You have a wicked sense of humor."

I bowed low. "You are most kind, your grace." Louie bid me good night and wandered on up the street. He stopped momentarily under the street light at the corner and, as I opened the front door to head off to bed, I could hear him laughing.

Tuesday morning was fairly busy. We had a large number of guests checking in and out on the same day, and the amount of work to turn the rooms is immense. In addition, we were flying a party that afternoon but leaving earlier than usual. Finally, the phone simply would not stop ringing.

I was working the front desk while Tony and Scot turned the rooms. I had just recalculated three different bills for contentious guests when the phone rang. It was my brother telling me that he would be coming back down on the ninth. The pharmacy chain he worked for had a store on Bertha, and they were looking for a new pharmacist. He had put in for the transfer and was coming down to meet with the store manager. I told my brother I was happy for him, wished him luck, and then promptly hung up on him. I answered two more reservations calls, and helped one of the guests fish her Pomeranian out of the pool. I then ducked into the back room to get a fresh ream of paper for the front desk printer when I heard someone repeatedly pounding the service bell.

"May I HELP you?" I fairly shrieked as I came out of the storeroom, only to see it was Louie. "Louie, if you don't stop pounding that bell, we may be throwing your wake for real."

He didn't seem to hear me. He waved a few sheets of paper at me. "You, my boy, are *brilliant*. These are, quite possibly, the funniest things I have ever read. We will most definitely be using your idea. In fact, we are going to go one better. We are going to throw this party for charity."

"Good, Louie," I replied absently as I loaded paper into the printer. "Which obituary do you want me to put in the invitation?"

"Oh, Fruit Nation, definitely. That was the funniest of the three. But don't you worry about the invitations right now. I will need you, however, to come to dinner tonight, so we can make some plans."

"Uh, dinner is out. How about if I come by later?"

He looked a little disappointed but waved his acquiescence gaily nonetheless. "Afterwards is fine. We will be receiving at the Palace all night tonight." The phone rang and I answered it while pantomiming to Louie that I would definitely be there. He wandered up the walk, and I turned my attention to the caller.

"Hi," a familiar voice said. "I'm trying to reach Aidan McInnis."

"This is Aidan," I told the voice. "How can I help you?"

"Hi Aidan. This is Phoebe." I stopped what I was doing. I had not seen or heard from Phoebe since Thanksgiving. Honestly, I hadn't really even thought much about her at all.

"Hi Phoebe. How are you?"

She was fine. Her reason for calling was that her attorney was coming to Key West in two weeks to depose me. She thought she might also come along on the trip. Jason had not been to Key West for almost two years, and he was bugging her incessantly about it. She asked if I had any rooms available. I was able to book her in on the nights she wanted, conveniently tying up the last available nights we had in March. We chatted briefly for a few more minutes and then hung up.

That evening, I made my way over to Louie's house. Since the day had been so crazy, I didn't feel like walking all the way around the block to get there. Instead, I went behind the guesthouse and hopped the fence that separated my property from the royal grounds. I was barefoot, and I had to avoid a lot of broken glass as I crossed the yard. For some reason, various members of Louie's entourage insisted on smashing wine glasses. In the fireplace, in the pool, random spots in the street. I narrowly avoided slicing my foot open on some smashed Waterford, and climbed up the back steps and knocked. No one answered. I knocked again. I tried the knob and it was locked.

That was odd. I had never really thought about it, but Louie's doors were never locked. There was usually always a crowd around. But lately, Louie had been without his entourage. I came down off the porch and walked around the house to the front door. I rang the bell. Still no answer. I tried the knob. It was locked also. I stood back and looked at the house. To the left of the door, one of the throne room windows was open. I walked over to it and yelled inside. "Hey! Louie! You home?"

There was no answer. Figuring that I had been stood up, I started back around the house towards the back yard. As I crossed the porch, I glanced to the left through the dining room windows. The light was on in the kitchen. A slight movement caught my eyes. I glanced back. Through the butler's pantry, I could see Louie lying on the floor in the kitchen.

"Oh shit." I crossed back to the throne room and let myself in through the window. Running through the house, I got to the kitchen. Louie was lying on his chest. He was breathing, but it was a shallow, raspy breath. I put my hand on his back. "Louie?" He stirred slightly. I felt for his pulse. It was light and irregular, but it was there. "Louie?" I asked again. There was no reaction. I jumped up, grabbed the phone and dialed 911. After a moment, the dispatcher answered. I gave her the details, and she told me an ambulance was on its way.

I returned to Louie. He still didn't respond. I wasn't sure what to do while I waited for the ambulance. I sat there for what seemed like an hour (but was probably only thirty seconds), wondering what I was supposed to do with an unconscious monarch. I got a glass of water and splashed some in his face. It had no effect, except that I now had a *wet*, unconscious monarch.

Where the hell was the ambulance? There was no part of the island that was more than a five-minute drive than anywhere else. How long could it take to get here? I got a towel and dried Louie's face off. "Okay, Louie. This isn't going to prove you right and Albert wrong. You need to wake up now."

After a geological age, I heard the ambulance sirens. I opened the door and two paramedics came in. I answered the standard questions. No, I didn't know if he was sick or had allergies. Yes, I was a neighbor. Yes, he was like this when I found him. Yes, I tried to revive him.

One of the paramedics broke an ampoule under Louie's nose. He made a face and stirred but didn't wake up. They brought a gurney in from the ambulance and loaded Louie on it. Then they loaded him into the ambulance, and they were gone.

I wasn't really sure what to do next. I locked the front door and closed and locked the throne room window that I had let myself in through. I considered getting in touch with Olivia, but knew she would want details, and I had none. I finally decided to follow him to the hospital. I ran back across the back yard and hopped the fence. In the house, I got my car keys and drove to the hospital.

I arrived at the hospital shortly after Louie did. I ran into the emergency room and started to ask the admitting clerk where they had taken Louie. She glanced behind me and said, "You mean you aren't here for you?"

I was confused. "No. Why?" She looked behind me again and I turned to see where she was staring. A single line of bloody left footprints crossed the lobby, stopping at my left foot. I looked at the sole. At least three jagged pieces of glass protruded from the bottom. I started to feel faint.

Twenty minutes later, I was in an examination room with my foot sitting in a tub of soapy water. A very attractive resident named Samantha wrapped it up. We talked for a while and really hit it off. When I asked her about Louie, she told me she had admitted him, and that he was upstairs resting. She said he would probably be there for a couple of days. When I asked what he was suffering from, she shook her head. When I asked if I should notify his daughter, they told me she had already been called to get permission to admit him.

We made a date for the following Saturday night while she was giving me a tetanus shot.

As I was signing myself out, Samantha handed me a prescription for an antibiotic salve. "Ordinarily, we would fill it here," she told me, "but we're without a pharmacist at the moment."

I made a mental note to tell Bart about that, and then drove myself home, carefully favoring my bandaged foot. It was after ten when I got home, and Tony and Scot had both retired upstairs for the night. I decided not to call Bart that night, but thought I should check in on Olivia.

I found her phone number in my phone book and dialed it. She answered the phone in a husky, suspicious voice that five years in the northeast taught me to expect when I call New Yorkers. "Hello?"

"Hey, Liv. It's Aidan."

"Oh, hey. How are you?"

I glanced at my bandaged foot, but didn't answer. "How are you?"

"Okay, thanks. Thanks also for taking care of Louie. The hospital told me you were the one who found him."

"No thanks necessary. What else could I do?"

She laughed unnecessarily. "In that house? Throw a party over his body."

It was my turn to offer a courtesy laugh. "Do you need anything?"

"Not really. The doctor said he was stable. I'm flying down tomorrow. If you could look in on him in the morning, I'd appreciate it. But I'll be there by five."

"Sure. No problem. You want me to pick you up at the airport?"

"Yeah. That would be great. Comair 545."

I wrote it down. "Anything else?"

I could hear her think. "No, I don't think so. I'll see you tomorrow evening."

"You got it. Sleep well."

"Thanks." I started to hang up when I heard her add, "Oh, Aidan?"

"Yeah?"

"Thanks for not asking. He has a brain tumor. Inoperable."

"Oh." I said. "Oh."

"Yeah. See you tomorrow."

"Yeah." We hung up.

The next day, after I finished up the morning chores, I drove over to the hospital. At admitting, I was greeted by a rather bovine clerk. Actually, *bovine* really is an understatement. I was greeted by a cow in a Laura Ashley smock. Not fat, mind you; relatively normal build, in fact. But, a face that you would honestly expect to see hanging over a fence chewing cud. I asked the cow about Louie's condition. The cow told me he was awake and stable. I inquired about seeing him and was informed it was restricted to family only. "Are you family?"

"I am," I lied. "I'm his nephew. His brother Albert's kid."

The cow picked up the phone and called someone. I glanced at her nametag and thought, if you are going to be cow-faced, it's a shame to have to go through life with the name Elsie. Nonetheless, for a cow living in a human world, she seemed extremely professional and goal oriented. After several moments, she hung up and told me I could go to room 314.

I found my way to his room. The door was open, so I knocked and leaned in. "Louie?"

He was sitting up in bed, looking very alert. He turned towards me and raised one eyebrow. "My *brother* Albert's kid?"

I walked into the room. "It was either that or your daughter's fiancé."

He looked me up and down. "I guess I'll take Albert as my brother."

I sat on the side of his bed. "How are you feeling?"

He shrugged. "Like a damn fool. If I'm going to die, I'd rather be spared the ignominy of dying on my kitchen floor. Killed by Fruit Nation is the way to go." He gave me a sidelong glance. "You know?"

I nodded. "Liv told me last night."

He rolled his eyes. "I'd rather have no one know," he growled.

"I'm sure," I told him evenly. "There is nothing worse for a career eccentric than giving the world an easy explanation. 'Oh, he's not all that unique. It's just a brain tumor.'"

He blinked, clearly shocked. Slowly, a look of recognition spread across his face. Then, he began to laugh. Deep laughs that started somewhere down in his chest. "Duke Aidan, you...are...*right.*"

Before we could say anything else, a male nurse who bore a striking resemblance to a puffin—the walk especially—interrupted us. "Time for your medicine," the puffin announced and placed a small cup on Louie's bed tray. He then filled up a cup of water at the sink next to the bed, and put it on the tray as well. He was pleasant enough. He took Louie's temperature and wrote some things on his chart. "You need to take your pills," he reminded Louie.

Louie committed to the nurse-puffin that he would take them immediately. The nurse left. He picked up the cup of water, grimaced at it, and handed it to me. "Dump that," he commanded. I complied. From behind me, he instructed me to give him back the empty cup and hand him his shaving kit. Again, I complied.

"The real problem with being terminal," he told me as he unzipped the bag, "is that there is no hope of a grand exit...without a suicide, that is." From inside the shaving kit, Louie produced a saltshaker, a lime wedge, and a silver flask. "You know, I never fancied myself as a 'die quietly in his sleep' type; more of the phenomenal, untimely death type." He opened the flask and poured a shot of the contents into the cup. "I certainly never imagined myself as someone who is going to expire in a hospice while loved ones gaze on."

The smell of the contents reached my nose. "Louie, should you really be taking your pills like that?"

Louie fixed me with a gaze that clearly showed he thought it was a stupid question. "What's the worst that can happen, Aidan?" He screwed the top back to the flask. "Besides, there really is no other way to take medication."

He licked his left hand, and poured the salt on it. Then, he picked up the pills, licked the salt, tossed the pills into his mouth, and slammed the tequila. He put the cup down, wincing, and bit into the lime. Then, he put the remains in the cup, zipped his shaving kit, and handed everything back to me for handling.

"You have really hit it on the head, young Aidan. When you've spent your entire life developing and refining your personality, there is nothing worse than giving people a convenient way to pigeon-hole you."

"Well, to a certain degree, it's natural. I remember a psych professor once telling me that the only way human beings are able to deal with all the stimulus that they encounter during the day is by stereotyping."

Louie settled back into the pillows. "I've heard that too. And you know what I say? *Bullshit!* People are not *entitled* to stereotype other people. I used to have a friend. Brilliant architect. Worked for years to learn his craft. Designed some absolutely *phenomenal* art galleries. Happened to be gay. One time, we were at the dedication of a gallery he did in Miami. I overheard this old broad from Boca say…*actually say*…'well, of course he's creative. He's a fagella.'"

He shook his head. "Can you imagine? Having your talent, *your passion*, reduced to…to…an ancillary feature of something so *superficial* as your sexual preference?"

"Or your health?"

He shook his head. "Or your health," he admitted. An awkward silence followed.

"How did you get the tequila?" I asked.

He smiled. "Aidan, I only hope you are as lucky as I in having the same number of friends who look out for you." Suddenly, he was all business. "Since I am going to be in here for a couple of days, I am going to need your assistance in putting this wake together." He motioned to the sink and ordered me to pick up the paper and pencil sitting next to it.

"Uh, sure."

For a largely mad eccentric, he could certainly put together a party. A stream of directives issued forth as though he had been planning wakes for twenty years. "You are going to have to handle the invitations for me. On the desk in my studio is my Rolodex. Everyone in it gets invited. I want the invitations to be ivory card stock, and I want the Fruit Nation obituary included as an insert. If you take it over to Farrel Nimoy at Kinko's and tell him what I'm looking for, he will put it together.

"Since it's Saint Patrick's Day, I'll want Irish fare. Call Jennifer at Cape Catering and tell her you are calling on my behalf. I will want my usual size party. Corned beef and cabbage, smoked salmon, beef in Guinness, barm brack. Oh, and what's that thing Albert used to make that was a specialty of your grandmother's? Belfast constable?"

I laughed. "Dublin lawyer."

"That's it. Then, you're going to need to call Bernie at Biscayne Bottle. Tell him I'm having a party and I want my usual order, plus ten cases of Guinness."

And so the conversation went. I came away with two pages of instructions; mostly, directions to call people and tell them 'the usual.'"

I spent perhaps another ten minutes with him, and then excused myself to get back to work. Over the course of the day, I found time to make all of the calls. No one seemed surprised by the orders. No one seemed put off by the short lead times. Even the caterer, who was normally booked months in advance said she would juggle her schedule. When I expressed surprise, she responded simply "Hey. You *do* for the king."

Louie spent another three days in the hospital, and then came home to be clucked over by Olivia. The week wore on, and soon it was Thursday, the ninth. It was a day much like any other day except for the fact that I had to drive to the airport to pick up Bart. His flight from Chicago was delayed, so I wandered over to the hangar to check on the plane.

The hangar was dark and silent. For the first time, it occurred to me that it was the one-year anniversary of Albert's death. The plane sat exactly where it had a year ago. That was possibly the only thing that *hadn't* changed in a year.

I walked up to the plane and touched the propeller on the number two engine. I could see my face reflected in the brightly polished chrome blade. In the blade, I did not look all that different than Albert had at twenty-nine.

So much had changed, I thought again. I was no longer mad at Albert. Still confused, mind you, about what he had intended leaving me the plane and the house, but still deeply grateful to have had them. They had certainly helped me get through the year that followed the loss of my job. And, oddly, for the first time, I felt Albert's presence in my life changing.

For most of my life before college, Albert was a distant, enigmatic person. I knew and knew of him. But seldom saw or spoke to him. In college and afterwards, he was a larger-than-life hero. Someone who I idolized, but I now realize didn't really *know*. Now, a year after his death, I found that I was beginning to feel closer to him than I had ever felt when he was alive.

Bart arrived eventually, accompanied by that wonderful sense of joy and camaraderie that he brings into my life. As he settled into the house, I told him about the job opening at the hospital, and he made plans to call them and check it out. He had two other interviews lined up as well. Over the course of the week, his time was divided between going to the interviews, lying by the pool, working on his tan, and spending time with Ross.

I saw little of Olivia or Louie over the course of the week. When I did, they were usually at each other's throats, so I assumed everything was normal. Louie resumed his evening walks on Tuesday. I also noted that I saw Olivia out walking each morning, following largely the same route Louie took, only in reverse. I thought that reflected well on their personalities.

On Thursday afternoon, the sixteenth, George's mammoth, ancient, black Town Car temporarily berthed itself in my driveway, and Phoebe, Jason and someone I could only assume was her attorney, disembarked from it. Jason, I noted, had grown an inch or two in the

six months since I had seen him, and bore even more striking resemblance to my side of the family than the first time I had met him.

They made their way to the desk where I checked them all in and
got them the keys to their rooms. As I did the paperwork, Phoebe
looked around the yard wistfully. "You guys have really done a lot with
this place. I would hardly have recognized it. Albert would be pleased."

I offered to help Phoebe with the bags, and we started across the
yard towards the guesthouse when Jason let out a surprised, "Oh."

"Something wrong, Sport?" I asked. I wonder how many times
Albert had called me "Sport."

"Uh, no," he stammered. "I thought we would be staying in the
house."

It had never occurred to me that he would have been accustomed to
staying in the house. It was, after all, his father's house, and the only
place he had ever stayed in Key West. Phoebe and I exchanged looks. It
had obviously never occurred to her, either.

"Well," I offered, "If you would rather stay in the house, I'm sure
we could find a place for you."

"Aidan," Phoebe began. "You don't have to do that."

"It's no problem," I replied, and turned my attention to Jason.
"You'd probably be on the couch in the library."

Jason smiled. "That's fine." He glanced at his mother. "Do you
mind?"

"You're sure you don't mind?" Phoebe asked me. I assured her I did
not. "Well, okay," she told Jason.

"Great!" Jason replied. We helped Phoebe to her room, and then I
took Jason to the house. We entered the kitchen and nearly collided
with Bart, who was coming out.

Bart had been forewarned that Phoebe was coming and fully briefed
on all Albert's admonishments that Jason was to be kept away from the
rest of the family. Still, there is no hiding that we're brothers since we
look so much alike, so I had decided to downplay it to Phoebe. Bart,
however, was clearly not prepared for how much Jason looked like him

and me. He took a step backwards and kept looking from Jason to me and back again. "Wow!"

"Jason," I said, "This is your cousin, Bartholomew. Bart, this is our cousin, Jason."

Bart held out his hand, and Jason took it, shyly. "'Lo." Jason offered.

"Hi," Bart responded. "I think I would have known you immediately."

"Why?"

"You look just like your cousin Aidan did when we were kids."

Jason looked at me. "So I'm going to grow up to look like you two?" he asked innocently.

"Horrifying thought, isn't it?" Bart replied.

Jason immediately blushed and became flustered. "No, I meant..." He realized that both Bart and I were laughing, and admitted weakly, "I guess there are worse people to look like."

"Damned with faint praise yet again," I told Bart. "Jason is going to bunk in the library."

"That's cool," Bart replied. "I'm going out to jump in the pool. Catch ya later, Jason."

Bart disappeared outside and I led Jason through the house. He stopped in the foyer and looked through the arch into the living room. "Where's all of my dad's *stuff?*"

The living room was, indeed, bare from the way Albert used to keep it. "Most of it was sold when he died," I told him. "I got the house but not a lot of the stuff."

"What did they do with the money?"

"It went to your aunts and your Uncle Jeff, I believe."

He made a look of distaste. I can only imagine Albert didn't think any more of his brother than the rest of us did. We continued into the library. I opened the glass doors, and Jason's face immediately lit up. "At least this room is still the same."

I put my hand on his shoulder. "It is. I wanted one room that would always remind me of your dad." I put his duffel bag down on the sofa. "I'll get you some sheets and a pillow later. Is there anything you want right now?"

"I'd kind of like to go jump in the pool."

"You know, I think that's a capital idea," I told him, wondering why I was talking like Sebastian Cabot. "Why don't you change and I'll meet you outside?"

I walked back out to the patio. Bart was on the float, reading a magazine, and Scot and Tony were getting the bar set up for happy hour. I went over and helped them out.

"Man," Tony observed, "Jason looks just like you and Bart."

"Pretty scary, isn't it?"

"For him," Scot shot back. I threw the wet bar towel in his face.

The back door opened, and Jason came down the back steps, wearing his bathing suit. He walked over to the part of the pool farthest from Bart and tentatively slipped into the water. Bart heard him, and leaned over to see who it was. When he saw it was Jason, he said something to him, and Jason smiled. Bart threw his magazine to the side of the pool and rolled off of the float.

Tony noticed me watching them and told me "Go join them. Scot and I have got things covered here."

"Thanks," I told him. I came around the bar, pulled off my shirt and cannonballed into the pool.

About forty-five minutes later, Phoebe came down from her room. Bart, Jason and I were in a rousing game of keep-away in which I was going to clearly come out the loser. I tried to institute a new rule, "no dunking the pool owner," but to little avail. Phoebe showed up just as the two of them were letting me up for air.

She walked over to the bar and met Tony and Scot. While she got a drink, the game devolved into a grudge match between Bart and I. I had just managed to pin him when Jason jumped on my back. I went under again. Jason suddenly disengaged. When I came to the surface, it was apparent that Phoebe had told him to stop it, because Bart was telling her, "Oh, he's fine. There's just something about Aidan that makes you want to hold his head under water."

As I wiped the water from my eyes, Phoebe was staring at Bart. I told her, "Phoebe, meet my brother, Bart. Bart, this is Jason's mother Phoebe."

Bart swam to the side of the pool and shook her hand. "Holy shit," Phoebe exclaimed. "Hell, does every man in your family look alike?"

Bart and I both laughed. "Not everyone. Uncle Jeff and our cousin Roy look like rats. Just us."

Bart got out of the pool and dried off. While he talked to Phoebe, Jason and I fooled around some more. Eventually, they were joined by her attorney, Feldman Nesslehut. I got out of the pool and got Feldman a drink. Phoebe and Bart had hit it off, so it was eventually decided that all of us would go to dinner. About an hour later the five of us, with Tony and Scot in tow, walked up Duval to Wang's & Juan's, a chino-latino restaurant that I am particularly fond of.

Jason sat between Bart and me at dinner, and seemed to really enjoy the attention from his two cousins. Bart spent a lot of time explaining to him who Caitlin, Roy, Valerie and assorted other family members were. While he did, the conversation for the rest of us turned to Vivian's custody battle.

"What I don't understand," Feldman asked in his thick, Cajun accent, "is why Vivian would go to the trouble to sue for custody instead of just challenge the will."

"Easy," Bart replied as he used one nacho chip to heap salsa onto another. "This is not as much about money as it is about control."

"Come again?"

Bart popped the chip into his mouth and immediately began loading up another. "Look, Vivian's not poor and she's not stupid. She's been involved in enough litigation to know that Albert's estate could mount a legal battle that would last long enough to use up all the money. Vivian is all about familial control. Albert created a life that didn't involve the family, and she's going to take control of it."

Since Bart knows I don't like Vivian, we never discuss her. I was, therefore, amazed to listen to his cool, impartial assessment of our aunt.

"You remember that old saying, 'you can't choose your family'?" he continued. "Well, that's what Vivian trades on. She takes the role of being the oldest child very seriously. And our mom and Uncle Jeff pretty much let her get her way on everything because it's easier. From what I understand, our grandfather was the same way as well. Albert wasn't willing to let everyone have input or authority over his life, so he left. Grandfather and then, after he died, Vivian were never able to re-establish family control over him. My guess is that this is much more about family matters than money." He waved to the waiter to bring a fresh basket of chips.

"So she goes straight to a custody suit?" Tony asked. "That seems a little like overkill."

"Oh it is, absolutely," he acknowledged. "But you've got to realize what the stakes are for Vivian. She doesn't have any friends to speak of. Her husband is about as warm and animated as a stack of lumber. The only real social interactions she has are with her family. And Albert took, perhaps in her mind *maliciously,* a part of that social interaction away."

Phoebe refilled her margarita glass from the pitcher and said pensively, "You almost make me feel sorry for her."

Bart shrugged. "I'm not sure she deserves *sympathy.* Admittedly, she's a lonely woman. But the major reason she's so lonely is because she's an acid tongued, manipulative, controlling bitch who holds her family hostage in order to have a social circle."

"Aidan, you're unusually quiet on this subject," Scot observed over his beer.

I smiled. "Bart is a more objective source of information on the subject."

Bart shrugged again. "Vivian leaves me alone. In her mind, though, I don't think you are much different than Albert. You moved away, and always rebelled against letting her have any control over your life. The more you rebelled, the more she tried to control you. And, then, when you re-established diplomatic relations with Albert, that validated in her mind that your were the same as him." The waiter arrived with our meals, and the conversation drifted off to other, happier topics. We did not come back to family matters.

That night, I kept turning Bart's comments about my aunt over in my mind. Phoebe was right. I almost felt sorry for her as well. For a moment, a small glimmer of light emerged in my soul, and I thought that maybe she wasn't such a bad person after all.

I immediately found that little light and stomped it out.

Whatever the circumstances, I could not allow maudlinism to overshadow what had happened and what was happening. After all, this was the woman who had threatened to contest the will, knowing full well I didn't have the money to defend it. This was also the woman who was looking to break up my cousin's family. I could take no solace in thinking that her motives might have been driven more by loneliness than greed. In fact, I found that more troubling and dangerous.

My deposition was the next morning. Phoebe and I were shown into the small conference room in George's office when we arrived. Soon after, George, Feldman, Vivian's attorney, Aaron Newkirk, and a court reporter all crammed into the room with us. It was a cozy little deposition.

Vivian's attorney began the questioning. For the first hour, most of it was extremely straightforward. I discussed my background, my education, and how I wound up in Key West. He asked about the nature of my relationship with my aunt, and the rest of my family.

After a quick break, the questioning continued on a very different track. He began to probe the nature of my relationship with my uncle. The questions were very straightforward at first, but soon the tone and direction began to change.

"Mr. McInnis," Newkirk asked. "What did you know about the nature of Mr. Fitzgerald's business?"

"Albert was in the import/export business."

"Do you know what he imported and exported?"

"Imports, largely rum. Some seafood and textiles. Exports? Anything that there was a market for in the Caribbean. Lots of SUVs."

"Were you ever aware of him importing anything illegal?"

I shrugged. "After the revolution, I think he ran some rum occasionally, and I believe he always had a stash of Cuban cigars. Otherwise, no."

"No narcotics?"

I laughed. "Narcotics? Nah. Albert was not subtle enough to import narcotics."

Newkirk did not smile. "What do you mean, 'not subtle enough'?"

"Albert was a loud mouth. He would be a lousy drug runner. He couldn't keep a secret."

"Really? But he did keep his son's existence a secret, didn't he?"

I was a little nonplussed. "He did."

"And he kept the sale of his business, the size of his estate a secret from you and the rest of his family, didn't he?"

"He did," I acknowledged.

"And he kept his relationship with Ms. Metior a secret, didn't he?"

"He did."

"So then, how can you say he couldn't keep a secret? It would seem that he was actually very accomplished at keeping secrets."

I struggled for the words. "Different kind of secrets. Albert was closed mouthed about his personal life. He was never closed mouthed about the business. He had plenty of opportunities to run drugs, but I don't believe he ever took them. Albert knew he did not have the finesse to keep his mouth shut in dangerous situations, so he simply didn't break the rules."

"He never broke rules?"

"*Never* is an awfully strong word. He certainly broke rules. And was extremely versatile at bending them. But drug running is a different level of rule breaking. Albert didn't take foolish risks. If the stakes were too high, he didn't play."

"So, you are reasonably certain he never ran drugs."

"Reasonably certain, yes."

"Have you ever run drugs?"

"*Me?* No."

"Having a private plane would certainly facilitate it, wouldn't it?"

"It would. However, having a plane doesn't necessitate it."

"But you've never run drugs?"

I glanced at George. "No. Never."

"The reason I ask is because you certainly seem to be well off financially for someone who lost his job last year."

I looked at him incredulously. "Well off? Based on what?"

"You own a vintage plane and an extremely valuable piece of real estate in the heart of a tourist community."

I nodded. "I do. And it takes scraping together every cent I can get my hands on to keep them."

"Perhaps. But wouldn't your lifestyle, and your uncle's before you, be much easier explained by some form of *supplemental* income?"

I struggled to keep my temper. "I'd say it's more readily explained by hard work."

Newkirk gave me a patronizing smile and then abruptly changed his line of questioning.

"You began visiting your uncle while in college, is that correct?"

"It is."

"Why?"

"Why? I guess because he lived in Key West, and it was a cheap place to go for spring break."

"That's your only reason? Because he offered cheap accommodations?"

"Not my only reason, no. I guess because I had also always had something of a romanticized image of him. In our family, Albert was frighteningly exotic. I wanted to meet him."

"What made him 'frighteningly exotic'?"

"He left Chicago. He lived in the tropics. All of the stories in the family about him were interesting. He did something besides live in the suburbs and shop at Sears."

"So you idolized him?"

"That might be a fair characterization."

"Did you have a romantic relationship?"

George had warned me that the deposition might take an unexpected or even unpleasant direction, but I was totally unprepared for that question. "*What?!?*"

"Was there any romantic or sexual component to your relationship with your uncle?" This question was delivered in such an even, slightly mocking tone, that I almost slugged him.

"I heard you. I just can't believe you would ask that. No! There was no such component to our relationship."

"Why is it so hard to believe?"

"Because there is no reason for anyone to expect it."

"Why not? Key West has a large gay population. You were of age of consent. It's not so hard to believe…"

"You fucking son of a bitch, *he was my uncle!*"

"Aidan…" George began.

"It's not unheard of," Newkirk said. "And, seeing how your uncle had so deliberately and completely cut himself off from the family, yet inexplicably welcomed your presence, it's a logical question."

"No it's *not* a logical question. One has nothing to do with the other."

George interrupted at this point. "Let's all take a break." He looked at the court reporter. "We're off the record."

George led me out of the conference room and into his office. "What the hell was that about?" I demanded, hotly.

George shrugged. "Don't let it get to you. They're fishing around for dirt. They want to prove that Albert was a dirt-bag so they can demonstrate that Phoebe must be a dirt bag for associating with him, and is therefore an unfit mother."

"Is 'dirt bag' the technical, legal term for it?"

He winked at me. "Listen, Feldman tells me your brother had a very interesting perspective on things last night."

"I guess. It is certainly a different perspective from mine. He thinks that Vivian's basically doing this to reinforce her claim to the role of *mater familias*."

George nodded sagely. "Think it would be worth the effort to depose him?"

"I'm not sure what value he would bring. He might be useful for establishing a strategy, but not for actually demonstrating Phoebe's worth as a mother." George nodded but said nothing.

The remainder of the deposition went pretty much the same way. It finally ended after about four hours. I went home and made myself a stiff drink. I filled Bart in on all the details and told him George was thinking about having him deposed. He nodded but didn't think he would be of much use, either.

"Jason's a pretty cool kid," he volunteered as we walked downstairs. Bart had spent most of the day with him.

"That he is," I agreed. "I wish I could see more of him. While I guess I can understand Albert wanting to protect him from the family, I think he really threw the baby out with the bathwater. I don't see that there is anything so horrible about the McInnis side of the family that justified all the secrecy."

Bart nodded. "I can't say I disagree with you. I think the greatest sin we commit is living in proximity to Vivian. It would seem to me that Albert could have maintained some level of control over interactions with Jason just based on the physical distance between Chicago and New Orleans. I guess you could argue that we wouldn't be in this bind now if Albert had been upfront with the family all along."

"Not sure I agree with you on that one," I said as we headed into the kitchen. "Nothing says Vivian wouldn't have tried this stunt even if she had known about Jason before Albert died."

We walked out into the back yard, where Jason was floating on a raft. "Hey Jase!" I called from the top of the steps. "We're heading over to King Louie's. Wanna come?"

"Sure," he replied and rolled off the raft. A moment later, we were out in the street, heading for the Palace in Dayglo.

I had seen party preparations at Louie's before but nothing of this magnitude. The entire palace was awash in activity. Workmen, caterers and florists swarmed over the old house like so many carpenter ants, and the results of their work were dramatic. The throne room had literally been transformed into an Irish pub, complete with three red-haired bar maids. In the back yard, an Irish band, which had been imported from Miami, was busy setting up their equipment and doing a sound check. The entire house was festooned with thousands of green carnations.

We wandered through the house looking for Louie. Bart admired everything with a sort of wide-eyed bemusement. Jason was more dazzled. Eventually, we found Louie in the backyard, giving directions to three workmen as they hoisted a huge, plaster leprechaun onto a pedestal by the pool. Olivia sat in a rocker on the veranda, sipping a glass of wine.

"He certainly seems to be in his element," I told her, after being greeted.

"He is," she acknowledged. There was something wrong with her voice, and it took me a moment to figure out what it was. It contained a genuine tone of warmth. "My father is always at his best when he can show off how creative he is. Nothing, but *nothing*, gives him as much pleasure."

"I've always wondered what motivates the creative process," Bart observed. "Maybe it's recognition."

Olivia took a sip of her wine. "I've lived in the middle of the 'creative process' all my life. My experience is that several things can motivate it. Sometimes he's motivated by the need for recognition, and sometimes he's motivated by the need for money. On rare occasion, he's motivated simply to get me off his back."

"*Rare* occasion?" I smirked. She ignored me and continued.

"But a chance to show off brings out a totally different side of him. Whenever he locks onto something that no one else has ever thought of, he's more like a man possessed."

By this time, Louie had succeeded in getting the leprechaun placed exactly where he wanted it, and had noticed us on the porch. "Duke Aidan," he called as he came strolling purposefully across the lawn. He strode up on the steps but suddenly came up short when he saw Jason. "My God. There're three of you."

"Louie," I said, "You remember my brother Bart. And this is my cousin Jason."

"Master Bartholomew," Louie said absently as he walked over to Jason. Jason held out his hand hesitantly, but Louie apparently did not see it. He cupped my cousin's chin in his right hand and held his face up so he could gaze into the kid's eyes. "My God…" he said again. It was one of those persona-shifting moments that not many people got to experience. Some moments he was the king, sometimes he was just Louie.

Jason looked slightly terrified. "What?" he asked nervously.

"And I thought that Aidan looked like your father," he said, wistfully. "You, my boy, are the spitting image." He suddenly released Jason's chin and immediately shifted back into the King. "Master Jason, we welcome you to court. You will, of course, be joining us tonight."

"Um…" Jason glanced at me, unsure of himself.

"Louie," I intervened. "Jason is here with his mother. We probably need to run it by her."

Louie nodded, but continued to address Jason. "Well, you must impress upon her that there is a limited number of Irishmen on this island, and we require all of them at court tonight to help us mourn appropriately."

Jason glanced at me again. "Mourn? I thought it was a party."

Louie laughed. "A party? Why, dear boy, *it is.* It is a celebration of my life. And a tragedy it was too, cut down in the prime of our life like we were..." He put his arm around Jason's shoulder and led him down the steps. Jason glanced over his shoulder at me, clearly looking for some direction. I shrugged to indicate that he was on his own.

They spent the better part of an hour walking the back yard discussing something, although clearly Louie was doing most of the talking. Later, as we walked back to the house, I asked Jason what the subject had been.

"My dad," Jason said offhand. "He was telling me stuff about my dad."

He didn't seem to want to elaborate, so Bart and I didn't push it. However, when we got back to the house, he was extremely animated with Phoebe, indicating the strong urgency that they attend the wake that evening.

"Wake?" Phoebe said to me, with one eyebrow cocked.

I explained the important nature of the wake, the nature of Louie, and the rather intrinsic role he had played in Albert's life. Not surprisingly, she had never heard of him, either.

That evening, Bart found me digging through my closet. "Do I have to wear shoes tonight?" One of Bart's favorite aspects of Key West is that he is able to go almost anywhere barefoot.

"You probably should," I explained over my shoulder as I dug through my footlocker. "Generally speaking, there can be lots of broken glass in his backyard. I learned that the hard way."

"Hey, seven stitches was a small price to pay to get me a job lead." I found what I was looking for and stood up. "Aidan, what in the *hell* are you wearing?"

What I was wearing was a pair of flowered surfer shorts, flip flops, my old tuxedo shirt, black tuxedo coat with tails, a bright red bow tie, and an old costume Iron Cross that I had picked up in college. What I had been looking for was a sash of the McInnis tartan (procured on a trip to Ireland during my early years at the airline), which I now draped over my right shoulder and across my chest. "*Duke* Aidan, thank you."

"Okay, *Duke* Aidan. What the hell are you wearing?"

I feigned a lack of comprehension. "I'm a Duke. We're going to court. Got to dress the part."

Bart shook his head. "You, son, are becoming as loony as that old coot." It was not said unkindly.

Scot and Tony met Bart and me at the bottom of the stairs. For their part, they were dressed festively as well. Tony had on his best set of Mardi Gras beads, and Scot had, someplace, found a very real and lethal looking scimitar to strap to his side. In the back yard, Ross was making polite small talk with Jason and Phoebe, but also had a costume component. He held a very heavy looking knight's helmet under his right arm.

"Oh God, I'm dating a lunatic," Bart said as we descended the stairs. He kissed Ross lightly. Living in Key West, two men kissing is not an uncommon sight. In the McInnis and Fitzgerald families, however, it is. I resorted to the tried and true family coping mechanism. I repressed.

All of us walked up the street together. As we exited Monarch Court, we joined a steady procession of other, costumed, revelers on a loud and boisterous pilgrimage to the Palace in Dayglo.

Even for Louie, this party was a spectacle to behold. So many people were there, I wondered who on the island was left to look after the tourists. As we arrived, several dozen of Louie's friends, dressed as priests and nuns (and one as a bishop) were standing on the porch intoning some form of Latin and waving a very real looking censer of incense. One of the nuns hit us up for five dollars each for the local AIDS hospice.

"My God," Phoebe said, inhaling deeply. "They're using real frank-incense. Where did they get real frankincense?"

"Knowing Louie, he's got a connection at the Vatican." We pro-ceeded inside.

I warned Phoebe, "Some of this may be a bit risqué for Jason."

She shrugged. "Can't be any worse than anything he would see at Mardi Gras. I'd rather he see his first debauch with me to look out for him." Then we saw Louie. He was dressed in full royal regalia. Long purple robe with an ermine collar, gold crown that looked deceptively like the one kept in the tower of London, scepter. If it wasn't for the martini, you could almost picture him in a renaissance painting of the Tudor court.

"Duke Aidan," he called out and did something he had never done before; he hugged me. "We're having a wonderful wake. *Marvelously* civilized custom you Irish have come up with. We couldn't have done this without you."

I stood back from the embrace and made the introductions. "Your royal highness, Miss Phoebe Metior of New Orleans. Phoebe, I present His Royal Highness, Louis Of Robideau, Monarch of Key West, Pan-creator of Highway One."

Phoebe, proving that she was always game for anything, held out her hand, and then dropped into a low curtsey as he kissed it. He winked at me approvingly. "Miss Metior. Welcome to court."

"Thanks, your highness. Aidan tells me you and Albert were close friends."

"As close as anyone ever got to the sonofabitch," he said warmly. Phoebe laughed knowingly.

Over the next hour, they spent a good deal of time together during which Louie flirted shamelessly. I speculated to Olivia that, perhaps, Albert had been smart to keep her away from him.

"More likely," she said with a wry smile, "he's trying to piss Albert off. He'd like nothing better to have Albert storm up to him at the Gates of Heaven and tear into his ass."

During the next hour, the party moved outside. A copious amount of liquor was served. Louie, being dead, took the rather unusual action of creating several knights, Ross, Scot and Tony among them. They became, respectively, Sir Ross the Romantic, Sir Scot the Smiling and Sir Tony the Cranky. After Tony's strenuous objections that he was never cranky, merely very serious (which no one believed), the king relented and changed his title to Sir Tony the Terribly Serious. Tony was inordinately pleased with his title.

Soon after, we were treated to the arrival of Fruit Nation, as several dozen of our neighbors came over the fence, led by Elizabeth and Andrea of House Diana. They were all bedecked in combat fatigues and adorned with fruit. More impressively, much of the fruit was also bedecked in fatigues. To this day, I still cannot forget the sight of a guava wearing a camouflage headband.

Fruit Nation stormed up onto the veranda and loudly claimed responsibility for Louie's assassination. Louie immediately pardoned them all, his royal powers apparently transcending the great beyond. "We're sure we deserved it," he told them magnanimously.

The party settled down for a while at this point. Well, settled down may be a bit of an overstatement, what with all the terrorists and new knights and melons dressed as Che Guevara. Let's say that the guests were left to their own devices for a while.

I found myself perched next to Jason on the edge of the veranda, beside the French doors that opened into Louie's studio. I was drinking something the bartender explained was a martini, but was a rather unsettling shade of blue. Jason was nursing a Coke.

"This place is crazy," Jason volunteered.

"It is," I replied. "That's why I like it."

"I meant the party, not Key West."

"I meant both."

We talked for several minutes of the meaningless things that are quite meaningful to teenagers. Finally, Jason observed, "I'm surprised that my dad never mentioned any of this."

I said nothing but motioned for him to continue.

"I mean I never knew about you or about Louie or about these kind of parties. I'd have thought he'd mentioned *something*."

Out on the lawn, I could see Tony and Scot vying for the attentions of a recently *dame-ed* doyenne. "I know how you feel. He never confided any of this to me, either."

"I don't understand it. It's like he didn't want to share part of his life with us. Like he wanted to keep us on the outside."

I could hear the frustration in his voice and came, for the first time in my life, face to face with the decision of whether or not to be an adult. I opted for the high road.

"No, I don't think that's it. I think your dad just didn't want to compete. He knew he was my hero and he didn't want to risk that I might find anyone else more interesting. I think, maybe, he had the same fears with you. I think he liked being the *only* hero and didn't want to share the spotlight."

He rolled his eyes. "If that's so, he didn't have to worry. Louie is a little too weird to be a hero."

I smiled. "Really? Oh. Well, I'm not sure I agree with you. I'd say he's one of mine."

The attention span of pubescents being what it is, he drifted off onto another subject. Then he abruptly decided he wanted another soda and took off. I sat and contemplated my martini for another moment or two. The French doors into the studio were open to admit the air. From the darkness inside, I heard Louie's voice say quietly, "When the hell did I become the *Pancreator of Highway One*?"

I stood and walked to the doors. From the lights in the yard, I could just make him out, enormous martini in hand, sitting with his feet propped up on the desk. "I felt like you needed an additional title, something that expanded the empire, so I came up with it. Kind of

Romanesque, don't you think?" He stared at me, unmoving. I shrugged. "You weren't supposed to hear that conversation, by the way."

He took a sip of the martini. "Aidan McInnis, what on earth about me would you think is remotely hero-like?"

I walked inside and sat on the stool in front of his easel. Prince Noritake gazed serenely at me from the canvas. "You live life to the fullest, Louie. You have fun. Ever since you asked me at Christmas if I was happy, I've been aware that I'm not. You are. You are more full of life *dying* than I ever have been alive."

Louie opened up the humidor on his desk and removed a cigar. I thought about reminding him that he wasn't supposed to smoke but thought better of it. "Aidan, you may have noticed something about me." He bit the end off the cigar and rummaged around for his lighter. "I never tell people what's wrong with them. I may ask questions, I may hint. But frankly I don't like hearing what other people think is wrong with me, so I don't force my opinions on other people." He found his lighter, and made a great show of lighting the cigar, "That said," he took a deep drag on the cigar and sat back in his chair. "That said, I'm going to tell you what's wrong with you."

The problem with having a close personal relationship with an insane old man is that you never know if you are going to get a pearl of wisdom, or a clam full of crap. I said nothing.

"Your problem is that, since life hasn't made you happy, you are going to manage the shit out of it instead. Life may not be fun, but by god, it will be organized. You've heard the old saying, 'can't see the forest for the trees?' Painters have a slight variation on that. You're so busy painting the grass blades, you're missing the sunrise.

"Aidan, the secret to happiness lies in you taking responsibility for it yourself. You keep looking for happiness to be the byproduct of your circumstances. Instead, your circumstances are the byproduct of your life. Focus on enjoying your life, and the circumstances will work themselves out."

Jackpot. Pearl of wisdom.

"I guess the problem is, I don't know how to do that."

"Do you believe in Satan, Aidan?"

That's an odd question, I thought. "No, not really."

"I'm not sure if I do or not. But I've always had a theory. If there is a Satan, I don't believe his sin was blasphemy. I believe it was trying to control circumstances. He damned himself by refusing to believe that the universe doesn't *need* a system imposed on it.

"You don't need to know how to just be happy any more than you need to know how to breathe. You don't know what makes your diaphragm work, and it works just fine without your management. Trust me. Your life is every bit as self managing as your diaphragm is."

My catechism flashed through my mind. "'Consider the lilies,'" I mused aloud

He ignored me, opening his desk drawer. He removed a velvet bag. Leaning across the desk, he held it out to me. "Here. I want you to have this."

I opened the bag. Inside was Albert's sextant. "Louie, I can't take this."

"Yes you can. Albert gave it to me because he found his course. I've also found mine. It's time for you to look for yours."

I started to protest, but he would hear none of it. I started to thank him, and he abruptly stood up, grabbed me by the shoulder, and dragged me outside onto the veranda.

The party was still in high gear as Louie called for attention. The Irish band obediently quieted down, and the king took the microphone.

"Dear and beloved subjects, we wish to thank you for coming tonight. As a charitable event, we've raised well over five thousand dollars, and that's a noble success." Everyone cheered and applauded. "We have a couple orders of business to discharge tonight. First of all, a wake is a celebration of life. I think it is only appropriate that we remember others who have gone ahead of us and drink a toast to their life." He raised his martini. "So, to all those good men and women, I say *salud*."

I thought of Albert, raised my glass and joined the chorus of "Salud."

He continued. "The second order of business is to thank someone. Mr. McInnis, please join me."

I was standing off to the side. Reluctantly, I took a step closer to the king. Having no patience for shyness, he reached over, grabbed my arm, and pulled me next to him.

"Duke Aidan was the creative force behind this party tonight. He conceived of Fruit Nation, and wrote the obituary, and did a good bit of the legwork during my unfortunate incarceration in the hospital. And I think, seeing as this party is a rousing success, we owe him a rousing round of thanks." The crowd cheered politely.

Louie's ability to create unique titles always impressed me. The fact that he could remember everyone's titles (and there were well over a hundred of us who had them) amazed me. What he did next left me stunned.

As the cheering died down, he did not relinquish his hold on my shoulder. "As many of you know, we have always believed we are immortal. We firmly believe that the fact that everyone has died so far is just an incredible coincidence.

"That said, we have recently begun to consider that, perhaps, we need an heir, in the highly unlikely case that we are wrong. We have, therefore, decided to designate Duke Aidan here as our heir apparent." There was the mandatory, surprised but appreciative murmur from the crowd. He turned to me and instructed, "Aidan, please kneel."

I did so, having no other idea what I *could* do. Louie produced his scepter from somewhere.

"Aidan McInnis, Duke of Disrespectful Daughters, Baron of the Biscayne Skies, we do hereby declare you the Heir Apparent to the Monarchy of Key West, and bestow upon you," the scepter touched my left shoulder, "the royal title," the scepter touched my right shoulder, "His Royal Highness, the Crown Prince."

The crowd applauded and I had my own, small cheering section from the guesthouse contingent. Louie produced, a ridiculously small crown, about the size of my fist, and placed it on my head. My friends immediately began shouting, "God save Prince Aidan. God save the King."

I stood back up and the cheering continued. As it died down, I mumbled my thanks and acknowledge the fact that I truly didn't deserve this. Louie overruled me and instructed the crowd to "continue in their revels."

As the band started up again, I leaned close to him and asked, "What the hell are you up to?"

He put his arm around my shoulder and guided me back towards the veranda. "Granting your wish, my boy."

"Louie, c'mon," I protested. "I don't have the right personality to be the monarch." We walked into the long hallway that connected the veranda to the foyer. A number of people patted me on the shoulder and offered me congratulations.

"Yes, my boy. You do." We walked to the foyer and ascended the stairs. At the top we were alone and he turned to face me, laying both his hands on my shoulders.

"Aidan, thirty years ago, I became the monarch at a party because everyone else was drunk enough to agree with me. I have no legislated authority. There is no long-standing tradition. I am a harmless old eccentric that these people indulge because they like the idea of having a harmless old eccentric monarch."

I started to protest, but he waved away my comments before I could make them.

"And there's nothing wrong with that. Because, during all these years that I've been this harmless old eccentric, I've managed to convince a lot of people to do a lot of good under the guise of making it fun. The Order of the Conch has raised almost a hundred and fifty thousand dollars for charities over the last thirty years. People in the order have started clubs and social activities that other people have desperately needed to join. Every person out there that I've ever given a title has received it because they needed it. And everyone so far, has never disappointed me. They may have needed it, but they wound up deserving it.

"Aidan, when I die, no one out there will ever realize what they were part of. They accomplished an immense amount, all the time thinking they were part of one big party. But, none of them will step up and become the next Monarch. So, I'm giving it to you. What you do with it is up to you. You can let the Order die, and no one will care; probably, no one will miss it. Or you can keep it alive, continue to make it fun for them, and they will accomplish wonderful things."

He let go of my shoulders and took a step backwards. For the first time, it registered with me exactly how frail he had become. I couldn't bring myself to say anything, and was desperately afraid to blink, lest he see the tears welling up in my eyes.

"I'll tell you something else, Aidan. You say you want your life to be fun? Well, I promise you if you abandon yourself to this silliness, every day will be the most fun you ever had.

"Now my boy, the king is tired and going to go to bed. As his heir apparent, get downstairs, make apologies for him, and take over hosting this party."

He turned and walked towards his bedroom door. Over his shoulder he called, "Goodnight, Olivia."

I turned and saw Olivia standing on the landing. While I still fought to hold back tears, her cheeks were wet. She smiled the warmest, most open smile I have ever seen, and called back, "Good night, Daddy."

I turned back to see Louie's door close with a gentle click of the latch.

After a moment, I wiped my eyes and descended the stairs to the landing. I didn't say anything, but she kissed me on the cheek and said, "Welcome to the secret legacy of Louis Robideau."

I didn't see Louie very often after that night. The brain tumor began to sap some of his energy, and he required more sleep. He still took his constitutional around the neighborhood, but his hours became a little less predictable.

I did, however, receive notes regularly from him suggesting I attend certain charitable functions on his behalf or join him at some other social occasion. I complied as often as my schedule would allow. And, while I wouldn't say the Order viewed me as an acceptable surrogate, they did make me feel welcome. And, after a few months, I began to receive invitations on my own.

Bart returned to Chicago. Before he left, Feldman Nesslehut did subpoena and depose him. Most of the questioning focused on Aunt Vivian. Almost immediately after he returned to Chicago, he received a job offer from the hospital. He set a tentative start date for June 1 and then quit his job. Ross put a lot of pressure on him to move in. Bart, to his credit, was still adjusting to being out of the closet and didn't think he was ready to make a commitment. Ross was frustrated but took it well. Bart would, instead, move into the only unoccupied room in my house, a basement room under the library. It was only temporary, he said, while he looked for a place. He planned to move his few personal belongings down in May.

Phoebe and Jason returned to New Orleans, and I occasionally received updates on the progress of the lawsuit from George. Jason began to send me emails and hinted around at being invited back during the summer.

In April, I received a package in the mail from the court reporter containing the transcript of my deposition. The reporter asked me to review it, note any mistakes or anything I would like to change, and send it back to her.

Almost immediately after I received it, I also received a thick letter from Aunt Vivian. True to my Aunt's nature, although it was written on bright, deceptively cheerful looking stationery covered with daisies, it contained the most ruthless, vindictive diatribe I had ever read. In her letter she denounced my deposition as untruthful, cruel, misguided and wrong. She issued accusations, epithets and slurs. It ended with her critical skepticism of how a woman as saintly as my mother could have produced such misanthropes as my brother and me, and expressed her wish that I stop being such a horrid, wretched disappointment to her.

Oddly, I felt almost nothing reading it except a sad emptiness. In the past, I would have sent the letter to my mother with a note exclaiming "See?!? See?!? I told you she hated us." Now the thought scarcely crossed my mind. Let Mother keep her delusions about her siblings. I carefully placed the letter back in its envelope, and slid it into the back of my desk drawer.

I spoke to Bart later that week. During the conversation he told me he had received his deposition as well. "Got a letter from Aunt Viv, too," he added offhand.

"So did I." That was all that was ever said between us. It was all that ever needed to be said.

Bart's furniture arrived during the second week in May. Bart did not accompany it. Preliminary custody hearings had begun in New Orleans. George told me I would not be summoned, but that Feldman Nesslehut had decided the judge needed to hear from Bart. Bart would stay in Chicago for two weeks, and then appear in New Orleans the first week in June. The hospital had been extremely accommodating and allowed him to change his start date to the second week in June.

We had another arrival during the second week in May. Our friend from Boston, Mike, showed up at our front desk the day after Bart's furniture had. He was unshaven, unkempt, and apparently soon to be unmarried. As soon as we checked him in and got him into a room, the three of us huddled in the library while I pulled out my old day timer.

"Three years, two months, fourteen days." I said after a moment of calculation.

"Yes!" Tony exclaimed. Scot and I each opened our wallets and handed him a twenty. Tony had said they would break up before their fourth anniversary. Scot said sixth. I said tenth. What do I know?

We soon discovered that Mike had recently turned down a promotion at the airline to continue flying. Turning down promotions apparently did not sit well with Susan. Things had deteriorated steadily ever since. "I do bring you some good news," he told us as we were well through a pitcher of beer at Sloppy Joe's. "The airline is making money again. They're planning to start recalls next month. You guys could come back if you wanted to." He stretched languidly and bent backwards to get a better look at a girl in a bikini top and Daisy Duke shorts walking by. "Not that I could imagine why you guys would want to."

The three of us exchanged glances but didn't discuss it.

Mike had taken a one-month leave of absence from work for a couple of reasons. First of all, he wanted to get away from Boston while the lawyers hammered some things out, and he didn't want to be someplace where Susan could call him to complain about the lawyers. Secondly, he wanted to reduce his income for the year to help the alimony settlement. While he was in Key West, he would fly a couple of trips with us, and we'd pay him under the table. I welcomed the help since Ross was off in Chicago helping Bart move.

During the last week in May, Louie went into the hospital. He was suffering from pneumonia. I spent a couple hours with him and Olivia every day that week.

June first marks the start of hurricane season in the North Atlantic. The month began with a tropical depression in the gulf, and my brother discussing my aunt's emotional state with a judge in New Orleans. He and Ross were due to drive from New Orleans to Florida after his testimony, but the judge held him over for a second day of testimony.

On June first, Olivia also found out that she had to be in New York for the week. Although her company had been extremely cooperative with giving her time off to be with her father, they needed her to help close a deal. She asked me to look after Louie while she was gone and promised to be back by the fifth. She flew out that night.

All hell broke loose on the second.

Louie and I were seated in his room, watching the news while I tried to get him to eat some lunch. He was alert, but not hungry, and I got the impression he was not enjoying my company at all. The lead story on the news was about the tropical depression that had, all of a sudden, very rapidly compressed into a hurricane. It was a small hurricane, but they issued watches for the entire gulf coast from New Orleans to Key West.

I needed to cancel about three charters, since the storm was centered not far from Runner's Key. Louie was more than happy to excuse me, although I promised him I would return that night.

Over the next two days, the hurricane rapidly increased in magnitude from a Category One to a Category Three. It began to move towards the Florida coast, and hurricane watches were revised to stretch from the Florida panhandle to Key West.

I went ahead and cancelled the charters for the rest of the week. It made sense since tourists were steadily departing the island and only a trickle were flowing back in to replace them. I also went over to Louie's house and took the liberty of sinking all of his lawn furniture into his pool and closing all the storm shutters on his windows.

On the evening of the fourth, the National Weather Service determined that the hurricane was going to make landfall somewhere between Key West and Sarasota, and hurricane warnings were issued. They estimated landfall sometime in the next thirty-six hours.

Over the course of that evening, I spoke to several people, including Olivia at least four times. I'm sure she called several times more while I was on the phone with other people and silently cursed me for the fact that I refuse to carry a cell phone or have call waiting.

Olivia's flight had been cancelled as the airlines pulled planes out of Florida. She was going to get herself as far as Atlanta and then determine what to do next. Most of the patients in the hospital would be transferred to Miami. But, since the hospital was one of the safest facilities in Key West, and since Louie was deteriorating pretty rapidly, she made the decision to keep him there. She had told Louie that on the phone but wasn't certain if it had completely registered with him.

I also talked to Bart on the phone. He was trapped in Pensacola. He couldn't get farther down the coast since everyone was being directed inland. He and Ross were going to sit the storm out there unless it shifted course and they had to evacuate.

He did have time to share one bit of family gossip. "She lost, Aidan."

"Who?"

"Vivian. She lost. Well, for all practical purposes."

"You're joking! How?"

"Well, after reading all the depositions and talking to both her and me, the judge said that, before he would allow the case to continue, he wanted Vivian to have a full psychological profile done."

"You're kidding!"

"Not at all. Well, naturally she refused, and the judge refused to allow further consideration until she did so. She apparently hopped back on her broom and flew home to Chicago."

"'Before someone could come along and drop a house on her,'" I mused.

"Indeed. I'm guessing even she is worried about some of those bats she keeps up in that belfry. Anyway, Mom says she's pretty hot with me, but that she'll get over it."

"In about ten years."

"That soon?" He sounded disappointed.

We didn't linger on the call for long since there was work to do. The guys managed to secure some plywood and boarded up as many of the guesthouse windows as we could, and then taped the rest. We sank all of our lawn furniture in the pool, and secured all of the exterior doors. We disconnected the washer and dryer and the ice machine, and moved all of the computers and other equipment from the small gazebo that served as the front desk into the garage. We moved all the liquor into the kitchen.

The house itself was much easier to secure. Whoever had built it a hundred years ago intended for it to withstand all nature had to throw at it. We bolted the heavy storm shutters over the windows and battened down the hatch to the widow's walk. We found the hurricane kits and the flashlights, the generator, the batteries, and located all of them in the small hallway between the basement stairs and the garage. And then it was time to leave.

Or so I thought.

Scot and Tony decided that they were going to stay and ride the storm out. "It's only a Category Three," Tony explained. "I've been through much worse before."

"Guys, that's crazy," I told them. "We're supposed to get off the island."

"Lots of people are riding it out," Scot explained. "We're going to be better off if someone is here."

"No," I commanded. "We're all going."

Commanding didn't do much good. We argued about it for about twenty minutes. I finally relented when Tony said, rather hotly, "Look, Aidan, you've got your house. You've got your plane. All we've got is *our* business, and we want to stay here and look after it."

"I've got to get the plane off the island," I said meekly.

"Then go," Scot said. "No one is saying you have to stay. Take care of the plane."

I didn't know what else to do. I got Mike and we drove to the airport. I filed the flight plan quickly. We would be the last flight out before they closed the airport entirely. We pulled the hangar doors open and pulled the chocks on the plane.

And I couldn't go. For the first time since Albert died, I felt like I had to make a choice: the plane or the business.

Please understand, my plane represents everything I love in life: freedom, control, peace. It does not represent commitment to me. Sure, it's a lot of work, but it's a labor of love. The business, on the other hand, represents commitment. I had made a commitment to the guys, and I needed to stay with them.

I handed the keys to Mike and told him to take the plane. I had filed a flight plan to Atlanta to pick up Olivia. I told him where to meet her, and to bring her back to the island as soon as the storm was over.

Mike didn't try to talk me out of it. I think he understood that there were bigger things going on in my head. We pushed it to the apron, and he climbed aboard, pulling the hatch shut behind him. I could hear him flipping switches in the terrible stillness outside. After a moment, the prop on the number two engine slowly began to turn.

Through the windshield, I could see him radioing the tower for permission to taxi. The other prop began to spin. Then he looked out the window and gave me a thumbs-up. I gave him one back, and my plane slowly began to taxi away from me.

I walked a few steps and watched her roll to the end of the taxiway and turn onto the runway. She pulled into position at the end of the runway and began her takeoff.

She was heavy with fuel but no passengers, so it didn't take her long to come to speed. The tail lifted smoothly, and about two hundred feet farther, the main gear left the runway. She made a long flat spiral to the right and straightened out heading northeast on a direct line for Orlando Center.

I slowly pulled the hangar doors closed. I think that was the first time I had ever been in the hangar without the plane. It felt chilly, empty and lonely.

I got back in the car. The storm was now projected to hit Key West sometime before midnight. The vast bulk of the evacuation had taken place, although probably a third of the population remained on the island. The bulk of the traffic was now on Highway One somewhere around Marathon. They would make it to Miami long before the storm hit land.

The island was quiet. Most people were busy finishing boarding up their homes or businesses, so there was hardly anyone on the street.

Except for one lone lunatic walking up Bertha.

I squealed to a stop next to him. "Louie!" I snarled. "What the *hell* are you doing out of the hospital."

He turned to me and smiled. "Prince Aidan. How good to see you. Would you be so kind as to escort us to the Palace in Dayglo?"

"I'll escort you to the morgue, you senile old coot. We're going back to the hospital."

Louie's face fell. Wordlessly, he turned and began walking away from me.

"Hey!" I drove along side of him. "Get in the car."

"Thank you, no."

"Louie!" He kept walking and ignored me. "Louie?" He continued to ignore me. I finally calmed down. "Louie? I'm sorry. C'mon and get in the car."

He turned and leaned on the passenger door. "Do you give me your word as the future Monarch of Key West that you will not take me back to the hospital?"

I nodded. "But I can't take you back to the Palace. I've already boarded it up."

"Fine." He got in the car. "Then we will ride out the storm at your place."

I sped off. "You need to be in the hospital."

He rolled his eyes. "Aidan, I'll go back to the hospital tomorrow. I love hurricanes, and I'm not about to miss my last one. It is all the majesty of nature laid out before you, and I refuse to enjoy it doped up on Seconals."

I gave in. "Fine. Whatever. But you're staying with me. Do you at least have your medicine?"

He patted his jacket pocket and smiled wickedly. "I do. Do you have tequila?"

We pulled up at the house and I was just able to wedge the car into the few remaining feet of floor space in the garage. Tony and Scot were both surprised and pleased to see me. Nothing was said about what had happened earlier, but the message now was clear; we were all in this together. For the record, I don't think they felt at all surprised to see Louie. The last year had made them used to him popping up unexpectedly.

Having everything fully secured, we made margaritas and sat outside, listening to the radio and waiting. Key West was silent. Amazingly, alarmingly, unequivocally silent. The whole island sat and waited in anticipation.

At about eight o'clock, the winds began to pick up and the first clouds started to roll in. The National Weather Service upgraded the storm to a Category Four. Scot, Tony and I exchanged nervous glances. It was too late to leave now. Louie rubbed his hands together in gleeful anticipation.

At eight thirty, it began to rain. We sealed up the front door, much to Louie's dismay, and watched the storm from the kitchen. The back door had a wrought-iron grill on it, so we weren't able to cover it. We indulged Louie by leaving it open, and he sat on the back steps with an umbrella, sipping his margarita and watching the sky.

At nine thirty, the storm began to pick up. When his umbrella blew inside out, Louie retreated to underneath the porch roof but refused to come inside. Landfall was now predicted at 11:45.

At ten, we had thirty mile per hour winds. I was worried that Louie, given his frail state, would blow away, but he was good at reading the winds and shifting himself out of their path. He still refused to come in.

At eleven, we lost power. The winds were up to thirty-five knots. Louie finally came inside, but still stood in the open doorway. Tony,

Scot and I scurried to find the candles, flashlights and the transistor radio. The temperature in the house began to drop.

At eleven thirty, Louie closed the back door.

The storm came ashore at midnight.

My house, charming old brick pile that she is, seemed to relish the storm. As the winds howled around her, I prowled from room to room and floor to floor looking for problems. I was able to find a small trickle of water coming down the flue into the library fireplace, probably due to an ill-fitting damper cap. In the garage, water began to leak in under the garage door. Otherwise, the house creaked and groaned but did not seem to mind the havoc around it.

By one o'clock, there was a sizeable puddle of water in the garage. I put a barrier of towels against the door into the hall to prevent the water from getting into Bart's bedroom and ruining his stuff.

At one forty-five, the winds were about fifty knots. Through a gap in the boards covering the garage window, you could see that about a foot of water was standing in Monarch Court and lapping at the base of our driveway.

Things that neighbors had not tethered down began to crash against the house with alarming frequency. It started out small when a terracotta pot came careening against the front steps, startling all of us who were sitting in the kitchen. In the pale light given off by the emergency lamps glowing on the guesthouse, I saw a chaise lounge come flying through the bamboo thicket that separates our yard from our neighbor's. It crashed against the door of room four, but we couldn't hear it over the noise.

For a while we amused ourselves by identifying what had crashed against the house. Garbage cans were easy, as were flowerpots. Lawn furniture was a little harder. We spent several minutes trying to guess what made a high-pitched squeal followed by a crunchy sounding "thwock," only to discover the next morning it was someone's pool rake, flying handle first, and impaling itself though the laundry-room door.

The eye of the storm passed over at about two thirty, and we walked outside to survey the damage. The back yard was a mess, but the guesthouse looked soundly intact. In the front yard, the neighbors had lost a palm tree, which now lay listlessly against their front gate. The water level in the court was now about halfway up the driveway.

It took about an hour for the eye to pass. The stars winked out with a suddenness that was terrifying, and we retreated into the house just as the wind picked back up. It took three of us to force the door closed again.

I had always heard that the front half of the storm was the worse, so I began to relax. I returned frequently to the basement to make sure the water, which was rapidly advancing up the driveway, had not made it to the garage yet.

Tony and Scot also seemed relaxed as I came back up the stairs and into the kitchen. Louie, of course, was always relaxed, no matter what was going on. I took a sip of my very warm margarita, when the wind suddenly rose to a fevered shriek. Even Louie seemed unsettled by it, and we all glanced at each other uneasily.

At that moment, a piece of PVC pipe crashed against the back door. The end of it was small enough to fit through the wrought-iron grate, and it shattered the window. We immediately scrambled to fit something over it, and a piece of wood was retrieved from the basement.

We fought against the wind and rain as they poured through the broken window. As we attempted to secure it, a sudden gust blew it back in and the three of us tumbled to the floor.

And then we heard the crack.

Perhaps *crack* is not the right word. It was a loud bang followed by a rapid succession of snapping sounds. This is, of course, the sound a tree makes as it breaks off at the trunk. The tree in question was a large mangrove that sat at the back of Louie's property, next to the guesthouse. Through the open window, we could just make out the tree, which was about forty feet tall, as it fell slowly forward. For a moment, it looked as though it was going to fall harmlessly to the ground next to the guesthouse. Then the wind took it, and it crashed with force into the side of the building. We could see the wall of room number four buckle inward slightly.

"Oh shit," Tony said.

"Let's go out and see if we can't prop it up," Scot suggested.

Louie laid his hand on Scot's shoulder. "Don't chance it, son. You're more likely to wind up beneath the building if you go out there. It may be able to ride out the rest of the storm."

We managed to get the broken window partially blocked, and then took turns mopping up water and watching the guesthouse through the window. The next hit it took was when a palmetto that the mangrove had hit snapped and swung around like a pendulum. Tony pointed it out to us just as it struck the support for the second-floor balcony. The corner of the balcony sagged and Louie kept his hands on our shoulders, trying to physically repress the instinct to run outside and do something.

The sagging stopped after a minute, and we were able to entertain a brief hope that everything would be fine. But then the roof broke free of the gazebo and smashed into the support next to the one that just broke, this time on the first floor. The balcony sagged alarmingly.

At that moment, the back door burst open. I can only guess that, somehow, with all of us moving back and forth to mop up water, we must have hit the latch. All of us tried to close it and were standing together as we heard the long, low moan come across the yard.

Without the two supports holding the roof down, it lifted off the building and flipped backwards into Louie's yard like the top of a toy box. Losing the roof further unsettled the balcony, which now slid sideways and collapsed, folding down over the first floor rooms.

All of us just sort of stopped struggling with the door at that point, and we watched the inn go through its death throes. The front wall of the second floor collapsed inward, and we could see towels, linens, and one chair go flying up and out. A moment later, a mattress followed.

There was another loud groan, and the sounds of repetitive popping. We could faintly see the back wall pull away from the building and collapse. Without the back wall the upper floor drifted almost lazily backwards, collapsing downward like so many playing cards.

We stared in stunned silence for several minutes. Finally, Louie regained his senses and helped us close the door. The storm lasted for about another hour, but the worst of it was past. It drifted out to sea and set a southeasterly course for Cuba.

None of us could say anything for the better part of an hour. Finally, Scot wondered aloud, "Should we try to go salvage anything?"

"Don't bother at this point," Louie answered. "Let insurance pay for it."

The storm abated, and all of us drifted off to different rooms to try to sleep for a couple of hours. I put Louie in my bed and slept on the couch in the living room. I slept like the dead.

The next morning, we walked outside to survey the damage. The guestrooms themselves were a total loss, as was the gazebo. The bar, the laundry room and storage room were all still intact and looked fine, except for the laundry room door, of course.

Louie came outside and laid a hand on my shoulder and asked quietly, "Are you okay?"

I shrugged. "We have good insurance. We should be." I looked at him. He looked tired and worn. "I need to get you back to the hospital."

He nodded. "You do. I've seen the power of nature once again. And, I'm afraid, I am succumbing to it."

Bart and Ross made it back to the island first. They were there by that evening, although I didn't see Bart since he went directly to the hospital and started work. Olivia and Mike made it back the following afternoon, shortly after the airport reopened. Olivia was mad as hell that I didn't take her father back to the hospital, but given the circumstances, was smart enough not to say anything to me.

Scot, Tony and I discussed going back to our old jobs in Boston briefly, but none of us really wanted to. Scot put it succinctly enough. "This is home."

"As natural disasters go, if you have to have one, I recommend having one like we did. Our insurance was sound; our home survived in tact; the most expensive of our equipment and supplies came through just fine." I recounted all this to Louie the following week, during one of my daily visits.

Louie looked very frail now. He lay in the bed, and had breathing tubes in his nose. He was still alert, however. That was the interesting thing about Louie's brain tumor. With his personality, it had always been impossible to discern dementia.

"My only regret is that I won't sustain whatever legacy Albert was trying to achieve by leaving me the inn."

"Are you still on that?" Louie asked incredulously. "I thought you had decided I was your only legacy."

"For all practical purposes, you are. At least you left me with instructions. I have some idea what *you* intend by leaving me the monarchy."

Louie gave me a disgusted look. "Do you know why we celebrate the sunset every night on Mallory Square?"

"For the benefit of the tourists," I speculated.

"We celebrate it *because*. It's not like it's an unpredictable event. We celebrate it because we want to. Or because we've had a great day. Or because we don't know what else to do. There's no reason. There's no plan. There's no pre-ordained fate. Just like life.

"Albert gave you no plans, because he *had* no plans for you. Albert gave one thing to both you and Jason. He gave each of you the freedom to make life whatever you want.

"You're a writer. Let me ask you this. When you compare the story of your life now to your life in Boston, how's it different?"

I thought for a moment. "It's a lot more interesting. The plot may not be easy to follow. It may not always be fun to read. But God knows it is not predictable."

"And are you happy?"

I smiled as I saw where he was going. "I wouldn't have it any other way."

"That's Albert's only plan for you. He gave you freedom, but he *didn't* make it easy for you."

Louie's life came to an end in a way he never wanted, but in a way I certainly think he appreciated. He fell asleep shortly after lunch on June 10th. I received a call from Olivia at about two.

"Aidan, I think it's time." Her voice was curiously peaceful.

"I'll be right there," I told her.

The three of us had been cleaning up the wreckage of our business. The insurance people had just cut us a check, and we were meeting with demolition crews to determine how much it would cost to have the wreckage removed. As a result, I was pretty grubby.

I told Tony and Scot that it was time and bolted back into the house and ran up to my room. I washed my hands and face quickly and changed into a pair of floral shorts, a blue-and-white awning stripe jacket, a yellow tank top, and one of Louie's bowlers that I had secretly purloined. I had planned this to be my own, personal salute to him, so I was surprised as I descended the stairs to see both Tony and Scot dressed much the same way.

We drove to the hospital, and went straight to his room. Olivia was outside the door, talking softly with George. George looked very old. She turned and saw us, and a smile lit up her face. "It's Mr. Blackwell's honor guard!" she exclaimed.

I hugged her, and she squeezed my hand. "He woke up a few minutes ago and asked for you."

All of us walked into the room, and I stepped forward and sat on the bed. His eyes were closed and his breathing was extremely labored. He had refused a respirator earlier, so he at least could still talk and move his head. I silently applauded him for preserving his dignity.

I took his hand and began to stroke it. He didn't move. Olivia came up next to me and put her hand on my shoulder. "I'm sure this goes without saying, but I hope you know you're the eccentric son he never had."

"Or wanted," I added. Everyone chuckled, and I saw a small smile cross Louie's face. After a moment or two, he opened his eyes and looked at me.

His eyes were tired, very tired. But there was still the same sense of mischief. He tried to say something, but couldn't. Finally, he mouthed a word that looked like "ready."

"Ready?" I asked.

He lowered his eyes ever so slightly in confirmation.

"I know you are, Louie."

He raised his hand slightly and pointed at me.

"Am I ready?" I asked. He nodded with his eyes again.

I smiled. "For this long, strange journey? It doesn't really matter, does it? At least I've got the togs for it."

He smiled again, and lowered his eyes. He held his left hand out, and Olivia came around the bed and took it. "I'm here, Daddy."

He mouthed the word *love*.

"I love you too, Daddy," she said through her tears.

Louie took a deep breath, then another, and then a third. I felt his hand relax in mine, and then his arm. And then he was gone. A moment later, his heart realized what had happened and the heart monitor alerted us that it had stopped.

A nurse had come in at some point, and she switched it off. We all sat there in silence for a long time, until Tony said, quietly, "Ladies and gentlemen, the king has left the building."

All of us laughed. I got up from the bed and wiped the tears out of my eyes. Olivia stood up and did the same. "I guess there's only one order of business left," she observed as she walked around the bed.

She placed her hands on my shoulders, looked me squarely in the eye and said simply,

"The king is dead. Long live the king."

EPILOGUE

▼

We laid Louie to rest much the same way we had with Albert. He, too, was cremated, and George, Olivia, and I took him up over the ocean to spread his ashes. This time, we flew east towards Key Largo, and Olivia did the honors. It was a peaceful moment.

The Order of the Conch acceded to Louie's dying wishes, and a month later, I was "officially" crowned HRH Aidan the Airborne, Monarch of Key West. The coronation was an elaborate affair that took place in the backyard of the Palace in Dayglo, overlooking the now condemned wreckage of our guesthouse. Tony, Scot, Ross and Bart served as my knights errant, and Olivia herself placed the crown on my head. As she had reconciled herself with her father, her moments of good humor had become a little more frequent, and she was a good sport about discharging her father's instructions to her in his will.

I had made my choice and Key West was now home. I had hoped that Olivia might consider relocating back to the island as well, but she was a New York girl at heart, and was itching to get back to Manhattan. Before leaving, however, she made an interesting business proposition.

She had no need for her father's house; it was entirely too large for her. But she didn't want to lose her connection to Key West altogether, either. A business deal was struck in which she became a partner in the Ocean Nights Inn, which would be relocated into the Palace in Dayglo. The only caveat was that her childhood bedroom and bathroom, along with her father's studio, were to be kept for her exclusive use. We moved the inn operations in as soon as the will was settled, and used the insurance money to clear the wreckage from my back yard and pay off our business loans. With the inn on more solid financial footing, we were able to pay ourselves decent salaries, and Tony and Scot moved out on their own, leaving me to rattle around in this huge house by myself. Although I thought I would miss the noise and hubbub, the fact that it was just beyond my garden wall instead made this place a comfortable retreat, and appropriate staging ground for *court* functions. And, with the guys gone, Bart decided to stay with me on a more long-term basis while he and Ross decided where their relationship was going.

My parents retired that year and moved to St. Petersburg. With them in Florida, but the rest of the Fitzgeralds still in Chicago, I found I truly began to enjoy their company. It did not appear that I would ever have any more direct dealings with my aunt or cousins, apart from occasional updates via my mother.

For Fantasy Fest that year, the Order of the Conch conducted the largest fundraiser yet, raising almost $10,000 for charity. The theme was the annual Wake for King Louis Of Robideau.

I had collected enough stories about my uncle, and Olivia helped me get them published. *A. Fitz: Finding the Man who was Uncle Albert*, while far from a critical success, sold well. I made enough off of it to encourage me to keep writing. I gave Jason the first copy. I also sent one to Aunt Vivian. I doubt if I will ever know if she read it.

Jason came to stay with me during his Christmas holiday that year. Louie had left me the painting Albert did of Cuba, but I decided to give it to my cousin. I kept the sextant for myself. I built a special teak holder for it and kept it on the flight deck of the *Biscayne Voyager*, always next to my left hand. I still wasn't sure where my life was taking me, but until I figured out my course, I wasn't letting it out of my sight.

About the Author

Over the course of the last twenty years, D.M. Paule has been an aerospace engineer, financial analyst, company controller, marketing consultant, speechwriter, disk jockey, librarian, television producer, corporate officer, entertainment critic, cartoonist, college professor and stand-up comic. He is rarely classified as *focused*.

The youngest of five children, he was born and raised in Dayton, Ohio. He managed to secure a BS in Aerospace Engineering from the University of Cincinnati and an MBA from Georgia State University despite the serious misgivings of each institution's faculty. In 1989, he joined Delta Air Lines, which has given him a wealth of opportunities to work and travel all over the world. It is also the longest relationship he has ever had, and quite possibly the most co-dependent. He is the author of the narrowly read novella, *Amidst the Brownstones,* and the play *The Sisters.* He lives in Atlanta.

0-595-22290-0

LaVergne, TN USA
16 December 2010
209004LV00004B/2/A